A WALLFLOWERS IN LOVE NOVEL

Lady Wallflower in Love
A Wallflowers in Love Novel
By Emma Sutton, Georgia Sutton

This is a work of fiction. Names, places, characters, and incidents are the
product of the author's imagination and are fictitious. Any resemblance
to actual persons, living or dead, events, or establishments is solely
coincidental.

*Possible Triggers: Threat of Sexual Assault (to FMC, by non MC), Physical
Violence (non between MCs), Death on Page (not of an MC), Portrayal of a
Panic Attack.*

This is a work of **adult** romance fiction. Intimate acts between
consenting adults appear on page in **full-length, often detailed,
description**. If medium-high level spice books do not appeal to you, this
may not be the read for you.

Safe and happy reading, everyone!

Lady wallflower in Love

A WALLFLOWERS IN LOVE NOVEL

EMMA SUTTON
GEORGIA SUTTON

GS BOOKS

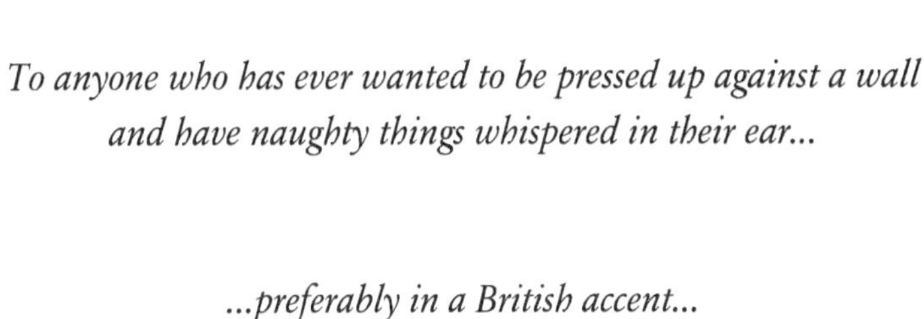

*To anyone who has ever wanted to be pressed up against a wall
and have naughty things whispered in their ear...*

...preferably in a British accent...

...this one's for you!

Chapter One

Lady Evelyn Pricewinters drew in a nervous breath as she let her eyes fall over the crowded ballroom. She'd never liked these things, and nearly *six seasons* had done nothing to fix that. If anything, it had only made her taste for London society sour further.

This year, especially.

She crinkled her nose as she passed a trio of young ladies, heads bent in what could have been innocent conversation, but for the titters they barely contained behind their silk fans.

She huffed out a sigh, smoothing her hands down her own silk skirt, trying to stem the rising irritation. There was every chance the gossip was about her—a suspicion she felt more certain of when one of the young ladies turned, her eyes going round as though caught in the act.

Evelyn felt herself bristle, wanting nothing more than to march up to her so-called peers and give them a piece of her mind in righteous anger.

But that was how she had gotten herself into this mess in the first place.

She forcibly cast her eyes away from the ladies and pressed past them. She needed to at least try to remain calm if she didn't want another scene before she left London.

She looked out again at the ballroom, at the matching lines of dancers in their finely tailored jackets and swishing skirts. But she knew full well what her traitorous eyes were truly searching for.

One very specific sweep of gilded hair.

Piercing blue eyes, set into an elegantly handsome face.

Calm. The reminder did little to slow the thumping in her chest. *You must remain calm.*

Evelyn fidgeted with the thin gold chain around her neck.

It was easier said than done.

Especially beneath the shimmering light from the crystal chandeliers. That brightness flickered and danced, making her dizzy and lightheaded. And the stuffiness of the room was just bordering on unbearable.

It felt like her head was swimming.

You're having a fit of nerves like an old dowager, she scolded. *Get a hold of yourself.*

She could place the blame on the twinkling lights or the mad crush of people until she was blue. But the truth was, the only reason she currently found herself spiraling was because of one couple in the crowded ballroom.

She blinked.

One couple that her eyes landed on just then, as the two pretty dancers swayed almost *too* close together.

Evelyn struggled to swallow past the emotion clogging her throat. She wouldn't call it jealousy, *per se*. Certainly not if anyone asked her.

No. Not jealousy.

It more closely resembled the embarrassment she'd felt two weeks ago, when her *suitability* in the marriage game had taken a sudden and unexpected plummet—off a very tall cliff. Lady Whitaker's ball had been the most anticipated event of the season, and was now surely remembered, almost exclusively, for Evelyn's complete and utter humiliation.

Now, she watched the dancing couple helplessly, tracing a slow circle along the periphery of the ballroom, as if unable to take her eyes off them, even if she tried. But she couldn't bring herself to look at *him*, even if her gaze kept being yanked in his direction like a magnet. So, she kept her eyes glued to the young woman he danced with.

It was an exercise in humility, watching Miss Burville's graceful dancing. Pale blonde hair, bright blue eyes, the flawless skin of a porcelain doll, and young—Henrietta Burville was, in all regards, a pearl of the first water. And it made Evelyn's stomach sour to watch her pretty, heart-shaped face tilt up with that worshipping expression as she stared at *him*.

With a heavy exhale, Evelyn braced herself, then forced

her gaze to pass from the sparkling flower of a girl to the man beside her—the one Henrietta was now smiling so sweetly at.

Nigel.

Even in her head his name sounded like a sigh. Though considering the way every young lady of marriageable age cast him furtive glances when they believed no one was looking, she didn't think anyone would blame her for it.

Or they wouldn't have, until Lady Whitaker's.

Breathe.

Just seeing him made her feel like she was adrift at sea.

Breathe.

She hated it.

Breathe.

It felt impossible though, when his every graceful movement brought back memories—memories of the way his mouth moved over hers and the feel of his lithe fingers at her waist.

Memories too of the hurt and disbelief when she'd heard about his betrothal. Then the crushing humiliation when he'd loudly claimed in that crowded ballroom—in no uncertain terms—that he had *never* made any vow to her.

It had come as a complete shock to Evelyn, who could still distinctly recall those very same whispered promises. Admittedly, there had been nothing said or done in any official capacity. But how else was one meant to take an impassioned pledge of *forever*?

Evelyn frowned, feeling her brow pinch as he watched them. Thinking about it still sent flutters of rage through her belly.

Her ultimate mistake had been giving in to that rising fury two weeks ago and confronting him in a crowded ballroom.

Evelyn exhaled a heavy breath and forced the furrow from her brow.

Much like the crowded room I am prowling through now.

She forced her eyes away from the two—away from the way Nigel watched his affianced with such smug satisfaction. And why wouldn't he be so puffed up? Lord Nigel Sedley had gotten everything he'd wanted. And *she* had been reduced to a laughingstock.

If I am lucky, that will remain the worst of it, she thought.

It was difficult to forget the vilest whispers. The ones that accused her of having questionable morals.

Or the ones suggesting she would have been *better off* compromising herself—at least that way she could have secured a husband. Unlikely, given his cold, selfish greed.

She shuddered. *I need to be rid of these vipers.*

After tonight, she hoped to never set foot in a London ballroom again. She would just have to convince her mother first.

Dragging her eyes from *Lord Nigel's* aristocratic profile, she scanned the lingering faces at the edge of the ballroom. She had only come tonight to see Maryann and instead she was acting like a lover scorned.

Maryann's bright, copper curls flashed like firelight against the glass paned doors as she fanned herself against the room's heat, even so close to the terrace.

"Maryann," Evelyn called.

The young woman flinched, as if startled, then slowly blinked her attention to Evelyn.

"Evelyn! You made it." She smiled, recovering quickly. "I didn't know if you would."

"And miss seeing you before you left town?" Evelyn waved a hand, brushing aside the very idea.

"I wouldn't have blamed you."

Evelyn shook her head. She wouldn't have abandoned her friend like that.

"You would have just come to visit."

Evelyn considered that. "I have missed Bath," she mused. "When do you leave?"

Maryann tried to hide the frown that clouded her face. "Two days."

Evelyn's eyes went wide. "So soon?"

Her friend nodded, those shadows still heavy in her eyes. She cast a glance back out at the dancers again, too quickly for Evelyn to make out what held her attention.

They had been friends since that first year in London, when they had each had their presentation before the queen. Two overwhelmed ladies, too young to fully grasp the importance society's mammas put on *the season*. They had both carved out their space along the walls, flouting those expectations, much to their own mothers' chagrin.

Though the way Maryann kept half her awareness now on the people crowding the ballroom seemed more proof her friend's position as *wallflower* was not so much by choice.

Unlike Evelyn, who could have happily gone unnoticed by the lot of them forever if not for *Nigel*.

Dancing. She suppressed a shudder when she thought of the country dance she'd been forced to endure with the aging Lord Tavish her very first season. That was the last time she'd defied her mother by bringing a book to a ballroom. Lady Sampford could get quite creative with her children's punishments.

The man spewed more spit than speech.

"Papa has already found a tenant for the London home."

Lord Blake had moved quickly then. Maryann's brother, Valentine, had only convinced their father to take such drastic measures recently—mere weeks ago at best.

"That is it then?"

"For now," Maryann sighed, one last glance at the mingling guests. "But I am excited for the change," she assured her.

"Yes, I am looking for a bit of a change as well," Evelyn muttered.

"You really should come to visit. There will be endless entertainment!" Maryann's eyes sparkled. She was looking forward to Bath at least.

Evelyn didn't point out that the *endless entertainment* would likely be in pursuit of security for Maryann. Or that Viscount Blake and his wife were unlikely to want an earl's daughter tagging along while they tried to repair their family's fortunes.

For all she was a joke in London, next to the daughter of

a penniless viscount, she would still be unwanted competition.

"I will think about it," she said instead.

"Oh, please do," Maryann begged. "It will be so much more fun with you there."

Evelyn didn't know how true that was, but she smiled anyway.

"I promise."

It was still dark when Evelyn climbed up into the family carriage, taking the seat next to her mother. Her brother, Edmund settled into the space across from her with a great, languid stretch, earning him a reproachful look from Lady Sampford. Evelyn hid a laugh behind her gloved hand when he responded to their mother's disapproval with an insolent yawn.

"What a splendid evening," her father declared as he took the final seat, next to Edmund.

Evelyn turned to the covered window with a roll of her eyes. What did it matter to her father that the sounds of early morning had begun out in the darkened streets, when time was all but immaterial to him. And to nearly everyone they knew.

She pulled at the curtain to glance at the stately home they had just left. Inside, the dancing would continue long after their departure. It would likely go on for another hour at least.

While the rest of London labors around us.

She shifted in her seat. It was an uncomfortable realization—one that struck her now, but not one she typically spent much time thinking about.

"Evelyn is about to tell us that it isn't evening at all,"

Edmund teased, and she sent him a scathing look.

But her father only chuckled. "Right you are, Evie."

Her childhood name. One that made her feel safe, indulged.

"But 'splendid middle-of-the-night' doesn't quite have the same ring to it." When the Earl of Sampford smiled, he looked ten years younger.

It was an infectious sort of delight. One impossible to ignore and Evelyn chirped an uncontrolled burst of laughter right alongside her brother's answering chuckle. Their mother eyed them both and then her husband, sighing exasperatedly, though it was mostly farce.

"Oh really, Sampford. Now look at what you've done." But a smile tugged at her lips.

Lord Sampford's charm was effortless, and evidently still held sway over his countess.

Evelyn caught the lingering smile her father gave his wife and turned back to the window. There was something tender and intimate in the look they'd exchanged. Far too personal to intrude upon.

The sort of devotedness that came from years at each other's sides—and a magnetism that had not weakened over the decades.

It was not at all surprising. The marriage between the Earl of Sampford and his countess was the against-all-odds, love-at-first-sight sort of love story Evelyn secretly wished for. She could have laughed at herself for it.

It was a dream that was at direct odds with her distaste for society. After all, how many matches had been made by the lady burying her nose in a book?

And her recent hiccup was bound to keep her too far from the London social whirl to change things.

The thought struck like a blow to her chest. She might not enjoy the dancing and the flirting. She might detest the shameless gossips. But there was a part of her that had hoped she could stumble into some sort of future—some sort of *happiness.*

The thought that her fleeting attachment to Nigel could have the sort of lasting effects to deny her that—

A few stolen kisses hardly seem worth it.

"Don't forget we have the Giffords' ball tomorrow night," Lady Sampford said, continuing a conversation Evelyn had all but drowned out.

Tomorrow night, she thought.

She would have one day's reprieve before being thrust back into the viper's nest. And if she didn't say something now, she was afraid she would shy from it, and find herself dragged about London for the remainder of the season.

"Mamma." She had to force out that one, single word. "I do not wish to go tomorrow night."

Her mother startled, turning to her daughter in apparent shock. She looked as taken aback as if Evelyn had suddenly declared the sky was violet.

How do I explain?

It wasn't that her mother was unsympathetic to her discomfort, but Lady Sampford held onto the belief that the only way past society's tittle-tattle was through, leaving no room for running away. That was how Regina Venables, daughter of an impoverished baron, had dealt with the venom of her own peers when she'd unexpectedly become the Countess of Sampford.

Edmund cleared his throat from the other side of the carriage, giving Evelyn a moment to collect her thoughts.

"I think I should like to skip the festivities tomorrow night as well," he said, and Evelyn narrowed her eyes at her brother.

Her father scoffed and turned his eyes on Edmund, while Lady Sampford tossed her hands up in the air in aggravation.

"What is this?" she declared, sounding vexed. "Sampford, please get control of these children."

"This wouldn't have something to do with a Miss Caroline Gifford?" their father asked sternly.

Evelyn swallowed and looked away. This conversation was destined to become one she wasn't meant to hear. She might pine silently for romance and love, but Edmund was happy to test the waters wherever he found a welcoming smile.

It was a truth she was meant to know nothing about. But ladies talked, and talk was that her brother was a terrible rake.

Her father must have been exceedingly displeased to bring the subject of *Miss Caroline Gifford* up in Evelyn's presence.

The gossips had begun whispering far worse implications about Caroline and Edmund than they did about Evelyn.

"My reasons are my own," Edmund replied, and Evelyn winced at his cavalier tone.

This was not going to go over well.

She chanced a peek at her father who looked absolutely furious. Her mother held her tongue, but glared at her son with such angry fire, she thought he might combust on the spot.

"Not when your reasons have the power to embarrass this family," Lord Sampford bit out.

"Oh, come now," Edmund said with a hesitant laugh, trying to win them with the smile that showed off the dimple in his right cheek.

His smile faltered when he saw it had little effect on the tension in the carriage.

Edmund had spent all twenty-five of his years charming their parents into overlooking the worst of his antics. It seemed the limit on that particular skill had finally run out.

She turned to her mother again, all too aware of the heated conversation across from her and the chaos it had set off in the carriage. Perhaps she could turn Edmund's disruption to her favor. She might make more progress with her mother while she was half distracted by her son and husband.

"Mamma," she implored again. "Please. The last few balls have been unbearable for me."

She was unwilling to let her chance at freedom slip away.

Her mother patted her hand absently, eyes still firmly glued to Edmund with heavy disapproval. "It will pass, dear."

Perhaps using the distraction had not been such a good idea.

Damn. She cursed her brother for hijacking the conversation. And all for the sake of avoiding his latest presumed *lover.*

It was viciously unfair. He could cavort about town and suffer little more than a feeble slap on the wrist and their parents' passing reproach. He would certainly never be vilified by society.

Evelyn felt herself puff up with her irritation. *He* was not currently debating the merits of fleeing to the continent and braving Napoleon's forces just to escape the *ton*.

"I will not attend another London event!" She all but shouted it, and flushed wildly as she became aware of her sudden outburst.

All three sets of eyes turned to her, wide as saucers.

"I'm sorry," she demurred, looking down at her hands, clenched in her lap. "I don't know what came over me."

"I should hope not," her mother chastised.

"It's just that I cannot face another London ballroom," she pleaded, hoping they would understand.

Edmund cleared his throat again for attention and Evelyn fought the urge to reach over and pinch him. He must have seen the violence in her eyes because he raised his hands in appeasement before he spoke.

"Perhaps it would be best for *both* of us to spend some time at Haythorne House, away from the eyes of London," he suggested.

"It certainly would be best for you," their father muttered.

Edmund had the good sense to look shamefaced. His cheeks even looked a touch pink.

"Please," Evelyn begged.

"But Evelyn, the season is already more than halfway

gone." She looked at Evelyn imploringly. "There is so little time left to fix this."

Evelyn doubted her mother's best efforts could manage to fix things. If she'd yet to find a husband in six seasons, what were the odds she would be successful in the next four months, after Nigel had made every effort to decimate her reputation?

She did not think staying would have such a very different effect than leaving.

Lady Sampford watched her daughter, then shared a glance with her husband. "I suppose there is always next year," she murmured.

"Mamma, I'm nearly twenty-four," Evelyn said on a whisper.

She frowned. Her age had never bothered her before, but it was starting to feel like there were armies of eighteen-year-olds—just like Henrietta—coming out each year. So, her age *was* a valid argument against her chances on the *marriage mart*.

Her mother clasped her hands together where they rested in her lap and looked out the window at the blackness outside. With another sigh, she turned back to Evelyn.

"If Edmund is willing to retire to Norfolk, then I suppose you may return with him."

For the first time in two weeks, Evelyn felt a moment of blessed relief.

Chapter Two

The morning room at Haythorne House was a large room, with high ceilings accentuated by the colonnade that ran flush against the walls. The pattern was broken by floor to ceiling windows that in warmer months would open wide, bringing the feel of the garden inside. With the current chill in the air, the windows had been firmly shut since she'd arrived. But the morning sunlight still reminded her of spring.

Evelyn looked forward to that tease of warmer weather as she stepped into the morning room. She flexed her grip on the book in her hand. Edmund had run off back to London, and she would finally have a moment's peace—

"Aunt Dorothea!" Her step faltered just past the threshold. "I didn't expect you until tomorrow."

Her aunt had made record time to get to Norfolk so suddenly, and all to keep an eye on Evelyn. She eyed Aunt Dorothea suspiciously. Likely to drag her back to London too.

"I prefer to keep a quick pace when I travel," her aunt said with a wink. "I'm not in my dotage quite yet."

Evelyn flushed.

"I didn't mean to imply—" she stammered, but Aunt Dorothea smiled over her teacup.

"I'm only teasing, dear."

Evelyn swiped a small honey cake from a platter before lowering herself into a chair. She had been depending upon the extra day to think up reasons to stay at Haythorne House. Now that Edmund had deserted her, her mother would force her back to the Sampford townhouse.

"I couldn't help but notice Edmund's absence." Evelyn frowned. There was no mistaking the hand of her mother in this. "Has he returned to London for good?"

Evelyn panicked and sucked down a gulp of tea, nearly draining her cup in one swallow. Her aunt quirked a brow.

"Yes," she admitted. Elaborating was unlikely to help her.

"I can tell from your expression—you know the reason I'm here."

Evelyn felt her hand tense on her silverware until her knuckles went white. If the fork hadn't been so sturdy, it might have snapped in two. She put it down firmly on the table.

"I cannot possibly go back yet," she pleaded. "I've only been gone from London a matter of weeks—hardly enough time for the gossips to move on."

"Yes. It's my understanding the rumors may have gotten a mite worse after your sudden departure."

Evelyn's face heated as she sank back against her chair.

This is just great.

How could she face her peers now? She'd fled London to avoid the worst of the ballroom chatter and had only succeeded in making matters worse for herself.

"I can't go back," she whispered. She hated the weakness in her voice, but she could do little to chase away the sense of defeat creeping in.

"Yes. I imagine that's why my sister sent me."

Evelyn's back straightened. Her aunt had spent the better part of a decade taking advantage of the sort of freedom that came with being a widow. She tended to travel quite a bit.

Maybe she'll let me join her.

"Do you have any plans, Aunt Dorothea?" she asked.

She tried to sound only passingly interested, not wanting to seem as desperate as she felt.

Aunt Dorothea chuckled. She was apparently as transparent as a pane of glass.

"I leave in a week to visit cousins," her aunt said with a sly smile. "Would you like to join me?"

Evelyn shifted again on the carriage seat to stave off the numbness creeping up her leg. She had never traveled farther than from London to Haythorne House and this was easily twice that distance. She was thankful Papa had insisted they take the family carriage, but even plush cushions and a spacious interior couldn't alleviate the aches of four long days of travel—and the tedium was beginning to wear on her.

"You look dissatisfied," Aunt Dorothea said baldly, jolting Evelyn from her sulk. "Though I think it might be too late to reconsider this visit."

"No, it isn't that." Evelyn shook her head. "I just wonder if I'm not making things worse by running away, yet again."

Aunt Dorothea shrugged one shoulder, the movement making the swath of silk wrapped around her hair shift, just a touch.

"In all likelihood, it will," she said. "But eventually, even the worst scandal has to die down, and you've hardly caused a scandal."

"That isn't how it feels."

"That is only because you've never been embroiled in *real* scandal. Things could always be much worse."

Evelyn shrugged her own shoulder. The only difference between this and a real scandal was that she still had her virtue intact. But if the gossips got any more out of hand, she didn't know if anyone would even believe it.

She sighed. Instead of buoying her, the conversation was coming out rather depressing.

She was nearly twenty-four with nothing to show for it but a public humiliation and a questionable reputation.

"I have a confession to make," Aunt Dorothea said with a frown. Evelyn wrinkled her brow. "Cousin Arabella knows you are coming."

"Yes," Evelyn said, confused. "You told her before we left

Norfolk."

"No." Aunt Dorothea shook her head. She watched Evelyn, as if waiting to gauge her reaction. "I mean that she knows *exactly* who is coming."

Evelyn sat up, ramrod straight.

"That cannot be!" This was a disaster. "You were going to tell her I was someone else."

"Evelyn, darling." Her aunt heaved a sigh. "I could hardly tell her *Evelyn Price* was coming with me to visit, but not my niece, simply someone else with a suspiciously similar name."

Evelyn deflated a little. "I suppose it is a silly name." But wasn't the rule to keep as close to the truth as possible when concealing a lie?

Coming up with a wholly different name sounded like a great way to immediately be caught out.

"I did explain a bit of the situation," Aunt Dorothea continued. "Not all of it, mind you. But enough to convince her to keep quiet about who you are."

There was a glint in her aunt's eye that made Evelyn think there had been more *coercion* involved than just sharing some of her story. She decided she did not want to find herself on her aunt's bad side.

"Her lips are sealed. No one else will know the truth."

"Really?" Evelyn cringed at the unvarnished hope in her voice, but it sounded rather too good to be true.

"It wasn't easy. She was quite excited at the idea of having an earl's daughter under her roof, and letting the world know it."

"She wouldn't be if she'd seen me in London," Evelyn muttered, peering out the window.

"Yes, well, I promised her you would spend time with her daughter, to make up for the deception."

"Augusta?" Evelyn asked. She had met the Hardings and their daughter only once, and she didn't remember liking the experience.

"Yes, you remember her, don't you?"

"Hmm," Evelyn hummed, and nodded. She did remember Augusta Harding—pretty, blonde, and shamelessly spoiled. "She didn't strike me as the type to keep a secret."

"She doesn't know."

Evelyn's brows leapt in shock. "But I've met her."

"She was a child then. She won't remember you. To her, you will just be a distant cousin, bringing a touch of London culture to Porthaven."

It sounded absurd. Especially if they were meant to spend any amount of time together.

"But surely the name is too similar? You said so yourself."

"Her mother does not seem to think it will be a problem." Aunt Dorothea fought a smile. "Perhaps she isn't overly bright."

Evelyn hadn't known she could choke on air. "That's hardly charitable!" she spluttered.

Her aunt laughed.

"She's nineteen now and home from school. Her mother is hoping you can provide any touch of polish—something beyond the abilities of a finishing school."

Evelyn raised one eyebrow. Mrs. Harding truly knew nothing about her if she thought she could be of any use to her daughter's *polish*.

She was more likely to teach Augusta how to avoid society in favor of novels than put her on the path to winning connections and landing a husband.

Aunt Dorothea gave her a sympathetic, knowing look and reached across the carriage to pat Evelyn's hand.

"Well dear, you'll do the best you can."

Aunt Dorothea was fast asleep by the time the carriage began rolling through the outskirts of Porthaven. Evelyn kept her sights glued to the changing scenery out the window, as much for the adventure of it as to drive out the consistent hum of the older woman's light snores. She chanced a glance over her shoulder at her aunt, stifling a grin at the careless way she was slumped in her seat.

I could manage so much rigorous travel too if I slept through half of it.

She turned back to the window with a smile. She was grateful for this trip—her first opportunity to experience the freedom of giving up on the marriage mart.

It was of course, the bitter freedom of failure, but a freedom, nonetheless.

Evelyn blinked through the glass and into the sunlight. It was the far side of noon and they'd gone all through the morning without pause. She could use the sleep just as much as her aunt, but the jostling of the carriage wheels over tamped dirt had made it impossible. And now that they were nearing the city, the thrill of excitement wouldn't let her rest her eyes.

The city came on gradually—wild green giving way to the occasional cottage, then short rows of terraced houses. The bump of cobbles was the first sign that they'd entered the city proper, followed by a sudden claustrophobia as the streets narrowed abruptly and towering buildings seemed to blot out the sun.

"Are we here already?" Aunt Dorothea asked.

She stared out the window, as composed as if she had been awake and alert the entire time. If Evelyn hadn't heard the noisy breaths herself, she never would have believed her aunt had spent half the trip slouched against the squabs. She didn't know how anyone could manage to look so fresh after travel.

Evelyn looked down at her own creased skirts with a grimace.

"I think so," she said, staring back out the window. "The streets are very narrow."

Aunt Dorothea hummed as she peered out at her side of the carriage.

"Yes, I vaguely remembered that."

"Hmm," Evelyn murmured. "I didn't realize the roads would be paved here."

She flushed the moment the words left her lips. She would need to learn to curb her tongue in front of the Hardings.

Evelyn frowned. She wished she could curb her thoughts if they were going to be so impolite.

"An effort to make these cramped lanes less unbearable,"

Aunt Dorothea hazarded, then gave Evelyn a wry smile. "Though I wouldn't say so to anyone we meet."

Evelyn forced a smile. She smoothed her hands over the rumpled lace of her skirt.

"And who am I going to meet?" she asked.

She picked at a loose thread on one of the lace ribbons.

"Don't forget, on-the-shelf relations spend a fair bit of time squiring their eligible young cousins about."

Evelyn choked on a laugh.

"Are you trying to dissuade me from accepting my fate?"

Aunt Dorothea's reply was an unladylike snort.

"I do believe we're here," was all she said.

Evelyn peered back out the window. The view had turned from cramped city streets to a large stretch of open parkland on one side and a row of fine houses on the other. She looked up, trying to get the scope of the Harding house. In the small frame of the window, it looked massive, akin to the houses she knew in Mayfair. But when the carriage door swung open, she could suddenly see all of its edges.

It was new looking, in that geometric, modern style everyone seemed to favor, but with more ornamentation than its neighbors. It reminded her of a large dollhouse, placed just so on its miniature square of green lawn and white stone pavement. She hesitated on her way out of the carriage. How would they manage to visit without being underfoot?

It's good that Mr. Harding is leaving for London so soon, she thought.

The front door opened then, and Evelyn raised startled

eyes as it swung wide. But instead of a butler's somber black, the couple who greeted them—framed by the crisp, clean lines of the doorway—were a riot of bright color, like a wildflower spring. Evelyn felt a smile tug at her lips.

These were her cousins.

Arabella and Solomon Harding.

"Arabella, dear, it is so good to see you," her aunt fussed as they were ushered into the house.

Evelyn stared at the pale ceiling. Someone had painted a blue sky across the width of the hall. It looked out of place in the small space, and cut off abruptly where an odd, long walkway extended down to the back of the house. If Evelyn peered just so, she could make out the footman bringing their trunks in, around to where the servants' stairs must be hidden away.

She looked up again at the puffs of cloud stippled across the light blue plaster.

"Finest painter in all of Porthaven." Mr. Harding's voice was a boom that bounced off the tight walls.

She nodded, trying her best not to let her eyes round into saucers.

"I may have him come back to do the drawing room too," he boasted.

"Don't you have business to attend to?" his wife asked.

He barked a laugh. "I'll leave you ladies to it then." He bussed a kiss across his wife's cheek that had Mrs. Harding turning a shade of scarlet that rivaled the flowers on her shawl.

"Oh, that man," she muttered, then ushered them to the next room.

They entered the drawing room in question, the walls papered a deep green-blue. Evelyn couldn't imagine how the space could benefit from a painted ceiling. She looked around the space.

Or paint anywhere, really.

Even the window frames were decorated with little, trailing vines carved into the wood. It was a wonder so much ornamentation could fit into such a small space. She was reminded again of her earlier impression of the Harding house as a dollhouse.

Like a child's toy.

Mrs. Harding watched Evelyn with narrowed eyes, making her worry she had said the words out loud.

"So, *Miss Price.*"

Ah, Evelyn thought. So that was it. *She has not gotten over the disappointment of my secrets.*

Mrs. Harding trailed her gaze down the length of Evelyn's rumpled dress. She fidgeted beneath her stare.

Or perhaps she has realized how useless I will be at helping her daughter.

That was beginning to seem more likely.

"Thank you for having us," Evelyn murmured. "You have a beautiful home."

That seemed to mollify Mrs. Harding, at least for the moment. She turned with a haughty smile, preening as she showed Aunt Dorothea the wallpapering.

Her aunt dutifully praised the spaciousness of the room. Evelyn wondered if she could toss a stone from the front hall and hit the morning room at the back of the house.

She smothered a smile.

"You must both be tired from your trip." Mrs. Harding's voice brought Evelyn back to current company. "Let me show you up to your rooms."

"That would be wonderful," Aunt Dorothea said. "Thank you."

Evelyn nodded and followed behind the two older women as they started for the stairs. Her aunt cast her a knowing look of reproach as Mrs. Harding continued on about the house, and Evelyn felt the keen prick of shame.

Her cousins were proud of their home, and she was silently ridiculing them for it.

I cannot help where my thoughts go. It was a weak excuse that rang hollow in her ears.

I cannot change what I have grown accustomed to. It did nothing to make her feel better.

She had never considered herself snobbish or rude, and she suddenly felt like both.

I must be tired. This is surely exhaustion.

She quietly followed them up to the second-floor landing, glad when Mrs. Harding pointed her to a door on the right. She wanted nothing more than to slip away and hide from her aunt's wise gaze. At least until she could recover enough to banish any misplaced pompousness from her mind.

Breakfast with the Hardings began promptly at eight o'clock and lasted until just before nine, when Mr. Harding gave his wife a peck on the cheek and left the house to conduct his business. Evelyn appreciated the structure, though the hour was beyond un-godly.

She raised her hand to cover a yawn, too tired to care that someone might see as she crossed to the window. She normally enjoyed breakfast, but all she'd been able to manage was a bite of toasted bread. It had been that way all week. She doubted she would ever adjust to her new schedule.

It is so damned early. She cast her eyes about her skittishly as if she had sworn out loud, but she was completely alone.

While the teal drawing room was small, it boasted a row of windows overlooking the street and the park beyond. It was as lovely a view as the canvas hanging in the drawing room at home. And with the way the early morning sunlight filtered through the leaves, the brick walkway outside looked like burnished gold.

Evelyn smiled to herself. There were already people out in the street, making their way through the park and across the pavement. She imagined they must be working people, like Mr. Harding. She yawned again.

No one else could have any sort of reason to be out at this hour.

Evelyn leaned against the edge of the window, peering down as a breeze rustled through the young trees lining the park.

Though it does look peaceful.

She toyed with the ties of the pewter-colored window

treatments, debating the merits of exploring Porthaven now, when the morning had barely begun. A cart rolled slowly along, down the street, two young women darting across behind as it passed.

Here, it seemed morning had already begun. At home though, she doubted the curtains had even been drawn.

A sliver of determination straightened her spine as she watched outside the window. She'd been here nearly a week and had done little more than laze about. If the city was awake, what was there to stop her from being out in the middle of it now?

Expectations?

Propriety?

Evelyn Price may go where she pleases.

It was an intoxicating thought, and her hands clenched at the bubble of excitement it brought. She wasn't in London. No one cared what she did here. They certainly would pay little heed to what time she ventured out into the city.

That alone was pull enough and mind settled, she marched to the entryway and the little corridor beyond.

She hardly expected her maid to be loitering in the hall, but still she peered around as though she might find her there. Instead, she went to the tall, well-dressed servant fading into the hall's wallpaper.

"Tell Marie we're going out," she rushed out, already turning on her heel to dart upstairs. She paused on the step, peering back to thank the young man, not wanting her enthusiasm for escaping the confines of the stifling house to push her to more rudeness.

The look of surprise that flittered across his face told her all she needed to know about the way her young cousin treated the staff.

I wonder if she would be so poorly behaved if she knew who I was.

She breathed a laugh. It hardly seemed likely. Evelyn let the question fade from her mind. And she was hardly likely to find out the answer anyway.

Chapter Three

The sun was just as brilliant outside as Evelyn had expected from the drawing room window. Little motes danced in the light slipping through to the tree lined pavement, and across the street was a sea of green—another time she would have to explore the park.

Evelyn let Marie lead them through the winding streets, making their way past rows of homes and picking through the streets that connected the residential neighborhoods to the bustling center of the city. There, the narrow lanes opened to a large square, each side boasting little shops tucked into each available space.

"Is there a book shop near here?" she asked, making a full turn on the cobbled walkway as she scanned the shopfronts.

"Across the square," Marie said with a nod. "With the green awning."

Tucked in at the end of a row of stores was a little green shade, neatly running parallel to the row of large windows at the front. The sun was too bright to peek inside, but she could see the lettering painted across the glass.

Books.

"Come, let's see what they have."

She ignored Marie's blatant chuckle, too excited to care, and stepped into the square, hurrying across to the other side. Marie's mother had worked in the Sampford household since before either girl had been born. As a child, Evelyn had found making friends a difficult task, but Marie had been a steady companion. As a result, the other woman was more than happy to say what she thought, and Evelyn was more than happy to put up with it.

She was as much a friend as a maid anyway.

A bell tinkled overhead as she opened the door, announcing their entrance. It was warm inside, warmer than the early spring chill outside, and Evelyn was glad she wore her yellow walking dress instead of a proper jacket.

It did the job well enough without suffocating her in heavy layers.

Evelyn turned to look around the shop as she tugged the ribbons free from beneath her chin. She could hardly see anything past the wide brim of her bonnet, and the shop itself was small, squeezed into a tight space at the end of its row of storefronts. Still, the shelving ran all along the walls, from floor to ceiling.

Oh, my. It was the like the comfort of coming home. *I think I could live here quite comfortably.*

Marie would undoubtedly think she was crazed.

She smiled as she walked the rows and rows of books. There was a little bit of everything here.

Histories. Botany. Politics. She trailed her finger along the spines. It was an eclectic assortment. *Novels.*

She paused with the pad of her fingertip pressed against the spine of one book, feeling the smile tug at her lips. Her mother would roll her eyes. Her brother would accuse her of rotting away her brain.

A romance.

She reached up on tiptoes and tugged the volumes down from the top shelf. She would have to come back when she had more time and explore these shelves more freely, but this would certainly do for now.

And if the weather continues like this, I can read in the garden after luncheon.

With the primrose bonnet ribbons looped hastily around her arm and books stacked in her hand, Evelyn imagined she looked like a rumpled mess stepping up to the counter, though the little white-haired man at the money box only smiled. She flushed when she pulled the small fortune from her reticule to pay. It felt wildly extravagant to pay so much in ready money for a book, but the guilt only half struck her. And when the proprietor grinned at her, she felt somewhat vindicated in her purchase.

"Thank you," she said as she collected the books—two tied up in a single ribbon, volume one already opened in her hand.

The man nodded as she stepped back towards the door.

"Enjoy this weather while it lasts," he said with another smile and a wink. "We'll be in for rain later."

She paused, peering from the blue sky outside and back to the man. "Is it likely to rain today?" she asked.

"We're overdue for it," he said with chuckle. "And my knee always pains me before a downpour."

She smiled to herself at his casual familiarity. She imagined this was what it felt like to live in a small town or village. One where everyone knew each other and each other's business. But without the viciousness of the *ton*, or the cloying, fake niceties that accompanied it.

"I will keep that in mind," she said with a broader smile, and lifted her hand in a small wave before leaving the shop.

Evelyn lifted a hand to shade her eyes when she stepped back outside. The sun was certainly still shining brightly just then, the sky so blue it was blinding. But if she squinted against the light, she could just see the haziness of clouds creeping in from the horizon.

Maybe he does know what he's talking about, she thought bemusedly.

Her eyes trailed back to the open page in her hand, and she lifted the book for a better view of the printed words. She'd always been a fool for these dreamy romances, and if she'd really lost her chances of finding her own love story, she'd just have to devour more of these. She would live vicariously through fictional heroines—*shamelessly*.

I should most likely save my reading for once we've made it back.

It was probably unwise to walk all the way back to Linden Street and the Harding house with her face buried in a book, but she'd been hopelessly bored the last few days, with nothing but letter writing to entertain herself.

She looked around at the midmorning rush, then down again at the book. *This is so ill advised*, she grumbled.

Yet she fumbled to turn another page and continued anyway. Boredom and desperation made her do foolish things.

"Do be careful," Marie groaned as she sidestepped out of Evelyn's way.

"I will stay close to the buildings," Evelyn conceded. "This way I can keep a straight line."

Marie stifled a snort but nodded, letting Evelyn pass her to follow the line the windows. She struggled trying to turn another page and huffed. Her gloves made it difficult to turn the pages, so she wiggled her fingers inside the kid leather, trying to loosen them free.

When that didn't work, she carelessly placed the tip of a finger between her teeth and pulled. She exclaimed quietly when her hand popped free.

She flexed her fingers against the cold air before turning the page. It felt odd with one hand encased in warm leather, so she repeated the awkward maneuver with the other glove, not caring who saw the unladylike behavior. She tucked the gloves into the bonnet swinging from her arm and shifted her focus back to the book. She barely avoided colliding with a pair of giggling, shopping ladies as Marie led her aside by the elbow.

She crossed to the other side of the square at Marie's urging, glancing up only briefly to get her bearings. She was nearly across when the sky darkened, one of those far off clouds reaching out to blot the sun behind shadow. She shivered as the temperature dropped without direct sunlight to warm her, and lifted the book closer to her face, as if the pages would protect her from the breeze.

How large is this damned cloud? she wondered as she waited for it to pass.

But it never did.

Instead, she walked face first into an immovable wall—and had the immediate realization that it wasn't really a wall at all.

She blinked and peered up—and up—at the shadowy face looking down at her from atop a set of broad, hard shoulders.

Her mouth went dry.

They're the broadest shoulders I've ever seen, she thought deliriously.

It couldn't possibly be true. But she had certainly never been so close to shoulders like that, or—

She blinked down again at where her hands still held her book, crushed between the decorative cover and a—expensively tailored—large, well-muscled chest.

Oh Lord.

She squeezed her eyes shut, feeling her face flame like never before, but she didn't seem able to move, frozen in place where she'd collided with the stranger, still pressed against him. Mortification swept her when she heard him clear his throat.

This is really happening. There would be no slinking into the shadows to hide from this embarrassment.

And then she looked up again and swallowed.

He is the shadow.

There had never been a cloud, just this large, imposing man, and with the sun angled behind his head, it took a moment of blindly blinking up at him before his face came into focus. Evelyn drew in a sharp breath and only hoped she didn't *squeak* when her mouth popped open in surprise.

He wasn't what she would have called traditionally attractive by London standards. Even smartly dressed, he looked too rough, too savage beneath his elegant veneer.

His eyes were fierce and penetrating, his hair a bit long, almost wild where it brushed his starched collar. And he was far too big to fit the lithe athleticism favored by the fashionable men of the ton.

Though she suddenly wondered if it wasn't simply that the lazy Lord Nigels of London didn't have the right kind of dedication, because there was something staggeringly masculine about this.

"Excuse me," she chirped as she attempted to take a step back. She needed to disentangle herself from his heat, which was undeniably intoxicating. Remaining so close for any longer was inadvisable.

She forced herself to take a step back, but her toe caught in a gap in the cobbles, and she stumbled with a gasp.

She couldn't seem to keep her feet today and it was beyond

embarrassing. But then her gasp turned into a sudden, shaky inhalation when she felt warm, shockingly gloveless hands grasp for her upper arms, preventing her fall.

"Thank you," she said breathlessly. His eyes roved over her face, concern wrinkling his brow.

"Are you alright?" he asked, his voice deep and smooth.

He had nothing of the city in his voice—if she closed her eyes, she might have mistaken him for a London gentleman.

"Yes. I'm so sorry I didn't see you."

Inwardly she cringed.

I didn't see you?

As far as excuses went, it was beyond terrible. She craned her neck to look at him. He was practically a giant. How could she possibly have missed him?

"Is it any good at least?" he asked, but she stared back at him wordlessly, mouth parted like a fish. She could barely make sense of what he had said, let alone formulate an answer. She blinked.

He released his hold on her arms and let one hand fall to tap against the spine of the book still clutched in her hand.

"Oh!" She felt her face heat. "I don't know. I only just started it."

He nodded. "I might have guessed. I saw you leaving Mr. Balfour's."

Mr. Balfour's? she wondered silently.

A hint of a smile teased his stern features before he clarified. "The bookseller."

Heat crept up from her beneath collar. Thinking of this

man watching her carelessly walk all this way with her nose in a book was too much. It made her feel suddenly foolish.

"Of course," she replied.

Still, that little smile did odd things to her equilibrium.

She caught a glance of Marie from the corner of her eye, the maid shifting her feet in what might have been physical discomfort—or the pain of Evelyn's continued awkwardness.

Either way, they needed to return to the Harding's. She should excuse herself and go, though it seemed a shame to leave without his name.

"Thank you again, Mr.—" she hedged, feeling bold and reckless.

Something sparked in his eyes, and it made her tilt her own away. "Gabriel Stone," he said, the deep baritone of his voice low and hypnotic.

"Mr. Stone." She liked the way it sounded. "Evelyn Price," she added haltingly, nearly forgetting her name.

But being *Miss Price* was proving intriguing. *I would even say, exciting.*

Marie fumbled with her package of wrapped books and Evelyn darted her eyes to the maid once more. She hid it well, but there was definite bemusement in her downcast eyes.

"Happy to be of service, Miss Price." His voice drew her back to the firm set of his lips.

His eyes flickered with something she couldn't name, but it made her skin tingle all the same.

"We're expected back," she said, glancing again to Marie. "I've been visiting family." She could feel his eyes on her face and babbled on nervously. "They'll be wondering where I am. I have a tendency to wander, especially when reading."

Why did I say that? She could have crawled into a hole in the ground. *As if he needs any more convincing that I'm a feather-brained ninny.*

"The one thing I wish I had more time for," he said, the corner of his mouth finally lifting up into something resembling a real smile. "Reading and having the spare time for it—it might be the only thing I miss from my school days."

He chuckled and Evelyn tried to hide her sudden intake of breath. It was too trite to say it transformed his face, but when he really smiled, it even lit up his eyes.

If she didn't leave soon, she might get lost in those eyes. "It was a pleasure to meet you," she breathed.

"Indeed," he said with a tilt of his head, the hint of a smile still playing over his features.

She pushed herself to step around him, nodding with a blush to Marie as they started back the way they'd come. It felt as if her heart was going to beat out of her chest. Surely everyone could hear it.

I am surprised they cannot see *it.*

She glanced back before they rounded the corner, unable to forfeit one last look. He was still standing there watching her, so tall he practically blotted out half the sky. When she caught his eye, he gave a nod of acknowledgement before turning to leave. She watched while he slipped into the shadow between buildings, on his way to wherever he'd been going before their collision.

"Marie, remind me never to walk with a book in my face again," she uttered as they turned their own corner.

"Are you sure?" Marie quipped. "You didn't seem to mind so much a moment ago."

Evelyn couldn't help her startled laugh.

Gabriel frowned, trying to dispel the grin he felt splashed across his face, as he walked down the next street on the way to his banker.

Evelyn Price.

The fact the girl was beautiful had been evident the moment he'd seen her step out from under the green awning at Balfour's. Porcelain skin, flushed from the cold and radiant in the sunlight, bright eyes, and the richest brown hair curling around her gently rounded face. She didn't possess the doll-like features that were so fashionable, but she was young.

Too damn young, he thought with a groan. If it hadn't been obvious from her careless distraction, up close the smooth perfection of her features was enough to confirm it.

He wondered who her family was, and who she was visiting. With two sisters of his own, he knew her dress was well made. She likely had connections in the same circles he traveled in—it stood to reason their paths would cross again.

Selfishly, he hoped they did. But he shook his head with a groan.

It had been a moment of madness that had placed him directly in her path. He had seen the way she'd walked without any attention to her surroundings, the way her maid cut her looks that fluctuated between concern and exasperation.

He imagined the two were close, or as close as a servant and her mistress could be.

It had been pure foolishness that prompted him to change course across the square. The way her full lips had parted while her delicate hands had pressed against his chest had made it well worth it, though it made him feel like the worst kind of rogue.

As did the tempting vision of her walking away, the sway of her hips still imprinted in his mind.

Gabriel shook his head, forcibly dislodging the image. He should be focusing on his business troubles, and the devil knew he had enough of those lately.

There were difficulties inherent in any sort of business, and wine was no different. His grandfather had built his company on the network of well-placed relationships developed over years in trade. Simon Stone's son, Henry, had expanded from the small local enterprise he'd inherited to an independent import company of considerable size.

The pressure Gabriel felt to uphold that success was sometimes suffocating.

And now one of my ships is missing.

The Starling had been due back in port over a week ago. In all likelihood, Captain Reid had been forced to sail through the devastating squall reported off the coast of Spain. Normally, he would stake his life on Reid's sailing ability, but some things just couldn't be overcome.

In three days, The Starling, its men, and cargo would be

missing for two full weeks.

It felt like some equalizing punishment cast down from the Heavens. He knew it was foolhardy to continue his trade straight on, unhindered, even in the face of the damned war. But the world moved on—and people wanted wine, whether the continent was a riotous mess or not. He'd been lucky thus far, though he knew of many others who had not. He sighed.

And now this.

The heavy loss of imported wines would hurt, but Gabriel could weather it until his next shipment. It was one of the assumed risks in any international trade. But he had a solid foundation and enough revenue to ride out most disasters. The possible deaths of all those onboard troubled Gabriel far more. They were good, honest men employed on The Starling, and many had families. Losses like these were always hard to accept.

And it was just more distressing news in already uneasy times. He cursed under his breath when he thought of it.

It had been nearly three months since Stuart Talbot had come to him, begging he investigate the dockside thefts. Those warehouses had apparently become the hunting grounds of some local delinquents, though it hardly seemed the work of any criminal mastermind.

More likely the hooligans had gotten lucky.

And then Franklin had found the discrepancies in Gabriel's own accounts—missing inventory that stretched back at least six months. There was no one to blame for the oversight. Gabriel reviewed the books himself almost weekly. Whoever was stealing from him had started small, but had grown more brazen in recent weeks.

It would have been no more than a headache—a nagging complaint at the back of his head—if he didn't already know Constable Evans. The man was the walking embodiment of ineptitude. If anything was to be done about the thefts, Gabriel couldn't leave it up to that man.

Thankfully, he had enough influence and money alike to stop it, even if he had to track down the culprits himself.

Chapter Four

Mr. Balfour had been right after all. By two o'clock, the skies opened, and they were treated to an onslaught that didn't seem likely to let up anytime soon. A fire was laid in the drawing room, an unflinching defense against the creeping cold. It left Evelyn little choice but to join her aunt and cousins in the compact space.

With four ladies stuffed in like sardines, it was very nearly suffocating. Still, it was better than shivering in her room—and she had plenty to occupy herself with, alternating between her new novel, the letter she was writing to Maryann, and memories of Gabriel Stone's expansive chest.

She could practically feel the hard slope of muscle shifting beneath her hands now.

Evelyn, you are being wicked, she admonished.

But no one had ever made her so aware of her femininity before. Certainly not *Lord Nigel Sedley*.

He'd stirred some sort of interest in her of course, but if this was what attraction was meant to feel like, she would have been better off ignoring Lord Nigel the first time he'd swept her into the gardens.

"You should sit farther from the fire," Aunt Dorothea said with a heavy sigh, her voice shaking Evelyn from her thoughts with a start.

"Pardon?"

Aunt Dorothea gestured between the fireplace and where Evelyn sat just to the left. "Perhaps the chair by the window," she suggested, though Evelyn doubted it would make much difference—every seat in this room was in spitting distance of the licking flames.

Vulgar now, too.

"I don't want you fainting dear," she said.

Augusta barely contained a chuckle behind her needlework. Evelyn narrowed her eyes at the younger woman, then back to her aunt. It was then she remembered where her mind had wandered, and the color that must be burning across her face.

"The window does look more comfortable," she forced out. Inside she thought she might die from embarrassment.

Augusta sniggered again behind her hand, but Evelyn would prefer they all think she was too delicate to sit near the fire. It was better than seeing inside her increasingly indecent thoughts.

She caught Aunt Dorothea's eye again as she settled into her new seat and felt her face flush darker. The others might believe the heat had been too much, but the glimmer in her aunt's eyes gave her away—Aunt Dorothea, at least, didn't believe a word of it.

"The rain came on quite suddenly," Evelyn said by way of conversation.

"It always rains," Augusta sulked. "It's one of the things that makes this place so unbearable."

It seemed to take Mrs. Harding every ounce of strength not to roll her eyes at her daughter. "It rains in London too, Augusta. It isn't a different country."

"It feels like it," Augusta grumbled in response.

Evelyn hid her smirk behind her book. Her cousin's girlish pouting reminded her of her young sister's own melodrama. But Penelope was barely fifteen, and Augusta thought herself ready for marriage.

It does feel a bit like a different country though.

Or perhaps she was the only one different here.

Whatever the reason, be it her assumed name or the general anonymity of a new city, Porthaven presented a chance for freedom that she had never experienced in London.

She frowned down at her book, a sigh slipping from her lips. It would be difficult to give that freedom up when it was time to return to London.

She peered out the window at the rain obscuring her view of the garden and sighed again.

I'll just have to enjoy it while I can.

Dinner was served at five o'clock, always as promptly as breakfast. Marie helped Evelyn dress, selecting one of her simpler gowns—rose crepe over rose silk. Evelyn thought the color was flattering at least, though now that she was cinched in, she thought it a bit snug.

It was already a year old—or was it two? She had a hard time giving up the few pieces of clothing she actually liked, a fact that caused her mother a mountain of grief.

"I think this one is getting too small," she lamented into the mirror. It was really too bad, because it looked nice and was exceptionally comfortable. "Maybe I should stop eating at luncheon," she muttered.

Marie stuck a pin in Evelyn's hair and scoffed. "Starving yourself hardly seems like a solution." She patted Evelyn's hair, eyeing her handiwork in the mirror. "Besides, it looks perfect— as long as you can breathe in it. You can breathe, can't you?"

"Yes," Evelyn said with a laugh. "You don't think it accentuates me a little too much?"

"I think if you'd been wearing this today, Mr. Stone would have been struck mute," she said so bluntly, Evelyn nearly choked on her own tongue.

"Marie!" she exclaimed but couldn't suppress a surprised laugh—or the warmth that spread in her belly at the thought.

Marie shrugged, a wry smile turning up one side of her mouth as she busied herself, tidying up the room. Evelyn attempted a severe look at her in the mirror but ruined the effect by once more eyeing the close-fitting bodice with a bewildered laugh.

She turned, placing a finger at the scooped neckline, seeing the way her chest strained against it. She'd never thought to look at her clothing through the male eye. She tilted her head. Maybe Marie was right.

Not that she'd ever have the chance to meet Mr. Stone again.

The rain continued for two long days—days when Evelyn was trapped inside with Aunt Dorothea's knowing eye and Augusta's shifting moods. When the sun shone brightly midweek, she jumped at the chance to escape.

"Marie," she called as she came back up from breakfast. "Let's explore the park today."

Marie paused in her folding and looked Evelyn up and down. "I'll find something better for you to wear."

Evelyn eyed herself in the mirror. "What's wrong with this dress?"

Marie gave her a quelling look but said nothing else as she turned to the trunk.

"Fine," Evelyn conceded. "But I don't need a bonnet."

Marie narrowed her eyes. "You need a bonnet. What would your mother say if she knew you were going out without one?"

Evelyn smiled. "My mother isn't here."

"If you'd like to hear that tirade when you return to London, freckled and sun-tanned, then by all means. But I'm bringing it for you if you won't."

"Fine." Evelyn grumbled, snatching the straw hat from Marie's hands. "But I won't keep it on."

The maid laughed. "I never expected you would."

Out in the streaming sunlight, Evelyn was secretly glad for the bonnet's wide brim, though she'd never tell Marie. It was a beautiful day, made doubly special after the dismal grey of the past two days.

They walked along the main path, following where it curved through the rolling expanse of green. It was like a little oasis here in the middle of the city, but without the crush of carriages and people that dominated Hyde Park.

"I should have brought my book," Evelyn said as she eyed the shade beneath a large oak tree.

Marie choked back a laugh. Evelyn peered at her in her periphery. "Something to add?" she asked.

Marie shook her head with a poorly concealed smile and they both knew they were thinking about her collision in town. There was hardly anything quite so absurd as the apparent danger of a book in Evelyn's hands.

She was a walking disaster, given half a chance.

"I promise never to read while walking again," she said with mock seriousness.

Marie answered with a skeptical huff. "We'll see."

The park was larger than Evelyn had first realized. From the Hardings' home on Linden Street, it looked like the sort of small city garden you could skip a stone across, but green lawns extended so far, the buildings at the other end where little more than hazy grey blocks peeking through the trees.

"I wonder what's on the other side," Evelyn mused.

Their path had taken them along the edge of a fishpond somewhere near the midway mark. Evelyn peered into the water as they walked.

"More houses," Marie guessed.

"Hmm," she replied, absently fiddling with the ribbon ties of her bonnet. The brim might be effective at shading her face, but it was damned itchy beneath her chin.

Evelyn watched a brown feathered duck fly over the pond to land near the water's edge. It ruffled its wings with a little splash. Marie coughed lightly, but Evelyn hardly noticed, too busy watching the little duck preen.

When her maid reached over and pinched her arm, she jolted.

"Ow," she said accusingly. Marie opened her eyes wide in warning, making Evelyn frown, but still she whispered, "what? You pinched me. That hurt!"

Marie flicked her eyes back towards the main path.

"I thought you might like some warning," she said under her breath.

"Warning?" Evelyn mouthed as she turned her attention to the path, then felt her eyes go momentarily wide before she managed to compose herself.

Gabriel Stone was walking towards them, a surprised smile pulling up one corner of his mouth.

"Don't do anything embarrassing," Marie muttered as she

took two steps back.

Evelyn didn't have the chance for a witty retort, not when Mr. Stone was already so close. Goodness, he was breathtaking. *No, more than breathtaking.*

He looked absolutely commanding, like he controlled the very ground beneath his feet.

A breeze rustled through the trees and over the grass, playing with the loose ends of his hair—no fashionable style or greasy pomade for him. It made him look barely civilized, even in his fine black coat. He had the simple, refined dress of a London dandy, but Evelyn thought he wore the molded black superfine and buff breeches far better than any gentleman she knew.

He bowed his head when he reached her.

"Mr. Stone. I didn't expect to see you here," she said. Her voice came out tight, clipped.

She was too aware of his physicality.

She released a heavy breath, trying to calm herself. She hoped he couldn't tell how sharply he affected her.

He gestured to the stretch of park behind him. "It's a more direct path to my office," he explained. "I prefer to walk it most days."

"It's very beautiful here," she agreed.

His answering smile made her warm inside, despite the breeze. "When the weather holds," he said wryly.

"Mr. Balfour warned me it would rain, though I didn't expect quite this much of it," Evelyn said with a half grin.

Mr. Stone looked pleased that she'd remembered the old bookseller. It felt unnervingly pleasant to have his approval.

"Yes, but he says it will rain at least eighty percent of the time." He chuckled, and her smile grew wider. "But I suppose he has to be right some of the time."

He stepped closer as a breeze blew across the field, sending ripples across the pond. The wind tousled his hair again, though it had little power over his closely fitted clothes.

Evelyn had no such luck, her skirts whipping around and pulling taught against her legs. Another gust tugged the ribbons on her bonnet free, and she gasped as it came off. She turned and reached for it, but it flew past her fingers, and she closed her hand around air.

"Oh dear."

She bent to pick it up just as Mr. Stone did the same, and his arm brushed against hers, sending a shudder of awareness through her. She stumbled at the contact, but a hand at her waist prevented her fall.

"I'm sorry," he said, though he didn't move his hand. It stayed at her waist, his fingers firm at her back. "Are you alright?"

She nodded, her eyes level with his cravat. It was remarkably white.

He must spend a fortune in bleach.

Evelyn cleared her throat and tried to look up, but only succeeded in reaching his neck, and the light shadow under his jaw.

"I would say I'm not usually this clumsy, but I'm afraid

that would be a lie," she muttered nervously, and chanced a glance the rest of the way up to his face.

He was much closer than she'd realized—close enough that if she tipped up onto her toes, she could press her lips to—

Another rush of air caught up her hat, sending it tumbling across the grass before tossing it up, up, and over the edge of the pond. It landed with a splash.

Evelyn felt something hysterical bubble up in her chest. She didn't know if it was his overwhelming nearness, her embarrassing clumsiness, or the sight of her pretty bonnet floating beside the ducks, but she couldn't help the giggle that escaped.

She brought a hand up to her lips, as if pushing the noise back inside. She had never been a giggler—that was for ladies who gossiped and flirted, things she'd never been very good at.

Mr. Stone eyed the straw bonnet with a calculating eye, as if trying to work out how to get it out from the middle of the pond.

"I'm not going to make you retrieve it," she said with a breathy laugh.

"I don't think I could possibly salvage it anyway," he chuckled. "Though I do wonder if I ought to give up my trip to the office to keep an eye on you."

His teasing tone made Evelyn's face heat.

First giggling, now teasing—

Were they flirting?

"I should be heading back anyway," she said, nodding in the direction of Linden Street and the Harding house. "We've been out all morning." She looked up at the bright sun. "Besides, I freckle terribly."

"I can't imagine anything looking terrible on you."

She sucked in a breath at his hushed compliment and defensively forced out a laugh, uncertain what to make of the giddy, tingly feeling in her belly. She turned away slightly, just enough to catch Marie's eye.

They would have so much to talk about when they got back.

Beside her, Mr. Stone straightened and cleared his throat. When she looked back, he appeared stiff. She wondered if she might have disappointed him by all but ignoring his compliment, but she hardly knew what to say.

"I should really get going too. I have business to attend to," he said, and she couldn't help but feel she had broken whatever moment had been between the two of them. It was a keen loss that she didn't like, and it made something in her chest clench.

"Would you walk with me?" she asked hesitantly. "I am going that way too."

She held her breath and kept her eyes glued to the swaying grass, afraid to see rejection on his face.

She remembered Nigel's haughty sneer at Lady Whitaker's ball when he'd rebuffed her. It was an unpleasant reminder, but the truth was he hadn't wanted her, and he had known who she was—who her father was.

What could *this* man possibly see in her?

Especially when I am simply Miss Price.

"It would be my pleasure."

She peered up, shading her eyes from the sun with a hand. He was so very striking from this angle. It reminded her of their encounter in front of the bookstore.

"Thank you," she muttered when he offered his arm, but still she hesitated.

They hadn't even been properly introduced and now she was going to walk across the park with her hand tucked against his arm? It was so very bold. But what good was pretending to be someone else if it didn't afford her the freedom to *be* bold.

She hooked her hand around his arm without another thought. Her fingers flexed and she stared at the spot where they touched. She didn't know what it was, but she liked the feel of his strength beneath her palm.

This isn't London, she reminder herself. There were no tittering gossips watching her, waiting for the Earl of Sampford's daughter to misstep. No one in Porthaven knew who she was, and they certainly wouldn't have any opinions on who she walked with.

She looked up at his profile again. It was too bad she would eventually have to leave and go back to those horrible vultures in London.

I'd much rather have more of this.

"I thought you didn't know how to flirt."

Evelyn hurriedly pressed her bedroom door shut, falling back against it as if she could physically keep out any listening ears.

"I don't," she bit out.

"You could have fooled me." Marie turned towards the wardrobe to hide her smile. "What color for dinner tonight?"

She shrugged. "You choose."

She crossed the room and tossed herself onto the bed. She'd been flirting with Mr. Stone—*flirting*.

And giggling.

It was absurd. She didn't know how to flirt. She'd never flirted—not even with Nigel. At least she didn't think she had.

He'd always been the instigator in their trysts. Not that there had really been anything sordid about it. Some kissing in the garden and that one time he'd grazed her breast hardly constituted an affair, although she could imagine the spin society would put on it.

And never mind that I'd expected an engagement at the end of it.

This, now, was a different story entirely. She sighed, covering her eyes with a fling of her arm. Here she was, playing the coquette with a man she had no chance at a future with.

She rubbed the space just over her breastbone. She didn't know how long she would be in Porthaven, but she already didn't like the idea of leaving for London when her stay was over, and not only because of what she would be returning to. If only she had ever felt this way about any of the men at home.

"How about the green," Marie suggested, holding up a dress the color of sea glass.

Evelyn wrinkled her brow. "I didn't think I packed that one." She propped herself up on an elbow. "I don't even remember ever wearing it."

"You haven't," Marie said wryly. "Your mother packed it—and six others."

"No wonder I had so many trunks," Evelyn muttered as she dropped back onto the bed. She peered at Marie again from the corner of her eye. "What do you think of him?"

"*Him* who?" Marie asked archly.

"You know exactly who I mean," Evelyn said and tossed a pillow across the room. The small, frilly thing barely brushed Marie's arm.

"Hmmm," Marie hummed with a barely contained grin.

Evelyn sighed. "Mr. Stone," she hissed with a glance at the closed door.

"What do you think of him?" Marie countered.

Evelyn looked up at the ceiling. The stark white color reminded her of his bright cravat, and that brought thoughts of the hard muscle underneath. She flushed.

What do I think of Mr. Stone?

It was a difficult question to answer when there was so much context to think of. How she felt didn't mean the same thing for Lady Evelyn as it did for Miss Price.

"He doesn't even know who I am."

Evelyn felt the shift of the mattress as Marie perched on the edge of her bed. She didn't know how she would have managed here in Porthaven, let alone London, without Marie. She was almost more companion than she was maid. She reached for Marie's hand.

We even read together at Haythorne House, she thought with a half-delirious laugh. And there were few people she could talk so freely with, without the shadow of propriety hanging over her head.

What do I think of him?

"I think I like him," Evelyn whispered up to the ceiling, barely audible, but she knew Marie heard her.

Chapter Five

Little stones crunched under Evelyn's slippered foot as she turned to make another circuit of the garden. She brushed a curl from her face and sighed when she tilted her head back. The sky was clear—a crisp blue without a cloud in sight. The sun was nearly too bright, but it was warm on her face and that was enough to make her glad she'd discarded her hat. It had been so frigidly cold lately, she wondered if they would skip right over spring altogether.

At least it isn't raining, she thought wryly.

It was a welcome change from the excessive rain. Every other day seemed to be grim and wet, making it a sort of frigid, damp torture—especially when the weather kept her forced into the company of her cousins, with no chance of escape.

Augusta's pouting alone could make Linden Street feel claustrophobically cramped, like a gilded prison.

She sighed and tipped her face back up to the sun, closing her eyes against the brightness. It felt as if she had been trapped inside more often than not since arriving in Porthaven. She supposed they would be enjoying a flurry of social engagements back in London—anything to beat back the dreariness of this cursed weather. She was glad at least to be missing out on that.

She glanced back down at the letter clasped in her hand and sighed again, bringing it up for another read. She frowned down at Maryann's familiar penmanship, feeling a little crease form between her brows. It was just an account of what her friend had done since arriving in Bath, and an open invitation to visit—nothing to explicitly suggest anything was wrong. Yet—

Something is most definitely wrong.

She huffed out a frustrated breath and flipped the letter over, continuing onto the other side. It would be easier if she had something concrete to go on, but the letter itself was completely innocuous. It was the feel of it that was off—there was a melancholy in the writing that didn't match Maryann's excitement before leaving London.

Something had happened in the last month. Evelyn just didn't know what.

She folded the letter back up, holding the little square of paper tight between her fingers as she walked across the garden. It wasn't like she could ask Maryann outright what was suddenly wrong, but perhaps she could give her a little push, show her unwavering support by writing, and maybe leave a small hint of her concerns.

Like dropping breadcrumbs.

She paused as she considered it. But where would she even begin? She sighed and dropped herself onto the garden bench. Evelyn had never liked a problem she couldn't solve, but first she needed to know what she was dealing with. Teasing out what this one even was would be difficult. She had no notion what was on her friend's mind. Maryann had been careful to leave anything of the sort out.

Even with the bright sky, the garden became chilled as the sun passed slowly overhead. A breeze dipped into the garden, sending a shiver though Evelyn as it went. She tugged her shawl tightly around her shoulders and stood to peer back into the house. It was a shame to leave the sun for the dimness waiting inside, but her fingers were beginning to prickle with the cold.

It was hours still until dinner, and she had little else to do to pass the time.

I might as well write to Maryann.

Or at least start something, even if she didn't know where to being to offer help.

I will write, and simply hope she shares what is bothering her in the next letter.

It was the best she could do at the moment.

She bent to pick up her hat from the garden bench, gripping it by its pale green ribbons. It swung like a pendulum from her hand as she walked.

Perhaps I should plan a visit to Bath soon.

It wasn't a terrible idea.

She leaned into the doorframe as she took the step up. The doorway opened to the small hall at the rear of the house, just off the morning room where they breakfasted. The large glass windows let in a flood of light to reflect off the pale walls, giving the temporary illusion that she was still outside. She closed her eyes, inhaling deep. There was no rosy perfume in the air yet, but there was still the bright smell of early spring.

Opening her eyes, she turned towards the front of the house, where the staircase rounded up to the second floor. It took her eyes a moment to adjust—the rest of the house was gloomier, without windows lining every wall.

She took another step and nearly collided with a servant, hurrying through with a two-person tea service in the direction of Mr. Harding's study.

"Excuse me."

Evelyn peered towards the front of the house but couldn't see past the dining room from this angle.

No matter.

She glanced back down at Maryann's letter as she rounded the corner. She hoped whatever plagued her friend wasn't anything too dreadful, but she worried. The Selwyns were already suffering financial strain—they didn't need more trouble compounding it.

The sound of male voices drifted back from the other end of the house. She looked up as she approached, ready to slip up the stairs unnoticed, and cringed at Mr. Harding's booming laugh. His companion wasn't nearly so boisterous.

She could only see the back of his black coat and dark hair, but it was a somber contrast to Mr. Harding's garishness. The man chuckled, then said something in response, but Evelyn couldn't make out the words because the sound of the smooth, familiar voice made her thoughts jumble.

Her delicate slippers somehow made enough noise as she slid to a stop for the two men to notice, and she watched, frozen, as Gabriel Stone turned to face her.

He was already nodding politely when their eyes met and he paused, eyes going momentarily wide, before a surprised smile tugged at one corner of his mouth.

"Miss Price," Mr. Harding called with a tremulous laugh when she had paused long enough to be unavoidable.

The name sounded awkward from his mouth and he looked to be struggling with what to do now. She had all but forced the introduction on him by lingering awkwardly, but she could imagine he was having trouble introducing a man of business to his wife's *lady* cousin.

"Mr. Harding," she replied with a distracted smile as she tried her best not to openly stare into Mr. Stone's handsome face. She took a slight step forward and hoped it was enough for Mr. Harding to take the hint. After all, if she was only *Miss Price*, there was no major impediment to an introduction.

She peeked at Gabriel through her lashes and caught his eyes trailing the length of her pale dress in a way that made her skin tingle, though she wished she was wearing something more flattering than the pale muslin. She gave him a faint smile.

It suddenly felt imperative that she have this introduction.

Mr. Harding cleared his throat and straightened to his full height. He still didn't come near to Mr. Stone's stature.

"Miss Price," he started, coughing to clear his throat. "May I introduce my friend, Mr. Stone?" Mr. Harding's spine seemed stiffer with resolve, and he had regained some of his usual bluster. "He's one of our more prominent men here in Porthaven."

"It's a pleasure to meet you, Mr. Stone." She felt warm inside, especially when his eyes danced with their intensity.

"You've already met Lady Carr," Mr. Harding said. "Miss Price is her niece."

She smiled. Though Mr. Harding could have introduced her as a butterfly, and she would have agreed. Something in Mr. Stone's dark eyes made her thoughts scatter so thoroughly, she felt like a little fool.

"The pleasure is mine." His deep voice was warm but made her shiver, and she gripped the square of paper in her hand more tightly. Evelyn prayed Mr. Harding couldn't see into her thoughts.

She would rather Mr. Stone not see them either, to be honest.

"I wouldn't want to keep you from your important business," she murmured, with a small, shy dip of her shoulders.

"If you are staying with the Hardings, perhaps I will see

you again," he said.

"Yes," she muttered, blinking up at him as she stepped backwards, towards the stairs. She was afraid she was making a spectacle of herself in front of her cousin, but Mr. Harding didn't seem to notice her fumbling at all.

As she turned to go up the stairs, she heard him say, "she'll be here long enough to keep Arabella and Augusta company while I'm away, but I'm afraid she's back to London after that."

So, he is already trying to head Mr. Stone off.

That was to be expected, but it pinched something in her chest anyway.

She peered down the stairs before she lost sight of Mr. Harding's study. Mr. Stone was staring after her while Mr. Harding spoke to him, a heat in his eyes that she prayed went unnoticed by the other man.

Evelyn felt warmth creep into her own cheeks at his attention, but she smiled to him once more before rushing up to the second floor. With any luck, she would see Mr. Stone again, and soon.

I can only hope.

"I've invited Mr. Stone to dinner next week," Mr. Harding announced at dinner, his voice loud over the clatter of dishes.

A servant pulled off the last cover on the platter before Evelyn, revealing a very large fish that stared boldly back at her. She recoiled slightly from the shock of that gaping mouth. She had always hated the look of roasted fish. At home, the servants knew to keep that particular dish at the other end of the table.

She looked at the shiny eye, watching her unblinkingly, and suppressed a shudder. Then she registered what Mr. Harding had said and startled all over again.

"Next week?" Mrs. Harding wife asked, flustered.

She fingered the necklace at her throat as though overcome by the insurmountable task, but Evelyn could see excitement in her sparkling eyes.

"So little time to prepare," she fussed.

She glanced down the table at her daughter. "This is the perfect opportunity for you to meet him, Augusta."

There was calculation in those eyes too.

Across from her, Augusta did not look nearly as impressed. She frowned instead at the unexpected announcement, her eyes narrowing as she stared down at her dish. Augusta hadn't said a word, but Evelyn could see the hot emotion simmering in her cousin's eyes. She was surprised the food on Augusta's plate didn't go up in flames under that glare.

Mr. Stone's eyes were like fire.

The thought hit her unbidden and she flushed. She could still feel them on her from that afternoon.

It's too bad he isn't here now.

She was wearing her prettiest blue gown, and while she'd never cared about her dresses before, she thought she would much prefer to feel his eyes roaming over this one than the old morning dress she'd worn earlier.

"He will be happy to meet you, Augusta," Mr. Harding said more brightly, then chuckled. "All these years and to think you've never been introduced. Even Miss Price has met him this afternoon." He waved his hand in Evelyn's direction, and she tried not to let her color deepen as all eyes turned to her.

"You've met Mr. Stone?" Mrs. Harding asked.

When Evelyn nodded, her cousin smiled conspiratorially. She had the uneasy feeling she was going to be roped into some scheme for Augusta's sake. She didn't like that it concerned Mr. Stone.

"He's a fine young gentleman, isn't he?" Mrs. Harding directed.

"Mother, he's thirty-six—hardly *young*," Augusta bristled.

"Thirty-five," her mother corrected, still looking expectantly at Evelyn.

She had to imagine Augusta had never seen Mr. Stone before. If she had, Evelyn doubted the girl would have been so opposed to the idea. She didn't see how anyone could be immune to that *pull*.

"He seems very kind," she offered mildly.

If Augusta didn't see Mr. Stone's appeal, Evelyn certainly wasn't going to be the one to point it out for her.

Logically, it made sense to support a match between her young cousin and Mr. Stone. She knew she wouldn't be in Porthaven forever, but that didn't mean she liked the idea of warming Augusta up to him.

She glanced at Mrs. Harding, who looked a little disappointed she hadn't said more. She wasn't about to tell her young cousin all her thoughts on Mr. Stone—especially not the ones that centered around the intensity of his eyes or the breadth of muscle beneath his coat.

That I will keep to myself.

It was bad enough that she wouldn't be able to do anything with this growing attraction of hers, but it was far worse to think that seeing him in a week would also give Augusta the chance to see what she might be missing.

Gabriel leaned back in his chair with a groan. The sun had long since set and his office was dark, even with the candles burning. He sighed, running an agitated hand through his hair. The losses from The Starling were greater than he'd anticipated—lives and goods alike. It had been a headache going over the numbers and calculating the small fortune that had sunk into the gulf.

The Bay of Biscay now sported a hoard of the finest port along its seabed.

He peered down again at the list he had been reading for the fifth time. This one was the crew list, and it was far more troubling than the loss of wine. He didn't want to forget the true tragedy here, so he'd spent the last hour going through each name. It was a weighty burden, but it was his to shoulder. He let the paper fall back to the table and looked out the window.

He needed a break.

Pushing up from his chair, Gabriel rubbed a hand over his eyes, then walked to the large windows. It would have been impossible to see outside if not for the abundance of lamps lining the streets. It might not be London, but they thrived on modernization in Porthaven, all the same.

From this vantage, he could just see the edge of the park in the distance. The walk from Solomon Harding's house to his office had been a short one—the line of trees in the distance, visible in the lamplight, was testament to that. Knowing now that Miss Price was just a few short blocks away was more distraction than he needed.

"Fuck," he muttered.

He wasn't one to let womanly allure get to him, but something about this one was different. He looked forward to seeing her the next week at dinner, though he hadn't missed the way Solomon had tried to steer him away from Miss Price and towards his own daughter that afternoon.

She lives in London. He reminded himself. *She will be going home soon.*

There was no future in this attraction he felt, and he should nip it in the bud before it proved more difficult.

He flexed his fist against the table. Not that his body seemed to care. Hell, he could hardly get his brain on board.

A brain now consumed with thoughts of Miss Price in her off-white dress with little flower springs dotting the muslin.

He frowned out the window. He'd wanted to trace his eyes over every speckle of color—his hands too. He only hoped she hadn't realized the direction of his thoughts. Those clear green eyes of hers looked sharp and perceptive, but innocent. He didn't want to scare her off.

She was young—*too young*, he told himself, yet again. Not so young as the Harding girl, but he still had more than a decade on her. Solomon had confirmed she was only twenty-three. It was the same age he'd been when he was engaged to Jane Thomas.

Look at how well that went.

He was jaded, and he knew he came across severe, even brooding. He wasn't the bright romantic a woman like her ought to have. He thought of the little smile that had played across her lips when she'd looked at him.

Twenty-three was far too young.

Entirely too young, something like his conscience insisted, but he didn't know if he could bring himself to care.

Chapter Six

"There are two more shipments expected this month." Franklin Little's voice droned as he read through the lists of cargo planned for each sailing.

The first was already en route, having left the shores of Portugal a full two days prior. It was blessed timing too, after the recent blows he had taken. The report if The Starling's loss had already been printed in the papers and seeing it in black and white only made the blade drive deeper.

"When do we expect The Herald to make it to port?" Gabriel asked distractedly as he fiddled with his watch. He looked up to see the other man make a face.

"It's been difficult to say," his foreman started. "The conflict on the peninsula has complicated matters."

Gabriel grumbled and snapped the watch closed.

"It seems the journey now involves a stronger need for evasive maneuvers than the previous runs."

"The French are seizing more ships then?" Gabriel asked. "And with more success, I take it."

The foreman nodded. "So I have heard."

"Fantastic," Gabriel snapped. He glanced back up from the pocket watch to his foreman. "Sorry," he grumbled.

"No matter, sir."

Gabriel leaned back in his chair, letting his arms fall heavily on the wooden rests, and stretched out his legs to cross at the ankles. "Anything else?"

Franklin frowned, looking displeased. "Not about the shipments."

"The thefts then," Gabriel supplied with a beleaguered sigh.

Can't I catch a break?

It wasn't bad enough that he had to deal with rough seas, acts of God, and this damned war—he also had to worry about petty thieves robbing him blind.

"There have been another three complaints lodged this month alone."

"Already?" Gabriel asked, frustratedly. "The month has barely begun."

Mr. Little stepped forward and pulled another sheet from the small stack of papers he held in his arms. He dropped this one on the desk in front of Gabriel.

"And these are the losses I've noted from your own stores.

Since last week."

Gabriel picked up the page and scanned it quickly.

"All this, even with a guard posted?" he asked.

His foreman looked uncomfortable. "We've only been posting someone overnights," he explained, and Gabriel nodded.

They had been in agreement on that. It made the most sense for the thieves to be striking under cover of darkness.

"So, either someone has been neglecting their duties," Gabriel sighed. "Or they are hitting us during the day."

"It would seem so."

This was becoming a bigger problem as the days went by. He was more than ready to be done with it.

Franklin scanned another page, flipping it over to read the back before clearing his throat.

Such a waste of paper, Gabriel thought absently.

He remembered when Franklin first started working for him, how the man tried to reuse every scrap. Gabriel's excess seemed to be rubbing off on him. He should probably feel some sort of guilt over it.

"Constable Evans sent someone by the east warehouse yesterday," he said, looking back up. "He'd like to assess the situation with you at your next convenience."

Gabriel scoffed. "Oh, now he's ready to *assess* the situation? Where was he six months ago?"

The other man wisely kept his opinion to himself. Gabriel was grateful for it. He ground his teeth—he hardly needed any extra push to rage at Albon Evans. The man managed to bring out Gabriel's worst, all on his own.

He slapped a hand against his desk. He needed to get control of himself if he meant to get anything more done today.

"Tell Constable Evans I will see him at the docks on Monday. I should be able to set some time aside for him then—we can start from there."

"Yes, sir. If that is all?" he asked, and Gabriel sent him off with a wave of his hand.

Franklin shut the door behind himself, leaving Gabriel alone with his thoughts.

He would deal with Constable Evans on Monday, and he would put the petty thieves from his mind until then. He could only handle one crisis at a time. Right now, he was more concerned with these reports of ambushed ships.

How is a man meant to run a business?

The dining room was warm that evening, heated thoroughly by an ornate fireplace set into the far wall. With the unexpected heat, the burgundy walls and dark wood furnishings made the small room feel even more claustrophobic. And the branched candelabras on the table did little more than offer a warm glow that bled into the orange hues cast by the fireplace.

Evelyn looked down at her hands, folded in her lap. Mrs. Harding laughed at something her husband said, but Evelyn couldn't keep track of the conversation around her. She felt separate, like she sat outside the room with no clear way in. She shifted uncomfortably in her seat.

God these chairs are stiff.

And the fire was making the room too warm. She pulled at the lace edge of her sleeve. The frills on her dress were suddenly itchy, too tight against her skin. Though she thought it might really be that she was the thing that didn't properly fit.

She'd felt like an observer since her first night with the Hardings, when she'd lain awake in bed, staring up at the white ceiling and wondering how many of the little room she could fit in her bedchambers at home. She had felt horribly ill-bred for thinking it, but that hadn't stopped that sense of *otherness* from settling around her. That first week she had wondered how she would survive in this house until returning to London.

Now she felt oddly invested in Porthaven, but it was all tied up in a connection that could never lead anywhere, and it made her very much aware of how little time she would get to spend in the city before she was forced to return home.

And ever since the Hardings had set their targeted sights on Mr. Stone, that old feeling of not fitting had not only returned—it had doubled.

Especially since he's become the topic of nearly every dinner conversation.

Evelyn imagined the only reason his name hadn't been brought up that evening was because Augusta still hadn't made an appearance.

And there she is.

Mrs. Harding clenched her teeth as her daughter flounced in through the open doors.

"It was unbearably warm today," Augusta huffed in lieu of

any real greeting.

Mr. Harding snapped closed his fob watch as she sat down, leveling a reproachful look down the table at his daughter. He was not typically an imposing man, preferring the loud, happy boisterousness that seemed to disarm most people, over intimidation. But Evelyn thought she would quake to be on the receiving end of the look he threw Augusta's way just then.

Augusta, however, appeared unaffected and unconcerned by that look. She didn't even acknowledge it.

"Did you visit the Reads this afternoon?" Mrs. Harding asked, content to ignore her daughter's lateness.

It is no wonder she is so unbearable, Evelyn mused.

"Of course not," Augusta said carelessly, stabbing her fork into an asparagus stalk on the platter in front of her. "Papa had the carriage all day."

"It is close enough to walk, Augusta."

Augusta looked at her mother, aghast. "And risk freckling?" She cast a glance back across the table. "Like Evelyn?"

Evelyn forced her attention to her soup. She had enough thoughts crowding up her mind without putting herself in the middle of Augusta's war with her mother.

Nothing about that fight seemed worth it.

"There wasn't so much sun this morning," Arabella pressed, a surprising hint of steel in her voice now. "Never mind that you have more hats and bonnets than I can keep track of."

Augusta pouted. "I may manage to drag myself down to

breakfast at that awful hour, but you cannot expect me to be active so early in the morning."

"Well, I was out all morning and still barely had the time to get anything done," Mr. Harding interjected from his end of the table, putting himself between the bickering women. "I was held up for hours with my banker. Didn't manage to see any of my own clients and I leave in less than a week."

His upcoming trip to London was nearly all Solomon Harding had spoken about since Evelyn's arrival.

When he isn't talking about the upcoming dinner with Mr. Stone.

That was set to occur in just a few days and Evelyn found herself increasingly nervous at the prospect.

"Oh dear," Arabella exclaimed. "Are there very many you need to see tomorrow?"

Mr. Harding had been a simple solicitor when he had started his trade, though he'd managed to leverage it into a veritable empire from what Evelyn could see . His frequent travel was one of the reasons Aunt Dorothea had been invited to visit in the first place.

"Mr. Emory in the morning and Mr. Clarke as well," he said, making a gruff noise in his throat. He took a healthy swig of wine before he continued, looking pointedly at his daughter when he said, "then only *Gabriel Stone* in the afternoon."

Evelyn startled, drinking her own wine in an overzealous swallow that burned her throat. Tears pricked her eyes as she fought off a cough. She had foolishly thought they could avoid this line of conversation. At least until Augusta had been at the table for a solid fifteen minutes.

"—such a nice young man." She caught only half of Cousin Arabella's words but could see where it was sure to go. "Be sure to tell him how much we are looking forward to dinner."

"I'm sure he's looking forward to it just as much himself." Mr. Harding leaned back in his chair.

"I cannot imagine how he is still unmarried," Mrs. Harding mused. "Perhaps that will change soon."

Augusta looked uncomfortable on her side of the table and Mr. Harding barked a laugh at his wife's clear intentions.

"He is quite the busiest man I have ever met. Great for business, I'm sure. But he's hardly had time to think of frivolous things like marriage."

"Frivolous?" Mrs. Harding looked slightly wounded at the suggestion.

"No, no. You are right. Not frivolous at all," Mr. Harding corrected. "And of course, for a man like him, marriage would be the smart thing. Especially with that behemoth he calls a business," he chuckled.

"All he needs is the right candidate."

The Hardings made it sound as if they were conducting a business transaction. It made Evelyn wish she could sink away into the cushion of her chair.

"Indeed," agreed Mr. Harding. "But there's been nothing since that slip of a girl—what was her name?"

Or maybe the floor could swallow me whole.

"Jane Thomas." Mrs. Harding provided the name almost

immediately.

Augusta sucked a breath in through her nose and Evelyn saw her clench her hands into fists. She was clearly as uncomfortable as Evelyn felt.

Though presumably for a completely different reason.

"Ah but she is Lady Jane now, isn't she?" Mr. Harding added. "Married that Sir Gilbert fellow. Knighted, was he?"

"A baronet," Mrs. Harding corrected. "Passed poor Mr. Stone right over for a title—it nearly broke him, do you remember?"

Mr. Harding fidgeted with his napkin. "Right you are," he said, looking suddenly uncomfortable. "Well, he'd hardly want us dragging up his personal business at the dinner table."

"Oh, but it was so very long ago."

"Over a decade," Mr. Harding agree.

"He sounds absolutely ancient," Augusta grumbled.

Her mother closed her eyes and forced a steadying breath. "You will not embarrass us, Augusta. Mr. Stone would make any young woman a fine husband. You will remember that."

"Then maybe Evelyn would prefer to take him," Augusta quipped. "She at least is closer in age to him."

The Hardings darted their gazes between Augusta and Evelyn, looking as if they'd each been struck. Mr. Harding recovered first, disguising his obvious discomfort behind a loud cough, but leaving *that* explanation to his wife.

"Your cousin won't be staying long." Mrs. Harding gave Evelyn a measuring look, like she was just then realizing the competition she might present.

Evelyn tried to hide the heat that filled her cheeks and did her best to avoid eye contact. The older woman's calculating gaze narrowed, like she might see beneath Evelyn's attempts to hide her damning thoughts.

Mrs. Harding only sniffed at her, before turning back to her daughter.

"And she would agree with *us*," she continued. "Mr. Stone is by far a better fit for you."

She turned back to Evelyn, eyes still sharp. "Isn't that right, *Miss Price?*"

Evelyn swallowed but nodded.

Mrs. Harding's answering smile was so broad it made Evelyn blink, and she wondered for a moment if she had imagined the calculation in the woman's eyes as she had studied her.

"Well, you see? It is a perfect match." Mrs. Harding beamed at her daughter. "We must go shopping tomorrow. Surely, we can find something that can be made ready in time for dinner."

It would certainly be a rush. They had hardly any time before the dinner party, as Mrs. Harding continued to remind her husband near daily.

"And Miss Price can come with us," she added, making Evelyn jolt in her seat.

"Why?" Augusta asked baldly.

"I would love to hear her opinion on current fashions."

Augusta looked Evelyn up and down, as if to point out how little her cousin knew on the topic.

She is not wrong.

"Don't be so rude," Mrs. Harding hissed. "Besides, you'll finally get your taste of London, Augusta."

Augusta rolled her eyes so hard, Evelyn thought the girl might accidentally make them stick that way.

Evelyn tugged at the edge of her glove, wondering when it had become so damned loose fitting. It wasn't like her hand had mysteriously shrunk in the last year. She wiggled her fingers and sighed. Perhaps the leather had thinned from overuse. She turned her hand over to examine the worn tips. They were nearing the point of being useless. Soon they would be an embarrassment—her mother would undoubtedly already classify the gloves as an embarrassment. It was too bad.

I like these gloves.

"We are going to start at the milliners. I could use a new hat," Mrs. Harding said, then glanced at the footman. "John will carry anything back to the carriage."

Evelyn gave her glove one last tug. The last thing she wanted to be doing today was shopping for hats and baubles with Mrs. Harding and Aunt Dorothea, but ever since Mr. Harding announced Mr. Stone's invitation to dinner, her older cousin had been bubbling with nervous energy. She needed a distraction, and anything that got her out of the house—even in the company of her cousin's constant tittering about Mr. Stone—was welcome.

"I do wish Augusta had joined us," Mrs. Harding complained.

But there was only determination in the woman's posture. She was like a general, for all the scheming in her eyes. It set Evelyn's teeth on edge.

"No matter. I'll manage well enough without her here. Evelyn, you can teach us all about London fashion. She'll need the very best if she wants to catch Mr. Stone's eye."

Perhaps I was wrong, Evelyn thought.

Perhaps shopping with her cousin would be too much to bear after all.

"I wouldn't say I'm anything of an expert on London fashion, but I'll help however I can," Evelyn mumbled.

She was suddenly glad to be utterly useless at all things *tonish*. It made it easier to avoid helping Mrs. Harding in her quest to turn Augusta into a more desirable match—no flimsy excuses needed.

I cannot even identify rose from salmon.

Mrs. Harding did not seem to notice. Or perhaps she just didn't care.

"Mr. Stone will take one look at my Augusta and won't know what hit him."

Evelyn had always believed shopping with her mother was the absolute limit for what she could tolerate. Lady Sampford could spend half a day having Evelyn draped in every muslin, silk, and lace on offer until she felt like some stiff, marble statue.

Now, two hours and six shops later, she could appreciate her mother's agonizingly leisurely pace.

Mrs. Harding shopped like it was an occupation.

"Lift your arm a bit higher," she directed with a wave of her hand. "I want to see how it reflects the light."

Evelyn dutifully raised her hand, wondering if she looked as bored as she felt. She didn't want to offend her cousin with her disinterest, but she could not care less which shade of peach would look best with Augusta's complexion. Never mind that Augusta and Evelyn looked nothing alike.

"That one looks very nice with your hair," the young shop assistant offered hesitantly. Mrs. Harding tutted as she gave her head a little shake, and Evelyn lowered her arm back down with a sigh.

"My Augusta has gold hair—very pale," she said and stepped up to look at the color again. "No, this won't do. I want something that will showcase her youthfulness. You must imagine someone much younger."

Evelyn felt her face heat, but there was little she could say to refute that. Augusta was much younger, and the silk she was currently holding was too deep a color for the dainty nineteen-year-old. Still, she shifted her feet awkwardly and looked away.

"I didn't mean it like that," her cousin said gently as she took the swath of fabric from Evelyn's arm, but turned back to the selection of bolts too quickly for Evelyn to know how sincere she was.

"Perhaps Evelyn would prefer to explore a bit on her own. It must be boring with us old matrons dragging her this way and that," Aunt Dorothea chimed in from her seat near the window. "I'm sure we can get on just fine on our own."

Aunt Dorothea sipped from a teacup that the proprietress had materialized when Mrs. Harding had walked in with her cousin, *Lady Carr.*

Evelyn stepped down from the platform with a stretch, feeling her spine finally relax. She would not be venturing into the city with her cousin again anytime soon. Shopping with Mrs. Harding had been exhausting, and she hadn't even purchased anything for herself.

"I think you will find what you are looking for in one of these," the modiste said as she shuffled in from the back room. "They arrived only this week from London."

"Unfortunately, Miss Price has to leave us," Mrs. Harding said with a disappointed sigh, though her eyes were already narrowed on the woman's young assistant. "You have similar coloring to my daughter. Oh, and you are likely of a similar age!"

Evelyn smiled wryly to herself as she walked towards the exit. She'd seen the way the shop assistant's eyes had widened. The poor girl was about to be subjected to the whirlwind that was Arabella Harding.

Aunt Dorothea caught her smirk and raised her teacup to her as Evelyn approached, with a laughing glint in her eye.

"Would you like to take a seat?" she asked with a nod to the upholstered chair on the other side of the low table, then leaned forward and lowered her voice. "Or do you wish to make a run for it?"

Evelyn bit back a laugh, glancing behind her to make sure Mrs. Harding hadn't heard. She did want to leave right away—

partly to have time to explore more on her own, but also to ensure her cousin didn't change her mind about needing her.

She peered out the window over Aunt Dorothea's head. It was beautiful and sunny outside, and she didn't want to be trapped inside for it.

She could see a familiar green awning across the square and straightened. She hadn't recognized where they were before, too overcome with exhaustion no doubt, after their morning marathon of shops. Perhaps she should go in, to finally browse all the shelves, and see what Mr. Balfour kept them stocked with.

She traced her eyes across from the bookshop, to a small lane that cut between the brick buildings—more of an alleyway, really, than a street. She couldn't help the picture in her mind of Mr. Stone stepping into that gap, towards the shadows.

She wondered what he was doing now, and what it would be like when she saw him at the Hardings's for dinner.

Maybe I should pick out something new to wear myself, she thought, then cringed.

She would hardly look supportive if she suddenly made efforts to dress herself up, when the focus was meant to be Augusta. What would she even do in a new gown? Flirt?

She was supposed to be helping Augusta find a match, not daydreaming about stealing Mr. Stone from under her nose.

It isn't stealing if he isn't hers, she thought stubbornly, but it didn't make her feel any less like a thief.

Aunt Dorothea cleared her throat and Evelyn felt herself

physically jolt out of her meandering thoughts. Shocked, and more than a bit embarrassed, she smoothed her features, feeling the way she had begun glaring out the window.

"I think I will go," Evelyn muttered to her aunt.

Aunt Dorothea didn't seem the least bit concerned by her oddness, likely because of how frequently Evelyn let her mind wander.

At least this time I am standing still in a shop, and not walking.

It was less dangerous that way.

She thought again of colliding with Mr. Stone when she'd been too engrossed in her book—the way she'd fallen against him so easily and seemed unable to pull away.

The unmistakable feel of muscle beneath her hands.

Dangerous, indeed.

She swallowed hard and glanced again at her aunt. If anything of her indecent daydreams showed on her face, Aunt Dorothea didn't see it. She likely thought Evelyn was staring longingly at Mr. Balfour's new display of books.

Sometimes, she supposed, it was good to be predictable.

Aunt Dorothea leaned forward and winked conspiratorially, as though they shared some great secret. Then she nodded once towards the door.

"Quickly," she whispered, with a wry smile and that twinkle in her eye. "Go, before she changes her mind."

Evelyn smiled appreciatively and hastily ducked out of the shop, retying the ribbons on her bonnet as she went. She wanted to be far from the grasp of Mrs. Harding's fervor just as much as she needed to remove herself from her aunt's watchful eye.

I should be more careful, she scolded herself.

Especially at this dinner. She frowned. Otherwise, her wistful looks would certainly her away.

Chapter Seven

"**S**urely not this one too," Albon Evans exclaimed when Gabriel led him to the next harborside warehouse on his list.

Gabriel clenched his teeth but only nodded. Constable Evans knew exactly how many warehouses had been burglarized, or at least he very well should have—Gabriel had given him the stack of reports himself. He ignored Evans' complaining and leaned into the warehouse door, pushing the heavy wood so it swung open with a slow creak. He strode into the dimly lit space and waited while Albon teetered on the threshold.

Gabriel eyed the man's light coat and buff breeches and did his best to smother his smirk. There was a practical benefit to his preference for black, one that Albon Evans clearly did not appreciate. Still, his apprehension at each of their stops was beyond laughable.

"It's a warehouse, Albon, not a damned hole in the ground. You aren't going to get dirty just stepping inside," he grumbled.

The constable sniffed audibly, but followed Gabriel in. He walked with him across the warehouse floor, to a staircase set against the far wall. The few men working glanced their way as they walked through. Gabriel was well enough known around Porthaven, and he imagined one or two might recognize Albon.

One man hauling a cart of goods puffed himself up as he crossed in from of them. He had a hateful look to him, and Gabriel didn't take his eyes from the man until he was well out of reach.

Henry Watkins, he recalled.

The man was a nuisance at best—not the type he would ever employ in his own warehouses. He didn't know what Stuart was thinking hiring him on.

They reached the top of the stairs and Stuart Talbot came stomping out of his office in a huff, more aggravated with Mr. Evans's presence than anything else, by the look he leveled at the constable.

"This should have been handled months ago, Evans," he fumed, getting close enough that Gabriel worried he would strike Albon in his agitation.

"Stuart," he warned, and stepped closer to keep himself between the two men.

"I have had a tremendous amount on my plate, Talbot. I'm here now, aren't I?"

Gabriel grimaced at Albon's lack of tact. Stuart was a relatively mild-mannered man, but he looked fit to explode, his face had turned so red.

"And what could be so much more important than the lifeblood of this city? Who do you think makes these streets run?"

Apart from his unfailing laziness, Albon's one major fault as constable was his aversion to men he thought beneath him—even if those same men were the ones who kept the city going. Never mind that Stuart Talbot contributed more to the community and economy of Porthaven than Albon Evans ever could. The man came from common origins, and that was enough for Albon to peer down his nose at him.

Gabriel was another beast altogether. It didn't matter where his grandfather had come from. His enterprise seemed on the outside to be too big to fail, though that was something he worried lately wasn't quite true. Plus, he had rubbed elbows with the aristocracy when he'd been at school—something even the elite of Porthaven couldn't compete with.

Albon would never dare look at him the way he was currently glaring at Stuart.

"We are here now," Gabriel said and stepped firmly between them.

Tempers were high enough with the ongoing thefts. This tension needed to be diffused before the two came to blows. Gabriel watched as Stuart turned to him, and the man's face fell.

"They took a fortune in textiles this time, Gabe. I can't take much more of this."

Gabriel raked his hand through his hair with a sigh. He knew Stuart wasn't exaggerating. His warehouse was nearly flush with the harbor, and those stores seemed to have been hit the hardest, and the most frequently. He was plenty successful, but not enough to weather this situation forever.

"We're going to get to the bottom of this Stuart. I've placed extra men to guard my warehouse, day and night. Can you manage the same?" He thought it likely he couldn't, but he had to ask.

Stuart's look of distress all but confirmed it. Gabriel knew these thefts were hurting Stuart a lot more than they'd hurt him.

"Maybe for a little while, but if I suffer any more of these losses, I don't know how I'll manage to pay for round the clock guards." Stuart shook his head in defeat. "I don't know how I'll pay the workers I do have."

Gabriel glanced at Albon, who shifted uncomfortably on his feet. He was glad he'd dragged him around with him today. Maybe if he saw this suffering, he would be more inclined to do something about it.

He could do with a fire under him, Gabriel thought.

"I can help if you need it, Stuart," Gabriel said. He didn't like the dejection he saw on his friend's face.

"I just want this to end."

Gabriel put a steady hand to his shoulder. "I'll have this

sorted, Stuart. Mark my words."

Evelyn wrapped her arms loosely around herself as she walked. After midday, the sun had become warm, and she had found herself wishing she'd left her long pelisse behind. Here along the harbor though, she was grateful for the protection the light velvet gave.

The breeze coming off the water was chilled and damp from the frigid spray in the air. It was the sort of wet cold that would have been bone deep if not for the glowing sun overhead.

Still, she shivered against the chill, though she wasn't ready to leave yet—even to escape to the steady warmth of the city streets. No, not when the view here was so very worth it. She sighed as her eyes scanned the waterline again, out to the horizon beyond.

Large, gleaming ships lined the dockside, towering above the ground, as massive as the buildings lining the street. Evelyn thought they looked like ancient leviathans, rising from the waters. Their masts seeming to scrape the sky.

She had never seen anything like it before, or ever experienced such a sense of awe as she had when she'd first stepped out onto the brick-lined quay. After the cramped darkness of the surrounding streets, it had been like walking into a different world. One that glimmered in the salt spray, underneath a bright sun.

When she'd first left her aunt and cousin, she had thought to remain close, only going as far as the book shop, where Mr.

Balfour at the very least pretended to remember her. But she had left his storefront sometime later with the draw to *see things*, and had meandered lazily down the nearby streets, peering through windows at their displays as she went.

Porthaven seemed to exist in a state of urgency—the fervent bustle of the city no match for the easy pace of her side of London. Yet there was familiarity in the sight of well-dressed ladies and gentlemen strolling across the pavement, even if they did so with a singular sense of purpose.

Soon though, the wide, fashionable squares and shop-lined streets had given way to narrow lanes—so tight, the rising walls seemed nearly to obscure the sky. What began as a feeling of thrilling adventure had become more like the uneasy scrape of anxiety as she'd squeezed her way down increasingly claustrophobic streets. The buildings were no longer pristine and bright, and the flagstone pavement had given way to rough cobbled streets, then tamped dirt as she'd ventured farther into the mess of the city.

She had found it noisy too, the crush of voices in the swarming crowds bleeding into the air as much as the thick smell of smoke and soot. The buildings were aged and grime-smudged from the filth stirred up underfoot, but Evelyn had kept close to the greying bricks to avoid the worst of the foot traffic.

The tall walls let so little light down to the floor, she'd had the sudden, flighty impression of being deep underground. Evelyn had needed to force down a hysterical giggle at the thought as she'd sidestepped yet another worker lumbering his way down the road.

And then, like a great parting of dark clouds, the tight lane and its crush of traffic had opened to what had felt like a blinding burst of light.

It had taken a moment for Evelyn's eyes to adjust, but when they had, the harbor was before her, stretching as far as she could see.

She blinked even now, the sun reflecting nearly too brightly off the water and the wet bricks at her feet. It did nothing to stop her from staring at the ships, the people, the lapping water—it was like every time she swung her gaze, there was something new she'd missed, and she greedily took it all in.

Men carried large crates up and down the wooden gang planks and rolled heavy oak barrels. She watched a pair haul an oversized wheelbarrow down one of the lanes on the far side of the harbor, where it disappeared into that first line of tall, sentinel, brick buildings.

The warehouses, she guessed.

She wished she could stay there, tucked as she was against the side of one of the tall brick edifices, hungrily watching the flurry of harbor life. But she knew she should be getting back, before she caused any concern with her continued absence.

Evelyn blinked up at the sun. She was no sailor and had no skill at interpreting the sun's position in the sky, but she knew its slow descent would soon dip low enough to bring nightfall, and then she would be far too late for dinner.

Reluctantly, she turned and started back towards the tight

streets and crowded buildings that would bring her to the other side of Porthaven. The cramped, gloomy passage was anything but inviting, and she turned to cast one last glance back at the warm sunlight behind her. White sails shone bright in the distance, and she inhaled the briny scent of sea spray as it swept across on the breeze.

Evelyn distractedly retraced her steps, making her way back from the open harbor, through the winding streets. Men and women brushed past her as they navigated the city with direction, intimately attuned to the mazelike network of roads, some little more than trodden footpaths between buildings.

She hesitated, pausing at the edge of a street, tucked against a brick building as a larger group bristled by. She wondered idly how they could so readily differentiate the winding lanes when each looked all but identical to her.

One left, two rights, she recounted determinedly as she made her way back. *And another turn at the building with the large green door, straight up ahead.*

Only there was no large green door at the end of the street.

Evelyn stopped short, startled, and slowly spun in a circle, taking in the unfamiliar buildings around her.

Have I gotten myself turned around already?

The big, stocky buildings—oversized, square things with tall doors that loomed over her—weren't anything she remembered walking past before. She shivered. There was something almost menacing about the sheer size of the buildings, in the suddenly quiet, empty streets.

It was odd how the astounding size of the ships in the harbor, with their towering masts, had made her feel only a sense of wonder and excitement, but these massive buildings in the tight confines of the city streets made her aware of how small and vulnerable she was. She had the distinct impression of being like an ant, scurrying beneath the feet of giants.

Evelyn turned again. The dark maze of streets behind her offered no comfort. She worried that if she tried to navigate those twisting arteries again, she would only manage to get herself more lost than she already was.

Where am I?

There was the faint smell of brine in the air, and she wondered worriedly if she had somehow managed to turn herself so far around that she was back in the vicinity of the harbor. If so, she had absolutely no inkling how to get back to the far side of the city. She had thought she'd been going in the right direction the entire time.

She peered up at the large buildings again. They were utilitarian looking, with large doors that opened on a wide stretch of street, as if maneuverability had been the prime priority when construction had been done. And the smells and sounds of the dockyard seemed to float just in the distance.

These must be the warehouses, she realized, and that at least gave her some sense of where she stood.

Though she had no real perspective to say where the warehouses were in relation to the rest of Porthaven. Except that they seemed to sit somewhere just before the harbor.

Evelyn pushed forward. If she wasn't going to go

backwards, she reasoned, then the only option remaining was to cut through the warehouses and see if she could find her way back to familiar ground.

And hopefully by a more direct route, she prayed.

It was surprisingly quiet the further she went from the dockyards. Where there had been a flurry of activity surrounding the moored ships, here there was little movement here, and it made the solid, brick buildings seem more desolate, and more foreboding. It was a stark contrast to the congestion of the city streets that had brought her to the harbor too.

And then there was a sound, sharp and high, like the clang of metal against stone. It was loud in the relative silence, and Evelyn inhaled sharply, startled by the sudden noise. She put a hand to her chest to steady her breathing and reflexively peered around her.

The street was empty, except for herself and the few crates and barrels and odds and ends that were stacked alongside some of the warehouse buildings. Any one of those could have clattered and fallen to the dirt—on their own or helped by scurrying vermin, like the rat she stiffly watched scamper around a dark corner.

And, she reminded herself—no matter how desolate the street around her was, there were certainly workers indoors. Moving things around and loading and unloading goods.

She pressed her hand more firmly to her chest, willing her heart to cease its rapid beating.

It was nothing. Just the sounds of trade.

She was glad no one was near to see her act so skittishly.

Especially Mr. Stone.

The last thing she wanted was for him to see her so easily frightened. She would seem completely unsuited to life in Porthaven—the life he lived.

She shook her head at her girlishness.

Never mind that he *would never be suitable at all,* she thought.

The thought was an unpleasant one and she flinched. She did not like where that line of thinking was taking her, no matter how relevant it might be. It was a distressing realization and she wanted nothing to do with it just then.

She was reasonable. She knew had no real connection to Mr. Stone, apart from a few run-ins, and possible flirting. Yet stubbornly, she thought there was something there—something real, that she could almost hold on to.

Like the spark her mother always said had been immediately obvious when she'd first met Evelyn's father.

Bang, bang.

Another heavy clank of metal and Evelyn jumped. Then the swing of a large, heavy door, and distant voices.

They were raised and agitated, though not loud enough to make out clearly. She paused mid-stride, not wanting to intrude or snoop on the muted bickering.

She shook her head.

I am meant to be going back to the Harding home, not distracting myself with thoughts of Mr. Stone.

Evelyn peered up at her surroundings again. She was alone amid the large, intimidating warehouses, and quite certain she was lost—it was hardly the time to be worrying over Mr. Stone's eligibility for marriage.

Marriage! She stumbled with a gasp and shook her head. *Perhaps courtship.*

That seemed a safer topic to think on.

Evelyn hesitated at the next available turn and peered down the lane, a compact walkway that was no more than a back alley, tucked between one of the long, brick buildings, and a stretch of tall, wooden fencing.

She wasn't quite sure which way would bring her to Linden Street, but she thought this at least led in the right direction. At the very least, she should be able to find the familiar square with the bookshop.

As she walked, that looming warehouse rose up on her right, an uninterrupted, unforgiving wall that let little direct sunlight into the narrow space between it and the wooden fence. It made the corridor dark and cold, and Evelyn fought against the chill of a strong breeze that whipped its way through.

Even over the wind, the voices grew louder, and partway down the alley she realized they were coming from the warehouse to her right. They were still muffled, but louder now, coming through a half-opened door as it swayed on its hinges.

She had never considered herself particularly nosy and didn't typically resort to eavesdropping—except at society functions, where there was little else to entertain—but Evelyn paused anyway, unable to pass as a sudden impulse to lean closer gripped her. She felt foolishly curious, but if she strained just a little, she thought she might be able to make sense of the garbled words.

Maybe just a peek inside.

The warehouse was dimly lit, even next to the gloom of the grimy alleyway, and when she leaned her head inside, she blinked her eyes wide, struggling at first to see.

The warehouse was large—bigger than she had realized from the outside.

It must stretch all the way to the next street.

She tiptoed forward. Inside, the space was bisected into two tall levels, with a set of stairs at the back, and a dingy looking railing running the length of the second-floor landing.

Evelyn looked up, seeing the high, vaulted roof, which seemed capable from below of scraping the sky. She felt quite small, standing in the little doorway, especially next to the towering wood and metal shelving that ran in rows across the floor. They were filled, piled up with bolts of cloth in every color and style she could have conceived of—likely some she couldn't even name.

Mrs. Harding wouldn't know what to do with herself in a place like this, she thought with a wry smile.

She took a final step over the threshold.

A loud clang rang out, echoing against the walls, followed by a string of curses that were now clear enough for Evelyn to make out in profane detail. She peeked around the corner, down a long aisle with fine carpets rolled up against the wall.

There was a wheelbarrow pushed against the nearest shelf,

filled nearly to the brim with what looked like dark, glass bottles, and what might perhaps have been a small wooden cask.

Three men were huddled together, whispering hurriedly where they were pressed in around the cart. They were arguing, unaware of their sudden audience. One had unwound a cloth bolt and was beginning to pull a stretch of fine, coppery silk overtop.

Hiding the evidence, she realized instinctually, and her hand flew to cover her mouth as a shocked gasp escaped her lips.

Evelyn backed up slowly. Thankfully, the men were too distracted to have noticed her yet, and she hoped if she moved deliberately, she could escape the warehouse unseen.

And then she could go back to a life where she had never seen a criminal in person, let alone a crime being committed. At the very least, she could pretend.

But her heel caught on something small and metal that kicked across the aisle, ringing out as it clattered against the far wall.

She froze, wide-eyed.

The sound seemed to echo in the quiet warehouse, and she found herself wondering where all of the workers were. Why was there no one here to stop these men from stealing, or protect her from their notice?

Because if they hadn't noticed her before, they certainly did now.

Chapter Eight

The three men stilled, frozen in place at the ringing sound of the small, bouncing scrap of metal. They'd been caught, but Evelyn felt like the one cornered and trapped. She couldn't move—could hardly bring herself to breath. And when they stiffly rose, standing with tension riding their backs, panic gripped her.

What do I do?

She should run, yet she could do nothing to unstick her feet from where they felt glued to the floor.

Three sets of eyes scanned the room before settling on her face. Even from a distance she could see the glimmer of hostility as those gazes narrowed on her suspiciously. She swallowed against the lump forming in her throat, feeling certain that nothing good could come of this, but unable to do a thing about it.

The youngest of the men shuffled his thin frame in front of the wheelbarrow, as though to hide the evidence still clearly peeking out from behind his back. Though it would take a fool to believe there was an innocent explanation for the stash of corked, glass wine bottles they were trying to hide.

Especially when the warehouse around them held nothing but textiles.

The biggest of them seemed to recover first from his shock, glowering at her with a sneer that sent ripples of fear down her back. He took a lazy step forward, raking his eyes over the length of her in a way that made her skin crawl.

He was tall and broadly built, with the kind of bulky strength formed over years of manual labor. He looked as if he could crush her with his hands, and she swallowed the dread that threatened to choke her as he took another step towards her.

"Hey there, missy." His lip curled as he took another step towards her.

Oh, God. What do I do?

She backed up, instinct pushing her to do whatever she could to escape, but her back struck a wooden shelf. Somehow she had gotten herself backed into a corner, with nowhere to turn.

"You're a pretty thing, to be down in these parts," the big man drawled.

Her eyes darted, looking for a way out of—trying to recall

the way back to the street and the hope of safety. There was only another wall of shelves on her side.

Trapped.

She glanced futilely behind her, at the unmovable rack of shelves at her back.

"A long way from those fine, big houses." He inched closer.

Maybe if she feigned ignorance, they would see her as no real threat to whatever illegal activity they were involved in. Maybe they would simply allow her to leave.

"I must have gotten turned around somewhere."

She did not need to pretend to be fearful and out of her depth. Her voice shook on its own and her eyes blinked widely—innocently. But it did not seem to help. She was not so innocent to mistake the malicious intent in his stare as he advanced.

She swallowed nervously again and darted her eyes towards the exit.

She couldn't see the door from her position, but she could hear its hinges creaking loudly in the echoing silence of the room. Evelyn knew it wasn't far—if she pushed herself, she could probably make it out into fresh air.

She felt a shudder go through her even as she shuffled her feet, ready to bolt, thinking about the narrow alleyway along the warehouse where that door opened up to. She wouldn't just have to make it outside. She would have to outrun three men down those tight confines as well. And there was still no guarantee that anyone would be nearby to help her if she did.

The wide roads near the warehouses had been empty when she'd gone down them earlier.

Her feet shifted again, inching ever closer to the corner shelf that blocked the door from her view. The way the man chuckled as he watched her made the hair at the back of her neck stand on end. Like he knew what she planned to do, where she planned to go, and was wholly confident in her inability to escape him.

She slid her feet another step closer towards the door.

"Already planning to leave us? So soon?" the man tsked. "That seems rude. You only just got here."

"My cousins will be worrying about me."

He braced his arms over his chest, assessing her. He had all the self-important arrogance of a king and cast his eyes over her like he had every right. The way they trailed over the length of her again made her feel queasy, and she suppressed a shiver as fear gripped her.

For a moment she froze, her heart stuttering in her chest, and she pressed herself as close to the shelving as the protruding bolts of fabric allowed. If she could curl up on herself and disappear into nothingness, she would. But at least he had stopped advancing towards her.

He smirked, a cruel tilt to his thin mouth, and her stomach dropped.

"Don't worry. I promise to take real good care of you." He snickered, the other men echoing his sickening laughter.

She nervously glanced at the wheelbarrow behind him and his eyes hardened. She swallowed again, her throat dry and scratchy as she tried to come up with a plan. She darted her eyes towards her exit.

"I won't tell anyone what I've seen," she whispered when she realized he knew she'd seen their hidden contraband. She felt her hands shake and tightened her fists in her skirts. "Please. I'll go quietly, and no one will know."

He laughed darkly and took one menacing step towards her. "I don't need you to be quiet."

He glanced back at his men.

They had stopped what they'd been doing, leaving the cart forgotten in favor of watching her with a sick sort of interest.

"Get that out of here, before someone sees," he shouted, waving an arm fervidly. "I don't want any of those self-righteous pricks looking into our activities."

"Right, boss."

"We've got it Henry," the younger of the two men muttered, before they both made haste hauling the wheelbarrow away.

Evelyn could hear the slap of the wooden side door as they pushed through into the back alley.

The one they called Henry scowled after them as they left, and without his eyes boring into her, it was like a tight band had been unwound from her chest. She inhaled a deep breath and felt air refill her lungs.

When he swung back around to sneer at her, that iron grip constricted her breath again, and her heart thundered in her chest.

She took an automatic step sideways, closer to her escape.

"You," he grumbled and sucked his teeth in agitation.

She couldn't help the whimper that escaped, and he chuckled. "Yes," he crooned sinisterly. "I think I'd like to hear you scream." His wolfish grin suggested horrible things.

Her lip trembled.

"Underneath me," he clarified, eyes ravishing her again so that she felt sick. "Maybe you'll even like it."

No! her mind protested.

She jerked to one side, ready to bolt, but he mirrored her movements and she hesitated, fear gripping her.

He laughed, a low, ominous sound. "You're a rather jumpy little thing, aren't you?" He eyed her again, sneering. "No matter. Run. If you can in those pretty skirts." The taunting chuckle again.

"I'll enjoy chasing you."

She knew she couldn't wait any longer. There was no room for hesitation, not with this devil. Evelyn darted her eyes one last time down to the end of the aisle. The door was just around that corner, the same door the other men had used. But they would be distracted—enough that if she was quick, she could get somewhere safe. Henry's chuckle echoed off the walls.

Anywhere was safer than here.

She dragged in a shaky breath, feeling the air warble in her chest. Henry's eyes glimmered with delight, and for a moment, she thought he would lunge for her.

But she pushed from the shelf, dragging bolts of fabric

down and swinging them, as far as the heavy rolls of cloth allowed. He hesitated, wide-eyed, just long enough for her to run for the exit, the smooth soles of her boots helping as she slid around the corner towards that swaying door.

"Stop her!" Henry shouted from behind her, but when she slammed the door open, the wood crashing against the brick with a thundering clap, the other men looked up in surprise from halfway down the alley.

She turned away from them, her shoulder landing against the tall fencing until she pushed off, her feet stamping up dust as she ran for the wide street ahead.

"Get after her damn you!" she heard Henry bellow when he made it to the doorway himself.

There was scrambling behind her, feet stumbling against dirt and loose stones, but she didn't turn to look. Instead, she lifted her skirts and prayed the road was closer than she remembered.

The towering brick wall rising up on her left felt suffocating, and the ribbons on her bonnet grasped like fingers at her throat.

Why do I bother wearing these monstrous things?

It felt like it was trying to strangle her.

She tugged at the ribbons, frantically wrenching the useless frilled confection from her head, not caring as it fell from her fingers. Her mother would be horrified to see it trampled into the dirt, but Evelyn thought it would be worse if Henry or his men caught her. She swiped wildly at a stack of slatted boxes as she ran by, toppling them into the passage behind her.

She pressed forward with all her strength, seeing the open street up ahead. Her breaths were coming fast and ragged, her heart galloping in her chest.

Just a little farther.

The men were gaining on her. She could hear the wooden crates clattering as they crashed through them, undeterred by the hurdle she'd tried to set in their path. It sounded as if they'd simply kicked them aside.

She had to fight the impulse to peer behind her, but if she didn't get to safety now, they would be on her.

Just a few more steps.

She was so close. She knew it.

Like a shot, she burst out from the narrow alley and into the street. She stumbled, her own momentum working against her as she ran, skirts slipping from her fingers to tangle against her legs.

She finally let herself peek behind her, but wished she hadn't. The movement slowed her steps until she felt like she would stumble over her own feet.

The breath hitched in her throat when she recognized the two men racing up behind her. They were nearly at the mouth of the alley now. She cast her eyes around, but there was no one to turn to. The road in front of the warehouse was just as empty now as it had been when she'd first passed through.

She took a chance and turned up the street, running past the warehouse, away from the direction she'd originally come.

Perhaps if she went this way, she would find her way back towards civilization and safety, before those men could reach her. She doubled her efforts as shouts rang out behind her.

"You fools!" she heard Henry shout. "You couldn't catch a mere slip of a girl, between the two of you?"

Their voices didn't get any louder, like they'd given up pursuing her. Evelyn supposed if they continued after her, they'd risk giving up their ill-gotten loot. She didn't think Henry would be pleased by that, but still, she didn't allow herself to slow.

When the voices had dimmed and no footfalls joined hers to echo against the cobbles, she slowed, turning just enough to glance over her shoulder at the empty street.

They're gone. Thank God, they're gone.

She felt the first waves of relief wash over her in a heavy slump that pressed the air from her lungs. Her chest burned, her legs screamed, and her vision swam, just before she was brought up short by the solid wall of a man's back.

The abrupt collision knocked her shaky legs out from beneath her and she fell back numbly to the ground. She blinked, brushing a hand over her forehead as she steadied her breathing, and looked up.

"Miss Price?" the tower of a man standing over her asked, and she breathed out a shuddering sob to see Mr. Stone's face, distorted as it was in confusion and mounting concern.

He reached down to grasp both of her arms, hauling her up to her unsteady feet. She stumbled, fisting her hands in his jacket to keep herself upright. His hands slid to her elbows, his touch light, as if his fingers were conscious of the impropriety of his grip, but he didn't let go.

"Goodness Gabriel, is she quite alright?"

She hadn't seen the other man until the haughty, male voice interjected, and Evelyn tensed in Mr. Stone's arms. She turned to see a lean, elegantly dressed gentleman, with pale gold hair that reminded her of Nigel. The distasteful look on his face was a near perfect match as well.

She reached a tentative hand up to her disheveled hair. She didn't like the unwelcome reminder of London and Lord Nigel Sedley. It made her more aware of the nervous anxiety still bubbling inside her, and of the disgrace of her rumpled appearance.

Such a foolish thing to worry about when she'd just escaped those evil men. She was lucky to have her life and her virtue intact—what did it matter what her hair looked like?

Mr. Stone's thumb traced a comforting pattern on the back of her arm, drawing her attention back to him and away from the other man. She took a slow steadying breath, trying to dispel the fear still riding her.

"Are you alright?" he asked softly, bringing a hand up to gently clasp her chin, tilting her face up to meet his eyes. "Evelyn."

She startled at her given name. It was unexpected, but it sounded lovely from his mouth. And it made something in her chest tingle.

"Are you alright?" he repeated.

She tried to nod, but she felt herself shaking. Mr. Stone

turned to the other man as he put an arm around Evelyn's shoulders, protectively tucking her into his side. He was solidly built and the warmth of him made her feel dizzy. She seemed to tremble even more.

"Mr. Evans, if you'll excuse me. We'll continue this conversation another time."

Mr. Evans huffed with impatience. "Gabriel, really. I've wasted half my day coming down to this hellhole for you."

He cast another uncharitable glance at Evelyn, before catching Mr. Stone's eye and visibly cowering at whatever emotion he saw there.

"But if you think this is more important," he stuttered, then awkwardly tipped his hat to Evelyn. "Apologies, miss. I do hope everything is all right," he clumsily rambled. "Gabriel, I will see you in the morning."

Mr. Stone waved him off, shooing him away with a sound from his chest that rumbled like an angry growl. Wordlessly, he guided Evelyn farther down the street, to a sturdy, upturned barrel. She gasped as she felt his large hands circle her waist, his thumbs gently tracing over her back. Then he lifted her and settled her atop the barrel.

Mr. Stone—*Gabriel*—kept his hands at her waist, and she felt herself sag into him. It was impossible not to think of him with familiarity, intimacy even, when he held her like this. She breathed in the scent of him, feeling safe ensconced in him.

"Tell me what happened," he demanded, his voice rough with suppressed emotion, while he continued tracing delicate circles on her back.

She looked down at her hands, noting idly that her gloves were still spotlessly clean. She had fled, stumbling through the streets of Porthaven, running for her very life, yet even aged, her gloves were pristine. They were the gloves of an earl's daughter, and she hated the sight of them.

They mocked her, a gleaming reminder that she could never escape who she was, no matter how hard she tried.

She impulsively tore one glove from her hand, gripping the leather between her fingers and tugging, almost violently, until it pulled free. She threw it to the ground before peeling off its mate and tossing that to the side as well. All the while, Gabriel held her, gentling her with his touch.

She frowned down at the fine kid leather, bright against the cobbles. She didn't want to go home to London just to return to the ballrooms of the *ton*. She didn't want to *fix* things.

She sighed and looked up at Gabriel. He was still waiting for her to speak. She swallowed against the uncomfortable memory and darted her eyes to the side, watching the low sun reflect off the large windows of the warehouse across the street.

"I got lost coming back from the harbor," she explained. "There were three men, in one of the warehouses back that way." She pointed over her shoulder at the direction she'd come from.

He nodded, urging her silently to continue.

"I tried to leave without being seen, but I caught them stealing and they knew it."

"How do you know they were stealing?" he asked stiffly.

"The warehouse they were in was full of textiles, but the

cart they were dragging away was filled with wine bottles."

Gabriel bit out a dark, "fuck," before catching himself.

"I'm sorry." He sighed, looking up at the still, blue sky. "That means they've likely hit my warehouse again. I'll have to check with Franklin in the morning."

"You sell wine?" she asked tentatively, and he nodded, still frowning. "I'm sorry. It looked like it was quite a lot."

He stared at her a mute moment and then breathed out a laugh. His hands flexed on her waist, and he stepped closer, his legs brushing against her knees.

"I import wine. Great, heaping boatloads of it," he said with a wry tilt of his lips that made her stomach flip delightfully. "Three men couldn't cart off enough to hurt me. I'll survive."

But then he frowned again, reaching up to trace the line of her jaw. "What did they do to you?" he asked, concern making his dark eyes look bottomless.

"Nothing," she said with relief. "I ran as fast as I could. But one of them—he said horrible things."

Gabriel tensed, but she continued anyway in a small voice, needing to get it out.

"I know he wanted to do things," she muttered, feeling her face twist in disgust, and she shook her head, as if she could shake the thoughts out of her mind forever. "Vile things."

His fingers stilled on her back, tensing as his hands gripped her tightly, drawing her closer to him, as if he could protect her now from the thing that had nearly happened in that warehouse. She leaned into him, forcing him to step closer so she could rest her forehead against his chest and the steady pounding of his heartbeat. His hips shifted closer, his legs slipping between hers, until he stood flush against her.

She should be terrified still, but when she was surrounded like this by Gabriel—his chest at her front, arms circling her—she felt safe, protected on all sides. His arms tightened and he leaned down to plant a firm kiss to the top of her head, then she felt him turn his face to rest against her hair, holding her close.

"I won't let anyone hurt you," he growled. "Ever."

She sighed against his chest, and then, feeling bold, shifted her hands to fall inside of his jacket. She felt his sharp inhalation as she flattened her bare palms against his waistcoat, her fingertips splayed against the fine linen shirt underneath. Gabriel's arms tensed around her, as if desperate to drag her closer still, and Evelyn tucked her face more tightly against his chest.

They stayed like that in silence for a heartbeat, then another, his heat chasing away the creeping afternoon chill while Evelyn breathed in the scent of him.

"You are alright, aren't you?" he asked softly into her hair, then pulled back just enough to peer down at her.

She nodded but didn't turn her face towards him right away. She didn't want to break the moment between them, but he slid his hands up to her shoulders and forced her to look at him again.

She flushed, embarrassed by the swell of desire she felt even after suffering such a terrible, frightening thing. But it was impossible to extinguish, heightened by the electric vibration that seemed to thrum beneath her skin now that she knew she was safe.

She didn't like the worried crease in his forehead, bisecting his brow, and she reached up a finger to sooth it away. Gabriel's eyes flickered closed and her own were drawn to his lips as they parted on a sigh.

She dropped her hand, but only made it as far as his jaw, her fingers tracing the firm line, and the muscles tensed as her touch feathered over his skin. When his eyes flashed open, need flared there, raw and intense. Hot enough to burn her.

Would I survive being burned?

She absently wet her lower lip. Gabriel's eyes tracked the movement of her tongue. It was the only warning before he descended on her, covering her mouth with his own.

The sudden contact was so shocking she stilled beneath him, flush with need but too stunned to act. A sudden sense of vertigo assaulted her, as if she were perched atop one of the tall city buildings instead of a short, upturned barrel.

His lips are soft, she marveled—surprisingly soft against her own, defying the tight line of his mouth.

And they were persistent. Dragging, pressing, caressing. Coaxing her into the sort of all-consuming kiss that a lady would be wise to avoid—but Evelyn only wanted more.

She felt Gabriel's big hands slide back down her arms, suddenly hot against her tingling skin, searing her through the layers she wore as if there was nothing between them. This was what she had been wanting, needing—for longer than she was likely to admit.

The realization sparked something desperate inside of her and she sagged against him, hands fisting in his waistcoat.

Finally, she thought with a breathy sigh.

Her fingers crushed silk against linen and the hard, unyielding muscle beneath. She felt a smile tickle the edge of her mouth. He would be terribly wrinkled after this.

Christ, almighty.

Gabriel groaned when he felt Evelyn's dainty fingers dig into his chest, like she was afraid to let him go. She needn't worry—he was never going to let her go. Not now—now that he knew her taste, when he had her honey and lilac scent on his lips.

He had seen the desire flare to life in her eyes, felt the way she'd trembled against him. And when she had touched him with those delicate, soft fingers, he'd thought it might be his undoing.

Her skin was cool without her gloves, and he'd fought the rude desire to feel that gentle touch on other parts of his anatomy.

Damn, but he felt like a brute.

She had just endured a horrifically frightening encounter—one that could have been so much worse. And here he was pawing at her like some beast, immune to all higher reasoning.

It was a predicament he seemed to find himself in whenever he was near her. It was a predicament he hadn't the will to drag himself out of.

He tilted his head, angling to slant his mouth more firmly over hers. She moaned lightly against his lips and his hands tensed, then edged up her back of their own accord. He couldn't stop them if he tried, and he wasn't of a mind to.

"Gabriel," she whispered against his mouth and like the fiend he was, he took advantage of her parted lips.

She was a gently bred young lady—that much would have been obvious even if she hadn't been related to the Hardings. But she didn't object to the liberty or react timidly. Instead of the slap he likely deserved, she whimpered, and he was met with the sensual glide of her tongue. She melted against him, and her fingers trailed up to fist in his hair. He wanted to devour her.

He groaned.

What he really wanted was to hike up her skirts and bury himself inside of her, but that was something he could never expect to deserve. As it was, he was overstepping the bounds of propriety by handling her so roughly in full view of the street.

It took every ounce of strength he possessed to pull back from her. The dazed cast of her eyes and kiss-reddened lips made it twice as hard. It also forced a stab of guilt into his chest.

"I'm sorry," he murmured. "I shouldn't have done that."

She blinked up at him, the dizzy befuddlement in her stare clearing before her eyes panned to the open street behind him. He stifled a wince. She must have realized where they were, and how very visible.

A gentleman would have simply walked her home.

Though he could hardly claim to be a proper gentleman now. If he had been, he wouldn't have kissed her so thoroughly, and he certainly wouldn't still have his hands wrapped around her waist.

"Don't be," she breathed, quiet enough that he might have imagined it. "I'm not."

His fingers flexed and all Gabriel wanted was to drag her to him again. But he forced himself to let her go, taking another small step backwards and offering his hand to help her down from her perch.

"Let me walk you home."

It wasn't meant as an offer or a request. If she stayed even a minute longer, staring up at him with those adoring eyes, he was bound to do something that she at least would regret. He would see her safely to the Harding's door, whether she wished it or not. Ideally with her reputation intact.

She thankfully did not resist.

"Thank you," she murmured, with another nervous glance behind him as she found her feet. Luckily the street was empty—hopefully it had been the entire time.

Evelyn flattened her hands down the front of the skirts beneath her brick red pelisse, brushing off dust and smoothing the worst of the wrinkles. She had come frighteningly close to danger, and it made a shiver of fear trail down his spine to think of it.

He scowled, unable to escape the weight of responsibility that struck him. And he cursed Albon Evans. If the man's investigation hadn't been so damned sluggish, there would have been no danger lurking in the warehouses.

But he could hardly blame Evans for his predictable behavior, not when Gabriel had known full well the thefts had never been a priority for the constable.

This was his own fault, for letting Constable Evans drag his feet. Hell, if he'd been of a mind to, Gabriel could have thrown time and money into the investigation himself from the beginning, instead of waiting as long as he had.

He couldn't let this stand, not any longer. Not when lives were at risk—lives of people he knew and cared about.

Care about? He hardly knew her.

He cleared his throat, realizing he had been glaring at the dirt beneath his feet while Evelyn patiently looked up at him, confusion and concern caressing her face.

"Come," he said, and dutifully offered his arm.

He forced a smile, though it was hardly a struggle with her hand tucked against the bend of his elbow.

"Let's get you home."

Chapter Nine

Warm fingers traced up her back, kneading through the fabric of her dress with their firm grip. They urged her closer, but she had already allowed herself to fall fully into his embrace, chest flush against his. There was nowhere closer to go, though she tugged her hand through his hair as if she could drag him into her.

His tongue teased the inside of her mouth, sending shivers through her as his hands curved around her back, pressing her close. He was so near, she could feel the heat of him between her parted legs.

Evelyn blinked, feeling her face heat as fire coursed through her at the memory. She had been desperate for him, memorizing every pass of his lips. And recklessly, she had wanted everything Gabriel had to offer, heedless of the consequences—unconcerned for her reputation. He had looked like sin, all heavy-eyed and brooding, and kissed like he wanted to devour her.

I would have let him devour me.

Evelyn fought to suppress the shiver that traced her spine, leaving her chest feeling warm, her skin tingly, and her fingers nerveless. Her fork slipped from her lax grip and clattered to the table, echoing like a bell in the ensuing quiet—the sudden, shocked silence was nearly deafening. With all eyes fastened on her, Evelyn's eyes grew wide, and she swallowed an audible squeak.

"Excuse me," she said, her nervous pitch bringing more attention than the tumbling fork.

She knew it was ridiculous to think they could read her thoughts, but she couldn't shake the senseless fear that all four knew what she's been daydreaming.

"Are you alright, dear?" Mrs. Harding asked, softly.

She briefly closed her eyes, begging her flushed face to cool, before forcing a placid smile and nodding. Her efforts satisfied the Hardings, who turned back to their meal. Only Aunt Dorothea seemed less than convinced, looking at her with increasing worry as Evelyn awkwardly attempted to avoid eye contact.

"You are sure?" her aunt prodded, then frowned as if covering a wince. "You have been a bit jumpy since coming back this afternoon."

A bit jumpy—

She froze.

Her mouth went dry, and she swallowed against the prickly lump in her throat.

Rather jumpy little thing, aren't you?

Her palms went clammy, and she wanted nothing more than to tug them to her lap, wrap her arms around herself to stave off the memory of that voice. But she had no plan to share that story with her aunt. She did not wish to experience it again so soon. So she forced a breath into her lungs and gripped the fork she'd recovered from the table between pinching fingers.

But *God* was it difficult.

It felt like the walls were closing in, and like the lights had begun to dim until they were nothing more than a hazy splotch in the gloom. And while the dining room felt increasingly tight and claustrophobic, her family seemed a mile away at the other end of the table.

Until she was back in the narrow aisles of that shadowy warehouse, struck immobile once more with fear.

"Evelyn?" her aunt pressed.

She shook herself.

"Yes?" she asked hollowly. "What was that?"

Aunt Dorothea's brow furrowed as she watched her, searching for the truth Evelyn was concealing.

"Are you sure everything is alright? You seem unwell." Now everyone was looking at her again, eyeing her askance.

It made her feel like a wild dog—like they worried she would either run away skittish or bite their outstretched hands.

"Yes," she said more firmly. "I think I am just a little tired from my walk today." Evelyn squeezed the fork more tightly in her grip, trying to force the man's leering grin from her vision. "I went farther than I had planned. I think I may have overdone it."

Mrs. Harding nodded sagely from her seat down the table, as she returned her attention to her food. Evelyn took a careful sip of her wine as she continued to avoid Aunt Dorothea's eye. She could feel her aunt's probing gaze from across the table— a weight only they two seemed aware of.

Mr. Harding broke the tension with his usual bluster.

"We may not seem as grand as London," he conceded, and leveled a pointed look at his daughter behind his boastful smile, "but Porthaven is a fine, large city all the same. It is easy to lose yourself down its streets."

Evelyn nodded and gave a small grateful smile to Mr. Harding for his unwitting rescue. She snuck another glance across the table. Her aunt had returned her eyes to the meal, but Evelyn could feel the older woman's attention still half on her.

She wasn't worried about her aunt learning the truth of what had nearly happened in that warehouse, though she had no interest in bringing it up. Lady Dorothea Carr was like a mother bear when it came to protecting her family.

But she was a bloodhound when it came to secrets. If Evelyn wasn't careful, what had happened *after*—that fierce, all-consuming kiss with Mr. Stone—would become her aunt's business. And then her family back in London would find out.

Gabriel.

Though his name set her skin tingling, she wasn't ready to

share *that* secret either. She eyed her aunt again, wishing she had ever developed that skill of keeping her thoughts and fears from her face. Because if the starchy stiffness of her spine was anything to go by, Aunt Dorothea knew Evelyn was hiding something, and had now been put on high alert.

"I see Diana, just down the road," Augusta called from the front window. She started towards the front hall, only stopping to huff at Evelyn, still seated in the drawing room. "Are you coming or not?"

It was late morning and Evelyn and her young cousin had been waiting nearly a half hour for Augusta's friend, Miss Diana Hughes to join them. After her *adventure* in the city the day before, Mrs. Harding had suggested a more sedate activity for this morning.

If she only knew. Evelyn shuddered and suppressed the memory, endeavoring to fill her mind with yesterday's encounter with *Gabriel* instead.

Those memories made her skin tingle for entirely different reasons.

She looked at Augusta, in her periwinkle dress and light blue pelisse. The colors offset her gold hair prettily, but Evelyn thought the long velvet jacket looked absolutely stifling.

The sun had finally brought a touch of warmth with it, and Evelyn had every intention to take full advantage.

"Marie is bringing down my spencer," she explained.

Augusta tapped her foot impatiently, then whirled with a sigh back to the front window to watch her friend's progress.

"I have it here," Marie announced as she rushed into the room.

Evelyn hopped up from her perch to meet her at the door.

With Marie's help, Evelyn slipped the light, short jacket over her arms and secured the hooks tucked cleverly along one side. She absentmindedly moved to the large mirror hanging near the hall to study her reflection. It struck her as she tilted her head that she had never bothered to fuss over her appearance much before.

She took in the length of herself.

What would he *think of this one?* she wondered idly.

She wasn't quite sure what made for fashionable attire, but she thought the close fit and crisp look of the green spencer made for a striking contrast to her white, patterned dress. And the military-style braiding across the front only seemed to accentuate the tight stretch of seamless twill across her chest. With the short jacket secured closed, it looked as if she'd been sewn into it.

She heard Augusta sigh again from the window. Evelyn gave a light cough and turned away from the mirror.

"I'm ready."

Augusta rose with a muttered, "finally," and led the way to the front door.

She at least hadn't seemed to notice anything out of the ordinary with Evelyn's new interest in her reflection, but Marie smirked at her as she paused to take her bonnet. Evelyn hid a smile and with a sideways glance back at Marie, followed Augusta to the door.

So long as the Hardings don't suspect at thing.

She didn't know what they would make of their guest involving herself with a man she knew they had designs on.

She suppressed a chill at the thought of Gabriel and Augusta together—while she was miles away, trapped with those vipers in London.

"Diana!" Augusta exclaimed when they met her in the street. "I have so very much to tell you."

She linked their arms together and the two girls started forward without a glance back at Evelyn.

She truthfully didn't mind, but Marie made a sound in her throat, loud enough to drag their attention backwards to Evelyn.

"Oh, yes," Augusta said, with barely a glance. "This is my cousin, Miss Price." She flicked her eyes to Marie and then turned back to Miss Hughes, adding, "and the maid."

Evelyn nearly chocked on the laugh that bubbled in her throat and when the two girls darted across the street and disappeared beyond the park wall, she couldn't help the surprised giggle.

"This is going to be an interesting outing," Marie muttered beneath her breath as she swung the heavy food hamper. "An earl's daughter, paired with the maid."

Evelyn looked over at Marie. "You know I consider you my friend."

Marie's mouth tipped in a smile. "I'm only teasing.

They watched as a team of horses pulled a carriage down the street. By the time they crossed, they had to hurry to catch up to the younger girls.

Augusta and Miss Hughes kept their heads huddled together as they walked, and Evelyn could just make out her cousin's agitated voice as they approached. Recently, Augusta's protestations about Mr. Stone had progressed to the sort of complaints that sounded more like bragging than anything else. It seemed his thriving enterprise was enough for her cousin to overlook his *advanced years*.

"She is going to go on about him all day, isn't she," Marie groaned. "She says she has no interest, but yammers on so much my ears ache."

Evelyn bit back a chuckle. "And I don't think she's ever even seen him." It was a bit easier listening to Augusta's prattling now that she could so easily remember the taste of Gabriel's lips.

She peered at the two young women for a moment longer, then leaned in, to whisper to Marie, "There's something I haven't told you."

Marie looked at her sharply.

"Something good, that happened yesterday." She frowned at the path, then peered back at Marie. "After something bad."

"Something bad?"

Evelyn shook her head and the thoughts away with it. "The good bit is much better."

Marie looked like she would ask more, but refrained, evidently thinking better of it. Close as they were, the line between mistress and maid wasn't always the easiest to cross.

With another smile, Marie glanced up ahead at the girls

again, then behind them, as if to make sure no one was close enough to overhear.

"About Mr. Stone?" she whispered.

Evelyn nodded, trying to school her features. A smile tugged at her lips no matter how she tried to bite it back. Marie swayed close and reached a hand up to pinch Evelyn lightly on the arm.

"Why didn't you say anything?" she hissed, as Evelyn covered a yelp with her hand.

She giggled, then swatted at Marie.

Why didn't *I tell her last night?*

She knew why. Evelyn sobered immediately, shivering again as the memory of what very nearly happened before she'd found Gabriel crept back in. Marie must have seen the shift in her emotions.

"What happened?"

Evelyn considered how she could explain—how she could share something so terrifying, while keeping her nerve. She watched the men and women walking along the park paths. It wasn't something she thought she could do easily in such a public place.

"I promise to tell you everything later." She glanced around nervously again. "Just not here."

"Is—is everything alright?" Marie worried. "Are *you* alright?"

She nodded. "I'm fine. I had a frightful run in when I got turned around," Evelyn muttered, and Marie blanched. She knew the sorts of threats that lurked in the darker parts of a city.

"But everything turned out just fine," Evelyn promised. "And that was when I found Mr. Stone."

Marie considered that. Again looking like she wanted to ask more but giving Evelyn the space she needed.

"So, he saved you?"

Evelyn glanced at her and nearly laughed at the dreamy-eyed look Marie affected. "It wasn't really like that."

Gabriel saving me.

It was certainly a better way to remember the ordeal than through that lens of fear and danger. The one that made her hands sweat and her heart thunder away.

"Although, I suppose it did feel like that at the time."

If she thought of it only as Mr. Stone rescuing her, protecting her, maybe she could move out from under the memory's weight.

They continued in silence, while Augusta and Miss Hughes giggled ahead of them. Evelyn could no longer make out what they were saying, the girls just out of earshot.

"Well," Marie finally hedged. "What *can* you tell me?"

Gabriel saved me.

The reminder did its job and her thoughts jumped to more pleasant parts of that afternoon.

She smiled and sidled closer to Marie as she thought of how to tell her—of what to tell her. It was a good thing she could no longer hear Augusta. If she couldn't hear her cousin, then her cousin likely wouldn't hear her.

"Well?" Marie prodded.

"He kissed me," she hissed, then felt that electric thrill

again, tickling her spine.

She couldn't remember feeling this way before, even with Nigel. But then, Nigel had never kissed her the way Gabriel had. He hadn't made her quite so breathless, and he'd certainly never sent her spiraling into this wellspring of need.

Even now, she could practically feel the pressure of Gabriel's lips on her own. She brought a hand up to her mouth as if to dampen the tingling sensation skating across their surface and giggled.

Marie gave her an appraising glance then tipped her head closer. "Not an innocent peck then," she concluded.

They shared a look, eyes twinkling. Giddiness suddenly swept her and she sputtered a laugh loud enough that the girls ahead heard.

Miss Hughes turned to peer over her shoulder, eyes narrowed, and Evelyn straightened, attempting to bring herself up, calm and composed—and failed miserably. She stifled another delirious giggle behind her hand when Augusta glared back at her as well. She felt as young as her cousin in that moment. With not a care in the world.

"The cheek," Marie muttered.

"To be fair, neither of them know," she whispered.

Marie rolled her eyes. "It would take a simpleton to not realize who you are."

Evelyn scoffed and waved a hand at her person. "What part of me screams *peer of the realm?*"

Marie laughed at that. "You're certainly dressed the part." She squinted at Evelyn. "Although you do look a little windswept and we've only just left. You should have let me do your hair."

Evelyn waved the idea aside. "Too much fuss."

Marie chuckled. "Fine. You've made your point."

Evelyn's grin only faltered when she realized that however much she might not *look* like her peers in London, it was a part of her she would never be rid of.

Augusta didn't know how lucky she was to be such a suitable match for Mr. Stone.

Marie saw the shift in her eyes and the way they trailed Augusta as the girls giggled ahead of them.

"Just ignore her," Marie whispered. She sidled as close as the large picnic hamper allowed. "Now, tell me about this not-so-innocent kiss."

The sun was bright as it beat down across the wide stretch of grass. Even the breeze was warm, and when the thin clouds cleared from the sky, it felt like winter was finally receding for good.

Evelyn sighed. They had settled as close to the shady trees as they could without sitting on top of the roots, while the branches stretched out protectively overhead. They rustled as another warm breeze rolled through.

She had chosen the one corner of blanket that sat in direct sunlight, and she stretched, enjoying the feel of its heat on her back.

With another hum of satisfaction, she settled her attention on the book in front of her and willfully ignored her cousin's continued prattling. For someone who thought Gabriel Stone was an *old man,* she'd certainly devoted an inordinate amount of time talking about him. It had gone on all morning. And all afternoon.

"My mother has all but made up her mind about him."

Evelyn wished she could block the conversation from her ears. She didn't want to hear how perfect Mrs. Harding thought her daughter was for Mr. Stone. All it did was serve as a reminder that Evelyn was anything but. As Miss Evelyn Price, she was little more than a poor relation. And as Lady Evelyn Pricewinters, she could never pursue a merchant.

Never? The word teased her.

"Can you not convince your father?" Miss Hughes asked.

Augusta shook her head. "Papa just goes on about how wonderfully successful he is." She huffed an aggravated breath so heavily, Evelyn wouldn't have been surprised if she'd stomped a foot to accompany it. "If he's so enamored with the man, maybe he should marry him himself!"

"Augusta!" Miss Hughes admonished, though she looked delighted.

Evelyn barely suppressed her own laugh.

Here she was, fighting a losing battle with her churning jealousy, and her cousin didn't want a thing to do with Mr. Stone.

She hasn't even seen him, she reminded herself. *Her feelings are bound to change at tomorrow's dinner.*

How could they not?

She must not have muffled her laughter at all, because she

could feel Augusta's glare at her back. She blinked over her shoulder, against the bright sunlight as Augusta and Miss Hughes rustled to their feet.

"Come, let's walk," Augusta said. "It would be nice to have some privacy for a change."

Evelyn watched bemusedly as the girls smoothed their skirts and Augusta refastened the bonnet strings dangling beneath her chin. Miss Hughes seemed to take her cue from Augusta and leveled another haughty look in Evelyn's direction before both girls swayed off.

"You would think she'd be more grateful," she heard Miss Hughes quip as they walked away.

This time Evelyn did nothing to stop the laugh that bubbled out of her. She imagined how horrified the snooty Miss Hughes would be if she knew who she'd been snubbing. She turned and caught Marie's eye, where she sat just beyond their picnic.

"A most interesting outing, indeed." Evelyn grinned—Marie had been right.

Evelyn rolled over onto her back, closing her book and leaving it to rest on her stomach. It was certainly more peaceful now, with Augusta and Miss Hughes removing themselves to someplace off in the distance. She peered after them, squinting to make them out. They'd gone so far, she could shout and they'd likely not hear her with the breeze.

She closed her eyes, feeling the sun wash over her face. Without Augusta's incessant prattling, she could pretend she was home at Haythorne House, basking on the lawn. She stifled a yawn. If she wasn't careful, she might even fall asleep.

She might have. She couldn't say. She didn't actually know how long she stayed like that, lying atop the grass with her eyes closed. It was restful, and she appreciated the solitude.

It felt sometimes like there was no escape from her cousins on Linden Street. It wasn't just that the house was small, though it certainly was. That was something she had adjusted to, though it had taken some time. It was the constant machinations of Mrs. Harding, and Augusta's incessant whining that pressed in on her. Especially when all conversation seemed to center around one man as of late.

Evelyn drew in a breath. She had no business being upset over Mr. and Mrs. Harding's interest in Gabriel. She had no claim on him and in a matter of weeks she would inevitably return to London, no matter how she tried to avoid it.

You must stop thinking of him as Gabriel. Thinking of him as more than the impersonal Mr. Stone was only feeding the senseless attachment she felt.

She inhaled deeply again, taking in a lungful of fresh air.

She shouldn't be thinking about ineligible men, she should be focusing on this—the sweet smell of the warmed grass, the thin fringe of it tickling her neck. She arched her neck, giving the bright sun better access to warm her face.

A whisp of cloud floated by, and when it had passed, she fluttered her eyes closed against the unfiltered brightness. She smiled as the light flickered and danced behind her eyelids.

Another shadow moved overhead, blocking the sun from her face, and she frowned, waiting for it to pass. But this one didn't move, and she blinked up at the sky as she smelled the faint scent of—

Oranges.

She shivered as she stared up, but whether from the cool shadow he cast, or his presence alone, she couldn't say. Gabriel stood above her with the proud, commanding air of some long-ago warrior—or a king.

Or a god.

It was impossible to be unaffected by him. She might as well be drunk.

"Mr. Stone, we keep meeting like this." She smiled lazily, shielding her eyes from the sun behind him with a hand at her brow. "I thought you were a cloud again."

"A cloud?" he asked, amusement in his voice.

A cloud? She flushed. *Is that the best I can think to say?*

There was a slight crinkle beside his eyes as he looked down at her, but his gaze was anything but amused—it was heated in a way that made her feel nearly naked where she lay against the warm grass.

"You are so very tall," she explained as she pushed to sit up. "You seem to blot out the very sun."

He reached down to help her stand, careful to avoid her ungloved hands. Still, his fingers sent a thrill through her, his steady touch warm even through her spencer—her spencer that hung half open from when she'd unbuttoned it earlier.

But her fingers were nerveless, and she couldn't have refastened it if she had tried. She felt wild and unmoored in his presence, like she was adrift at sea, yet Gabriel was the only anchorage she could find to grab onto.

Her own hands found him for support, resting lightly against the sleeves of his coat. She wanted to curl her hands into the smooth wool—to dig her fingers into his arms and drag him closer. His own fingers flexed against her, and she wondered if he itched to touch her as much as she wanted to reach up to him.

She would smooth out the stubborn furrow at his brow if she could.

"This is a pleasant surprise," she said when he had released her, and she'd dropped her own arms to her side.

If they were careful, they would only look like acquaintances meeting in the park. She felt color rising in her cheeks as she thought of their last encounter and the hunger he instilled in her now.

"I'm glad I please you," he murmured, his voice a deep rumble that made her face heat true scarlet.

She turned, looking out across the stretch of grass, where her cousin stood in the distance, and blinked. She needed to break the spell his eyes had cast over her if she had any hope of appearing composed at all.

Warmth settled in his chest— from the sun overhead or how close Miss Price stood to him, Gabriel didn't know. A soft breeze cut between them, tugging at the loose hair that must have slipped from her pins when she'd been stretched out on the blanket. He felt a hint of a smile as he watched her try to compose herself, and he wondered if she was struggling as much as he.

Impossible, he thought, and he swallowed a groan.

He had seen her from a distance and something in him had recognized her immediately. As he'd approached, he'd had the satisfaction of seeing her, stretched across the grass—vulnerable and undone, laid out like an offering. She had been peacefully oblivious, and he had been starved for her.

Her eyes flit to his face then darted back to the point in the distance.

"I came with my cousin," she said, and he realized she was looking not blindly into the distance, but at a pair of young women, deep in conversation. "It was meant to be a picnic."

That time he nearly did groan, imaging her as she'd been when he had walked up on her. She had been a banquet to his hungry eyes.

And she tastes like sunshine, he thought deliriously.

He rubbed his brow. He could kick himself for the ridiculous thought. When had he become such a sodding poet.

"I'm sure you must be very busy," she was saying, her eyes barely touching on his face before she glanced away again.

He was making her uncomfortable, standing there staring with the rudeness of an oaf, and all because he couldn't control his heated thoughts around her.

"Not too busy to check on you," he murmured, and reflexively stepped closer.

She had partially fastened her little jacket closed, but he could see the pale swell of her breasts in the shadow of the gaped collar. He cleared his throat and forced his eyes to her face.

"How are you?" he asked.

"I'm alright," she promised, then let out a heavy breath that he felt in his bones. "I was shaken yesterday, but I do feel better today. It's so much farther away now, in my mind."

She had been in danger yesterday and he was to blame. It was like a dousing of cold water over his head.

"I'm sorry. I didn't want to leave you," he admitted.

"You didn't," she said. "You saw me home safely. It was just my unsteady nerves that stuck with me."

She laughed at herself, and the sound dug into his chest. None of this was her fault.

"I blame myself," he said solemnly, staring down at her with the stillness of a statue.

"What?" she asked, rocking back on her heel. "You saved me. You very likely did," she insisted when he shook his head. "I'm sure they had still been following me when I found you. They must have given up when they saw you."

"They were my responsibility—are my responsibility," he grumbled. She frowned and he pushed on. "I've known about the thefts for months and I should have done something decisive about it sooner."

The admission stung him. He had waited and done nothing, always with the excuse that it was Constable Evans' problem, when he'd known full well the man wasn't doing a thing to help. It hadn't been more than an annoyance when it was just inventory that suffered, but now his delay had nearly hurt Miss Price.

"If I hadn't waited, you never would have stumbled upon them to begin with."

She shook her head at him and took that last step closer, until the front of his jacket nearly brushed her dress. She wanted to reassure him, comfort him—he could see it in her eyes.

"It wasn't your fault," she tried again. "You saved me."

But all he could think about was the state she'd been in, the terror in her eyes. And then he'd pushed himself at her and given into the desires that had gripped him.

"I took advantage of your vulnerability," he bit out.

She reached her hands up to gently brush the lapels of his coat, just once, a whisper of the pressure he wanted to feel of her hands, flat against his chest once more. His hands clenched at his sides so that he didn't drag her to him.

"I don't feel taken advantage of," she whispered, then took a breath, looking up at him with boldness in her gaze. "And if we were anywhere else, I would want very much for you to kiss me again."

Gabriel hissed in a breath. Someone so innocent shouldn't be such a great temptation, yet it was all he could do not to give her exactly what she asked for. Only, he worried if he so much as touched her, he would fall apart.

He tried to speak that to her in his gaze, to warn her of his faltering control—that if they were anywhere else, he wouldn't just kiss her.

He would ruin her.

Chapter Ten

She turned her head in the mirror, still skeptical of her gown choice. Marie forced Evelyn's face forward with firm fingers and huffed in exasperation.

"Please stop moving," she grumbled.

"I wish I hadn't wasted the blue last night," Evelyn said, and frowned as Marie pinned her hair.

Instead, she was in the rose silk.

She eyed herself in the mirror. She still thought the gown looked a little past its prime, but she hadn't had much choice. Besides, she didn't want to seem like she was competing with Augusta by wearing her best. Not when the Hardings had been very plain in their intentions to introduce their daughter to Mr. Stone tonight.

Evelyn sighed.

"The blue is nice, but you look lovely in this color," Marie assured her.

It did make her skin glow in a way the blue never could.

Besides, she could hardly forget what Marie had said once before about this gown, and secretly, she liked the idea of Gabriel being *struck speechless.*

Though with Augusta thrust under his nose all evening, as she was bound to be, would he even notice what Evelyn was wearing? They might have shared a passion-fueled kiss, but the brush with danger had sent emotions skyrocketing, and while he had look positively wicked at the park the day before, he had left before setting sights on her cousin. Who was to say his interest would remain when he was given a younger, more fresh-faced option.

Nigel had hardly needed any convincing at all, she thought with a frown.

She didn't want to compare him to Nigel. It seemed unfair to Gabriel to do so. But it was difficult to overlook the parallels of her current situation to the one she had run from, barely two months ago.

She twisted just enough to assess the bodice again and flushed. Marie tried to hide her smirk, but Evelyn saw it well enough in the mirror. She glanced away. It was clear Marie thought she held enough promise to keep Gabriel's attention, but Evelyn was losing the battle against her insecurities.

And then there was the guilt. She'd watched the way Mrs. Harding had run about the house, making sure everything was just so. It ate at her—that the Hardings had put so much effort into this dinner, when she knew things about Gabriel that she had no right to know.

She knew the way he tasted.

I want to know more.

She frowned and tried to force the thoughts from her head. The Hardings had given her a place to stay when she had wanted to be anywhere but London, and she was being a horrible guest.

Evelyn smoothed her hands down her skirts to calm herself. The truth was, her flirtation with Mr. Stone had no chance of going anywhere. She needed to remember that.

She was only prolonging the inevitable—when he found someone more suited to his life, and it was not her. And the longer this went on, the more she was going to hurt for it later.

He doesn't even know who I am.

It wouldn't matter if he did. Gabriel didn't seem like the type to be swayed by a title. If anything, she should be more concerned that he would take offense to her keeping a secret for so long.

That gave her pause and brought an entirely new kind of guilt to worm beneath her skin. She huffed out a frustrated breath.

None of it really mattered.

She would be gone from Porthaven in less than a month and life would go on. She wouldn't fool herself into thinking Mr. Stone would dwell on some idle flirtation once she was gone.

She looked at herself in the mirror again, holding her own gaze steady.

She could do this. She could do the proper thing and allow him his future, with someone suitable. And it would be a way to pay back the Hardings for the damage she had very nearly done. It would have been unforgiveable if she had ruined Augusta's chances with Mr. Stone, when she could never have him for her own.

Never.

It still didn't sound right in her head, but what could she do? She swallowed and watched the line of her throat move.

She needed to keep her head down, to not draw attention away from her cousin. To allow things to progress the way they were meant to—the way her family and society expected.

She just needed to be sure the Hardings didn't see through her and realize how sourly she had already betrayed their trust.

She thought she would lose her nerve the very moment Gabriel stepped into the room. He managed to suck up so much of the air around him with his very presence, she felt pulled to him like a magnet. And the effort it took to maintain her resolve only doubled when he finally moved to greet her.

Those eyes, she thought with a sigh as she tried to keep her face blank.

Those eyes had stared searchingly into hers for an alarmingly long time. She needed to keep her head or all of her careful plans, and the efforts she was making to do right by her cousins, would be for naught.

And so, dinner was spent in a moody sulk, where she poured every ounce of focus she could muster into studiously ignoring him. It was either that or be hopelessly distracted each time he so much as *breathed*.

It was utterly ridiculous how affected she was by him, but she could not help it. She was aware of each little movement of his across the table. He lifted his glass to his mouth and she tracked the movement, even as her eyes were fixed to the table before her. His hand dwarfed the glass, as his fingers had done to her waist when they'd spanned sheer across her lower back, as he'd held her to him outside that warehouse.

She fought the heat rising up her neck.

Thoughts of his hands only brought to mind thoughts of his *lips* and the way his tongue had teased the inside of her mouth.

She swallowed a long sip of her won wine and kept her eyes carefully averted. She couldn't even look at his hands without becoming a wanton little fool. If she tried to make eye contact, she might fall into his lap.

Much as Augusta seems determined to do, she grumbled.

She took another drink of wine. It hadn't taken long for her cousin to accept that her parents knew what was best for her—once she had seen Mr. Stone for herself.

"It is sure to be well attended, with the weather improving."

Evelyn's eyes snapped to the young gentleman seated to her left. He was reasonably attractive, if not young and a bit overeager for conversation. He had spent all evening chattering her ear off in his attempt at it.

"Are the assembly balls held often?" she asked, trying to recall what he had been speaking about.

It was needlessly rude, but she couldn't seem to listen to a word he said—not with Gabriel seated just across from her. If she looked up, she risked being caught in those piercing eyes that seemed to burrow right into her soul.

What is wrong with me?

She had never been so silly before in her life.

I sound worse than a fool.

Then again, she had never experienced such raw promise in a man's kiss before.

"Oh, yes. If you are here to attend, it would be my honor to request a dance at the next one."

She forced her attention back to the gentleman. It shouldn't have been so difficult to remember his name—not when he had spent all evening talking to her. But she was distracted by her efforts to keep her eyes resolutely off of Gabriel. It was beginning to feel like a Herculean task.

"That would be lovely."

Mr. Carter? she wondered. *No, Mr. Calvin?*

It seemed useless to even *try* to remember.

She smiled blandly at him, though he seemed pleased by her response. She couldn't imagine what he saw to encourage him in that smile. She couldn't even remember his name. She was hardly enthusiastic about dancing with him.

"I would claim a dance as well."

Evelyn's gaze shot up to Gabriel's with wide-eyed surprise,

and she saw his fingers clench on his glass at the shock that must be on her face. And the stares from around the table.

From her periphery she could see Mr. and Mrs. Harding exchange a glance, before the mother cast a pointed look at her daughter. If their intentions for this dinner hadn't been glaringly obvious already, Augusta's coy, questing smile up at Gabriel certainly cemented it.

"Surely you mean with all of the ladies present," Evelyn offered in a small voice.

Anything to stem the murmurs between Mrs. Harding and her husband, and the cool, probing stare she felt from her aunt.

His eyes seemed to narrow on Evelyn's for just a moment, then he cleared his throat and smiled warmly down at Augusta, where she all but clung to his side.

"If the ladies do not mind."

He turned then from Augusta's batting eyes to cast an appeasing glance at the Hardings, his mouth lifting at one corner in that small smile Evelyn was already becoming familiar with.

It was amazing how someone so controlled and self-possessed—severe, even—could be so effortlessly charming.

The gentlemen stayed in the dining room after dinner, while the ladies retired to the drawing room. Evelyn stood near the threshold while the others rested around the room, feeling too unsettled to enter the small space when conversation had already turned to conquest.

Aunt Dorothea eventually made her way to stand beside her, leaving Mrs. Harding and Augusta to sit perched on a settee, heads bent together like schoolchildren. Seeing Gabriel at dinner had done just as Evelyn had feared and set her young cousin's mind firmly on thoughts of matrimony. It made Evelyn feel a bit queasy.

"They are a bit much, aren't they," Aunt Dorothea whispered when she stood beside her.

The two eyed the Harding women from their vantage as mother and daughter plotted excitedly together.

"You might not see it from your position, but it would be an exciting match for them."

Evelyn nodded but didn't respond.

"They made an attractive pair at dinner," her aunt added.

Evelyn felt a pit open up in her stomach—one large enough she was afraid it would suck her inside out until she fell into nothingness.

Then her aunt turned from the Harding women to the clock on the mantle.

"It has been nearly a full hour. Why don't you go to the kitchens to check on refreshments. I'm sure the men have had enough time with their port by now."

Evelyn nodded again and let herself slip from the room.

She fidgeted as she walked, fingering the seam of her glove where the fabric creased at her wrist. She had been so motivated before dinner to give up these feelings for Gabriel and let him go. It was the right thing for everyone, she knew that, but especially for her cousins, who had allowed her into their home with no real benefit to themselves. Mr. and Mrs. Harding had even kept her ridiculous secret, just so she could have some peace as she hid from society.

I am like a child, she thought. *Running from my problems instead of facing them, head on.*

And just like a child, she selfishly did not want to give up Gabriel.

It was a senseless form of cruelty, to insinuate herself somewhere she could never stay, and prevent the people around her from finding happiness. She was only visiting, dipping her toes in the waters here in Porthaven. She was never meant to cross this line and submerge herself so far from home, so far from her own society. There was no future for her here.

But seeing him tonight seemed to undo all of her resolve. One look at him and it was like a fist had squeezed in her chest, and it was dragging her towards him.

As she passed the dining room door she wondered what they were discussing inside. Had conversation already taken the same turn as the one in the drawing room?

Her cousin had been beautiful tonight. Augusta was always beautiful, but the dress Mrs. Harding had ordered rushed from the modiste seemed to set her young cousin aglow in the candlelight. And she was certainly a better flirt than Evelyn had any chance of being.

She thought of Nigel and pretty Henrietta. It certainly wasn't unimaginable that Gabriel would have opened his eyes to Augusta's charms when they had been presented in such stark contrast across the dinner table from her own.

And that was besides the fact that her parents would never allow it, even if Gabriel did by some miracle choose her. Or at least, her father would be firmly against it. She tilted her head in thought. Her mother certainly wouldn't be thrilled with the match.

But would Mamma really stop me if it was a matter of my happiness?

She doubted the Countess of Sampford had ever imagined her eldest daughter falling for a tradesman, but she had never really begrudged Evelyn anything. Mr. Stone wasn't exactly the same as a peculiar penchant for reading, but perhaps the principle was the same?

And Papa can always be brought around, she thought.

If anyone could do it, it was her mother.

She paused near the door to the back garden. Perhaps this wasn't as hopeless as she had feared. She wasn't exactly from a marriage-of-convenience promoting family. If anything, the Pricewinters were hopeless romantics—though they understandably expected their children to fall hopelessly in love with members of the *ton*.

But Evelyn had never been one for expectations, especially of the matchmaking variety. With as many unsuccessful seasons as she'd had, her parents ought to know that by now.

She looked at her hazy reflection in the glass panes of the door. There was still the problem of her name.

She didn't know how Gabriel would react to having been lied to all this time. She would have to find the nerve to tell him the truth if she had any chance of truly pursuing him.

Am I really considering this?

It was absurd. But it was rather thrilling. And it felt, maybe, *right*.

The feel of fingers banding at her wrist made her gasp and turn. She pulled a little at the grip until she saw Gabriel standing behind her and froze in place, wrist still firmly grasped in his hand.

"I thought I spied you through the door," he said and stepped closer.

"What are you doing? You're meant to be drinking, or whatever it is men do at these things," she said with half a laugh.

Gabriel leaned in as if to share a secret and her breath caught at his nearness.

"I wished to speak to you," he said.

He was so close she could feel his exhale against her ear as he spoke. She shivered and felt her back stiffen, afraid she would fall against him if she wasn't careful.

His hand dropped from her wrist, leaving a chill through her glove, where his fingers had been. He took a step back, putting a more respectable gap between them.

She turned nervous eyes to the hall, expecting to see one of the Hardings standing there, but they were still completely alone. She looked back at Gabriel, confused by his abrupt distance and the sudden, severe look in his eyes.

"Did I misread things?" he asked from behind his solemn frown.

She started, caught off guard by his words, not knowing

what to think let alone what to say. Had he misread things?

What things?

She didn't quite know what he was talking about.

"I'm sorry. I tend to be very blunt, but I'd like to think you already know that about me," he said in apology. "Was I mistaken in thinking there was some interest here?" he asked, as blunt as he'd warned.

He gestured vaguely between the two of them.

She swallowed, suddenly feeling like her mouth could not have gone drier.

What could she say?

This morning, she had come to terms with the fact she would never have a chance with this man and that the right thing to do was to give him up. Now she was, for the first time, considering the possibility of a relationship with him—*marriage*. It was exhilarating, but an utterly terrifying thought.

Her eyes flickered between his while he watched her steadily with that unwavering intensity of his. Her skin grew hot, and she felt like she could hardly catch her breath, but then she opened her mouth and breathed, "you were not mistaken."

His eyes widened a moment, as if he hadn't expected her answer, then a smile curved one corner of his mouth and he was stepping back towards her, making the space feel smaller than it already was. His closeness was nearly suffocating, but it sent such a thrill through her she hardly cared.

"Then why haven't you looked at me more than once this evening?" he asked, his voice soft and low.

She swallowed again. She wished she'd drunk more of the

wine at dinner. Maybe then she wouldn't be swimming in nerves and self-doubt.

He was standing so close, his attention so intense she should have all the evidence she needed that this attraction wasn't one sided. Yet still, the doubts bubbled up to cloud her vision.

"I'm sure you've worked out the Hardings's intentions for this dinner?" she asked, struggling to meet his eye.

He made a gruff sound in his throat—dismissive, like Mr. and Mrs. Harding's intention made little difference to him.

Perhaps they didn't.

He reached a bare hand up, but only to her shoulder, where he paused, hovering just above the little puff of sleeve. She wished he would touch her.

"Tell me," he commanded. "Do you prefer Mr. Clarke's conversation to my own?"

She looked at him, puzzled at first, unsure who he meant. Then she remembered the extra gentleman at dinner.

"Mr. Clarke! That is his name," she gasped.

Gabriel looked down at her with that wry tilt to his lips, his eyes glimmering with humor, and chuckled.

"Do you mean to say, you sat next to the poor man all evening, and couldn't remember his name?"

Evelyn flushed and put a hand to her face. "My mother would be mortified," she admitted.

Although truthfully, when would her mother have expected her to have dinner with not one, but two, unmarried, middle-class men?

The thought made her want to giggle, as did the giddy hope that while her mother wouldn't have expected this, Evelyn could at least make her accept it. But she looked back up to catch Gabriel's eyes and the heat there made every thought in her head scatter.

He blinked and slowly grazed his attention down from her eyes to her lips, along the slope of her neck, to rest where his fingers now brushed the pink silk, where the edge met her skin.

"So, then what did you occupy yourself with all through dinner?" he asked in a deep whisper. "If you weren't interested in Mr. Clarke's conversation, and you paid no attention to me."

Her face warmed until she was sure she glowed red. Between the rasp of his voice and the heat of his chest so close to her own, she felt lightheaded. And the way his fingers were now playing with her sleeve, tracing with slow, deliberate passes, made her heart pick up speed. She held her breath, waiting for his fingers to reach her skin.

"I was only paying attention to you at dinner," she admitted in a rush.

"You hardly looked at me," he protested.

She frowned down at the base of his cravat, too vulnerable to stare anywhere closer to his eyes. His fingers were still trailing back and forth at her shoulder. She could feel the pressure of each pass through the silk, until she thought she might go mad. It made her feel reckless and a little bold.

"You had plenty to hold your own attention, on your side of the table." She could hear the jealousy in her own voice.

He only chuckled though, the sound low and sonorous.

And then his fingers did touch her, slipping up the scant distance from silk to skin.

His hand was warm and seemed to engulf her, palm stretching over the curve of her shoulder, fingers dipping as far as they could to her back. She felt like she was on fire.

"I'll tell you now, I have no interest in your cousin." He leaned closer and Evelyn's lips parted on a sigh. "And my attention was firmly on you. All evening."

She swallowed the thickness in her throat, feeling his breath again, against her temple, her ear, her neck.

"I'm glad for it," she murmured.

He was standing so close now she couldn't imagine there was enough air for the two of them to breathe, and certainly her head felt irreversibly dizzy at the sheer size of him, looming over her. She drew in the scent of him—the port he'd been drinking, but something warm too. Like sandalwood. And oranges. She thought she might never regain steady footing.

He looked up and his eyes snared hers, just for a moment, before he stared back down at his fingers, banding across her pale skin. His hand trailed to her arm, carefully finding the bare stretch above her glove. She swayed on her feet.

When she rocked too close, and would have lost her balance, his other hand came up so that both slid across her back to span her waist. Evelyn sucked in a breath at the firm pressure of his hands through the thin silk. The snug bodice was constricting, squeezing her, and she felt the material digging in where it framed her exposed skin.

Gabriel noticed too.

His eyes hungrily traced her neckline in a way that made her instantly grateful she'd worn it.

"I like this gown," he murmured, eyes continuing their trail along the dipping neck.

 She felt like she could hardly swallow, her mouth had gone so dry. "I felt very plain in there, compared to everyone else."

He shook his head slowly. "You could never look plain."

Gabriel shifted his hold on her, smoothing his hands so that they braced the sides of her ribcage, just beneath her bust.

"I'm sorry," he murmured, as one thumb inched dangerously close to skimming her breast.

But he did not move his hands, and she watched him wet his lower lip as his eyes trailed over her.

"I'd like to kiss you again," he whispered. "May I?"

She nodded. She wasn't capable of responding any other way.

He smiled softly and his words swept over her lips. "I never did ask the last time."

When his mouth claimed hers, it wasn't the frenzied clash from their first kiss, when danger had been on her heels and any second wasted had felt like a moment lost forever. This was slow, and leisurely—a gentle, feather-like caress that set desire to a low simmer that would surely continue until it boiled over and consumed her whole.

And it was nothing like the kisses she'd shared with Nigel. Those had been utterly inconsequential compared to the current pressure of Gabriel's lips on her own.

How had she ever thought there was feeling with Nigel? *Was I blind?* she wondered.

There had certainly never been this sort of passion.

When Gabriel lightly passed his lips over hers yet again, she moaned and fisted her hands in his jacket, letting her weight pitch the rest of the way forward to press against him. She was impatient for him.

The one thing she could credit Nigel with——she did have the experience to understand the mechanics of kissing at least, even if he had never managed to make her tingle all the way down to her toes. Hesitantly, she dabbed her tongue against Gabriel's lower lip and felt him freeze beneath her.

She did it again, emboldened when a groan tumbled from his chest. This time, she swept to taste the breadth of his lip, then pushed up on tiptoes to press farther, until she tentatively brushed against his tongue. He coaxed back, drawing her against him and taking control of the kiss.

When she was breathless, he pulled back and pressed a soft kiss to the corner of her mouth. "And here I was worried I'd moved too quickly for you, the last time."

She didn't know why she answered. She could have reclaimed his lips then and continued the gentle embrace he had started. But she didn't want gentle.

He had lit a flame in her belly, and it had grown into an inferno—one that demanded something as unrestrained and wild as she now felt. So, she let her lips part beneath his, breathing her words into his mouth—soft and slow, but as sharp as a taunt.

"But it wasn't the first time I'd been kissed," she goaded.

"Oh?" he asked, and pulled back just enough that she could see the answering hunger flare in his eyes. "And how were you kissed, before?"

She had no desire to answer that, and instead reached for him to kiss her again, but he used his height to keep just out of reach. A sly smile spread across his face as he watched her strain, and he lifted a hand to trace a finger down her cheek.

"Tell me," he insisted, maintaining that hairsbreadth of distance, and she would have been embarrassed by the whimper that escaped her if her head wasn't so fuzzy from his heat. "How did he kiss you, Evelyn? Like this?"

He took mercy on her then and leaned to bridge the space between them. She sighed against him as he slanted his mouth over hers, claiming her with the sort of soul-searing passion she felt in her bones.

No, definitely not like this, she thought.

She clutched at him as he teased his tongue between her lips, and it was all she could do not to moan at the invasion. She felt him smile against her lips, before he swept against her tongue again, drawing her closer with the hand splayed across her back.

When he pulled away again, it was just enough to catch her eyes and quirk a questioning brow.

"Well?" he pressed, but she struggled to make sense of the word, let alone remember what he was asking.

He brushed a whisper-like kiss across her lips.

Have I been kissed like this?

The answer was a resounding no—her only experience before had been with Nigel, and she was quickly learning he'd only been an adequate kisser, at best. Certainly nothing like Gabriel. But she didn't wish to give him the satisfaction of an answer just yet.

"Sort of," she breathed.

"Sort of?" he repeated, his eyes gleaming with challenge. "This beau of yours, who *sort of* kissed you," he started, and brushed a hand up her side until his fingers settled just beneath her breast. His eyes darkened as he watched himself stroke her. "Did he touch you?"

She flushed, but the pleasant tickle of his hand made her bold. "A little. There," she indicated where his fingers were currently tracing back and forth, just beneath the line of her bodice.

She tried to firm her voice, but it still sounded reedy in her ears. "Although I never cared for it very much."

Back and forth, back and forth. His touch was like a flame to her desire, and it lit something to scorching inside of her. He surely must be able to tell from the way her eyes glazed over at his continued caress.

"No?" He continued that mesmerizing motion with his fingers. "So then, you do not like this?" he asked and ran his hand up to cup her breast through the silk of her gown.

She could feel her nipple stiffen almost immediately and mewled at the touch, leaning into the pressure.

He tilted his head to watch her reaction, drinking in each panting breath as his fingers toyed with her. She could hardly believe she was allowing him to touch her like this, exposed as they were in the open hall. He dipped his fingers just beneath the neck of her gown, enough to sooth the skin marked by the tight-fitting edge. His touch sent tingles rippling across her flesh.

She peered up at him in astonishment from beneath her lashes. Apart from the burning hunger in his eyes, he looked as in control as she'd ever seen him. Something about it excited her, but she didn't have time to consider why before he bent his head, hovering just above her exposed skin.

"And I don't suppose you would like this?" he asked, shifting both hands to span her ribcage.

The challenge was still in his eyes, and he watched her intently, almost daring her to stop him.

But she didn't and he bent the rest of the way, his breath like a caress against her flesh. And then he darted his tongue out against her skin, in a sensual drag along the swell of her breast, tracing the tight neckline.

Her hand reached out of its own accord to grip at his arm, and she stifled a gasped moan behind the other. She felt Gabriel's chuckle against her skin.

"Gabriel," she whimpered, startling herself.

It was the first time she had used his given name aloud.

Gabriel.

She liked the way it sounded on her tongue, almost as much as she liked her name on his lips as he ran them up the column of her neck, trailing his kiss all the way.

"Evelyn," he murmured against her skin, lips hot where

they nuzzled, just beneath her ear. "Believe me when I say, I do not want your cousin."

A lingering kiss beneath her ear.

"I want you."

Chapter Eleven

Mr. Harding departed the following morning to little fanfare. Evelyn imagined it was the frequency of his travel that dimmed his exit to a string of brief goodbyes just after breakfast. No one seemed overly preoccupied with his leaving. Mrs. Harding rushed out almost immediately to make morning calls, and Augusta disappeared off somewhere soon after. It left Evelyn alone with her aunt for the first time in almost two weeks.

And so, that morning she found herself seated at the round table in the morning room, staring out at the garden through the tall windows lining the walls. The early light filtered through, casting ribbons of sunlight across the blonde wood floor. Her eyelids fluttered briefly, the sheer brightness outside bringing moisture to her eyes.

Evelyn turned from the window. She should be finishing her letter anyway. She blinked again, looking down at the sheet of paper in front of her as her vision cleared.

"Ah, no!"

She groaned when she saw the spreading drop of black staining the paper. She moved to dab it away, but only managed to spread the puddled ink. She leaned back in her chair with a sigh and peered out the window again.

It was no use. She could not seem to string three words together, no matter how she tried. Instead, Gabriel's face kept swimming in her vision, and when she closed her eyes, she could feel his hot mouth on her neck. She shivered at the memory and forced her attention on the fresh, green growth out the window.

Not the brand of Gabriel's tongue.

Stop this, now. It was easier said than done. *Aunt Dorothea is bound to notice something.*

She took a steadying breath.

Now that Spring was upon them, the garden was beginning to look invigorated. The roses hadn't bloomed yet, it was still too early for that. But the abundance of flat, green leaves and curling vines brought life to the small space, all the same.

Evelyn let a smile spread across her face. The cheery color sat nicely against the pale brick and the white-framed windows across from her.

What room is that? she wondered.

The organization of the house was set like a square, but she could not seem to make sense of layout at times. It was not at all similar to the Sampford townhouse in London.

It had not the slightest bit in common with Haythorne House.

Evelyn blinked against the sunlight through the glass. There was a cluster of new buds she could just see, that would be perfectly visible from that far window. It would be beautiful when they bloomed.

It must be the drawing room, she realized.

Her eyes widened the slightest bit at the thought, and she blinked again, but this time in disbelief. Then she panned her eyes from the sash window, across to the other corner of the garden. She could see the drawing room windows from where she sat, but the morning room wasn't actually in its direct line of sight. No, that was the rear hall, with its tall, glass paneled door and oversized windows. The disbelief turned to distress.

Oh God, no.

Evelyn tracked the line from drawing room to hall, and back again. As if she could somehow force the layout of the house to distort until the sightline was obscured—or better yet, obliterated.

No one had said anything the night before, when she'd slipped back in from *checking on the refreshments*, but now she felt worry take hold in her gut.

And it was fast rising, creeping up her throat as she thought of what might have been spied from that very window—with the curtains drawn, and the hall's hazy light so much brighter against the nighttime darkness of the garden.

She was faintly aware of Aunt Dorothea speaking to her, but she was too distracted now to listen, and whatever words were said passed straight past Evelyn, unintelligible.

This was more than unease. Evelyn swallowed, feeling her hands shake, and she clenched her fingers in her lap. This was panic—not just that she could have been seen and judged for her behavior, though that was certainly a concern. But she feared her carelessness would make her lose this chance she was just beginning to consider a possibility.

"The tongue was a bit much," Aunt Dorothea said, and Evelyn felt all color drain from her face.

She coughed, feeling about ready to choke on her *own* tongue.

"What?" she squeaked, with a pained look she tried her best to disguise.

"The beef tongue," Aunt Dorothea said, not looking up from her embroidery. "These Porthaven breakfasts are too rich for my tastes. I can hardly stomach it."

She glanced up at Evelyn's continued rasping. "Are you quite alright?"

Evelyn nodded, her eyes watery.

"I'm fine," she assured her. "Just a speck of dust."

Aunt Dorothea looked speculatively about the spotless room. "Mhmm," she hummed noncommittally, but returned to her needlework.

Evelyn sputtered a final cough and put a hand to her chest, trying to compose herself. It would be no good if she was this on edge all of the time. Eventually her family would realize something was wrong, and she would be found out. She wasn't ready for that.

He doesn't even know who I am.

There were so many confessions that had to be made first—to Gabriel, and to her parents.

What will Mamma say?

Evelyn looked down at the half-written letter in front of her. There was only one way to find out how her mother would react. She shuffled the ink-stained sheet aside and grabbed another. She would write to her mother. She exhaled heavily. She would write to her mother and beg for her approval.

Dear Mamma, she began.

Aunt Dorothea's bored sigh startled her, like she had already forgotten her aunt was in the room. She looked up as the older woman gently tossed her needlepoint on the seat beside her.

"This is mind numbing," Aunt Dorothea said with a wry smile to Evelyn as she plucked the little spectacles from her nose.

Evelyn swallowed a nervous laugh and hastily restacked the papers, hiding the unfinished letter to her mother at the bottom.

"What do you think my cousin is up to this morning?" Aunt Dorothea asked, amusement in her voice.

"Visiting friends, I think," Evelyn said with a frown.

It did seem peculiar that both women would rush out alone so soon after Mr. Harding had left.

Aunt Dorothea gave a dry laugh at that. "I'm sure she's traipsing all over town telling anyone who will listen about her brilliant catch."

"Brilliant catch?" She was preoccupied again with what to write to her mother.

She wanted to hurry upstairs where she could pen something in the privacy of her room.

"Mr. Stone."

Evelyn's breath hitched. Aunt Dorothea didn't seem to notice and continued with a low chuckle to herself.

"I bet Augusta is doing the same. It didn't take long for her to change her tune, did it?"

"Oh," Evelyn sputtered. "I suppose so."

Aunt Dorothea tapped her spectacles against her arm. "He seems a fair match for her."

She still seemed oblivious to Evelyn's discomfort.

"Yes," she agreed tightly.

The turn in conversation was beginning to prove painful.

She looked down at the sheaf of papers now clenched in her stiff fingers.

"Oh dear," she announced, standing suddenly. "I've spilled ink on half of these."

Her aunt frowned up at her from her seat. Evelyn didn't care how flimsy her excuse was.

"I'll need to get more in my room. Do you mind if I go?"

Aunt Dorothea waved her on with a hand and looked out the window. Evelyn didn't want to stay any longer than necessary and moved quickly towards the door.

"I may sit out in the garden, in a little while," Aunt Dorothea called after her. "You're free to join me, when your letters are done."

"Yes, thank you," Evelyn murmured, managing to turn and give her aunt a placating smile before she left.

Then she slipped out the door and rushed for the stairs.

Gabriel blinked away from his work and pushed the stack of papers across his desk with an aggravated sigh. He'd been staring at inventory reports all morning—so long that the neat scratchings of Franklin's penmanship had started swimming across his vision. He closed his eyes for a moment's relief and cursed when rows of text and numbers flashed behind his eyelids.

I need a fucking break. He sighed and glanced at the windows.

Those blasted windows.

The sun was bleeding happily in through the glass, while he felt as if he'd been festering in the drudgery of work for a fortnight. Or at least four days.

Four long days.

He tipped his head back with a groan that rumbled up his throat. He felt caged.

It had been like this since the damned dinner party at Mr. Harding's—when he'd followed Miss Price into the hall and pressed himself upon her, like the great, big brute that he was.

His mind and his body couldn't seem to agree on how to react to that memory and it made him want to throw things like a petulant child. He vacillated between missing her—needing her—and hating himself for his coarse, ungentlemanly treatment of her.

Not that she had seemed to mind. She certainly hadn't protested.

He shook his head and a humorless laugh sprung from his throat. No, she had begged with the way she'd said his name. Like she was as desperately on fire for him as he was for her.

He groaned and dropped his forehead to his fist. He was a rogue to think it, but all Gabriel wanted was the feel of her soft breast in his hand once more, the tight peak of her nipple pressing beneath his fingers, demanding his attention.

Four days.

He had been like this for four days.

Three days, twelve hours, and forty-three minutes, he corrected himself, looking at the tiny hands of the clock.

And he was a useless, distracted wreck, hardly able to focus on anything important, because of his foolish insistence on thrusting his attentions on Miss Price's innocence. But then, he seemed unable to be anything but a fool around her.

God, but I want her.

He wanted her so badly it hurt. He peered at the blue sky through the windows.

Those infernal windows!

They were a taunting reminder of how close she was, a short walk across the park, but a lifetime away for all the good it did him. It wasn't as if he could waltz over to Linden Street and drag the poor girl into another searing embrace, just because he desired it.

Oh, the things I do desire.

He wanted so much more than the teasing touches she'd already allowed. He thought of the way she'd moaned his name, the way she had clung to him with her whole body when he'd kissed her that first time. He wanted to run his hungry mouth all over her willing body, clutch her close to him, and drive himself between those welcoming thighs.

God, he hadn't remembered being this depraved before.

He was a man still in his prime, and he had healthy appetites. Ones he sated, without shame or regret. But never had he craved a woman like this—to distraction. And certainly not a gently bred innocent like Miss Price. She was not the type of woman you bedded. She was the type of woman you married.

Marriage.

The word still felt sour on his tongue.

It had been years since Jane Thomas had abandoned him—tossed him aside for the type of pretty lifestyle he hadn't yet been able to afford.

If he was honest, it was a lifestyle his money still could not buy. He would never have a fancy title, never be the son of an exalted line, tracing his lineage back to the bloody conqueror.

That wasn't in the cards for him. He would always be the rough, unpolished spawn of Simon Stone—a man too stubborn to understand that the vaulted echelons of the aristocracy would never accept his son.

Though he'd certainly tried, Gabriel sneered.

Eton, Oxford, tutors, fencing, Latin, fucking Greek.

He'd had all the education of a little lord, but none of the breeding to make it matter. None of it had mattered to Jane in the end.

Not when she'd had a baronet on the hook.

He rested his head in his hands, pressing his weight against the desk as he bit back a snarl. Now his need was making him depressingly maudlin, and there was nothing he hated more than this pointless exercise of self-pity.

"And what has you so distracted?" came a voice from the door.

Gabriel looked up from where he slumped at his desk, eyes no doubt wild and vicious with his frustration. He started in surprise at the sight of Theodore Brook, recently Baron Hilgrave, standing at the threshold to his office. He would have been happy to see him, if not for the smug smile tilted across the bastard's face.

"Who is she?"

"None of your business," Gabriel muttered.

Teddy laughed, then crossed to the low backed sofa and sprawled across it. Even before he'd inherited his unexpected title from some distant, forgotten relative, he'd been insufferable. Naturally, they'd been friends since boyhood.

"She's really done a number on you then," Teddy said with a shake of his head.

Gabriel grumbled and pushed to his feet. "If you insist on being such a bother, make yourself useful and walk with me to town. I could use the idiotic entertainment."

Teddy took no offence, just laughed at Gabriel's foul mood and returned to his feet. "Good to see you too," he teased.

"I don't see why you needed to accompany me," Augusta pouted as they stepped into another shop.

"I am leaving for a few days and your mother would like to make use of my opinions before then," Evelyn said, though she was as unhappy about the arrangement as her young cousin.

Why on earth would she want to help Augusta pick fashionable clothing with which to entice Mr. Stone? She would be glad to leave the Hardings behind, just for a few days, while she went to see Maryann.

Her friend's letter, asking for her to come visit, had only just arrived with the post a few days ago. It was quite a last-minute thing, but no bother with Bath barely a stone's throw away.

"If she hasn't noticed by now that you know not a whit about fashion, Mamma must be blind."

Caught off guard, Evelyn laughed. Uncharitable though it was, it certainly wasn't untrue. She'd spent more time sitting in silence while Augusta shopped than contributing anything useful to this outing. But if the illusion of having an earl's daughter at her disposal made Mrs. Harding feel better, who was Evelyn to argue?

"Oh, this one!" Augusta exclaimed, darting away from Evelyn and leaving her alone by the windows. "Mr. Stone will be sure to notice this one."

Mr. Stone is a man, and therefore unlikely to notice any of your hats, Evelyn internally scoffed.

She turned to the window. The day had been horrifically boring. She didn't simply not know a whit about fashion, she didn't care in the slightest. Especially now that she knew she could entice Gabriel with the very oldest of her gowns.

She stifled a giggle. How fortunate that he wasn't moved by expensive gowns and towering hats.

"Oh," she breathed, as she stared out the window and spotted a tall, familiar figure across the square.

"What is it?" Augusta asked, suddenly at her elbow.

The girl peered out the window and Evelyn knew from her swift inhale the moment she saw Gabriel for herself.

Augusta turned to the shopgirl. "Wrap up the pink and the yellow," she instructed. "My cousin will take care of it."

"Augusta," Evelyn chided when she moved to exit the door. "You shouldn't go out there alone to meet him."

"Of course I should," Augusta sniffed. "We've already been introduced. This is Porthaven, not your stuffy London."

She looked exasperated and impatient when Evelyn's frown deepened. It took a concerted effort not to laugh—it was interesting how quickly London became stuffy when it served Augusta's needs.

"It is a busy, public square. I will look perfectly respectable," Augusta huffed.

You will look perfectly like a hopeless flirt, Evelyn thought. She rolled her eyes.

"You are an unescorted young lady, and he is a man—two

men," she corrected when she saw his companion. She sighed. "Just wait one moment and I will go out with you."

Augusta ignored her.

"I will be just over there," Augusta said in condescending tones, as if speaking to a child, and left through the door.

Evelyn pursed her lips, contemplating the sickening combination of aggravation and jealousy that pooled in her belly.

"The hats, ma'am?" the shopgirl asked shyly. Evelyn turned to her.

Yes, right, she mused wryly. *Evelyn the spinsterly companion, here to help her eligible young cousin with her packages.*

Outside, she handed the hatboxes off at their carriage. It was an unnecessary convenience for as short a trip as the one from Linden Street to the center of town, but Mrs. Harding had insisted. She'd been concerned for the armloads of purchases Augusta was sure to need if she was to pursue a betrothal with Mr. Stone. Evelyn thought it altogether silly.

She paused beside the carriage and looked up to see Gabriel and Augusta in conversation—Gabriel, who even from a distance looked like he'd stepped out of her daydreams. Her heart fluttered so wildly, she thought she might willingly purchase senseless yards of fabric as well, if she thought it would somehow win him.

A breeze blew in, picking up speed to whip at her skirts as she stepped out from the protection of the carriage's shadow. She put a hand to her bonnet as she walked across the square, aware of the way the wind tugged at the ribbons. She seemed constantly to be in a state of disarray around Gabriel, unlike her cousin, who's hat sat perched atop perfect curls that defied the very weather.

He was laughing at something Augusta had said and staring down at the girl with a gentle indulgence that made Evelyn's stomach flop. A thin finger of cloud crossed the sun, distorting the light and sending it dancing. Evelyn bit her lip.

The light looked like a glowing halo around them. They made for such a romantic tableau, her stomach felt dragged up to somewhere in the vicinity of her chest, as if in a fist that then squeezed.

Then Gabriel's eyes lifted and caught hers, and she saw the benign look there twist into something darker, hungrier. It made her chest squeeze in an altogether different way. The intensity of that stare was so enthralling, she had to remind herself to keep moving forward.

She could see Augusta giggling at the other man, but Evelyn could hear none of it—not the laughter, nor the conversation that went on, muffled, around her. It was all just meaningless buzzing in her ears while she stared up at Gabriel.

"Miss Price," he intoned, blithely interrupting Augusta. He didn't even seem to notice. "It's a pleasure to see you again."

"And you," she replied, feeling almost out of breath as he angled himself towards her.

It was such a slight motion, but she felt the weight of his attention like a blanket across her skin. His eyes glittered down at her, making her feel flush all over. She suppressed a shiver.

Those eyes were dangerous. They offered things a decent lady would run from. They shamelessly promised more of what they'd started the other night at dinner.

"Miss Price, allow me to introduce you to my friend, Lord Hilgrave," he said, and his mouth tilted up at one corner. "He is newly a baron, but we shan't hold that against him."

"Indeed," said Lord Hilgrave, with a nod. "Gabe has such an aversion to titles, but he puts up with me for the sake of nostalgia."

"I swear, I do not know why I bother." Gabriel affected a scowl, but Evelyn could see only affection for the other man. She wondered how long they had been friends for. "You still haven't greeted her properly," Gabriel grumbled.

"Apologies, Miss Price. It is a pleasure to meet you." Lord Hilgrave flourished a more dramatic bow.

"It's a pleasure to meet you." She laughed and bobbed a courtesy.

She peeked at Gabriel again to see him staring down at her with such heat in his eyes, she didn't know how the other two hadn't notice.

"An aversion to titles?" Augusta puzzled sweetly. She gave a breathy laugh. Evelyn didn't need to look at her cousin to tell her tone meant trouble. "Whatever do you mean?" Augusta asked.

It is not directed at me, Evelyn assured herself of Augusta's syrupy tone. *She does not know my family's title any more than he does.*

The way Augusta's eyes slid from Evelyn and back

confirmed she at least had noticed the emotion in Gabriel's eyes, and more importantly, who it was directed at.

"He's always been this way," Lord Hilgrave interjected, before Gabriel had a chance to answer. "He downright hates us poor nobles. No doubt it was the years of being beaten and bullied by our schoolmates."

"I'd hardly call you poor," Gabriel scoffed, his eyes darting away.

Evelyn watched the hard set of his jaw and unreadable expression and wondered if he wasn't upset with Lord Hilgrave's candor about his school days. Not many men would enjoy having his youthful losses announced in mixed company.

Gabriel cleared his throat. "I do not have much opportunity to engage with the aristocracy though, do I? So, it hardly matters."

"No, indeed," agreed Augusta.

Evelyn swallowed. She felt like she might be sick.

"Not many titled fellows here in Porthaven," Teddy replied, then pressed a hand to his own chest. "Present company excluded."

Gabriel wanted to dash the man about the head.

He could tell by that look in Hilgrave's eyes that he'd seen whatever it was between himself and Miss Price, and the aggravating man had been compelled to tease. Now he was playing at his favorite game—goad Gabriel. When they were boys, it had almost always led to scrapping in the schoolyard. Now Gabriel ground his teeth to stop from giving his friend a good thwack.

Beaten and bullied.

Who announced something like that so casually in front of ladies?

Gabriel frowned. He'd hardly been beaten and bullied as a boy. Not for very long anyway. Verbal punches, yes—he had certainly been a victim of those. But he had grown rather bigger for his age than his classmates, and the little lordlings had quickly thought better of hitting Gabriel when Gabriel might hit back.

His eyes slipped impulsively to Evelyn. Conversation had continued around him, and she looked uneasy, but he couldn't say why. He had missed at least half of the exchange.

She fidgeted, her fingers tangling where she clenched them at her waist. He watched her cast restless eyes at Teddy. Gabriel didn't think it was some developing fascination with Lord Hilgrave. He bristled at the thought. She didn't seem the type though.

Miss Harding, on the other hand—

He could have laughed at that, at the way the girl had all but glued herself to him at the Hardings' dinner party, but now was fluttering her lashes so prettily up at Teddy.

"They tend to get squeamish about traveling farther than Bath."

Still talking about lords then, Gabriel groused.

"Oh!" Miss Harding exclaimed, eyes rounding to match the surprised *o* of her mouth. She turned wide, longing eyes on Miss Price. "Maybe you'll be lucky enough to mix with them in Bath."

Evelyn shook her head and gave her cousin a look Gabriel didn't know how to interpret. "I'm going to Bath to visit my friend, not to go socializing about town."

Gabriel frowned. He hadn't known she was going to Bath—to visit friends or otherwise.

"You're going to Bath?" he asked.

She blinked up at him with a nod as a pink flush filled her cheeks. "Yes," she said faintly. "The invitation was rather last minute."

Her eyes darted again to Lord Hilgrave, though Gabriel couldn't tell if it was in shy admiration or some sort of fear. Either way, he wanted to hit his friend each time her eyes landed on him.

Teddy coughed, though it sounded to Gabriel more like he had attempted to cover a laugh. He narrowed his eyes at him and saw the man's poorly concealed smirk.

Gabriel knew why. He'd all but admitted with his intense, brooding stare that Evelyn was the woman who had *done a number on him*. And now she seemed to be apologizing for her imminent departure, when there was little obvious reason for her to do so.

Gabriel however was more interested in knowing when she would return than worrying about Teddy seeing through him. As long as the man left Miss Price alone, Teddy could think whatever he wanted. Gabriel glared at him before shifting closer to Miss Price.

"When do you leave?" he asked.

"Tomorrow morning." She peered down at her hands.

So soon.

It was nonsensical that the news would make his heart stutter. Especially when he knew she would have to return home to London eventually.

Only by then I'll have given her a reason to stay.

He mentally shook himself. What was he thinking? That she would stay—that he could convince her to *marry* him?

"For how long?" Gabriel asked, swallowing hard at the invasive thoughts.

"Only for a couple of days. I'll be back before the assembly."

She gazed up at him and he thought she looked suddenly breathless. Was she thinking about his offer to dance with her?

"Good. I'll look forward to our dance."

Look forward to it?

He remembered the way she'd felt beneath his hands.

I'm practically salivating for it.

Thank God she couldn't tell.

Chapter Twelve

Evelyn stepped down to the street, happy to have her feet on firm ground once more. The worn flagstones felt as sturdy as solid oak after the incessant jostling of the carriage.

She flexed her toes in her leather boots, willing the feeling back into her feet. She had thought the long journey from Norfolk to Porthaven uncomfortable, but two hours in the Hardings' carriage could do nothing to compare to the plush comfort of the Earl of Sampford's private coach, and she was suddenly aware of the luxury she had taken for granted.

She took a step and winced at the prickling in her leg.

Painfully aware.

"Evelyn!"

She looked up to see Maryann hurrying towards her.

Evelyn smiled.

Maryann must have been watching at the window, or else had heard the carriage pull up. Seeing her now felt like a weight had been lifted off her.

She hadn't realized how much she had missed her friend. It was not the same having only Marie for a confidante, no matter how close they'd always been.

"Maryann, it's good to see you." Evelyn reached to hug her, and Maryann clung with the weight of her worries.

It made Evelyn's heart ache for her friend.

"I was so glad you agreed to visit," Maryann confessed as they separated.

There was a note of desperation in her voice that matched the despair Evelyn saw in her eyes.

"And I was overjoyed to receive your invitation." She gave Maryann's hand a squeeze before letting her lead the way to the Selwyns' townhouse.

Evelyn didn't know how things had developed for the Selwyns since London, but it didn't seem for the better. She watched Maryann's profile as they walked, with a frown. Her happiness at seeing Evelyn was shadowed by the strain in her eyes, and a tiredness beyond her years.

I was right to come when I did.

She only wished she had come sooner. But the unpleasant truth was that she had spent little time thinking about Maryann's burdens since she'd been in Porthaven. How could she when her mind was consumed with thoughts of one charming gentleman.

Not that he's always behaved like a gentleman, she thought with a delicious shiver.

The memories that assailed her sent heat spiraling to places that made her cheeks burn hot with wanton desire. She peered again at Maryann and felt herself turn a deeper red, now with guilt. If Maryann hadn't sent that letter all but begging Evelyn come see her, would she have remembered her conviction to help her friend?

A footman marched past to collect her small, leather luggage from the carriage and Evelyn forced her attention back to the here and now. She should not let her mind wander so easily back to Porthaven. So she did her best to firmly lock the door on the pervasive need she felt for Mr. Stone.

At least while I am visiting Maryann.

It was, she decided as they took the step up to the Selwyn's front door, the right thing to do.

"I will admit, I'm a touch envious—I've missed Bath. My parents haven't taken us back in years," Evelyn admitted as she peered out the tall windows, angling until she thought she had a glimpse of the Sampford townhouse. "The house is just sitting there, empty."

"But they're coming up from London in just a couple of weeks."

That was news to Evelyn, though it was possible the post had arrived after she'd left. She had likely passed her mother's letter on her way to Bath.

If Mamma is as close as Bath, I will have my chance to speak with her, she thought.

"And then you can come back to Bath for a proper visit. Instead of being stuck in that city," Maryann said. "Honestly, I can't imagine what there is to do in a place like that."

Maryann wrinkled her nose as she poured Evelyn another cup of tea. She said it as if Porthaven was some remote, foreign land, with strange customs and peculiar people.

"There are plenty of things to do." Evelyn tried not to appear too offended by the skepticism on Maryann's face.

It wasn't Maryann's fault. Evelyn's own experiences were similarly limited in scope—from the ballrooms of London to the ballrooms of Bath. But to think that without the influence of the *ton* there could be no entertainment was laughable. Especially when she and Maryann had always been utterly miserable at London parties in the first place.

"What sort of things?" Maryann frowned. Her mind seemed to be circling for its own answers.

"Maryann, it is just another city," she said bemusedly. "I cannot imagine it's been so very different from your stay in Bath."

Maryann scoffed as she picked up her own cup. "I don't think anyone's experience has been like mine."

"What do you mean?" Evelyn asked at Maryann's dry tone. "I thought you were excited for all of this."

"I was," she agreed. "Until I realized just how many balls there would be."

Evelyn winced. "That many?"

"And more," she groaned. "It never seems to end, and I am

exhausted."

"I am not envious of that," Evelyn said wryly. "There is an assembly in a week, but I haven't attended a ball since London, and I am grateful."

"So, what do you do in Porthaven?" Maryann looked genuinely at a loss.

Obsess over a man who doesn't even know my full name.

She felt her face heat.

"Hmm," she considered. "Honestly, for such a busy city, it has been quite restful for me."

She wondered what Maryann would think of her situation with Mr. Stone, and what advice she might have.

"There was a dinner party before Mr. Harding left for London, but otherwise my time has been my own."

"That does sound nice," Maryann agreed, then shook her head. "But truthfully, I think I would be bored without all the entertainment."

"Even after your exhausting string of parties?" Evelyn laughed.

"I admit, I would prefer something in the middle." She sipped at her tea and frowned. "Though most of all, it's the pressure that has been the worst of it."

Evelyn had wondered how to broach the subject of the Selwyns' current position. It was like a large, unsightly figure in the middle of the room that they were both aware of, but wary of mentioning.

"How has it been?" Evelyn asked hesitantly. She could feel that Maryann's answer would be an unpleasant one and part of her wished to remain insulated from it. She had never had to taste the bitterness of suffering—she wasn't even familiar with the threat of it.

"I've had an offer of marriage," Maryann murmured. She looked up at Evelyn. "It would save my family."

It did not sound like Maryann wanted any part of it though. "You do not need to accept though, right?" she asked gently. "They aren't going to force you."

"A good daughter wouldn't allow it to come to that." Maryann touched her fingers to her temples, lowering her gaze and letting her head droop. "A good daughter would be happy to accept. I am not a good daughter."

Evelyn reached to lay her hand on Maryann's arm. She didn't like the hopelessness she felt in her friend's words.

"Who is it?"

"The Marquess of Stanton," Maryann muttered.

"Lord Stanton?" Evelyn exclaimed.

She reeled back, feeling for a moment as if she were truly struck speechless.

"But—but he cannot be a day under sixty!"

Maryann fidgeted anxiously, the very thought seemingly enough to make her uncomfortable.

"He is recently widowed, and his late wife gave him only daughters," Maryann continued, as though Evelyn hadn't interjected. "I am told he is eager for an heir."

Evelyn frowned, shaking her head as if she could deny the situation and banish it all to some far-off corner of oblivion. Maryann looked as if exhaustion had sucked the fight right out of her.

"Your parents will not really force you to marry him though," Evelyn muttered. "Will they?"

Maryann took a steadying breath. "It is better than the alternative."

She blinked upwards, catching sight of Evelyn's concern and confusion.

"There is nothing left, Evelyn," she whispered. "It is all gone—even this." She gestured at the finely appointed room around them.

"I don't understand."

"I only found out a few weeks ago, when Lord Stanton's intentions were made clear, and my parents thought it necessary to explain the importance of his offer." She exhaled a mirthless laugh. "Our new *tenant* has acquired not only the London townhouse, but this one as well." She said tenant like it was a dirty word. "We are only here on his kindness and charity."

"Who is he?"

Maryann shrugged and shook her head.

"Even my father does not know. It was all handled through the lawyers." She clenched her fingers into tight fists. "All I do know is that we are on borrowed time and soon we will likely find ourselves tossed from these walls as well. The only hope now is to save Longford for Valentine."

Longford Abbey had been the Blake seat for eight generations. It would be a heartbreaking sacrifice to give up. She knew how deeply her own family would mourn the loss of

Haythorne House. It didn't make the reality of Maryann's current situation any more bearable.

"Oh, Maryann." She didn't know how to comfort her friend.

What was there to say? If all their funds had truthfully dried up, where could they possibly turn? What comfort was there to offer under such dire circumstances?

Maryann was right—if the alternative was finding themselves on the street, it would be worlds better to submit to an undesirable marriage, even if it was to a man thirty years her senior. At least Lord Stanton didn't have a poor reputation, or a foul temper.

"Valentine is opposed to it," Maryann said finally.

Maryann's older brother was their father's heir, set to inherit Longford and the family fortune as Viscount Blake— that or a mountain of growing debts. If he opposed his sister marrying Lord Stanton, Evelyn thought it ought to count for something.

"I'm worried about him," Maryann said, with a sudden gravity that surprised Evelyn.

"About Valentine?"

During their first season, when Maryann and Evelyn had been hopeful and starry-eyed, Valentine had played the big brother for them both. It had been a welcome novelty, when her own brothers, though she loved them dearly, seemed always too distracted with their own lives for their younger sisters. She didn't want to think about him in some sort of trouble now.

"He's been sneaking out in the middle of the night when he thinks no one is awake to catch him. He doesn't realize I know."

"Maybe it is a woman?" Evelyn suggested, with a deep flush.

Her experience with carnality might barely brush the surface, but she knew the wicked pleasure of large, male hands on her body.

Gabriel's hands.

Maryann shook her head. "No, I don't think so. He has never looked dressed for socializing. Not even for *that* type."

Maryann wrinkled her nose in disgust and Evelyn understood her implication. Maryann did not think Valentine was *paying* for company either.

"Then what do you think—Where do you think he has been going?"

Maryann looked at a loss. The concern was still on her face, but it was now marked by a creeping despair. The powerlessness against her brother's situation, and the hopelessness of hers seemed to be crushing her.

"The first time I caught him was in London. So, whatever it is, he has found it here in Bath as well." She clenched her skirts, then said the thing Evelyn knew they were both thinking. "I just hope it isn't gambling."

"I do not think Valentine would be so careless as to gamble what money is left," Evelyn insisted.

"I do not know," Maryann confided. "I feel I do not know anything anymore."

Evelyn reached a hand to Maryann's shoulder, lending whatever sense of support she could. And wishing she could do so very much more.

Bath had not been the welcome escape she had hoped for. The Selwyns' predicament was more dire than she had realized, and her friend was in a prickly situation with no real way out, and no favorable outcome evident.

Evelyn had left Porthaven feeling uncertainty over her relationship with Gabriel—torn between her growing feelings for him and fear over her many lies. She did not feel much more steady now on her return.

Especially now that I know how he feels about the aristocracy.

He wasn't likely to find the surprise of an earl's daughter to be a boon. No, she was afraid he was more likely to be angry and resentful.

Evelyn swallowed past the anxiety that threatened to choke her. Her trip to Bath had only given her new things to worry about, and it had somehow managed to make her own troubles seem even more impossible, not less so.

In only three days she would see Gabriel, talk to him, dance with him. If they found any time alone, there was every chance there would be *more* than just dancing.

She flushed, thinking of his bold touch and expert kisses.

She didn't want Gabriel to be some secretive memory she left behind when she returned to London—not now that she knew the heart shattering emotions that went along with the stolen kisses and sinful desire.

I need to tell him the truth. There was no longer a way around it, nor any alternative. She couldn't quite voice the words to say what she wanted from him, but she knew it was nothing she could have without honesty.

"Should I wait to take that one?" Marie's voice cut through her reverie and brought her sharply back from her woolgathering.

"I'm sorry?" Evelyn looked down at the table, nearly surprised to find the unfinished letter before her and the pen in her hand.

I have met a gentleman...

She rocked back in her seat, face heating as she remembered the content of the letter she'd been writing—or trying to. *Again.*

Dear Mamma,

She put down the quill pen with nerveless fingers and hastily folded up the note.

"No, Marie. That won't be necessary," she muttered, as she gathered up the letter and held it clutched close against her waist. She fumbled for words. "I will finish this one later and post it myself."

Marie nodded, a questioning frown creasing her brow, but said nothing as she curtsied and left the room.

Evelyn stood clumsily. She could hardly manage to start a letter to her mother, let alone finish it. She wanted to speak with her about Mr. Stone, about her hopes—and her fears. She wanted her mother's advice about this *feeling* too, the one that pressed at her heart when she thought of him and compressed painfully when she thought of leaving.

"Ah!" She gasped and pressed the stinging pad of her thumb to her mouth. "Oh, damn. That smarts."

She could taste the tang of blood on her tongue and winced as the sharp twinge continued. Why did papercuts seem to hurt more than anything else?

She looked down at the offending square of paper. "Double damn," she cursed.

She wouldn't be able to post this letter anyway, even if it had been finished. The half-written missive to her mother was crumpled and streaked with crimson. It looked like she'd fished it from a crime scene.

Evelyn sank back into her chair. She wanted to come clean and make things right. She wanted to find a path forward that would guide her to the place where she could make something of this confusing jumble of emotions—a place where her father's title didn't matter.

She frowned, pushing the ruined letter with a heavy hand until it dropped off the desk. That crushing feeling was assailing her chest again. She rose again from her seat and tottered towards the bed. It felt like everything about fixing this messy situation was an insurmountable hurdle. She had dug herself so deep with a single lie that she didn't know how to drag herself out of it.

One single repeated lie.

She stopped in front of her mirror before she reached the bed. She looked exhausted. Not as tired as Maryann had seemed, but more weary-eyed than when she'd left for Bath.

The upcoming assembly was like a weight around her neck.

All she had been able to think about since she'd returned was the crossroads she now found herself at. She was hovering at the edge of a precipice, and whether or not she fell was entirely dependent on how Gabriel reacted to her confession.

And she had to make that confession. She couldn't put it off any longer.

She winced at the mirror, that squeeze making her chest hurt again.

Dear God! she marveled. *Am I in love with him?*

Her reflection only stared back, wide-eyed and gaping mouthed.

Oh dear, she thought. *Oh dear, oh dear, oh dear.*

Chapter Thirteen

Gabriel chuckled as he fumbled with his cufflinks. He was like a green youth going to his first assembly ball.

He laughed louder, startling his valet who showed it with only the slightest stiffening of his spine.

"Sorry James," he said, but couldn't help his grin.

Hell, he hadn't felt this nervous when he *had* been a green youth.

"I think I can see to the rest myself." His voice still held the reverberations of humor as he watched the lines of laughter play across his reflection's face.

He was a very serious man when it came to business, and business had been the center of his life for as long as he could remember. The only times he ever laughed with such lightness was likely when his sisters were home.

But this wasn't that kind of joy—this was something altogether different.

His valet sniffed and gave the black superfine at Gabriel's shoulder one last brush before leaving. Gabriel smiled.

James took his position very seriously, but Gabriel barely employed his services. Except for these social sorts of occasions. He might kit himself in fashionable black, but he wasn't some London dandy who needed a servant to dress him for his every day. But now as he anxiously fingered the buttons on his waistcoat, he was glad to have had the assistance.

He chuckled again.

He wondered if he should have dismissed James as quickly as he had. He was a fumbling fool, too preoccupied with the images of Miss Price—*Evelyn*—that danced across his mind.

Only she wasn't dancing in his imaginings.

He grinned slyly, unable to feel ashamed of the indecent pictures his mind conjured up, though he knew he should— pictures of the ways he'd like to see her and the things he'd like to do.

Once we are married.

That thought startled another laugh from him.

For someone who had been so skittish at the thought of marriage, he had certainly become rather entrenched in the idea.

He fiddled with the silk knot at his throat. Miss Price had left Porthaven for a few short days, and he'd become a desperate, slavering wretch for her.

He smoothed his hands down his waistcoat.

Good God, he thought with a huff.

There was every chance he would give anything if it meant she would marry him. The realization should have been far more alarming than it was.

He gave the sleeve of his jacket a final tug and went for the door.

"Smith," he called for the aged butler as he tromped down the stairs. "Is the carriage ready?"

He already knew it would be. There was no chance Mr. Smith had allowed it to be otherwise.

"Yes, sir," came the quick reply.

"Good." Gabriel paused at the door, just inside the threshold. "I will be out rather late. Take the rest of the night off."

"Very good, sir."

Gabriel tarried a moment longer. It struck him sometimes how very close his situation was in practicality to the very men he so disliked. Men like Albon Evans and Sir John Gilbert, and the long list of cretins who'd made his life miserable in school and now held seats in the *Lords*.

"Tell the rest of the staff as well," he added more gently.

Mr. Smith gave a bow of approval.

As far as Gabriel was concerned, the only difference between himself and Mr. Smith was that he'd had the good fortune to be born to the obstinate, bull-headed upstart, Simon Stone.

He couldn't allow himself to forget where he came from,

and the working classes that were still his people.

He strode purposefully across the gravel drive and jumped up into the waiting carriage.

At least he didn't need to mingle with those elitist toffs in Porthaven. It was easier to recall his place in the world entrenched in the milieu of industry.

The day of the assembly ball was unseasonably cold for spring, and while the house on Linden Street had none of the airy openness of her home in Norfolk, it still managed to be just as drafty. By the time they'd left that evening, the chill had settled deep within Evelyn's bones.

She shivered now as she was handed down from the carriage, tugging her velvet cloak more tightly around her shoulders. She smiled wryly as she was struck with a sudden eagerness for the sweltering heat of the crowded ballroom.

"Come, let's hurry Augusta," Mrs. Harding said breathlessly. "We must make sure you have your pick of dancing partners."

The two shuffled in, leaving Evelyn outside with her aunt.

"I thought they would leap from the carriage," Aunt Dorothea chuckled, forcing Evelyn to hide a grin behind her hand.

"They are certainly excited."

"Ha!" Aunt Dorothea exclaimed. "It has been the only thing they've talked about in days."

"Yes," Evelyn replied with a smile. "I suppose so."

Aunt Dorothea watched her, her face growing serious as

they continued their slow pace into the hall.

"I know you aren't much for dancing," her aunt noted. "But it would be good if you honored the offers you've already received." She paused to hand off her mantle at the cloak room. "Especially Mr. Stone. For Augusta's sake. We do not wish to offend him."

Evelyn turned, removing her cloak most deliberately as she tried to school her features into something neutral. She was looking forward to dancing with Gabriel, but not for her cousin's sake.

"Of course," she said as she turned back to the room.

"I am serious, Evelyn." Her aunt stopped her with a hand against her arm. "You have had the freedom to do mostly as you wish, but this is an important opportunity for Augusta. She does not have the advantages you have," she said delicately. "We must do our best to foster this match."

Evelyn scanned her aunt's eyes, searching for any recognition there of the emotions Evelyn knew must be shining in her own. Did Aunt Dorothea know what she was asking—what she was asking she give up for her cousin's sake? Evelyn didn't know, and she couldn't bring herself to enlighten her.

"I understand," she murmured, then turned deliberately into the ballroom, crossing the threshold into that whirling, riotous storm of music and colors and dancing.

It looked so much like the life she had left behind in London that she paused just inside the large arched doorway. Her stomach did a little flip.

The lights and laughter threatened to make her head spin, and she forced a string of deep breaths as she tried to steady herself. She hadn't expected her reaction to be so visceral.

"Excuse me," she heard from behind her.

She was blocking up the entrance, standing square in the middle of the one path to the dancing. She swallowed and ordered her feet to carry her the rest of the way into the room.

Like she was trapped in one of the ballrooms at home, she found herself sidling along the back wall, keeping herself as distant from the crush of people as she could. Her eyes scanned the space, and she fought to keep her breath measured, to stave off the dizziness creeping in at the corners of her eyes. She tried to focus on the differences in the room, instead of losing herself in the similarities. The many similarities.

I can do this, she told herself. She blew out a breath. *I can do this.*

"Mamma," she heard Augusta gasp.

Evelyn turned to find her cousins in the crowd. They stood just ahead of her, to the right, and Augusta was looking somewhere over her mother's shoulder.

"There he is."

Evelyn's eyes found him at the same moment Augusta said the words, and she sucked in a breath at the sight of him.

Goodness.

She thought she might forget how to breath.

If Gabriel Stone looked appealing dressed in his daytime black, he was absolutely devastating in full dress. The superfine of his black tailcoat was so perfectly tailored, it looked like a second skin. She could practically see the flex of muscle beneath the fabric, even from across the room. The crowd shifted ahead of her, and she felt her mouth go dry.

The rest of his clothes were just as fitted.

She watched him unabashedly, with greedy eyes—from his powerful form to that signature scowl.

How could he look so severe and still be so wickedly attractive? It was an absolute wonder.

Evelyn stared as he stilled, his head cocked as if he had heard some small noise. Or had felt her eyes upon him.

He moved slowly but with such steady grace. The men around him were like preening peacocks, but Gabriel, she thought in a moment of whimsy, was more like a predator.

Like a lion.

His gaze shifted, and Evelyn knew the moment he spotted her. It threatened to set her whole body on fire.

Gabriel's eyes widened when they fell on her, then traced from head to toe, possessively roaming the length of her. His mouth twitched, the barest hint of a smile, but it was enough to send that simmering heat scorching through her.

She instinctively took a step towards him, rocking forward on her slippered toes, but caught herself as she remembered where she was. It felt like nearly a hundred people had crammed into the ballroom and she wanted to run to him as if none of them existed, but she knew she couldn't.

It would be unseemly.

Gabriel angled his head to speak to someone just out of Evelyn's view, but his eyes never left her, keeping her entranced until he stalked forward. She felt herself quietly gasp as Gabriel ignored all social etiquette and moved to stride boldly across the floor, heedless of anyone who might be in his way.

He approached her like a missile, making a straight line for her, and giving no care to who might be watching his obvious display.

If anyone noticed, they said nothing, made no comment—they simply fell aside like rushes beneath his feet, as if they could feel the storm of him approaching. Evelyn shivered. That intensity sent tingles all the way down to her toes.

"Miss Price," he said when he stood before her.

She watched his chest expand with his next inhale—he looked as breathless as she felt.

"Mr. Stone."

"How was your trip?" he asked.

She flushed at the way his deep baritone rumbled through her.

"Good," she breathed. He was so tall she had to arch her neck just to look at him. "But I'm happy to be back."

Something bordering on delight danced in his eyes, like he knew the cause for her happiness was him, standing before her now.

"When did you return?"

"A few days ago."

She had gone into town twice since then, each time with the foolish hope that she would run into Gabriel the way she had so many times before. He tilted his head, too astute to miss her hesitation.

"What is it?" he asked. "Tell me."

She felt a deeper blush steal across her face. "I had hoped to see you in town one of those days."

She dropped her eyes to her feet, or tried to—he was standing so close, that instead she found herself staring at the buttons on his waistcoat. She felt his fingers brush across her gloved arm, near the crook of her elbow. She peeked up at him from beneath her lashes.

"Did I disappoint you?" he crooned. "I am sorry. I'm afraid I've been quite preoccupied with business matters." He let out a breath that sounded half like a rueful chuckle. "And, if I am being blisteringly honest, I have been doing my best to avoid your cousins."

"My cousins? Why?"

His mouth tipped into a half-sided grin. "I've found it has been easier to escape their machinations if I am nowhere near their persons to begin with."

Evelyn attempted to swallow her laugh, pressing her fingers to her lips to hide her smile.

"Has it really been that bad?" she asked.

His eyes glimmered playfully, even as his features maintained their usual stoicism. The sound of the musicians readying their strings reverberated through the room and Gabriel took hold of her elbow.

"Yes, it has really been that bad. Now come." He drew her towards the other dancers at the middle of the room. "I've yet to dance."

"Oh," she breathed. "I do not think I should be your first

dance."

"Nonsense," he replied. "And besides, I have it on good authority that the next is a waltz."

"A waltz?" she sputtered.

She knew she sounded scandalized, but she hadn't expected to dance with Gabriel just yet, let alone to something as intimate as a waltz.

"You are sure?"

He smirked down at her. "Yes, I am sure. I was the one to request it."

She stared at him wide-eyed. That was what he had been speaking to the other man about. He had sent a request for the next dance. The nervous heat in her face spread to her fingertips as he led her to the center.

"But everyone will see us," she muttered, taking hold of her lip between her teeth as she thought of all the ways this could backfire against her.

His eyes searched hers, his face etched with seriousness once more. "Do you want to dance with me?"

Yes, she wanted to say, to plead.

But she knew her family would be watching her. She could only imagine the sight they made together standing together like this, ensconced in their own little world. What would her cousins think if she waltzed with him? What would Aunt Dorothea think?

I want this.

She wanted more than this one dance. She wanted Gabriel with a fierceness she had never felt for anything before.

"Yes," she vowed, that one word holding more meaning than he could possibly know.

He placed her hand on his shoulder and held the other, more firmly than the delicate brush of fingertips she had seen at Almack's. His other hand found her upper back, and certainly the way his fingers brushed the exposed skin above the silk was unlike anything she'd observed in London. She swallowed the thickness in her throat.

"Have you danced a waltz before?" he asked.

"Of—of course not!" she stuttered.

His smile stretched to his eyes. "It really isn't all that scandalous," he assured her.

"I've seen a waltz, and it caused plenty of a stir in London," she protested. She flushed under his laughing gaze, and when his fingers flexed against her back, her breath hitched. "And this seems far more intimate than that."

"Yes," he agreed, unashamedly, "You'll find we are much less stuffy here than they are in London. I blame all those preening bluebloods, with their stiff propriety."

She forced a laugh. "You really have such a dislike for them?" she asked.

"I am plagued with strong convictions," he mused wryly.

His mouth tilted in an arrogant grin, but Evelyn could see the shuttering defenses in his eyes.

"I've met enough lords to last me a lifetime."

She swallowed heavily, carefully choosing her words.

"Then if you had the chance to pursue a true lady—?" She let the rest hang and dropped her eyes to his cravat.

She couldn't even say what precisely she wanted to know. *Would you be happy? Interested? Angry?*

He touched a finger to her chin, forcing her gaze back up to meet his. "There isn't a lady in all of London who could tempt me," he promised.

What about me? she wanted to ask. *Would you be tempted if the lady was me?*

Evelyn flushed.

Her face must be scarlet by now. Gabriel smiled as he slipped his hand back into hers and drew her into another turn about the room. It was easier to lean shamelessly into his hold and let him guide her through the dance than to think about his feelings on her class.

Let him think my discomfort is from his proximity.

It wasn't so far from the truth—not when each pass of the room seemed to bring her closer into his hold. By the time the musicians had made it halfway through the piece, she swore she could feel Gabriel's heart beating in his chest, just as clear as her own pulse thrumming beneath her skin. It made her feel lightheaded and giddy while the whirling steps of the dance spun her into an ever-dizzying fervor. She inhaled deeply at the exhilaration as they flew about the room.

"I hope I have not made you too uncomfortable," he murmured near her ear, his breath making the loose tendrils of her hair tickle her neck.

"No," she replied. "This is wonderful."

Her voice was a breathy whisper and her fingers gripped at his shoulder when his hand slipped along her back.

"Good."

The music swelled, swirling faster, like some living thing that carried them across the parquet floor. Evelyn had never been one for dancing, but suddenly she could understand the appeal.

She laughed with the vivacity of it—the surging music, the flickering lights, the pinks and blues and golds of swishing skirts. She looked up at Gabriel, smiling wide as he led her around another turn. And the open affection glimmering in his eyes made her feel absolutely breathless.

Gabriel didn't remember ever enjoying a dance as much as this one. But then, it had been a long time since he'd attended one of these things out of anything but a sense of obligation.

He didn't tell Evelyn that his last waltz had been with Mrs. Brooks, and the old matron had spent the entirety of their rather staid dance extolling the virtues of her unmarried daughter.

Gabriel had been bored to tears.

He wanted to laugh with the feeling surging within his breast now. No, he hadn't ever enjoyed a dance like this.

Gabriel looked down at Evelyn and the guileless delight on her face.

Though of course, he'd never held as appealing a partner in his arms before either.

He'd certainly never felt the irresistible urge to drag *Mrs. Brooks* deeper into his embrace.

He stifled the chuckle that threatened to rumble up from his chest. What a picture that made.

Evelyn though—

He might very well sell his soul just for the chance to haul her against him, and feel her gentle heat warm him. He wanted to groan at his own fancifulness.

God, I'll be spouting bloody poetry next.

They spun again and he took advantage of the movement to trace his fingers lightly against her back. His gloves were so thin he could almost imagine her skin was bare against his own. She fit so perfectly within his arms it made him feel reckless.

It's as if she belongs here.

He wished they were alone so that he could wrap himself up with her and see just how well they truly did fit. It was a delicious thought, but one she would likely be shocked by.

Still, he felt his fingers tense against her skin, as if desperate to make good on the impetuous thought. He gentled his hold and put an inch of distance between them. It was a grudging loss, but as it was, he was clasping her far too closely to be proper or decent.

I must be a fool—to have thought myself capable of dancing a waltz with her without losing myself like this.

It would have been wiser to wait for a country dance, or *anything* less controversial. But he had needed to feel her against him. His passions knew no logic or reason.

And she will pay for it.

He stiffened, the hand at her shoulder splaying instinctively as if to shield her from what was sure to come.

There would be talk after this dance—it was all but inevitable. Porthaven could be a gossipy place, as bad as any London ballroom.

Let them talk, he huffed. *It will hardly matter once we've married.*

He sucked in a breath and held it, still startled by this new preoccupation he had with marriage. It was an institution he hadn't considered for years.

Ten years—a decade.

Like the decade that fell between himself and the girl he now held so securely in his grasp. She was so very young—only a few years older than her cousin, and Miss Harding at least was in many ways still a girl. It felt like it had been a lifetime since he had been that young.

Since I was too young to know what I wanted, he rued.

Though Evelyn seemed to know her own mind. He could see that well enough. But marriage was a lifelong commitment, and one he couldn't take lightly.

Not after the last time.

Confusion stole across Evelyn's upturned face, and he forced the crease along his brow to settle until he was able to smile down at her again. These were worries for another day. He needn't be laying this pressure at her feet now, when they ought to be enjoying the intoxicating freedom of their waltz.

"Is everything alright?" she asked.

The music was winding to a close. The dance would end, and Gabriel would lose his only excuse to touch her. And he had wasted these last moments wrapped up in senseless insecurities.

Her age, her readiness for marriage—they are not senseless, his inner voice insisted.

He caught a glimpse of Teddy in the milling crowd.

Jealousy, money, fucking titles—

He caught himself before he tipped into *that* particular mental spiral.

"Everything is perfect," he assured her.

But the weight of uncertainty pressed into his gut.

Chapter Fourteen

Evelyn frowned as the music faded and the musicians prepared for the next dance. Gabriel's smile looked tight, the humor no longer reaching his eyes. She didn't know what had happened to cause the shift, but she desperately wished to see that hypnotizing gleam in his eyes again.

"Thank you for the dance," he said as he bent politely over her hand.

She wanted to ask him again if something was amiss, if something had changed during the course of their waltz. But the sudden distance between them stopped her.

Perhaps it was only her own discomfort, as the room closed back around them with a deafening crash of voices. Still, there was the plunge of disappointment when Gabriel stepped away with no more than a nod.

The glittering lights lost some of their magic then, flickering discordantly in a way that threatened to make her head pulse once more. It was like the calm wonder of the ballroom had disappeared the moment Gabriel's hands left hers.

Or perhaps when his eyes had turned distant. Either way, she could feel the pressure of the room again, feel the hot air and loud voices trying to drag her back, all the way to that ballroom in London.

It was too much—too much noise, too much movement. To her troubled mind, tender as a raw wound, it was all laughter and whispers and pointed stares.

It was a cacophony of sensation that left her isolated and alone in the middle of the room. She cast about her for something solid to anchor her in the here and now, to remind her she was far from London. But Gabriel had already disappeared back into the vibrating throng of people.

Did you really think I would choose you...

Her breath shook at Nigel's cruel words, and she turned again, but all she saw were those laughing faces that had haunted her for months.

...when I could have my pick of the season's hopefuls?

The swish of skirts had turned into murmurs and hushed giggles in her mind. She could hear the taunts and the snickering, as distinct as if they were here in the room with her now.

A flash of gold hair taunted her through the crowd, and

she was suddenly back in a different ballroom, in a different city.

Nigel is in London, she reminded herself.

There were plenty of young gentlemen with patrician features, and surely twice as many with blond hair. But her body didn't care what her mind insisted, and overwhelmed, blackness began to creep into her vision, her heart thundering as it threatened to jump into her throat.

She had thought she'd moved on from this. She had thought she'd left these feelings behind her in London.

"I have never seen such an indecent display."

Evelyn spun at the venomous words, hissed with the same disdain that contorted Cousin Arabella's face. She had expected some awkwardness with her family after that particular dance, but not the open condemnation she saw in her cousin's eyes.

"There were at least ten other couples dancing," she argued weakly.

She still felt panic gripping her in its claws, trying desperately to toss her in with the wolves in London.

Did you think I would choose you?

She shivered.

Do you think she is delusional or just desperate? The whispered viciousness.

Evelyn didn't know what made Nigel's rejections such welcome chatter for the gossips, except perhaps the boredom of an uneventful season. Her mother would say it was jealousy—that she was well-positioned, well-dowered, and pretty—but she thought it more likely that her staunch aversion to society for so many seasons made her an easier target than most.

Her gaze cleared again as she faded from the past back to the present and she tried to recall what was happening.

There were at least ten other couples dancing, she had said.

She didn't need to see the flash of anger in her Mrs. Harding's eyes to know that was hardly the point. This had nothing to do with Evelyn's reputation—it was about Gabriel, and only Gabriel.

She tried to find words that would ease the flicker of hostility she saw, but nothing seemed sufficient. Her lips moved wordlessly as she grew more flustered.

Mrs. Harding scoffed, her lips tilting in a sneer as she stared down at Evelyn from the inch of height between them. She infused such scorn into her stare that Evelyn felt as if she were barely three inches tall.

"It seems you find yourself embroiled in scandal no matter where you go," Mrs. Harding pressed.

"Excuse me?" Her voice was barely a whisper, and she blanched, feeling herself go white.

Her face felt numb. Just moments ago, she had been soaring through the most exhilarating dance of her life, and now she felt sick to her stomach over it. She didn't want to feel ashamed for dancing with Gabriel, and she couldn't stomach reliving the torture of London.

Not again.

It had been awful—being dragged from ballroom to ballroom, whilst every set of eyes sparkled with laughter at her expense. More than one lady had *whispere*d ugly rumors about her, just within earshot.

You don't suppose she—always the dramatic hitch, as if the accusation was too horrible to bear, but whispered loudly enough to ensure Evelyn heard every word. *Do you think she sullied herself, to trap him?*

She suppressed a shudder, her horror going bone deep. It was impossible for those whispers to have followed her to Porthaven.

Impossible.

It had to be. The only reason she had traveled to this damned city in the first place was to get away from those nasty vultures and their venomous rumors.

She saw the unkind glint in her cousin's eyes and dread sunk heavily into her gut. Evelyn tensed, bracing herself, as if she knew what she would say, even before Mrs. Harding opened her mouth. Still, the words fell hard, like a slap.

"You couldn't leave the scandal behind in London, could you?" she sneered. "You needed to drag that same wickedness to our doorstep."

"I—I don't understand," she sputtered.

"There are few reasons an *earl's daughter* flees London at the height of the season for an unfashionable city like this."

"Aunt Dorothea invited me," she murmured, her voice as small and weak as she felt.

"An earl's daughter?" Augusta's high-pitched outrage came from behind her.

Evelyn couldn't even turn to look at her, to see the betrayal that was certainly painted across her face, even as she stepped closer, speaking nearly into her ear.

"You are an *earl's daughter*? And you hid this from us?"

She couldn't look away from Mrs. Harding though. The cruelness in the older woman's eyes was bottomless and Evelyn had the fear that if she blinked, it would be like turning her back on a tiger.

There would be nothing left of her when the dust cleared.

"Did you know about this, mother?" Augusta snapped, but Mrs. Harding ignored her, advancing on Evelyn in a way that made her feel small and vulnerable.

She wanted to put her hands up and stop the words from coming, as if she could physically halt the vitriol and make all of this go away.

"Oh yes. I'm sure your sudden flight had nothing to do with that young lord's engagement."

"How did you know about that?"

"Word travels," she replied smugly. "Even so far from your *ton*." She took another deliberate step forward, and eyed Evelyn head to toe, dismissively. "Look at you. You were never going to be enough to steal away that lord in London."

Evelyn shook her head. "I didn't want to steal anyone," she insisted.

Nigel had lied to her—made a fool of her. How had things become so twisted, so mixed up.

So viciously misconstrued?

Mrs. Harding laughed. "I don't care what game you are playing at—it isn't going to work." She sneered. "Why on earth would you suddenly be enough now?"

Breathe, she told herself. *Breathe and don't cry. You didn't cry in London—don't cry now.*

"Arabella, that is enough." Aunt Dorothea's voice cut through like sharpened steel.

Evelyn sucked in a breath, amazed that she could breathe at all.

Mrs. Harding cast Evelyn another haughty look before grabbing Augusta by the elbow and spinning them both away to stalk across the room. Evelyn was glad to see them go.

She exhaled a pained sob as she turned to her aunt, grateful that someone had come to her defense. But there was no warmth in her aunt's eyes, only cold reproach, and Evelyn recoiled as if slapped.

"It was just a dance," she murmured.

"You knew the Hardings were looking to forge an alliance with Mr. Stone. You knew how important it was to them."

"But—" She wasn't given the chance to speak.

"You'll listen now, Evelyn." She looked up to the ceiling as if seeking some divine guidance. "Perhaps this is my fault— I should have been more direct with you before, but I thought I had said enough. I thought you would see reason. This isn't a game or an idle flirtation to Augusta. This is her future."

"Yes, but—"

"No, Evelyn. You may have enjoyed the attention, but is that enough to ruin all of their hard work? Arabella has been putting *everything* into securing this match. And then you put on that obscene display on the dancefloor."

"Obscene," she repeated, bewildered.

Aunt Dorothea's face hardened. "Perhaps I could excuse it if you were engaged to the man, but the way you clung to him, with everyone watching—" she shook her head in disappointment.

Evelyn felt herself sag, as if everything holding her up inside seeped out at those words.

"Is that what you think?" Her voice sounded small, like an echo from far, far away.

She stumbled backwards. Her cousin thought she was a grasping flirt, with a penchant for taking what wasn't hers. And Aunt Dorothea didn't see her as anything better.

Mrs. Harding's words had hurt, but she could excuse her hateful speech. She hardly knew Evelyn. But Aunt Dorothea should know better.

How can she think I would be so heartless—so careless with their lives?

She turned, unable to face the judgement in her aunt's eyes a second longer.

She fled.

She needed space, quiet, fresh air. The room had suddenly gone from over-warm to stifling, and the walls felt like they might close in around her.

She wove through the crush of people, her desperate exit feeling far too similar to her flight from Lady Whitaker's ballroom months ago. Back then, she had turned to see Nigel laughing with his vicious friends.

They thought they were so funny.

She was nearly at the doors that led out to the front hall—she could see the paneled walls and the dark night just beyond. But she turned for a similar, final glance at the ballroom, as if unable to stop herself from repeating the old, foolish impulse.

Her feet shuffled to a stop on the threshold at the sight of Gabriel, tall and imposing on the other side of the ballroom.

He had that serious look that so often graced his features and made him look stern but wickedly tempting. He seemed deep in conversation with Lord Hilgrave, who smiled with just as much enthusiasm as Gabriel scowled.

But it wasn't the contrast between the two that made her pause. It was the fact that she again had a needling sense of recognition when she looked at Lord Hilgrave. She had noticed it the first time Gabriel had introduced them, but she'd been unable to place either his face or his name.

Now she saw him through the lines of dancers, and it was like she caught a glimpse of him in another ballroom, behind swirling skirts and coat tails.

He hadn't been smiling then. He'd been frowning—following Evelyn with his eyes and looking on with pity as she'd rushed from the ballroom.

Oh God. The breath squeezed from her chest. *No, it can't be.*

But the longer she stared at him, the more clear the picture became in her mind. And the more firmly she found him rooted in the memory of Lady Whitaker's ball.

He had been there, for her horrible embarrassment. And if he had seen her then in London, it was only a matter of time before he recognized her here.

Has he already recognized me?

And then the thought that froze the blood in her veins.

Will he tell Gabriel who I am?

This fragile thing between them—already vulnerable from society and her secrets and her own family—would be over before it started.

She'd been so afraid of how he would react when she finally told him the truth, but how would he ever forgive her if he learned her secret from someone else? Would he even listen to her explanations then?

She rushed for the door, hoping to make an escape before she was spotted. Perhaps if Lord Hilgrave didn't see her again, he would forget her face. Then he would have nothing to tell Gabriel, no reason to even bring her up.

He saw you dancing with Gabriel, she reminded herself.

Obscenely, as per her aunt. How could he not have noticed her—recognized her?

She emerged into the night with a gasp. The late breeze was bracing, and she breathed the frigid air in big gulps.

Breathe. Breathe.

She pressed a hand to her chest. Her heart was racing, as if ready to burst from behind her ribs. She couldn't seem to make it slow, even as she willed it with every ounce of her being. Despair prickled at the corners of her eyes, but she couldn't cry—she vowed she wouldn't. She blinked, trying to dash them away, but her vision swam with tears.

"Evelyn!" Gabriel's voice was pleading, and she turned as

if tied to him, powerless to do anything else. "Christ," he cursed. "I didn't want to get you into trouble—tell me this isn't my fault."

He led her by the elbow to a darkened walkway alongside the assembly rooms, where no one could see as he gathered her into his arms. She let herself fall against him, her head to his chest as his steadying arms wrapped around her. She breathed in the scent of him and gripped her fingers tight in his coat.

She peered up at him, though she didn't loosen her hold. His brow was creased with the depth of his frown, and his mouth was set in a rigidly firm line. She blinked as he reached up a hand and brushed at her lashes, where tears still clung.

"It wasn't exactly the dance," she murmured. She was embarrassed to say more, especially with her aunt's accusations fresh in her ears. "You know the hopes they had for Augusta."

He sighed deeply, reaching to brush a hand through his hair, banishing any order there might have been to the messy black strands in his agitation. She let him go as he stepped back from her, leaning his weight against the brick side of the building.

"I had hoped my absence this week would put an end to that," he grunted.

"It seems not."

She clenched her fingers before her, and her shoulders hunched as she became more aware of the coldness in the air.

"I'm sorry Evelyn. I didn't mean to make things difficult for you."

She gave a shake of her head. It wasn't his fault. That fell entirely upon her shoulders. The secrets she'd been keeping—from him and from her family—had caused all of this mess. Their disapproval was aimed squarely at her, and it wasn't just the dance. In all honesty, it was hardly the dance at all.

And remorse wracked her for it, because when it came down to it, Mrs. Harding's accusations were exactly true, weren't they?

She was trying to take Gabriel for her own. It was just the specifics that her cousin had wrong.

"Evelyn, please. Tell me you are alright," he pleaded as he came forward, grasping her by the arms and staring searchingly into her face.

She nodded, but it hardly felt like *anything* was right. She could not tell him the truth now, when she felt suffocated by fear and guilt. And how could she explain the reason her family was angry with her without confessing everything to him?

She had wanted to tell him the truth, had planned to. But now, she couldn't bring herself to say a word.

"Gabriel?" she heard and turned to see Baron Hilgrave standing in front of the assembly hall.

Gabriel had been with him when she had run from the ballroom. He must have seen Gabriel follow her out, and now was looking for his friend, who had abruptly disappeared. She couldn't face Lord Hilgrave now too.

She shivered and Gabriel ran his hands against her arms to warm her. She didn't correct him to say that the trembling was more from panic than from the cold.

"Gabriel?" Lord Hilgrave asked again and stepped in their

direction.

His eyes scanned a distance off to the right and Evelyn did not think he saw them where they stood, huddled in the dark alleyway, but she feared him coming closer. She turned her face against Gabriel's chest, wishing there was a way to disappear into thin air and leave this entire horrid night behind.

"Take me somewhere we can be alone," she blurted, before she had a chance to think better of it.

She could feel the breath freeze in his chest, his body going unnaturally still. She could feel too her face go hot, even in the blistering cold.

"Please," she begged, unable to back down from the suggestion now that she'd made it.

"Evelyn," he whispered, and she could hear the uncertainty in his voice, though she avoided looking back into his face to confirm it.

Shame flooded her. It wasn't that she didn't want Gabriel—*God, how I want him*—but the overture felt too similar to the hateful insinuations she'd heard whispered in the London ballrooms.

Perhaps she should *have sullied herself.* A tittering giggle. *How else is somebody like her going to land a husband?*

Nigel likely wouldn't have offered for her anyway. He'd already been chasing Miss Burville long before he had begun wooing Evelyn in secret, though she hadn't known it at the time. *Gentlemanly honor* was not a much-used phrase in Lord Nigel's lexicon.

Gabriel on the other hand was a gentleman. If anyone

would feel beholden to honor, it would be him.

But it was a terribly grasping, dishonest scheme to play on him. It might give her the escape she needed from this disastrous night and prove a fool-proof means to secure Gabriel's hand—lies be damned—but at what cost?

If there was anything to feel ashamed for, it was the way she clung to the despicable idea. He would hate knowing he'd been lied to, might hate her if he found out the truth only after she had forced his hand.

I've already been dishonest.

Her face scorched impossibly hotter in the cool night air. She swallowed against the niggling uncertainty.

"Someplace quiet," she pressed. "Away from all of these people."

He angled himself for a better look at her face, but she kept it turned down against the wall of his chest. She traced the black-on-black pattern of his waistcoat with her eyes to distract herself from what she was asking.

"I don't know if that is wise."

His voice was low when he spoke, but she felt just how tenuous his grasp was on his control. It wouldn't take much to tip his hand into her favor.

She found strength in that indecision of his and forced herself to look up. A battle raged in his eyes, one fought for her honor in the face of such feverish desire she nearly gasped at the intensity radiating in his gaze.

That battle sent all doubts scattering from her mind like marbles. She no longer cared if Lord Hilgrave was looking for them, or if she'd offended her family by dancing with Gabriel—or what extremes she might be willing to go to, just to keep him as her own.

In that moment, all she knew was that she wanted him. And she wanted him just as fiercely as he wanted her.

"Please, Gabriel."

This time when she spoke his name, his eyes closed, and he exhaled a shaky breath. His hands tracked down her arms until they circled her wrists, and she held her breath as she waited for his decision—either to push her away, or to take her up on her suggestive offer.

"I can't seem to keep my hands off you when we're alone," he admitted.

It was a final resistance, but even as he said the words, Evelyn knew she had won.

"I know."

Chapter Fifteen

Gabriel cursed himself for being a fool.

He'd put on a good front, pretending he had any control over his reaction to her, when he had known the moment those seven precious words had left her lips that he was a goner.

Take me somewhere we can be alone.

Dear God, it was all he wanted—since the moment he'd followed her outside, since the moment they'd danced.

Since the moment he'd felt the sweet weight of her against his chest, that first time they'd met.

Take me somewhere we can be alone.

He didn't want to assume she meant the same thing by it that he wanted her to mean, but he'd tried to warn her away and she'd persisted. If she didn't want this, she would have said so. And like the masochist he was, he would continue to give her chances to deny him, to back herself out of her offer if she needed it. He would do nothing she didn't want.

Though Christ, if she wanted—

He descended upon her as if all control had been wrested from him, his mouth claiming hers with a wildness he could barely contain. She fell against him with a sigh that only spurred him on, urging him to wrap his arms around her and press her close. He ran his hand down her back until they were as close as could be, her lush body in unmistakable contact with his own. He felt shock skitter through her when she realized just how hard he was for her.

"We do not have to do this," he murmured against her hair, but she shook her head.

"Please," she said, for what might have been the hundredth time. "I need you."

Any meager restraint he'd had before incinerated at her proclamation.

"Come. This way," he urged, hand tight against her waist as he led her down the alleyway and across to another set of buildings.

He fumbled for the key in his waistcoat pocket, suddenly immeasurably glad he'd had the foresight to bring it. Not that he had envisioned anything of this nature occurring tonight— he never could have dreamed it. But he did have the unhealthy habit of sleeping in his office to start on work that much earlier in the morning. Tonight, that quirk of his had paid off.

They were only a scant few steps from the assembly hall,

and he ushered her inside once the door was open, as quickly as he could. He could hear the music trickling down the street from the ongoing ball, the murmur of voices seeping through the wall. It did not matter that he would surely marry her after this—if they were seen together here, her reputation would be in irreparable tatters.

"My offices," he explained, as they reached the top of the staircase, and he turned her towards the first set of doors.

He wished he had the time to take her back to his house, to his bed. It was unconscionable that her first time should be on the sofa in his office, but she couldn't very well disappear for an entire night, and well into the morning.

That would not go unnoticed.

"We can just talk, if you prefer," he offered once more. "Though I would happily kiss you again."

"I will not regret this," she said, with such certainty he thought his heart might stop beating. "Will you?" she asked.

He shook his head in a slow arc, back and forth. He could never regret this.

"Only if I hurt you."

"You will not hurt me."

He leaned down slowly, intent on her mouth, and Evelyn sighed as his lips found hers and he pressed her to his chest once more. He slanted over her, wanting to taste her deeply, to draw the essence of her into him so that he could hold onto it forever.

He let his tongue glide across her bottom lip, coaxing her to open for him, and when she did, he moaned with relief as he slid inside of that wet heat. He ran his hands across her back, up to her exposed shoulders and down to cup her rounded bottom.

Perfection, he groaned.

The only thing that could make the moment better would be removing the layers of clothing between them. He wrested the thin, white gloves from his hands. That was one layer he could take care of readily, and he dashed them to the floor.

Without the leather enrobing his fingers, he could feel her contours beneath her silk gown. Each little notch in her spine, along her back, the gentle swell of her hips in his hands.

He pressed his tongue again against her own as he trailed his hands up, up, in desperate anticipation, until he felt smooth skin against his work-roughened hand.

He might not need to subject himself to manual labor, but he knew his hands were not those of a leisure-seeking gentleman. He was too hands-on an employer for that. He wondered what his fingers felt like to her, against her soft, unblemished skin.

"You're perfect," he crooned. "Smooth and delicate, like porcelain."

"But I will not break," she breathed against his lips.

He cupped her face in his hand, watching the way his fingers nearly enveloped the elegant heart shape. She *looked* breakable. He took a step back from her, turning to light the scattered candles in the room as an excuse to give her space. He needed to be careful with her, gentle. He was too afraid he would hurt her without meaning to—or scare her away.

When he looked back at her, in the soft glow of

candlelight, she was standing near the windows, her fingers playing nervously with the low neck of her gown. And anxious as she was, she was still the most seductive woman he had ever seen—the way her eyes flashed to him, hiding nothing of what she felt, not even the fierce desire brewing within.

"It's warm in here, isn't it?" she asked, as he stepped nearer.

He moved around her, to one of the windows that ran behind his desk and unlatched it, pushing the pane open until crisp air swept inside. He peered down through the glass, between the bars of the iron trellis topping the decorative crenellation outside.

This side of the building faced the assembly hall, and he could see the street below, ensconced in the gleam of streetlamps. People milled about now, taking their nips of fresh air after the ceaseless dancing. He adjusted his neckcloth, feeling it squeezing at his throat as he recalled what Evelyn was risking being here with him, after they'd been seen dancing so closely by all those people.

It was less dancing and more an impassioned embrace, he corrected. *A very public, impassioned embrace.*

He was glad at least that no one could see them now. At the steep angle, he knew the view into this room was completely obstructed. The laughing figures below would be unable to see beyond the black metal bars standing sentinel outside the window.

He flexed his fingers and forced out a breath before turning back to her. He normally considered himself the picture of control, but he was wound much too tightly this evening.

"Is that better?" he asked, and she nodded.

He motioned to the plush green sofa across from the fireplace, which he was glad he had lit, now that the far window was spitting frigid air into the room. His eyes landed on the table in the corner.

What he needed was a drink, and by the look of Evelyn's fidgeting hands, she could use one too. He went and poured two glasses from the crystal decanter.

"I'm sorry, I don't have anything else—just the port," he confessed and shrugged as he returned with the glasses. At least he didn't still have the whiskey out. "It is my trade," he said in explanation as he handed Evelyn hers.

She smiled as she took it from him, her fingers brushing his and sending electricity racing inexplicably straight to his cock. He cleared his throat and shifted, before settling onto the cushion beside her. He fumbled for conversation.

The sudden nerves made him feel ridiculous. He could dance wickedly with her, and press himself on her with lips and tongue, but he could not sit here in intimate silence, it seemed, without succumbing to bashfulness.

"I've never had port before," Evelyn mused, and he watched her swirl her glass. "It's good."

He smiled behind his wineglass. "I should hope so. I've built my entire business around the stuff."

Gabriel drank deep from his wine. The lilt of her laughter made his chest ache with the need to hear that sound again.

It was as intoxicating as the port.

Evelyn tipped her glass back, draining its contents until that last drops of red were gone. It was her third glass—*or maybe the fourth*—and the heat coming off the hearth only heightened the muzzy feeling in her head.

Gabriel hadn't wanted to pour her this last one, but she had insisted. She was nervous. Not to be with him, or tie herself to him, but of the fallout that would surely come after, when he finally learned the truth.

He watched her now with worried eyes and she felt color steal across her cheeks. She wanted him, but she was at a loss as to how to show him, how to prove it to him. Four glasses of port and she'd only lost her nerve, instead of gaining courage.

Most days, especially sharing a house with her cousin Augusta, she felt world-wearied—tired of the social pressures she had left at home, and too old for the naïve hopes and dreams of her cousin's youth. But now?

What she wouldn't give to be someone more elegant, more refined, and sophisticated.

"And now it is warm again," she said, putting her glass down and fluttering her fingers against her throat.

She felt foolish and far too innocent.

She rose too suddenly, the room tilting on its side for a moment, but pressed through it, too fearful that Gabriel would notice and do the gentlemanly thing. She didn't want the night to end with him bringing her back untouched to her aunt's care. She didn't want to leave this room the same person she'd entered.

She wanted to be Gabriel's—truly and completely.

Evelyn moved to the open window, breathing in the soberingly cold air. It felt like icy snowflakes on her skin, and she tilted her face to the chill, smiling against the breeze.

"Let me take you back downstairs." Gabriel's low, rumbling voice was suddenly behind her and, feeling bold—and perhaps a little inebriated—she let herself lean back against the solid wall of his chest.

She could feel his sharp inhalation all down her back and it made her shiver with some unnamed anticipation. His hands went to her shoulders, and the breath that wheezed from his chest made her think he'd grabbed for her on instinct alone.

In for a penny, she mused and let a slow smile creep over her face.

She tipped her head back to his shoulder, peering up at him from beneath heavy-lidded eyes. The cold was bracing, but she still felt fuzzy from the wine and his nearness. And the startling feel of his male hardness sent a dizzying heat spiraling through her. She felt tingly and *wet* in places she'd never thought too much about.

Not until Gabriel, she corrected, blushing at the thought.

"Kiss me?" she breathed.

The wretched relief she saw on his face had her pushing up on her toes to bridge the distance between them.

He was still too tall, and she sighed mournfully. But he bent, with an enraptured half-smile, the rest of the way.

She was going to be his undoing.

Evelyn pressed back against him, and he groaned against her lips.

She might very well be the death of me.

He had tried to fight his every baser instinct to prevent this from happening. Tried and failed—repeatedly. She deserved more than to be claimed in his damned office.

But the wine had made her bold and when he felt her tongue slide against his own, he was lost. He was surely going to hell for corrupting such breathtaking innocence, but he could no longer find it in himself to care—not enough to stop.

We will be married after this. No damage will be done, he selfishly reasoned.

He leaned down and placed a kiss to the pulse at her throat.

"Do you know how long I've wanted this?"

Evelyn's breath stuttered in response, and he smiled against her neck, relishing the feel of her heartbeat racing beneath the skin. He dragged his hands up and over her shoulders, feeling the heat of her skin against his palms. She was still facing the window and he could see the faint reflection of her in the glass. He wanted to see more, wanted to see all of her.

Exposed. Bare.

Desperate and needy—as desperate and needy as he felt.

"I want to see you," he told her. "I'm going to remove this."

He said it like unchangeable fact, but he kept his hands still at her shoulders, watching her eyes in the window's reflection until she nodded.

Thank God.

His hands went to the tapes closing her gown at the back, loosening the ties until he could leave the silk to pool at her feet. In just a gossamer shift and stays, she stood in the shimmering blue pool of fabric—*Venus, rising from the sea.*

And like any good mortal, he was powerless to resist her.

"You are beautiful," he said reverently.

She shivered at his words, and her lips parted as he started on the laces holding her stays in place. When he peeled the straps over her shoulders, her eyes met his in the glass. She looked dazed. And lustful.

"I feel hot all over," she confessed, no doubt emboldened by the earlier wine.

He pulled her back against him until she rested again against his chest. Her shift was so thin he could see the pink of her nipples through the fine lawn, and peering over her shoulder like this, there was nothing obscuring the view straight down the wide neck. He wanted to touch her—to do something about that *hot all over* feeling she'd admitted to. But he didn't want to frighten her.

At an agonizingly slow pace, Gabriel inched the hem of her shift up, his fingers trailing lightly over the inside of her milky white thigh. She was so smooth and soft. He could stroke his fingers over her skin forever.

"Gabriel," she gasped, as his fingers slipped higher.

He couldn't help his groan when he felt dampness slickening her there. She was already wet for him, and he hadn't even begun to touch her.

He felt delirious, to finally have her in his arms, to feel her like this beneath his fingers. He didn't know what he had done in his life to deserve her, but he thanked his bloody stars for the perfection that was Evelyn Price.

"Do you trust me?" he asked.

"Yes," she mouthed, eyes wide—as if too eager and expectant to speak.

She tilted her hips just a little, an involuntary movement that brought his fingers closer to her center.

He could wait no longer. He needed to touch her. He needed to feel her fall apart for him.

Evelyn's gasp was nearly a squeak of surprise when she felt his fingers delve beneath the hem of her shift and brush against her *there*, in the space where she ached for him. He did it again and she helplessly tipped her weight against him, too shocked to be much good at holding herself up.

His other arm slid around her waist, keeping her upright as his wicked fingers touched her again, sliding between the wetness of her folds. His eyes held hers in the window's reflection, boring deeper into hers with each pass. When she felt one thick finger nudge at her entrance, she rose up on her toes—unsure if she wanted to get away from the touch or chase the rest of his hand to press against that single point that seemed to send pleasure radiating through her.

Gabriel brushed his lips against her neck again and chuckled against the skin, his tongue darting to taste her. As if he knew exactly what her body needed, he pressed his thumb firmly to that bundle of nerves while sinking his finger into her tight channel.

"Oh," she moaned, her head tilting to allow his lips better access to her throat.

He dragged his other hand from her waist to her breast, kneading through the thin fabric while he thrust between her legs.

"Gabriel," she moaned loudly, then flushed a deep red. "Oh God. The windows."

"Don't worry, they cannot see you," he assured her, punctuating his words with another curl of his finger.

He breathed in the scent of her at her throat and ran his tongue languidly along her neck. He smiled wickedly then against her skin.

"But I wouldn't make too much noise, just in case."

Evelyn gasped at his suggestive words, imagining just that—moaning with abandon, and being heard by one of the partygoers below.

The thought was sinful and depraved, and it made her inner muscles clench around his invading finger. He chuckled against her—lust turning her usually stoic Gabriel into a lascivious devil. And it made her wild for him.

"Did you like that sweetheart?" he asked, and curled his finger again in a way that made her eyes threaten to roll back. "The idea of being seen," he clarified.

She couldn't answer, even if she knew how. She was all sensation. And then she felt a second finger nudging against her entrance, alongside the first.

"I don't want to hurt you. Can you take a second?"

Evelyn didn't know what words came out of her mouth, just some incoherent mumbling as he slid a second finger into her, stretching her, all while his thumb pressed intoxicating circles around the apex of her sex that chased away the sting.

Something was building inside of her, like a wave—rising, intensifying, cresting. So close, and she squeezed her eyes closed, poised on tiptoes in her stockinged feet while Gabriel's fingers pumped in and out of her at an alarming pace.

The pressure built and built, and then it was crashing over her as she cried out, her inner walls convulsing around his fingers, which he held firmly inside of her. His thumb pressed unflinchingly against her pearl, dragging the sensation on as she shook with the force of it.

"Beautiful," he murmured at her ear, and she wanted to sob at the feeling rushing through her.

She was still panting as he withdrew his fingers from beneath her shift and turned her to face him. He was still fully clothed, and she fisted her hands in his coat.

"Take this off," she insisted, and he smiled wickedly down at her.

He did, unbuttoning the coat and waistcoat and sliding them from his arms.

"I want to see you too," she blurted.

"I still haven't seen all of you," he replied, even as he tugged the white linen shirt over his head.

Evelyn felt her mouth go dry at the sight of him.

He was large and imposing fully dressed, but unclothed, he was an entirely intimidating specimen. And he watched her like she was prey.

It was as intoxicating as the port, and Evelyn shuddered, wondering how she could still remain standing when her legs felt like jelly.

Thick muscle corded his body, slab upon slab, and she wondered what he did to keep himself looking like that. This wasn't a body honed by fencing, or riding, or running. He looked like what she imagined one of those pugilists looked like—hard and powerful.

"Your turn."

He reached for her shift, and she stood stock still as she allowed his fingers to push the material over her shoulders. It fell as easily as her dress had, and then she stood in nothing but her silk stockings.

Gabriel ran a hand down his face, in a way that made her think of her own reaction to his bared chest. Still, she itched to cover herself from his avid gaze, but she kept her hands at her sides, wanting to know he found her attractive. She certainly found him attractive. The fresh rush of wetness between her legs could attest to that.

She bit her lip to stop from moaning at the sensation of her slick thighs rubbing together, and the friction against her sensitive sex. He seemed to notice her helpless discomfort, and walked her to the sofa, taking mercy on her and laying her out across its plush surface. She watched with rapt attention as he undid the placket at the front of his pants. And then her dry mouth flooded when he pushed them down past his slim hips, letting his manhood bob free.

He's so very big, she noted nervously.

His fingers had stretched her almost to the edge of pain—she didn't know how that part of him was going to fit.

"Shh," he cooed, and sank to his knees on the sofa at her dangling feet. "I want you to come for me again first."

She felt stunned at his vulgar words, but then he lifted her legs to drape over his arms and heat stole across her face to think of him so close to the center of her.

"Gabriel, what are you—?"

Her words cut off when she felt his warm breath fan against her skin.

"Do you trust me?" he asked again.

She couldn't find words—could hardly think while he hovered there, looking up the length of her body from his position between her legs. She felt dizzy and her skin tingled everywhere he touched her.

His breath was hot against her as he leaned closer, and she could barely manage a quick nod as anticipation coiled in her belly. But nothing could have prepared her for the thrill of pleasure that coursed beneath her skin at the first slide of his tongue along her inner thigh.

"Gabriel!' she cried, and then she gasped and her back arched when his tongue dragged through her slit.

She choked out a moan, the sound raw and needy in her ears. He licked her again, so slowly she felt her eyes roll back, and teased the bundle of nerves at the apex of her thighs.

"You taste delicious," he murmured, then flicked that bud with his tongue in a way that sent her surging up off the sofa as she arched again.

She was panting by the time he pressed his fingers inside of her—first one, then two. She thought she would die from the overwhelming sensation of it, and when her climax crashed over her, she might have for a moment, the way she saw stars.

"This will hurt, and I am sorry for it."

He was already braced on his knees, stroking his hands down her sides as if gentling a wild animal.

She tilted her hips towards him, heedless of the pain that would surely come from someone of his size penetrating her delicate flesh. She had climaxed twice, but without the feel of him buried fully inside of her, she didn't think she would find relief from this heady ache.

"Please," she begged. "I want you inside of me Gabriel."

He gritted his teeth and then sheathed himself within her fully, in one fluid motion. He clutched her to him, holding her tensed body close and not daring to move a muscle.

"I'm sorry," he murmured over her hair. "I'm sorry."

She breathed through the worst of it, even as tears squeezed from her eyes. It wasn't just the pain, though that would have been enough. But she had never imagined she could feel so *full*. And she wasn't sure it was comfortable.

She felt not unlike a butterfly, pinned to a board, helpless beneath his bulk. But as he let her adjust to his invasion, and the sting of pain ebbed, she found she needed—something—and she wiggled beneath him, trying to discover what that something was.

Gabriel held most of his weight off her, giving her space to breathe beneath him, and leveraged himself up onto his outstretched hand, to draw himself out of her. The movement tugged at her insides with a ripple of pleasure, and she let out a surprised moan as her legs clung to him, desperate for him to stay.

He chuckled, the sound one half of relief, and dropped back to his forearms, bracketing her head, before sinking himself back into her slowly. She gasped at the sensation.

Then he did it again, slowly. Sawing in and out of her tender flesh in a way that set her nerve endings on fire with delicious sensation.

Her back arched and she groaned in wonder as she felt his ceaseless rhythm thrust her towards another growing crescendo. She had touched herself in the privacy of her own bed once or twice before, though never to completion, and God, she hadn't known such a thing was possible twice in one night, let alone three times.

Oh, dear Lord, she pleaded in her mind.

Nothing but gasps slipped form her lips as his steady strokes became harder, fiercer, his own lips finding her nipple and sucking it into his mouth. His teeth grazed the tight bud and she whimpered, then he laved at it with his tongue.

When her climax came upon her this time, she didn't just see stars, she floated amongst them.

She was still in that dizzy haze when she felt his pace grow more frenzied and erratic, then felt him bury himself so deeply, she convulsed around him through the triggered aftershocks.

He stilled, gripping her close as she clung to him, and she could feel the twitch of his release as he pulsed inside of her.

"Evelyn," he whispered against her brow. "God, Evelyn. I love you."

Chapter Sixteen

I *love you.*

He meant it, those three words.

With a heavy sigh, he flipped them over, so that he was beneath her, and she lay along the length of him. He would have liked to hear them whispered back to him, but for now he would settle for the weight of her in his arms.

"I didn't hurt you?" he asked, trailing his fingers up and down her back, thrilling in the way she shivered against him, snuggling closer.

He felt the shake of her head against him.

"No," then a pause, and she tilted her face to look up at him. "A little at first, but then it went away."

Her face flushed prettily, and he continued to stroke her

smooth skin. He smiled at her, tucking his other hand behind his head to watch her better. She hid her reactions to him even less here, in this haze of intimacy that they shared, and he didn't want to miss a single one.

"It will not, the next time," he promised her lazily.

She smiled impishly and pushed herself up for a better look at him. He couldn't hide the wolfish grin that stole across his face as he trailed his eyes down to the full breasts she revealed with her movement.

She followed his gaze and squeaked a gasp, dropping herself back down to conceal herself, to his disappointment. He gave her side a gentle tickle and reveled in her laughter.

"You are promising there will be a next time?" she asked, breathlessly.

"Hmmm," he agreed wordlessly.

He made circles across her back as he watched the flickering emotion in her eyes.

She looks happy.

It was a relief to him. He did not want to think of where he'd be if she had fallen into regret after.

She propped her face on her hand, supported by her elbow, tucked against his shoulder. She wiggled as she made herself comfortable, and he groaned at the unintentional torture of her sweet thighs against his shaft, her breasts still pressed against his chest for her modesty.

A sly smile tipped the corners of her lips.

Or not so unintentional, he realized.

He gave her bottom a playful slap and she squealed at the

sudden contact, a giggle escaping her.

"You may have me whenever you want, when we are married," he told her boldly.

He had hoped for more smiles, for teasing and laughter. Perhaps kisses, or other, more carnal exercises again. He did not wish to see the hesitation on her face, or the shuttering in her eyes. He did his best to ignore it, though it made his chest burn. Not one to back down from a confrontation he pressed on.

"I should like to speak to your family after tonight."

"No!"

Her reaction was like a slap.

She flushed though, looking shame-faced at her outburst.

"I just mean that I should speak to them first. After the way things were left at the assembly—" she broke off and he cursed himself for being an idiot.

Of course she would be hesitant after this night. Her family had brought her to tears over a mere dance—what would they do if he asked for her hand? Or if he revealed this night, his trump card, and forced their acquiescence? There would likely be no approval for Evelyn, not from them—not from the Hardings.

"Of course you should speak with them first," he agreed, apology lacing his voice as he held her more securely against him.

He would protect her from anyone's censure if he could, but he knew he could do little to stop hurtful words or accusations.

"I would like to write to my parents," she said, voice small and uncertain, as if this posed an even bigger obstacle than her Porthaven relations.

"Alright."

"I promise I will speak with them soon."

She looked up at him with some mix of emotions he couldn't name, but that he wished he could banish from her eyes. And he sighed—there was little more he could ask for.

He traced his fingers again down her spine, willing the moment and her place against him to be more permanent than it felt.

Evelyn fidgeted so nervously that she struggled to pull her gloves on over her trembling hands. She wasn't sure what worried her more—going back into that lion's den of a ballroom to face her cousins and aunt, or the promise she had made to speak with her parents.

She shuddered. Not to mention the pressing need to clear up the mess of lies she'd so carelessly strewn about.

"Will you be okay returning to the ball?" Gabriel asked from behind her.

She turned to him with a frown of indecision.

She likely should return to the assembly rooms and endure the prickly silence of the carriage ride home. She took in Gabriel's searching eyes, set in that handsome face. But Evelyn didn't want to give up her night with him just yet. She selfishly wasn't ready to say goodnight to him.

"I don't think I will be able to stand the ride back," she replied.

Her voice was pleading, begging him to save her from that discomfort.

He peered out the window as though in thought and cleared his throat.

"I will have a message sent to your aunt that you retired early." He looked back at her. "Let her think you returned home alone."

"Thank you," she muttered down to her feet.

"Come," he said firmly, with his arm outstretched towards her. "I'll walk you."

Outside they split ways long enough for Evelyn to fetch her warm, velvet cloak, and Gabriel to intercept an attendant to send her message to her aunt. He returned to her on the steps of the assembly rooms, looking elegant and formidable as he waited again for her to take his offered arm.

She blinked and for a moment she imagined them like this but in a different time, with all of the lies and unshed truth behind them—when they wouldn't have to wait for the dead of night to leave a ballroom arm-in-arm.

A time when they could arrive together too, and drive the matrons mad with scandalous outrage that Gabriel Stone would dare to waltz so intimately with his own wife.

She stumbled on the stairs, catching herself on Gabriel's side as he moved to keep her propped upright against him. She gave a slight shake of her head, not wanting to acknowledge the wishful thoughts that had sent her feet stuttering.

"I'm afraid the one downside to port is its potency," Gabriel chuckled. "Though usually that's more to the point."

She smiled and let him think it was the drink that had made her unsteady.

The park was strange at night. It felt bigger than she knew it to actually be. And it was unsettling, looking out into that darkness—a pitch-black void of nothingness. She shivered through her thick cloak.

It was too dark even to see the trees, but she could hear them by their rustling leaves. She had the impression of some wild, mystical beast, leering at her in the dark. It's mouth open, teeth bared, and the wind was its frosty breath. She knew she was being silly and quite gothic, but still Evelyn tipped closer to Gabriel's side.

He released her arm for the breadth of a moment, only long enough to slip a firm hand beneath her velvet cloak and coil his arm around her waist. His forearm was like a thick band across her back, and she leaned into the safety of him.

"I don't think I would have liked walking this alone," Evelyn murmured.

Gabriel's arm tightened around her. "I wouldn't have wanted you to."

He peered down, and she tilted her head to look up at him. He was fierce and imposing, especially in the dark, where his edges seemed to blend right into the blackness. She wanted him to kiss her again. The glint in his eyes made her think he wanted it as well.

He paused his next step, just as Evelyn's own feet stilled, and she shifted to face him. He angled himself towards her and bent to bridge the distance. His eyes never left her face.

Until a sound thumped off the path and Evelyn stiffened in his arms. Gabriel straightened, and he looked over his shoulder in the direction of the sound, Evelyn tucked against his side.

"Who's there?" he called into the dark.

There was no answer but for the shuffling of feet. Gabriel squinted in the direction of the noise, then rose to his full height with a grunt.

"I can see you."

Two shadowy figures scrambled in the dark, muttering between themselves as they hurried off. Steady footsteps sounded, after the other two had gone, the sound precise and methodical as they stamped closer. A third shadow appeared, coalescing into the shape of a man, though Evelyn could make out nothing in the dark.

She could hear the sneer in his voice as he spoke, but the sound was muffled. "Nice night, isn't it?"

Gabriel narrowed his eyes at the man. He at least seemed to recognize him.

"Watkins. Why am I not surprised?"

"Just having a stroll gov, same as you."

Gabriel scoffed. "I highly doubt that," he muttered. "What's with the cloth?"

He gestured towards the man's head and Evelyn realized the hushed voice was because of a mask of cotton across half his face. She could see little else, but the white of it was clear now in the darkness. She shivered. She couldn't imagine someone out for an honest walk disguising his features with a mask.

She sidled closed to Gabriel's side.

"Can't be too careful," the man said, though it sounded more like a taunt than an explanation.

"Mhmm," Gabriel hummed. "Come on," he murmured to Evelyn, shuffling her past this Watkins fellow, towards Linden Street.

He seemed on high alert as they made their way, vigilant until they'd left the confines of the park behind them, into the streetlamp lighted street on the other side.

"Promise me you will not venture out at night alone," he insisted when they were in front of the Hardings' mansion.

"I promise," she said. "I won't."

She shook her head, fear still trickling down her arms at the oddly menacing encounter in the park.

Hardly anything had been said, but there'd been an aura of something around the man and his exchange with Gabriel. Like there was some festering feud simmering between them.

"Who was that?"

"Watkins?" Gabriel asked, eyebrows raised. He shook his head. "Just a thorn in my side. I've dragged him in front of the constable so many times—I don't think anyone has spent as much time clapped in irons here in Porthaven as that man."

She sucked in a shocked breath and felt her arms tremble. Gabriel ran a hand down to her wrist.

"Nothing substantial," he reassured her. "He's mainly been guilty of petty theft. He's just always causing some manner of trouble or another, and he's been acting shifty lately."

He looked down at Evelyn warmly.

"But let's not worry about him." He huffed a dry laugh. "Unless you've a stash of wine for him to filch, he won't give you any trouble."

He gazed into her eyes a moment longer, as if he wanted to say something else. She thought he might lean down and kiss her. Instead of lowering his mouth to hers, his lips quirked up in a knowing smirk that made her flush to her toes. He tapped a finger beneath her chin, then stroked along the underside of her jaw before pulling away.

"Come," he said, gesturing to the walkway up to the Harding's door. "I should deliver you the rest of the way home."

The sound of the wooden door slamming behind him rattled in Gabriel's ears. His clerk jolted at the impact as he walked towards him, eyes momentarily going wide.

"Sorry, Thomas." He tapped his hat against his leg tensely. "I'm just heading out."

Thomas frowned. "Already?" he sputtered.

Gabriel hummed his agreeance, but paused near the end of the hall, tugging out his fob watch to peer at the face.

"Why? What time is it?" he muttered to himself, squinting in the light of the window.

He had to look at the narrow hands twice to be sure.

Nine o'clock.

He dropped the watch back into its pocket and ran an

agitated hand down his face. It was damned early, but it felt like he'd been at it for hours.

Probably because he had been.

"You've a meeting with Constable Evans in an hour and a half," Thomas interjected.

He scoffed at that. The thought of Albon being awake at ten o'clock in the morning, much less standing in Gabriel's office, was nearly laughable.

"I'm only popping out for a moment. I'll be back long before then."

He needed to stretch his legs, to get some fresh air.

After he'd seen Miss Price to her door, he'd hardly been able to sit still. It hadn't been worth going home just to wear a hole through the carpet and drive his staff mad.

So, after wandering Porthaven for longer than he'd like to admit, he had gone back to his office and spent the better part of the night reviewing documents by candlelight.

He blinked as he stepped outside and shielded his sensitive eyes from the sun. In retrospect, it might not have been the best way to spend the last six hours.

He yawned. He couldn't have gotten more than three hours sleep, crammed onto the sofa.

A rude smile tugged at his lips. That sofa would star in all of his fantasies from here on out. It had taken enormous will power to get anything done at all and not spend the wee hours of the morning reliving his night with Evelyn over again in his mind.

He turned at the corner and started down the next street.

He didn't know where he was going, he just knew he needed to move. It was impossible to contain the pent-up energy amassed during those hours hunched over his desk. The memory of Miss Price didn't help matters any.

Perhaps I should buy her something.

Gift giving wasn't something he was especially good at. He didn't buy much of anything, except presents for his sisters. He didn't think Miss Price would much care for pastels and watercolors.

Unless she would? he wondered.

He had to admit, apart from a mutual attraction and a seemingly shared affinity for each other's company, he didn't know all that much about her likes and dislikes.

I know she enjoys reading, he mused.

And she certainly didn't seem the type to preen over baubles and ribbons.

He smiled. No, the way she was forever abusing her hats seemed testament to that. A chuckle escaped his parted lips, unbidden.

"Now, that's a laugh I have missed."

He froze at the sound of the feminine voice behind him—so like a splash of cold water over his head. And for a fleeting moment, he considered not turning around, as if ignoring her would make her disappear.

Don't be a child. You're being rude.

He heaved a sigh and turned.

"Lady Gilbert."

Chapter Seventeen

Evelyn spent the better part of the following day locked away in her room. With the way things had been left, she didn't know if anything could induce her to sit in the same room with her family anytime soon.

She'd heard her cousins and aunt come in barely an hour after her own arrival and had kept herself tucked under the blankets in her bed, in case anyone thought to check on her. She didn't think they had, but she'd been so exhausted, she had fallen asleep almost as soon as her head had touched the pillow. The emotional turmoil of the night had taken its toll, and she finally woke well beyond the usual time for breakfast.

She's been relieved to have missed the family meal, requesting instead a light plate be brought up to her room. She spent that time at her writing desk, swathed in a yellow morning dress that she'd donned herself, avoiding even Marie while she worked through the events of the night before.

She had the letter in front of her, the one she continued trying to write to her mother—to confess all, and to ask for guidance on sharing that same truth with Gabriel.

By midday though, the hiding had gone on long enough. She felt trapped and claustrophobic, and she grew desperate to step beyond the confines of those same four walls.

She hadn't heard the sounds of the Harding ladies for hours and knew her best chance for fresh air and freedom would be while they were out. She also knew full well she'd have herself locked back inside her bedroom at the first sight of them, to avoid a repeat of the assembly.

It was quiet in the house when she reached the bottom of the stairs, and she breathed a sigh of relief at her luck. It was bright and sunny outside, light filtering through the windows in the hall and tracing lines across the walls and floor. Mrs. Harding and Augusta would likely take advantage of the weather themselves, and Evelyn was certain she could enjoy peace in the garden for at least an hour before her cousins returned home.

She hadn't taken her book, or anything else to occupy herself with. She was too preoccupied with what came next, and what the next few weeks would look like, in light of her assignation with Gabriel. She flushed, remembering the night in full detail—down to each gentle touch and firm caress.

Her shoes pattered against the stone flags, the only sound

in the hall as she crossed to the tall, glass-paneled doors. The wash of green outside was finally breaking at the nudging of snowdrop petals amid the grass. The little white flowers dotting the ground made the space look like a fairy oasis.

She pushed open the door and smiled as a warm breeze sifted into the house. It felt like true spring, unlike the bitter chill of the day before. Perhaps it was a sign of good things to come.

If there were ever a time that she needed it, this was it.

"Evelyn!"

She heard the voice calling from the morning room, and she froze, like a rabbit caught in a snare.

"Evelyn," her aunt called again.

Her heart thumped in her chest. She didn't want another confrontation. Especially when she was still sorting out how to muddle through the mess she'd made. She needed to find the words to explain things to Gabriel, not worry about justifying her behavior to her aunt.

I should have stayed upstairs.

At her aunt's third, insistent call, she sighed and stepped back inside.

"Aunt Dorothea," Evelyn answered breathily, as she found herself at the threshold of the morning room.

Her aunt looked up from her embroidery when Evelyn stepped in. Evelyn tried for coolness, but her fidgeting hands surely gave her away. Aunt Dorothea's gaze dropped to her fingers, but otherwise gave no notice. She let the square of linen drop to the seat beside her and clapped her hands in her lap.

"Good. You can be my distraction from this monotony," Aunt Dorothea pronounced.

Evelyn felt a twitch of humor tug at her lips. It would be easy to brush aside yesterday's disagreement. She could see that truth in her aunt's eyes.

If Evelyn apologized for her flirtatiousness and settled back into a more proper role, it could be like nothing had happened. But if she returned to London in a week or a month, she didn't want it to be as the same person she was when she left. She couldn't just sit back and watch her life reset.

She crossed her arms at her waist, hugging herself for strength as she stood tall, straightening her spine. That waltz had been more than a dance—it had been a declaration. And she would not relinquish these things she so desperately wanted.

"I wish to speak with you," she forced out, before she could lose her nerve. "About last night."

Aunt Dorothea sighed. "Yes. I should apologize for the way I spoke to you."

Evelyn dropped back a step. It was the last thing she had expected to hear. It took her so completely by surprise, she instinctively began shaking her head in disagreement.

"No, you needn't apologize."

"But I do," her aunt insisted, motioning for Evelyn to take a seat across from her.

Evelyn thought she might prefer to stand.

She hardly knew what to say. True, her motives may have

been honest, but her aunt had been right—she had planted herself firmly between Gabriel and Augusta, no matter the circumstances. It made accepting her aunt's abrupt apology difficult.

When it became clear that Evelyn wasn't going to sit, Aunt Dorothea continued.

"I may have overreacted—Arabella most certainly overreacted. It was *only a dance*."

Evelyn pressed her teeth into her bottom lip. She should allow her aunt to finish her apology, accept her words, and leave with as little fuss as possible. Then she could return to her thoughts on how to tie all the ends into neat little bows, and handle any fallout later, when she had Gabriel at her side.

She swallowed a giggle as the image of Gabriel Stone, head bowed, humbled and contrite, came to her mind. Thinking of him being scolded as she'd been the night before was nearly too much. She fought to keep her expression smooth.

More likely, he would have been grinding his teeth in agitation at being upbraided.

"We are visiting here in a strange city, so far from London," her aunt went on. "And you of all people deserve to enjoy a silly little waltz with a handsome gentleman."

Silly little waltz.

She thought it was perhaps the very farthest thing from the truth.

Her dance with Gabriel seemed anything but silly. After their night together, she saw it for the seduction it had been— a seduction they had both fallen victim to.

"I do not believe any permanent damage was done," Aunt Dorothea concluded. "This is nothing Arabella cannot salvage for Augusta. It was only a dance," she repeated.

Evelyn felt herself stiffen. She wasn't exactly surprised that her cousins would continue pursuing him. He certainly checked off all the boxes. But still it vexed her.

Is that where they are now? she wondered. *Attempting to throw Augusta in front of Gabriel again?*

"I suggested Arabella call on Mr. Stone this morning," Aunt Dorothea confided, then smiled conspiratorially. "I think we can confidently say there will be an announcement soon enough."

Evelyn felt herself flush at those words. She was sure there would be an announcement, but not the one they expected.

"I do not think—" She shook her head. She hardly knew how to explain without saying it outright.

"How can he not offer for Augusta? She is beautiful, young, from a good, local family—it will be a fine match."

"He has asked me to marry him," Evelyn blurted, then drew her hands to her mouth with a gasp.

She hadn't meant to say the words aloud.

"Who?" Aunt Dorothea asked with an incredulous shake of her head.

"Mr. Stone."

Her aunt scoffed. "Marry him? You?"

"Yes," she replied in a small voice.

"Oh, he sure has aimed high, hasn't he?"

Evelyn didn't like the insinuation. "He doesn't know who

I am," she admitted.

Her aunt's eyes whipped to her like Evelyn had reached out and struck at her.

"He doesn't know who you are," she repeated. "And who, pray tell, does he think he is offering marriage for?"

"Miss Evelyn Price."

Her aunt's eyes went wide. She looked dumbfounded and mouthed the name as if in utter disbelief that this had happened.

"How?" she began.

She didn't have any other words.

"I met him in town—that first day I went out walking. We've run into each other a few more times since then."

Evelyn kept her arms crossed at her waist and twisted her fingers into the skirt of her dress. If she clutched tightly enough, perhaps she could stay grounded, and not slip into hopelessness.

"Plus, the times here," she added in low tones.

Aunt Dorothea stared at her, unmoving and unspeaking, until she tilted her head with a look of suspicion in her eyes, sitting straighter.

"The night of the dinner party," she said accusingly. "I saw Mr. Stone leave the dining room. He followed you to the kitchens."

Evelyn didn't think she could flush any redder.

"Yes," she mouthed.

"Evelyn, this will not do." Her aunt's voice was clipped as she shook her head. "No, this will not do at all. You will have to fix this."

Evelyn began to protest but Aunt Dorothea only took a deep breath and went on.

"You will tell him the truth, end this silly flirtation while you still can, and leave the man to Arabella's matchmaking."

Evelyn was glad she hadn't taken the seat across from her aunt. She might have tipped the frail thing over, jumping up at such a ridiculous suggestion.

"I will not!" She shook her head. "It is not a silly flirtation. I care about him."

Dorothea huffed in disbelief. "You care about him? Is that why he doesn't know your name? You are an earl's daughter, Evelyn. You cannot expect to marry a—a—a tradesman."

Evelyn gritted her teeth. "He works for his success, yes. But he is very accomplished at it. And respected in this community," she added, defensively. "And he is kind, he cares about me. And I—I think I might love him."

She was surprised her aunt didn't throw her hands up in exasperation. The look on her face suggested she could have. But as Evelyn hugged herself tighter, something shifted on her aunt's face. She narrowed her eyes at Evelyn again, her features settling into something like grim determination.

Evelyn was not sure it boded well for her.

"You love him," she said dryly.

Evelyn nodded as her aunt assessed her with probing eyes. "You will have to tell him."

Evelyn knew she meant the truth. She nodded again. It had already been foremost on her mind.

"You will do it soon," Aunt Dorothea insisted. "And you will tell your mother about this."

Evelyn swallowed. "I will. I have already begun a letter to Mamma. I will post it—when it's ready."

"Your mother sent word that she and the Earl will be visiting Bath in two weeks. You may tell her then."

Aunt Dorothea picked up her embroidery and resumed her work, threading little flowers through the linen. She eyed Evelyn over the needlework, one brow quirking upwards.

"Thank you, Aunt Dorothea."

Evelyn turned and slipped from the room.

Dinner came much too soon for Evelyn, and she would have much rather skipped the meal altogether. There was just no feasible way to avoid her cousins while they were trapped at the same end of the table, no matter how intently she studied the silverware.

Aunt Dorothea at least served as something of a buffer, though Evelyn could have done without the reproachful looks she cast over the glow of the candlesticks.

"I nearly forgot!" Mrs. Harding exclaimed, as empty dishes were exchanged for the next course. "Mr. Stone is hosting a dinner in two weeks."

Aunt Dorothea's eyes caught Evelyn's. "Mr. Stone is?" She kept her gaze fixed on Evelyn.

"Technically, his aunt will be hosting," Mrs. Harding continued, oblivious to the tension at the table. "It's rather short notice, but Mrs. Gordon is an exemplary host. I doubt she'll have any trouble at all. And his guest of honor may not be in town much longer."

She seemed far too excited for this invitation to have *nearly forgotten*. Evelyn thought it more likely she'd been savoring the news all day. She seemed nearly to be busting at the seams with it.

"And who is the guest of honor?"

Aunt Dorothea could barely contain her exasperation. Evelyn had never known her to be one for theatrics and gossip.

"Lady Jane Gilbert," Mrs. Harding simpered. "It's remarkable—such a resemblance to my own, dear Augusta."

Augusta at least had the decency to look uncomfortable at her mother's declaration. Or perhaps at her tone—one that implied those similarities made her daughter as good as Gabriel's wife already.

"Things didn't work out so very well for Mr. Stone and Lady Gilbert, did they?" Evelyn's lips parted in surprise at her aunt's rejoinder.

"Not by his choosing," Arabella reminded them, with a pointed glare at Evelyn.

Chapter Eighteen

There are only six quails.

"Remind me why I am meant to find this news so worrying."

Gabriel frowned distractedly down at the report in his hand. It seemed his hunch had been correct, and Mr. Watkins had been up to no good of late.

"Gabriel, really," his aunt scolded.

He placed the papers back neatly on his desk. The reports would have to wait, no matter how desperately he wished to pore over them. He had this blasted dinner party to deal with, though the timing was terrible, and the guest list was hardly of his choosing.

Lady Jane Gilbert.

She was the last person he would desire to invite to dinner—let alone as the guest of honor.

"So, there are six quails instead of eight. What difference does it make?" he asked, gently as he could manage.

His mind was still squarely on the report sitting on his desk, and he found his fingertips brushing the stack of papers, as though themselves desperate to pick it back up. He glanced down at the desk, then quickly back to his aunt.

"I'm sorry, Aunt Clemmie. I have a lot on my mind." He stepped around to her side, so that the desk was no longer between them. "Tell me—what is the problem with dinner?"

She sighed.

"The quail, Gabriel. There isn't enough quail for the presentation Cook has planned."

He shrugged, frowning apologetically. It was hardly a problem he knew how to fix.

"It will leave the table looking unbalanced, I'm sure of it. And," she continued, before he could so much as think of a reply, "I have just learned we have no center-piece for dessert— the cake has been utterly ruined."

Aunt Clementine's voice had risen through her speech until she ended on a winded huff. Gabriel felt a stab of guilt at her expression.

She looked weighted down by the pressures of this dinner party and had for the last few days. She had been in and out of his house all week, seeing to preparations. Never mind that it all seemed a monumental waste of time to him, when there were more pressing matters to see to.

"It is just a dinner party." He did not want to disappoint her fantasies, but neither did he wish to see her put undue pressures on herself for this evening. "No matter its success, it will bear no influence on my," he cringed as Lady Gilbert's face swam in his vision, "matrimonial condition."

It pained him to see his aunt's face fall as it did, but he needed to disabuse her of the fanciful notion that he and Jane Thomas had ever been meant for each other. He could say with certainty that she had done him a service those years ago by choosing Lord Gilbert.

Still, he need not remove all the romanticism from his aunt's evening. He shifted his gaze and coughed, the realization hitting him that he had yet to speak the words aloud.

"My attentions belong solely to another."

Aunt Clemmie's eyes went wide, then her smile wider. "Oh, Gabriel! This is wonderful news." She paused in thought, then smacked at him with the narrow sheet of paper clutched in her hand—the menu, he realized with a laugh.

"Do not laugh, Gabriel. Why did you not tell me sooner? I would have sent an invitation!"

"She has already been invited," he said with a smile. "She will be attending this evening."

"Oh, thank goodness." She looked down at the menu. "Well, then I must make sure to sort out this mess with the menu. We cannot have a shoddy display for dinner when we've such an important guest."

"Two missing quails hardly makes for a shoddy display," Gabriel laughed, but his aunt waved him off as she turned from the room. "And I know you have three flavors of ice for dessert, and enough strawberries and melons to sink a small ship," he called after her.

He chuckled, looking for a moment back at the papers on his desk. He'd been eager to review the report, had felt vindicated, knowing he had likely been right to suspect Watkins.

He wanted this sorted and done with.

But the thought didn't have the strength to stand up against the vision of Evelyn that overwhelmed him—of her glassy-eyed and flushed with passion. He glanced at the mantle clock. She would be here, in his home, in just three hours.

He smiled.

The reports can wait.

"Damn and blast!" Evelyn uttered violently beneath her breath.

Still Marie heard her from across the room, and paused as she laid out another evening ensemble across the bed.

It was amazing her maid could come up with so many different options when Evelyn knew she had only brought a handful of gowns in the first place. The magic of the overdress, she supposed.

She huffed a breath to toss a wayward curl from her face and drew out a new sheet of paper. It felt as if she had been trying to write this letter to her mother for a year. Each time she managed to get anything scratched down onto paper, the words ran away from her, and she was forced to start over.

"This needs to be perfect," she grumbled.

"The letter to your mother?"

Evelyn nodded.

"I thought it was nearly done."

Marie stepped away from the bed and came to Evelyn's side. She sighed. She didn't know what she would do without Marie's familiar support.

"Every time I get anywhere, I seem to write the wrong thing." She let her head drop into her hands. "Imagine if I tried to speak the words to her," she moaned. "It would be worlds worse."

"I know it is a complicated situation," Marie offered, "but she has always listened to you."

Evelyn sighed again. "There is so much more at stake now than getting out of another season."

She looked down at the blank page, then up to the sparkling gauze overdress draped over the coverlet.

"Perhaps I should decide what to say to Gabriel."

She still had two days to find the right words for her mother, but she would see Gabriel tonight. It wasn't right for her to keep him in the dark any longer. And the more time she wasted worrying instead of telling him, the more all of her lies would feel like a betrayal.

My name is Lady Evelyn Pricewinters. My father is the Earl of Sampford.

It sounded so deceptively easy, but it had the power to blow everything up in her face.

She hadn't known of his feelings when she'd first given

him a false name, but now it had been months—months where they'd flirted, danced, kissed. She'd lain with him and still hadn't told him the truth.

I am plagued with strong convictions, he had said. Strong convictions regarding the aristocracy.

Strong convictions about me and my family.

And how would it look if she told him the truth only after she had permission from her parents? What would she say then?

I know I have lied to you this entire time, and I know how much you hate the aristocracy, but I am actually a lady, and my blueblooded parents have agreed to let me marry you, even if you are just a tradesman?

"Dear God, this is hopeless," she groaned, burying her face completely in her hands. "I should have been honest with him from the beginning."

What was the worst that could have happened? He was a Porthaven businessman with no connection to London or the *ton*. How likely was he to know her name or the talk that had plagued her in town?

He knows Baron Hilgrave. Is, by all appearances, close friends with him.

But at least if she had been honest, she could have addressed the nasty rumors if they came to light. Now she would have to come clean regarding so many things. Her name and her family, true. But also, the events that had led to her hiding away in Porthaven under an assumed name in the first place.

Evelyn forced in a deep lungful of air. Or as deep as her tight-fitted bodice and tightly wound nerves would allow. *I can hardly breath,* she inwardly grumbled.

"I cannot believe you are in that same old, pink gown," Augusta baited. "Even with the overdress—everyone will think you own only two."

Evelyn fought not to roll her eyes. She hardly cared if Gabriel's guests thought her the shabbiest dressed female in all of England. She tapped her fingers agitatedly against her knee and forced out another breath. She was only wearing this damned gown because Gabriel had commented on it the last time. Little good that would do if she passed out from sheer nerves when she tried to speak to him.

"No one there will have seen me wear it the first time."

"Mr. Stone has seen it. He might question our connections," Mrs. Harding sniffed.

If only, she thought.

She was far more concerned with him finding out that the Hardings had quite enviable connections.

I have to find the time tonight to tell him.

She flattened her hands in her lap, smoothing her skirt. The spangles on her netted overdress scratched at her palms.

I will tell him tonight.

"I suppose it hardly matters. His eyes will be on Augusta all evening."

Evelyn could hear the smug satisfaction in Mrs. Harding's voice, but she wouldn't be goaded. She had too much on her mind already.

She kept her gaze fastened to the picture out the window, the tedium of cobbles and flagstones far preferable to the conversation inside the carriage. Besides, the more she fretted over speaking with Gabriel, the more their voices faded into nothing anyway.

It was a short ride from Lindon Street to Mr. Stone's address, though it took them all the way around to the far side of the park. She blinked at the passing scenery.

It is so pretty.

Here, there was nothing of the Porthaven she had become acquainted with—there was too much green. It was as if the park had reached out past its confines to creep into this side of the city. After months of narrow streets and cramped edifices, she felt breathless seeing the open, tree lined lawns.

She heard the crunch of gravel as the horses turned and the carriage was pulled up off the road. The sun was low but still firmly in the sky when she stepped down, and it shone like a beacon on the house before her.

She swallowed and looked up. It was really more a manor than a house. She could hear Augusta's intake of breath behind her. She had never been intimidated by someone's home before. In truth, nothing in her mind had ever compared to Haythorne House, to think anything at all of another estate.

This was somehow different.

She couldn't say if it was the gravity of standing in front of Gabriel Stone's house, and the weight of knowing how completely her secrets could affect the course of her future. Or if there was an element of awe at play, having spent so much time now in the company of people who didn't know life inside the country homes of the upper class.

Regardless of the reason, the effect was the same—heady breathlessness that followed her in from the gravel drive, to the spacious entryway, and the drawing room beyond.

She found him instantly, standing tall and steady by the windows, his dark looks and staid expression even more brooding against the backdrop of Prussian blue curtains. It was like some preternatural force drew her to him, no matter where they were or who filled the room.

"Ah, that is her." Mrs. Harding's voice came from just beyond Evelyn's shoulder and she turned to see the cruel smile tugging at her cousin's lips. "She is strikingly beautiful, don't you think?"

Evelyn's eyes searched the room, looking for the woman who must be Lady Jane Gilbert, but it was like her eyes could not focus on anything before her. A feeling similar to panic crept up inside of her, and her gaze fell to the space next to Gabriel just as an older gentleman moved, bringing a breathtaking woman front and center.

Strikingly beautiful, don't you think?

Evelyn swallowed nervously. There was no denying her beauty, or the fact she clearly knew the affect her looks had on the men in the room. More than one gentleman tried valiantly to steal glances unnoticed when they thought no one was looking.

Lady Gilbert laughed, and Gabriel smiled at whatever she

had said, the expression chasing the shadows from his face. Evelyn could imagine the sparkle in his eyes as he grinned down at the lovely woman. They looked like close friends.

Or lovers.

Her steps faltered, and she halted just inside the room. She wanted to move closer so that he might see her, approach her. Give her any sense that the torment she had put herself through these past few days had been worth it—that he cared for her and would hear the truth in her apology, more than the lies she had told.

They have known each other for a long time, she reminded herself as she watched them together. *By all accounts they have not seen each other in years.*

The reassurances did not chase away the turmoil churning in her belly the way she would have liked. She clutched her hands to her middle, her fingers trembling as her vision wobbled and she saw another pretty, blonde girl standing in Lady Gilbert's place. Younger, more fresh-faced, her hair warmer than the pureness of that pale gold.

Did you really think I would choose you...?

Her throat felt dry as paper and panic threatened to grip her again, then the vision faded as quickly as it had begun, and the pair's features began to take shape again. Jane, a beautiful woman with kind eyes, but not Henrietta Burville.

And then there is Gabriel.

Evelyn fought the smile that now threatened to stretch clear across her face. She must certainly still be in the throes of hysteria if the urge to laugh supplanted the choking anxiety so easily.

But Gabriel Stone was as far from Lord Nigel Sedley as a man could be, and that gave her strength even in the face of fear and lingering doubts.

Then he turned, catching sight of her from the corner of his eye, and the look in his gaze, as it fell heavily upon her, scorched her with a fire that flared deep inside. His hands spread, clasping on nothing at his side and she did her best to hide the draw of her shaky breath.

She was not unaware that the heat flooding her was one she would have been unable to properly identify before *that* night.

The night when he'd touched her with those clever fingers, his mouth, and his tongue—until she'd been desperate and whimpering, needing more from him, in every sense of the word.

And he'd given her more.

"Miss Price," he said, drawing her to him with words alone. He turned to the other woman. "Jane, may I introduce you to Miss Evelyn Price."

"Lady Gilbert," Jane corrected. "It is a pleasure."

It was nearly a purr, and Evelyn had the distinct impression it was *not* a pleasure—that the only pleasure Lady Gilbert found was in Gabriel's company.

Perhaps her eyes are not so kind.

"Please excuse me Jane," Gabriel said, tipping his head closer to Lady Gilbert. "I have something to discuss with Miss Price."

"Oh my." Her eyelids may have fluttered.

Gabriel cleared his throat, seeing the unfriendly implication that passed over Lady Gilbert's face.

"Business," he clarified. "I have some questions about an investigation."

"Oh, Gabriel!" she chastised, relief supplanting that scandalized look, along with the sudden confidence that she remained the center of his attention. "At a social function?"

"It will be just a moment. Miss Price?"

Evelyn nodded and let him lead her to the far end of the room, where a recess in the wall made private conversation more feasible.

"What did you want to know?" she asked as Gabriel turned to her, but he shook his head with a faint smile, casting a final glance over his shoulder.

"Anything to get you alone with me."

Her face burned, but not with embarrassment, and when he leaned his shoulder casually against the wall, all but caging her in with his height, she felt lightheaded.

"Gabriel," she chided as the heat in her belly spread. "Everyone will know."

"What will they know?"

He seemed to take up all the space between them, though he maintained their distance. From the outside, they likely looked completely innocent, though his posture was a bit familiar.

If they only knew, she thought with a glance about the room.

If anyone made out the hungry look in his eyes, they would be exposed for certain.

"That I am thinking about your bare skin beneath my fingers?"

"You are trying to shock me," she breathed.

"It is what I will be thinking about all through dinner," he confided. Then he leaned close to her ear, company be damned. "That, and the taste of you."

Chapter Nineteen

Dinner in the large dining room was a grand display. There were so many dishes brought out for the first course alone, they should have overwhelmed the table, yet nothing felt cramped or crowded. At the far end of the room, Mrs. Gordon looked pleased, even proud of this success.

Evelyn did her best to keep her attention focused on her food. She had no talkative neighbor seated next to her to distract her from Gabriel, just a surly gentleman more interested in his soup than her acquaintance. It was not normally a thing she would have minded, except it barred her from turning to the right side of the table.

And Gabriel's position at the opposite head put him at the perfect spot to catch her eye each time she turned left to speak with her aunt.

"Did you try the quail?" her aunt asked. "I swear, it is better than anything in London."

Gabriel eyed her over the rim of his wine glass, looking famished in a way that had nothing to do with the food before him. Evelyn swallowed against the thickness in her throat and turned back to her own plate.

"Yes, delicious," she agreed, sparing one more glance at her aunt.

She could have sworn she caught Gabriel hiding a smirk behind his next drink of wine.

None seemed aware of his heady attention, but Evelyn felt his intensity like a brand on her skin. Her senses were overwhelmed and overloaded, a confusing mix of want and need mingling with the fear and dread still grasping at her heart.

She had wanted to tell him the truth, or some part of it, while they were alone before dinner. In fairness, it had hardly been the time to come clean with all she had kept from him, but she had hoped to at least let him know there were things she needed to discuss.

But time had gotten away from her, and they'd been called to enter the dining room much sooner than she'd expected.

Or perhaps his shockingly wicked confession had robbed her of all ability to think, to reason.

It was a side effect she was still struggling with. Each time he captured her gaze with his own, the tempest brewing there seemed to snuff out whatever new flicker of lucidity she managed to regain.

When had she become so utterly featherbrained around him?

When he began sliding his finger along the stem of his glass with that wicked gleam in his eye, as though slickening himself against me.

All while watching her with those eyes that promised even more wickedness.

She blinked away determinedly. She needed to speak with him.

Tonight.

And she needed a clear head to accomplish that.

He had always disliked dinner parties, but tonight felt like some cruel means of torture. Miss Price had been sat right there—close enough that he could see the pinpricks of color that tinged her skin when he caught her eye, but too far away to speak with her.

Unfair, he brooded.

Especially when he'd been subjected to Jane's brand of conversation all evening. He couldn't remember her being quite so shallow in her interests a decade ago. But then, she hadn't been a *Lady* yet, either.

At least he'd been able snare Evelyn's attention, no matter how hard she'd tried to look away.

He chuckled. It had been a valiant effort on her part, but where else could she turn? Mr. Sheridan was a terrible table partner, and about as riveting as drying paint. He'd sat there on her other side like a great, muttering oaf, with more complaints about the food and the company than any real attempts at conversation.

Gabriel glanced across the table at the man. He was grumbling into his glass even now, when dessert had long since been cleared away, and the men around him had taken to cards and drink. He couldn't say why his aunt had invited the man, except to even out the numbers.

Or as punishment for not telling her Miss Price's name, he mused.

Gabriel tossed back the rest of his port. It would be time to rejoin the ladies soon. He thunked his glass back on the table, then stilled with his hand on the stem. The room spun hideously, and his head swam.

Dear God, am I inebriated?

Wine had flowed freely at dinner—it was his trade after all. But he hadn't been drunk in years.

He peered down at the glass still gripped in his fingers. How many was that? He'd lost count at dinner, and that was before he'd broken out the stronger stuff.

It likely accounted for his behavior at dinner.

He conjured up the image of Evelyn's heated face. A proper gentleman should be ashamed of himself—goading Miss Price the way he had. A smile tugged at his lips.

Then he wasn't proper, or he wasn't a gentleman, because all he felt was the desire to see her naked once more and watch how far that flush traveled down her body.

All the way to her toes, if memory serves.

"Lady Gilbert still looks rather fine."

There was the clearing of a throat and sudden silence before Gabriel realized Mr. Ainsley was speaking to him.

"I suppose," he replied.

In his mind he was undressing Evelyn. Slowly.

I am most definitely drunk.

He wasn't normally such a lech.

Mr. Ainsley coughed awkwardly and made to continue. Gabriel ground his back teeth. The last thing he wanted to talk about was Lady Gilbert. But he kept his mouth firmly shut. It wasn't all too surprising that the man would bring up Jane when she was supposedly his guest of honor.

"Though the other one is quite nice to look at too," Ainsley added uncertainly.

"Yes," Gabriel agreed.

She is. Though you had better keep your eyes to yourself.

"Reminds me of Lady Gilbert when she was her age," the other man said.

He means Miss Harding, he realized.

Gabriel grunted. He didn't have anything to say about the Harding girl, except that he was glad she and her mother had shifted their venomous eyes from Miss Price to Lady Gilbert.

Their preoccupation with Jane had afforded him the opportunity to provoke Evelyn after all.

That stupid smile still teased his lips. He liked seeing her ruffled.

No doubt she would upbraid him for it later, though he hardly minded. He rose to his feet with the other gentlemen, feeling muzzy and tender headed.

It might have been the drink, but he thought he might like to make Miss Price blush again before she left. In places he wasn't supposed to see.

He stifled a grin. He would take any of her ire for more moments with her. Preferably ones where he could touch her wherever he pleased.

Evelyn thought the men would never return from the dining room. When they did, she felt like a suffocating weight had been lifted from her shoulders.

Gabriel looked as severe as ever—enough that she would think she had imagined his impishness at dinner if not for the glimmer in his eyes when they landed on her.

She tugged on her lip as she thought of the way he'd swiped a stray dab of wine on his lip with the tip of his tongue, almost deliberately. Everyone else had seemed oblivious, though he'd pinned her with his hungry gaze. That heat was still there now.

Perhaps it had been deliberate. She felt herself flush while her nipples pebbled under his scrutiny. She swallowed reflexively, her mouth going dry. She wanted his hands on her again. His mouth quirked in what was very nearly a smirk, and—*he knew*.

She looked away, suddenly fascinated by the pattern scrolled into the carpeted floor. She could not be caught undressing the man with her eyes.

"What do you ladies spend all that time talking about

while you are alone?" Mr. Ainsley asked as he settled back into a chair by the door.

He was a younger man, though older than she was—likely somewhere near Gabriel's age. He was attractive in a classical way, though she didn't favor men with such fair hair.

Not anymore.

"Just women's talk," Lady Gilbert said.

Evelyn breathed more easily when conversation shifted to include the newcomers to the drawing room.

As awkward as it had been to sit at dinner with Gabriel eyeing her suggestively, listening to her cousins gush to Lady Gilbert about Mr. Stone was nearly unbearable. It was like the women were trying to one up each other, and their encounters with the man were playing chips.

She supposed she should be grateful Augusta and her mother had all but ignored her since seeing Lady Gilbert in all her evening-worthy glory.

Almost.

"I hear there is a title somewhere on his mother's side," Mrs. Harding whispered, nodding at Mr. Ainsley.

Evelyn was surprised to realize her cousin was speaking to her, and more surprised when she angled her towards the other end of the room.

Gabriel and Augusta stood there in one corner, so close they nearly touched.

"Your people care about that sort of thing, don't they." It wasn't a question—it felt nearly like a threat. "And he does have that golden look you so very much liked back in London."

Evelyn blanched, feeling her skin go pale and clammy. She did not want to be reminded of Nigel while she watched Augusta sidle closer to Gabriel.

"Excuse me," she muttered.

Mrs. Harding tittered behind her as she rose, but Evelyn didn't look back. She slipped from the room and walked as fast as she could, as far as she could.

There was a door propped open at the other end of the hall that led outside and Evelyn drew a deep breath of fresh air as she stepped out into the briskness.

It wasn't cold, but it wasn't warm yet either. She would only last out here without her wrap for so long, but she needed the space to breathe, without all of this baggage suffocating her.

"Are you alright?"

She jumped at Gabriel's voice so close behind her and spun.

"What are you doing out here?"

"I came to check on you." He frowned. "You left in such a hurry."

Evelyn peered around him at the crack in the door and the fuzzy light from the hall inside.

"They will know you followed me," she whispered.

"So?" he challenged. "I will not feel ashamed for caring about you."

"Well then you should not be out here alone with me. We will be caught."

He traced her gaze to the door and turned, pushing it shut before taking another step towards her.

"If the worst to come out of today is a forced proposal, I would consider myself lucky."

She scoffed at him and took a step back. "You do not mean that."

"I have already given you my offer."

It was true. He had. And they had been in far more compromising situations than this one before.

But she wouldn't allow him to be trapped into marriage without knowing the full truth. He might not be so inclined to keep his proposal extended once he knew everything.

"Gabriel," she winced. "There is something I need to tell you."

"Is it that you want my hands on you as much as I do?" he grinned, then slid a hand around her waist, dragging her closer. "You know how much I love this dress."

"Gabriel?" she asked. "Are you drunk?"

He shook his head, but it did nothing to convince her. *No wonder he was such a devil at dinner.*

He reached a hand to rest gently at the base of her throat, his fingers caressing her pulse as he watched her. He trailed his fingers down, letting them slip along the swells of her breasts. She inhaled sharply, feeling like she might burst from the tight bodice as heat flooded her core.

"Gabriel." She tried to sound demanding, but it came out a breathy whisper.

"Alright," he admitted. "I might be a slight bit intoxicated.'"

She giggled. "You are. Absolutely."

She thought to reach up and swat his hand away, but instead her fingers fisted in his sleeve, holding him to her.

"I could take you here," he suggested, lips brushing her ear.

It sent tingles throughout her.

"Someone will come looking for us," she reminded him, though she leaned into his touch as his fingers slipped into her bodice.

It was so very similar to that other time he'd kissed her, at another dinner party, another night—down to the very gown she wore. But now she knew what pleasure tasted like, and all she wanted was to beg him to sink inside of her.

But they wouldn't be alone out here for long. The guests might not care where she had gone to, but a good number of them would mind that Gabriel had disappeared.

"Then damn them. I was going to marry you anyway."

She laughed at that but again cautioned, "Gabriel."

"Fine," he groaned against her neck. "At least let me touch you. Tonight has been torture."

She sighed, letting herself press against him, feeling the hard line of his arousal against her front. If there weren't another twelve people inside the drawing room right then, she might have let him have his way with her in the garden. The thought alone sent a flood of need coursing through her.

She nodded, then opened her mouth to say yes, unsure if Gabriel could feel her acquiesce. But he had.

His lips found her throat and he groaned, "thank God."

Chapter Twenty

***O**h God.*

She could barely think straight as Gabriel's hands fisted in her gown, pushing the silk and lace up with such violent ardor she worried she would hear it rip.

"I need to feel you." His tongue traced her pulse and she shuddered.

His hand found her bare thigh and tensed, fingers splaying as he gripped her so tightly, she wondered if she would have marks in the morning. An indecent part of her hoped she would.

"Please," she breathed, though she didn't know quite what she was begging for.

He slipped his hand higher, leaving a trail of fire dancing

in his wake.

"Please, what, Evelyn?" he asked, his lips trailing down to her collarbone as his hand traced higher beneath her skirts. "What is it that you want?"

"I—" her breath hitched as his fingers found her.

She felt the warm slide of his tongue, his mouth hot against the swell of her breast. "Yes?" he breathed against her skin.

"Touch me. Please." It was a needy whine.

"I've been thinking about this all night," he confessed. "Have you?"

Evelyn gasped at the sensations—his wet mouth on her skin, one hand teasing the peak of her nipple, and the other tracking through her slick heat.

Like the damned wine glass, she thought with a breathy laugh.

Then she whimpered when he teased her entrance.

"Have you, Evelyn?" he pulled back enough to watch her glassy eyes as she strained for him, needing him closer. "Did you sit all through dinner thinking about my hands on you? My mouth?"

He eased down the bodice of her dress and lowered his head, circling his tongue around her peaked nipple. "My tongue?"

"Yes, Gabriel," she moaned. "I thought about you all night." She huffed a laugh. "You were quite distracting."

She could feel his smile against her breast. "Did you like it?"

She chuckled more strongly at that, but the laughter died in her throat as he speared a finger inside of her. Her head tipped back, and her mouth fell open wordlessly as he thrust, teasing a spot that made her eyes feel like they would roll out of her head.

"Oh, God. Gabriel."

"It's just me sweetheart," he crooned, and closed his mouth over her nipple for a brief tug, before lifting his head to watch her again. "Can you take another?"

She didn't know if she could survive whatever this was, and he wanted to give her more? She felt delirious, senseless, lost so completely to sensation she was grateful when the hand at her breast lashed around her waist instead. She might have tumbled to the ground otherwise.

"I need to feel you all over me," he whispered. "I want you to fall apart on me before we go back into that drawing room and pretend nothing happened."

Somehow in her haze she nodded, though she already felt full. Almost too full. But then he forced a second finger in alongside the first and Evelyn felt like she might shatter at any moment.

"Oh, God," she moaned.

It was like she knew no other words.

How does he do this to me?

Making her unravel this completely, in a darkened corner of his garden. At his own dinner party.

"Oh, God." This time it was a groan laced with mortification, and fear of being caught.

"Shh," he gentled. "No one has found us yet. And they won't, so long as you come hard for me now on my fingers."

She could do nothing to control the breaths that came as gasps, or the way her eyes clenched closed. Or the way she arched into his touch, desperate for her release.

"Come for me," he murmured against her ear, and it was like a command she was helpless to ignore.

He pressed his thumb to that bundle of nerves, and like a switch flipped, she tumbled over the edge on a strangled moan. He covered her mouth with his, swallowing her cries as she rode out her pleasure, his fingers pumping inside of her even after she'd stopped seeing stars.

She was panting still as he righted the top of her gown, tucking a loose strand of hair behind her hair as he drew his hand away from beneath her skirts. A hand that glistened in the soft moonlight—from her. He didn't give her time to feel embarrassment though.

"If we had more time I would taste you properly again," he said, then brought his fingers to his mouth in a way that had her wide eyed in shock.

And then he put them in his mouth.

He watched her with a calculating stare that dug deep inside of her, beyond any proper façade. He brought his last finger to his lips, licked in a way that had her thighs clenching of their own will, then reached his other hand to gently grip the back of her neck.

His eyes sparked with a challenge as his thumb traced the line of her neck, up and down. Her eyelids fluttered but she wouldn't let them close. She wanted to watch him like he watched her.

He leaned closer, breath fanning her lips.

"Taste what I taste," he murmured against her lips as his mouth claimed hers.

He had become a debauched, licentious degenerate, with wicked desires and lewd ideas. And he didn't fucking care.

Not when Evelyn's tongue met his, stroke for stroke, and her fists clenched in his waistcoat, her sighs like a balm for his damned soul.

He could blame his drunkenness for his behavior, how far he'd pushed her, but it would be a lie. He might have been less inhibited with as much port as he'd consumed, but he would have wanted her like this, tonight, regardless. Even if he had been stone sober.

Riding my hand so wantonly.

He shuddered.

And now she eagerly kissed him, even with the taste of her fresh on his tongue.

"We should return soon," he murmured against her lips, wishing for all the world he could hoist her into his arms and carry her up the stairs to his bed.

One day.

"Yes," she conceded, and slowly they separated, though it was as if they could not physically let each other go.

He kept a hand resting at her waist, the other toying with a curl beside her face. Her hands held fast to the sleeves of his jacket, anchoring him to the space between her arms.

"Gabriel," she started, with a furrow to her brow. "There is something I meant to tell you earlier."

He frowned down at her. Her tone was too serious, too solemn, for what they had just shared. He touched a finger and thumb to her chin, titling her head back to look at him. He searched he eyes.

"What is it, Evelyn? Is everything okay?"

She nodded but didn't return the encouraging smile he gave her.

"I see my parents, the day after tomorrow. I plan to tell them about you, about us."

It was good news, so why did she look like the condemned?

"They are coming to Porthaven?" he asked with raised brows.

"No." She shook her head. "They are in Bath."

He chuckled, again searching her eyes for what made this such troubling news for her.

"Back to Bath so soon," he teased, finally earning a smile from her, though it barely tugged at her lips.

"There are just—" she looked so lost he wanted to drag her to his chest and hold her there until the shadows left her eyes. "I have not been completely honest with you about my family—who they are, where I come from."

He did pull her to him then. "I do not care who your people are," he swore. "I want to marry you Evelyn, not your parents or siblings or cousins. *You* are all that I want."

She didn't reply, but he felt her stiffen against him, her shoulders curling up to make her smaller in his embrace. He took those delicate shoulders in his hands and pushed her back from him so that he could look into her face.

"Evelyn Price. You are more than just a *want* for me. Your face is what I see in the first light of dawn, the warmth and fire of your soul carries me through my days, and at night—" he couldn't help the smirk that played across his lips as he stared down at her. "At night, I'm kept awake by visions of you breathless and gasping, coming apart for me, over and over again."

She choked on a laugh, her eyes misty and wide with what looked like wonder. He wanted to keep that look there, to have her always gaze at him like he could bring her the damned moon. He gripped her hands and took a step backward, watching that bewildered look in her eyes. He dropped to a knee as she let out a little gasp.

"Consider this my proper proposal, Evelyn. Believe me when I say that you are the one I wish to marry, the only one I wish to spend the rest of my days with."

He smiled up at her, waiting to see those doubts lifted from her eyes. She smiled so wholeheartedly, it felt like his chest might crack. As it was, a giggle escaped her parted lips, and he felt his ribs swell to contain the happiness there.

"I will put myself on my knees for you always if that is what it takes for you to smile at me like that."

"Oh, Gabriel," she breathed, and tried to pull him up to his feet on her own. He chuckled and rose, planting a chaste kiss to her lips.

"Gabriel Stone!" came a fierce hiss from the now open door.

His head snapped to see Aunt Clementine standing there, blocking much of the doorway with her body and obscuring the view through the doorway.

Evelyn jumped from him, her posture defensive, with her hands wrapped around her middle, as if to forcibly hold herself together. He whirled around, so that he faced his aunt, with his back to Evelyn, whom he now shielded with his person.

"Aunt Clementine."

Her eyes scanned from Evelyn to Gabriel and back again, noting their proximity to each other—her labored breathing and his sharp defensiveness.

"Lady Carr is looking for you," his aunt addressed Evelyn over his shoulder.

Gabriel shifted when Evelyn moved to walk around him. He could already see the defeated droop of her head, when just moments ago she had smiled at him. When it had only been mere minutes since she'd been eager and bold beneath his hands. He wanted *that* Evelyn back—he didn't want to lose her to whatever fears and doubts ate at her.

"There is nothing untoward here," he assured his aunt, as though his words alone could convince her when his face was surely as flushed as Evelyn's behind him.

Aunt Clemmie sighed in exasperation. "Just being caught alone out here is enough to make people think something *untoward* has occurred." She turned to Evelyn. "Miss Price, I would ask that you to return inside to your aunt so that I may speak with my nephew."

Evelyn scurried around Clemmie with her head down, reaching for the door like a mouse rushing off to hide in its burrow.

Don't leave me.

He didn't know where the words came from.

"Gabriel, what were you thinking?"

"She left suddenly, and I came to look for her. That is all," he insisted.

"And that is why you both looked as if I had caught you in some compromising position?"

"But you didn't." He wanted to end this now, but Clementine had never been one to back down.

"This will not go well for your chances with that girl inside," she clucked, and Gabriel frowned.

"The Harding girl?"

"Who else? You said you had intentions to pursue one of the young ladies present tonight." Her eyes widened for a beat and her hand flew to the necklace at her throat. "You cannot have meant *her*."

Gabriel bristled. "What is wrong with her?"

"Nothing, Gabriel." Aunt Clemmie made a face that suggested there *was* something wrong with Miss Price. "It is just that—she seems rather a bit too timid to make a proper hostess."

Gabriel scoffed. "I do not need a proper hostess."

She crossed her arms over her chest. "It is an important

part of business. Of *your* business. Your wife must be appropriately suited to the task."

"I do not particularly care if she is appropriately suited."

"We do not even know who her people are—she is some distant relation of the Hardings, yes, but what else do we know?"

Gabriel didn't have the time for this. He was a grown man. If he wanted to run off with the kitchen maid, his aunt had no right to put her nose in his business.

"She is traveling with her aunt who is a Lady. I hardly see how you can find her unsuitable."

"And you had a lady seated as guest of honor at your table tonight. A lady from Porthaven, whom you have a history with."

He thought he had explained this to her already. He had no interest in rekindling any old flame with Jane.

"It is a history I do not wish to repeat."

"Gabriel!"

But he was done.

This conversation had gone on long enough and he would not be moved. He had asked Miss Price to marry him—twice now—and he would have his way, so long as she remained agreeable to it.

"I am already determined in this, aunt." He walked to the door, holding it open for her. "Besides, I will know her family soon enough. They are in Bath. She will visit them in two days."

Aunt Clementine paused mid step at that. "You have been invited to join them?" she asked incredulously.

He did not bother denying it, though it was far from the truth.

"I plan to call on her father," he replied.

"Unannounced," she concluded, seeing past his bravado. "So then, you plan to ask permission to propose."

It wasn't a question. He knew there was no denying the resolve on his face any longer. "Or something."

He took a few steps into the hall then stopped, wanting to be honest with his aunt. "More like permission to *marry*. I have already asked her myself."

"Gabriel," she scolded lightly. "What sort of manners were you raised with?"

He smirked down at her, knowing he had worn her down. She would support him in this even if she did think Jane or Miss Harding would make a better match for him.

"Ones that lead me to respect the opinion of a woman as much as that of a man."

Chapter Twenty-One

The carriage arrived promptly at one o'clock, as per the ormolu clock on the mantle. Without it, Evelyn would hardly have recognized the time—not if the gloom out the window had been the only thing to go on.

"Raining, again," Augusta pouted as she flounced back against the leather squabs. "I am done with the wet and the cold. It is unbearable."

Evelyn would have liked to groan at her cousin's complaining, but it was impossible to argue when she was inclined to agree. It had been raining since they'd returned from Mr. Stone's dinner party. The door at Linden Street had no sooner shut behind them than the skies opened up, and a deluge had descended upon Porthaven. It pattered on the roof of the carriage now.

She didn't bother pushing aside the curtains—the endless sheets of dismal rain out the carriage window were much the same as the oppressive grey she had spied from the drawing room all morning.

"Do you think it will pass by the time we get to Bath?" Augusta asked.

She had been somewhat more bearable since Evelyn extended the invitation to join her in Bath. Spending a few days under the same roof as the Earl of Sampford and his countess had apparently healed most wounds.

She looked hopeful and Evelyn winced. "It is barely a few hours' drive. I think it unlikely."

"Wonderful," Augusta huffed.

Evelyn dipped her head as she hid a smile. Augusta's pursuit of Mr. Stone made the difference in their ages seem like an advantage for her cousin. It was easy to overlook how much younger she actually was. When she sulked like this, it was much more difficult to forget.

"What is that letter?" Augusta asked, nodding to the folded square in Evelyn's hand. "You have been gripping it like a lifeline since we left Linden Street."

Evelyn's eyes tracked to the letter. It was the one she had finally written to her mother. The one that detailed all of her feelings for Gabriel and expressed her desires to continue her life with him at her side. She flushed just thinking about the words she'd written, the way she'd penned her soul onto paper.

"It is for Mamma," was all she said.

Augusta's brow wrinkled. "Lady Sampford? But you are going to see her now." She shook her head like it was the most ridiculous notion she had ever heard. "I thought maybe it was some silly love note for Mr. Stone," she scoffed.

Evelyn's cheeks went from pink to red and Augusta's eyes widened in surprise, then narrowed suspiciously.

"It is *about* Mr. Stone then?"

She didn't respond. She didn't know *how* to respond. How did she tell Augusta that her visit this time to Bath was as much to ask permission to marry Mr. Stone as it was to see her parents?

"What can you possibly have to say about him?" Augusta wondered. "I know my mother made a fuss over your waltz, but I hardly see how it needs to be explained."

Augusta sounded genuinely perplexed. Evelyn frowned, wondering how much to say, or if she should just let the girl talk herself into circles and leave it alone.

"Your reputation is in no danger, and besides," she chuckled, "I cannot imagine the Earl of Sampford pushing you to marry a *tradesman*, even with the flirting and your little moon eyes."

"Moon eyes?" Evelyn sputtered. "I most certainly have not made *moon eyes* at anyone."

Augusta scoffed again. "You most certainly have. Just because you do not think anyone is watching, does not mean we are all so completely senseless." She scowled. "I know you must think me a fool to not have realized who you were."

"I didn't think that," she murmured, but Augusta brushed

her off.

"It doesn't matter," Augusta laughed. "It isn't as if you are going to steal him for yourself."

Evelyn froze and looked down again at the letter in her hand.

That is exactly what I plan to do.

"Augusta—" She clasped her hands in her lap and looked at her cousin. "Mr. Stone and I—" She frowned, leaning closer and wishing she had words that would lessen what she was about to say.

"No," Augusta interrupted, shaking her head. "Whatever you are about to say, no."

"He has asked me to marry him."

The words rushed out of Evelyn, much like when she had confessed to her aunt. It hadn't been any easier this time than the first. She worried it would be even harder to say them to her mother.

"I—No. He can't have—" Augusta looked lost. "When?" she demanded.

"I suppose the night of the assembly, but officially at his dinner party."

"I knew there was something suspicious when you both disappeared." Her mouth twisted into an unpleasant expression. "So, Mother was right after all—you couldn't manage to snare a *lord*, so you've settled for a *mister*," she sneered.

"No, Augusta. It is not like that."

"Then do tell me what it *is* like. He was meant to court *me*.

I am the one who is an appropriate match for him. Everyone says so," she snapped.

"I am sorry."

"He was meant to be *mine!*"

"He was never yours," she stressed.

Something in Augusta's eyes turned vicious, reminding Evelyn of the look Mrs. Harding had given her the night of the assembly ball. Only this time, there was nowhere to run to in the cramped carriage.

"I'm sorry," she said again quickly.

"Are the rumors true then? Did you *seduce* Mr. Stone the same way you tried to seduce that lord in London?"

Evelyn had known the accusation was likely on her tongue, but the words still battered her chest. "I did not seduce anyone."

But her voice came out as small as she felt.

What if Gabriel hates me when he finds out I've lied. What if he does feel forced into marriage—tricked, trapped, seduced—once the truth comes out?

Augusta huffed angrily and rearranged her skirts as she positioned herself to turn fully away from Evelyn. The rest of the carriage ride passed in tense silence.

A timid *knock* sounded on the door to his study, followed by another, slightly louder one.

"Yes," Gabriel called. "Come in."

A young footman entered.

"A caller for you, sir," he said, with a careful bow of his

head.

Gabriel sighed. He eyed the report he had been working through—his last before he escaped Porthaven to track Miss Price down in Bath.

This had better be important, he grumbled.

"Who is it?" His voice came out sharper than he'd intended.

"Mr. Evans, sir."

"Fuck," he snarled.

He couldn't hide the irritation from his voice. Albon Evans was the last person Gabriel wanted to see.

He had enough business matters to wade through this morning as it was, and he needed to leave before midday if he had any hope of finding Miss Price before she was otherwise occupied for the evening.

Calm down, he berated himself.

He leaned back in his chair with a sigh and let his eyes fall closed. When he opened them, he looked at the footman.

He'd been uncharitable to the man. Though the closer he looked, the more apparent it became that he was hardly more than a boy. He was new too, perhaps only in his employ for a week or more.

Jacob something, he thought. *Berkeley or Bexley*.

He couldn't recall, and that only served to sour his mood further. He had always made it a point to show his employees basic courtesy, at home and in his business. And that applied to knowing their damned names.

He wasn't a bored aristocrat—with too much time and not

enough brains—to go around forgetting the names of his staff. His own grandfather had started with hardly a shilling to his name. No matter how high Gabriel climbed, he didn't want to forget where he had come from.

Dammit.

But he didn't wish to make too much of a thing out of it now, especially after he'd snapped and snarled like some feral beast at the poor boy. He would have to ask his butler later—Jeffries would tell him and reserve any judgement.

He smiled at the boy. "Yes, thank you. Send him in."

He would give Albon *ten minutes*, and then he was kicking the insufferable man out.

To his credit, Mr. Evans had the decency to look shamefaced, intruding into Gabriel's personal study. He still bristled at the thought of the delay this would cause for his trip to Bath. He gave the other man the barest of acknowledgements before returning to the report in front of him.

"I hope you can appreciate how very busy I am this morning, Evans." He very much doubted it. "This had better be important."

Albon muttered something too low for Gabriel to hear, but he could tell from the tone that he'd offended the man with his dismissal. He knew if he looked up just then, Mr. Evan's pallid face would be mottled red. Perhaps he drew a little too much enjoyment from provoking Albon.

"I do run my own shipping business, you know," Evans

said, sounding affronted.

Gabriel scoffed, nearly rolling his eyes at the idea of Albon Evans as shipping magnate.

The man had one ship that he'd bought on a whim, and a meager import business run entirely by a hired man. He wouldn't know the first thing about actually running a business himself.

"Yes, of course," he said, placatingly.

He needed this to be over already. The last time Evans had called like this, it had led to forty minutes of wasted time and useless information—unless he was meant to find *usefulness* in the exciting discovery of feral cats living in an alley behind one of the warehouses.

The clock read half past eleven in the morning and the papers in front of him would take at least twenty minutes to sort through. He could not afford another aimless visit like Albon's last.

He peered up at Evans again, expectantly. "The reason for your visit," he prompted. "Or did you just wish to stand there whilst I work?"

He winced as soon as the words were out of his mouth. It wasn't Mr. Evans' fault Gabriel had been on a knife's edge all morning. The man did not know he was prolonging the time until Gabriel could present himself to Evelyn's family.

He was going to show up on their doorstep, unannounced and uninvited, and tell a man who had never met him and likely never *heard* of him that he intended to marry his daughter.

What could possibly go wrong?

He cringed. It was too late to back out now. He was already committed to the idea.

"We have a suspect—three. And a witness who can identify them."

Gabriel froze, wondering momentarily if he had heard correctly. The last report from Talbot had given him enough to think that Henry Watkins seemed more suspicious than anyone else, but a real suspect—and a witness? None of their prior leads had produced anything so promising.

"A suspect?" he asked dully. "A witness?"

Apart from Watkins, the closest they'd had to a suspect was the nest of feral cats, and their witness, a half-senile old dock worker so deep into his cups he hadn't known the difference between a full-grown human skulking in the night and a hissing feline.

Albon nodded, satisfaction at Gabriel's surprise evident on his face.

We have suspects. And a witness.

Gabriel would allow Albon to keep the smug smile.

"Suspects!"

He stood from his chair, excitedly slapping his hand down on his desk. He could feel the smile that split across his face.

"Well?" he encouraged. He was desperate for every scrap of information Evans had managed to find out. "Who do we have? Is it Henry Watkins?"

It had to be. Everything in his gut pointed to the man.

"Yes. With assistance."

The two others.

"And the witness?"

"The tally clerk from Talbot's warehouse says he saw a group of fellows skulking round the back of a building that turned up robbed the next day. He recognized Watkins on the spot."

"And?" He couldn't disguise the eager anxiety in his voice. "I presume he at least gave a description of the other men?"

Evans gave him a genuine smile at his question and Gabriel just knew.

Talbot's clerk hadn't merely given a description. He'd given names.

Evelyn twisted her fingers in front of her as she stared out the tall rectangle of a window, at the grassy slope across the way. She had always found it beautiful here—this view was what she had missed most since their regular trips to Bath had slowed, and then stopped nearly altogether.

It certainly wasn't the balls.

Those were no better here than they were in London. The only ball she could recall finding any enjoyment at was the assembly in Porthaven, and that night had led to hateful words and such high tension in the Harding home, she didn't know if it could really be counted as a success.

After the ball, however—

That was a different story entirely. She could feel the color spread across her face, as heat suffused her body.

That was a story she would do well not to think about in

the presence of her mother.

How am I going to tell Mamma all of this?

Even without the sordid details, it would be difficult to relate—and perhaps difficult for her mother to accept.

"Evelyn," came a gasp from the doorway.

Evelyn spun, spotting her mother standing just inside the room, hand to her chest in surprise.

"Are you alright, Mamma?" she asked, taking a step towards her mother.

Lady Sampford gave an embarrassed laugh. "Yes, I am fine. I'm sorry, but you startled me."

She walked the rest of the way into the room and took a seat near the window, beckoning Evelyn to join her.

It is now or never.

"I have missed this view," she said instead, keeping at the window and glancing down at the street again.

"The view in Brighton is even nicer."

Evelyn shrugged. "I like seeing the people here too."

Lady Sampford smiled. "You can watch the people just as well in London."

"Yes, but there, there are too many of them."

Her mother's smile widened. She was familiar enough with her daughter's affinities to have expected the retort.

"Now it is my turn to ask if you are alright," Lady Sampford said, a slight frown marring her face.

Evelyn nodded and offered a smile, but nerves kept it from reaching her eyes. She knew her mother saw it. She had always been perceptive—and deeply invested in her children's lives.

"It's nothing," she said.

She wanted to speak with her mother about Gabriel—it was largely why she was here—but she couldn't get the words to pass over her tongue.

"Is it anything to do with that man," her mother asked.

Evelyn sighed with an exasperated shake of her head. Months had passed and they were still stuck on Nigel Sedley. She had moved so far beyond Nigel her mother would be hard pressed to believe it.

"No. It is not Lord Nigel."

She remembered the conversation they'd had in the carriage coming home from that last ball in London. Evelyn turned back to the window and winced. She hoped Mamma wasn't still set on the idea of her returning for the little that remained of the season. She had no interest in mingling amongst the *ton* in search for a titled husband.

Her mother gave a raw chuckle that made Evelyn start at its genuineness. Not that her mother was ever insincere, but there was usually more artfulness to her manner.

"I do not mean Lord Nigel Sedley," she scoffed. "I mean this Mr. Stone of yours."

Chapter Twenty-Two

After a brief celebration, and instructions for Albon to proceed with the information he had obtained, Gabriel had ejected the other man from his home with as much grace as he could muster. Then he'd locked his study door and set to finishing his work.

He didn't think he had ever gone through such detailed reports in as little time. He would likely have to revise a thing or two when he returned.

His carriage jostled and the sound of the team's hooves became louder as tamped dirt gave way to stone beneath the beasts. A glance out the window confirmed they had made it to Bath, and before it had become too late. He pulled out his fob watch and peered at the numbers. He owed his driver some sort of boon—they had made record time.

They slowed as they turned from the tight city streets to a curving stretch of homes. From the other window he could see the wide expanse of verdant lawn that spread out along the far side.

The carriage clattered to a stop. He had given his driver instructions to let him out a few doors down from the address he had, wanting the walk to order his thoughts before placing himself in her family's hands like an offering. He still didn't quite know what he would say.

The door swung open and light streamed in.

It's too late to second guess this now.

He leapt down from the carriage, straightening his jacket as he stood.

He held his hat in one hand, too agitated to put it on his head, but wanting the option of looking fully respectable when he finally made it to her door. He looked down the line of houses that made up the Royal Crescent.

Not a poor relation then.

His aunt would be relieved to hear it. He felt a bemused smile pull at his mouth.

This will go well, he told himself.

Three days ago, he'd held Evelyn in his arms. The incessant rain had magically stopped overnight. And this morning he'd had Albon's outstanding news about their suspects. Now, he had the fortune to discover Miss Price was likely to be just as *suitable* as his aunt had hoped for him—as suitable as he had already deemed her to be.

Nothing could possibly kill his current mood.

"Mr. Stone?" Evelyn squeaked.

She looked at her mother with her arms wrapped tightly around her middle.

How could she know—how did she find out?

Aunt Dorothea had promised to give her this chance to tell her mother herself. Did she decide after Evelyn's *suspicious* disappearance the other night to take care of the matter on her own? It would have been short notice to get a letter out and into her mother's hands, but it was doable.

But her mother didn't offer those answers, just nodded.

Evelyn felt like she might faint and leaned back against the wall for support. What should she say?

Where do I start?

"Tell me about this gentleman," her mother said, patting the seat beside her.

She looked for all the world like this was the most natural conversation to be having in the world. As if the Countess of Sampford and her daughter sat in the drawing room to discuss men of trade frequently.

"I—"

Words would not come.

"Sit, Evelyn."

Evelyn's mouth snapped shut and she moved to her mother's side meekly. Perhaps obedience would be helpful in this situation.

"I do not know what to say," Evelyn whispered.

Her mother turned to face her, but Evelyn couldn't pry her eyes from her hands in her lap to see what emotion was there.

"Anywhere," her mother said. "Tell me anything about him."

Evelyn turned shocked eyes to her mother, finally seeing the gentle smile and compassion in her eyes.

What is happening?

"He is a wine merchant," she stuttered. The words came out one at a time, as though she wasn't quite sure of them.

Lady Sampford nodded again, encouragingly.

"I met him while in Porthaven."

She sounded like a dunce.

"And you have feelings for him," her mother said—it wasn't a question.

"I—yes," she admitted.

There was no use lying if Aunt Dorothea had already told Mamma everything.

"You are wondering how I know about all of this."

A sly smile stole over her mother's face as she reached into her sleeve and pulled out a folded square of paper tucked inside. Evelyn peered at the page, seeing the familiar scrawl on the front.

Mamma.

She flushed. Aunt Dorothea hadn't told her mother a thing.

"Where did you find that?" she asked.

"Evelyn," her mother said with a sigh. "You are my child.

I know everything there is to know about you."

Evelyn shook her head slowly, in awe.

"And you still hide things beneath your pillow like you did at twelve," her mother added.

"You went through my things?"

She tried to sound outraged, but she was still too much in shock for her voice to hold any conviction.

"Only because you have seemed out of sorts since arriving," her mother insisted. "Besides, it was addressed to me."

Evelyn dropped her head into her hand and laughed dryly.

"You've read the entire letter."

"You gave the young man a ringing endorsement."

Evelyn groaned. She repeated the letter in her mind, remembering each detail she'd felt worked in Gabriel's favor— all of the things that painted him in the best light to be well received by her aristocratic parents.

"I know he is not from a well-placed family," Evelyn began, needing to find the words to convince her mother he was still right for her.

"Evelyn, stop," her mother said with a shake of her head. "He is a very impressive gentleman. A thriving business, the respect and dependence of his community, an Oxford education." Mamma smiled gently.

But it is not enough.

She stood, unable to sit still while she watched her future slip through her fingers. She turned back to the window. A carriage was pulling up just down the Crescent. She watched the driver hop down to open the door for his master.

"Does he make you happy?"

Evelyn's head whipped and her eyes snapped to her mother. "What?"

Lady Sampford smiled. "Does he make you happy?"

His step lost some of its bounce as he made his way down the Crescent. These were clearly homes of important people, evidenced by the sheer grandeur of the structure, if not the people walking alongside him. They paid him no mind, seeing him as one of their own. But he knew that was his self-assuredness and a dash of his *proper* education that appeased them.

These were not his people in Porthaven. It was evident in the way they carried themselves, the precious jewels and adornments the ladies wore sparingly, and the pinched tones he remembered from his school days.

He was beginning to think Mrs. Harding had gotten the address wrong. That or she had intentionally sent him on a goose chase.

It is all I have to go on, he thought with a grimace as he approached the number he'd been given.

He could not imagine Miss Price living in a place like this, amongst these people.

The knocker thunked against the door and he waited no more than a moment before it swung open—enough to frame a man a decade older than him, wearing a grim expression. He made Gabriel's own severeness look whimsical.

The butler, no doubt.

"How may I help you, sir."

He sounded as if he wanted nothing more than to shut the door in Gabriel's face.

"Is Miss Price at home?" he asked.

It was amazing how the scrutiny of a house servant could make him feel so small and insignificant. He cleared his throat.

"There is no *Miss Price* at this address."

Gabriel had known it was a possibility, but he felt compelled to push on. "Miss Evelyn Price."

"Mister—" the man paused and quirked a brow.

"Stone."

"Mr. Stone," the butler drawled. He made the name sound like it belonged somewhere along the gutter. "There has never been anyone by the name of *Miss Evelyn Price* at this residence."

"Miss Harding, then," he pressed.

This gave the butler pause and he compressed his lips into a thin line, sucking in a breath, looking aggravated at Gabriel's very presence.

"I will see if she is here at present."

He unceremoniously shut the door in Gabriel's face.

Miss Harding is here, but Miss Price is not?

How could that be? It made no logical sense. Unless—

Gabriel shook his head. There was a reasonable explanation. Something that would ease his mind, perhaps make him laugh when he heard it. There had to be.

He didn't want to think of the alternative. He didn't want to think of the reasons that had nothing to do with misunderstanding or strange coincidence. He would not give breath to the festering doubts that tried to crawl up his throat.

Perhaps she has family that works in the household.

But then why would the butler know of Miss Harding but not Evelyn?

I have not been completely honest with you.

Her words from the other night rang in his head like a church bell, tolling over and over again, with all the violence of a thunderous clash.

Gabriel's vision swam with uncertainty. His head ached.

The door was opening again, the butler nodding primly to him, and then Miss Harding swept to the doorway like a fluff of pink cloud and golden sunshine.

He felt like he was in a daze. And soon, he would not be surprised if madness descended over him as his mind unraveled at the disaster playing out around him.

"Mr. Stone," she gushed. "What a serendipitous surprise!"

"Does he make me happy?" Evelyn repeated slowly, as if she couldn't quite grasp the meaning of the words.

"Is he kind to you?" her mother asked with a widening smile. "Do you like spending time with him?"

"Are—" Evelyn paused, too stunned to force words out. "Are you not upset that he is only a *mister?*"

"Evelyn," her mother scolded. Then she drew a breath and peered out the window as if collecting her thoughts. "Do I think your life would be easier if you found someone from our own social class? Yes. But," she turned to look pointedly at

Evelyn, "the last one you found for yourself was a scoundrel. And an ass."

"Mother!"

"Well, it is true! Lord Nigel Sedley is the last man I would want you to marry, after the way he behaved. So, tell me. Does your Mr. Stone make you happy?"

A sigh escaped Evelyn's lips and with it, a weight she hadn't realized had settled on her shoulders and wrapped around her throat, until it was gone.

Does Gabriel make me happy? She asked herself deliriously. "Yes."

The word bubbled up from somewhere hopeful and giddy inside of her and she felt tears prick at her eyes. She peered out the window once more while she collected herself, wiping away wetness that escaped past her lashes with a finger.

She moved to turn back to her mother when her eyes snagged on a man on the street, paused halfway between her door and the parked carriage.

It cannot be.

He turned as another tear dripped to her cheek, looking up at her window, as if he knew exactly where she stood. Her breath hitched.

"He came," she whispered. "Gabriel came to Bath."

Her mother came up behind her, looking out the window with her and surprised Evelyn again with an appreciative sound of approval.

"He is quite handsome, isn't he?" Lady Sampford said.

Evelyn giggled, feeling herself flush as she agreed with her mother. How could she not?

"And he followed you to Bath. That's very romantic."

"Yes," Evelyn whispered.

How in the world did he know where to find me?

"I should probably speak with your father," Mamma sighed. "He will have to come to terms with this quite quickly if your sweetheart is already here."

"Sweetheart?" Evelyn chuckled.

"I was going to say *lover*, but I thought you might balk at that one."

"He is not—we are not—"

Evelyn hardly knew how to respond to that, especially when the word *lover* was more than apt to describe what Gabriel was to her.

She thought of that night in the garden at his dinner party. The things he'd made her feel.

"Go to him," her mother said, laughing at her discomfort, and led her to the stairs. "Thompson has likely turned him away out of hand, and he is now roaming the streets of Bath alone."

"Oh dear."

Evelyn hurried down the stairs and rushed to the door. Augusta was stepping in, as if she had just been outside. She lookup up as Evelyn approached and gave her a syrupy smile.

"Evelyn, you just missed Mr. Stone," she said as Evelyn slipped by. "Oh, and Evelyn," she called at her back, making her pause at the open threshold. "I may have *accidentally* told him your full name."

Chapter Twenty-Three

He knows. It repeated in her head like a refrain. *He knows, he knows, he knows.*

It was what she wanted, what she had planned for. But not like this.

She could only imagine what Augusta had told him—*how* she had told him. Each option seemed worse than the last.

Evelyn frantically scanned the street, searching for his face, a glimpse of his back, just his *height* amongst the people strolling the Crescent.

Where is he?

She needed to find him and explain—to set straight any sour words or implications he had heard from Augusta's lips.

I cannot have missed him.

She pleaded with God and fate for it to be true.

There!

He was approaching the carriage—the same one she had spotted earlier from the drawing room window. She had seen him arrive and not even realized.

She quickened her steps, as much as she dared on the busy street. Already she received disapproving stares at her hurried pace.

Dammit! I wish I could run to him.

He was nearly to his carriage, the driver already hopping down to lower the step and open the door for him.

Damn them all, she thought with a last, nervous glance at a pair of simpering ladies.

She let her feet carry her.

He was so far.

She watched him tip his hat to his driver, his foot raising to take the step up to the interior. She didn't think she would make it.

"Gabriel!" she called when she was close enough for him to hear her.

He froze as he pressed down on the step, the carriage bouncing while his hand gripped the side. His back went stiff at her voice, and it seemed to take a herculean effort for him to draw breath as she came to a halt a few paces behind him. Her own breaths were labored.

"Gabriel, please," she said. "Do not leave yet."

He took a controlled step back, away from the carriage, another heavy breath raising his broad shoulders.

What had Augusta told him?

He turned, and she sighed to be able to see his face, to look into his eyes, and a smile lifted the corners of her mouth before she could stop it.

But those weren't the eyes of the man she had spent the last few days thinking about. Not anymore.

The severity of his features was set in such unforgiving lines, she almost thought she had imagined his smiles. Dreamed them up from nothing, because this man before her could not ever have looked at her with playfulness, kindness, *affection.*

"Miss Price." His voice was as flat as the contempt in his eyes. He scoffed. "Or should I say *Lady.*"

"Gabriel," she pleaded. "I was going to tell you. I *meant* to tell you."

She thought of the other night in the garden, when she had tried to confess the truth. But he had interrupted her with such tender words. And she had been eager to take the distraction, to give herself an out and go on just a little longer in the safe bubble she had created, where *Evelyn Pricewinters* couldn't hurt her.

"I don't know what Augusta told you—"

"None of this is Miss Harding's fault." He cut her off, his voice hard and wooden. He might as well have been talking to a stranger.

He looked at her like he did not know her, like he wondered if he'd *ever* known her. When he shook his head and stepped back to turn to the carriage, she felt a cry stick in her throat.

"I'm sorry, Gabriel."

He whirled back around, a fury she had never seen directed at her, contorting his face.

"You are sorry?" he demanded. "Tell me, *my lady*, what exactly are you sorry for?"

He advanced on her, menacing and fearsome.

"You are sorry that you lied to me, from the very *first* moment I met you? That you kept such significant information about *who you are*, a secret through every flirtation, and kiss, and stolen moment together?" He glanced around them, then leaned into her, head tipped to speak directly into her ear. "Even when I held you, naked, in my arms?" he whispered.

She shook her head, tears stinging the backs of her eyes. She could already hear the whispers around them, see in the periphery her peers conveniently pausing their strolling close enough to watch them.

"When I asked you to *marry me?*" he hissed.

Their audience was too far to hear the words he spoke, but they could see their faces, their expressions, and hear the heated temper in Gabriel's voice. She blinked back tears.

I will not cry in front of them.

"It was not like that, Gabriel. I swear it."

Already she could hear her name, whispered behind gloved hands, as she was recognized.

The rumors will be double now, she realized.

"I didn't use my full name at all while I was in Porthaven," she tried to explain. "I didn't want to be Lady Evelyn while I was there. I *needed* to be someone else."

"Yes, and you dragged me down into your playacting," he snapped. "You have humiliated me, woman."

"No. Gabriel, no. I swear. I never meant for it to go on for as long as it did."

His expression gave no room for her explanations. He would not listen, not now. Not when he thought she had played him in some awful way.

The whispers around them bled into her ears. *Who is he?* and *I do not recognize him.* She knew what they meant—*who is this* cit, *condemning Lady Evelyn?*

She didn't need to look at them to know their eyes would be gleeful.

She tried to speak, but Gabriel's eyes hardened, and she heard him huff an angry breath, his nostrils flaring with barely suppressed fury.

"Was it fun? Did you like your little game—pretending to be *common?*"

He was so close she could lean forward and fall against his chest. She wished he would reach for her, pull her to him and hold her close, even as he vented his spleen.

She flushed. He was silently raging at her and all she wanted was for him to kiss her.

When he spoke again, his voice was deathly quiet.

"Was it a great laugh to share with your friends at home? Your family? Your cousins?"

How could he think that of her? Had Augusta suggested such a thing? Or was it simply her title and station that blinded him to her heart now?

"Is that what Augusta told you?"

"Stop bringing Miss Harding into this. She is blameless in all of it. *She* spoke the truth to me."

His anger was a physical thing, radiating off of him as a living, breathing animal. It terrified her.

He sneered. "Perhaps I should consider her after all."

Evelyn felt like she had been slapped. She felt herself rock back on her heels, lips parted in shock and hurt.

"I—I had a difficult season in London," she admitted, hating that she had to lay the worst of her pain and fear bare, for him to believe her. "I was hurt and embarrassed. I needed a new start."

She looked down at his waistcoat—so close, but he might as well be a world away. "I thought this could be my new start," she whispered.

"A new start," he repeated.

"Please. I did not mean to hurt you."

He scoffed, taking a step back from her. The ice in his eyes cut like knives across her already battered heart.

"Do you really think you could have ever hurt me? *You?*" He laughed—a cold, humorless sound. "Run back to London, Lady Evelyn. Take your silly, little society problems far away from here, and leave Porthaven to those of us who belong."

He turned to leave, and she grabbed for his sleeve, knowing she was making a fool of herself, hearing the shocked gasps as people stared, but not caring. He needed to let her explain. He needed to listen. She needed to *make him listen.*

"Scurry back to your *people*," he said over his shoulder, loosening his jacket from her fingers. "We do not need your kind in Porthaven."

When she did not move, her hand still brushing his arm, he turned just enough to look her in the eye. "We do not want you."

Gabriel vaulted up into his carriage, sending the folding step dancing with the force of his escape. He didn't dare look back to where he'd left Evelyn, staring after him in open-mouthed shock.

He knew it would eat at him later, to think of the hurt in her eyes as he'd thrown all his hurt at her, but he couldn't face it now. *He* at least hadn't lied to her. That had been her sin, not his.

A lady, he fumed, as the door shut behind him. *The daughter of a fucking earl.*

How she must have laughed at his proposal.

In what world would the daughter of an earl ever truly consider an offer from a base brute like him?

He let his head fall back against the leather squabs while the wheels jerked him forward, as the horses began to move.

Fuck, but her tear-filled eyes were like a dagger through his heart. He was furious, nearly murderous with rage, and rightly so. But still he wanted to kiss the sadness from her eyes.

What is wrong with me?

For a moment, a more reasonable voice wondered if his anger was purely at Evelyn, or if it was exacerbated by Jane's unwanted attentions since she'd returned to town. She had deemed him unworthy when he was a younger man, the son of a coarse upstart, with no real place in Porthaven society to call his own. Ten years later, she seemed to have decided his success was worth the step down in address.

Evelyn lied to me.

He would not allow himself to forget that part. She'd had ample time to tell him the truth, endless chances and opportunities.

It had been *months* of their acquaintance. He had kissed her. He had held her, touched her. God, he knew what it felt like to be inside of her, and still she hadn't told him.

And now I am thinking about her naked, he grumbled. *Again.*

He could not seem to reconcile the anger he felt at her betrayal with the unholy desires that assailed him when he thought of her. If he reflected on it too long, he would likely go insane.

He groaned. There was nothing for it. He would endure the ride back to Porthaven. and he would lock himself away in his study. And then he would drink as much damned port as he wished.

Or better yet, whiskey.

The door shut behind her with a *thud* that seemed to shake her, vibrating through her body.

He left.

He had bounded up into his carriage without sparing a

glance in her direction. She had watched and waited, as the driver had climbed to his perch, picked up the reins, and set the team of four, sorrel-colored horses onwards. Gabriel never once looked back.

He does not want me.

She dashed the tears from her eyes.

"Did you find him?"

She started at her mother's voice, turning away to better wipe the wetness from her face, then look up at the staircase where the Countess of Samford watched her expectantly.

"I was too late," she lied. "I must have just missed him."

"Oh, dear!" She hurried down the stairs. "That is too bad." She linked her arm through Evelyn's and drew her towards the downstairs morning room.

"You will have to see him, straight away, when you go back to Porthaven."

Evelyn walked with her mother, trying not to drag her feet, though it felt like she was moving through shifting sands.

"I do not know if I will go back."

Her mother flashed her a shocked look of wide-eyed bewilderment. "What do you mean you will not go back?"

"Perhaps this was for the best," she muttered.

"Evelyn. Are you sure you are alright?"

Evelyn nodded. "It is just that I caused so much tension with the Hardings, giving Mr. Stone my attention as I did. It might be our missing each other here was more lucky than not."

Her mother did not look entirely convinced.

"Well, then. Where is the man?" her father asked from a chair in the morning room when they entered.

"Evelyn did not catch him before he left," Mamma bemoaned. "And now she says she might not wish to return to Porthaven to even speak with him."

"Evelyn," her father frowned. "I was prepared to meet the gentleman. Your mother made it sound as if an offer would be made."

They both looked at her with the same mask of confusion—confusion she felt herself.

How had it come to this?

"I just—I am enjoying Bath," she said and forced a smile. "I would like to spend this time with you here and worry about everything else after."

"If you are sure," her father said, the furrow between his brows deepening.

"Besides," she added, "it is a match that is bound to cause talk. I should think it over completely first, before speaking with him."

At that her father barked a laugh. "Evelyn, when have you cared what people *talk* about?"

She winced. It was true. And if things with Gabriel had gone differently, she would have faced the cruelest gossip with a bright smile, just to be by his side.

She remembered the stares and whispers that had surrounded her while Gabriel had fumed at her.

They will all talk anyway.

"Since Lord Nigel," she said, knowing she spoke the only

words that would force her parents to close the subject.

Her father ground his teeth at the name, and a shadow passed over her mother's eyes. She could only imagine the rumors and vitriol that had continued to be spewed through the London ballrooms since she had left. She didn't wish to think what whispers her mother and father had picked up on.

"Well," her mother said with forced cheer. "Then we shall enjoy Bath a little longer."

She strode to the window, then back again—as if standing still would force her to assess the inconsistencies in Evelyn's remarks.

"Lady Partridge is hosting a ball in a few days. You and Augusta will accompany us." She waved a hand at Evelyn's instinctive resistance. "It will be no bother, and we could all do with the diversion."

Evelyn tossed to one side, sheets tangling around her legs. She couldn't sleep. It had been like this since her confrontation with Gabriel on the streets of Bath.

She blinked up at the ceiling.

It was too dark to see anything. The curtains were closed, keeping even the moonlight from the room. She sat up, letting the bedding fall at her lap.

I cannot stand this.

She swung her legs over the edge of her mattress, not pausing until her feet hung over the side of the bed and then touched down on the delicately woven rug at her bedside.

The night air was cool, even with the windows shut and

barred, and she shivered in her nightclothes.

She pulled a wrap off the chair on the other side of her bedroom, slinging it around her shoulders and gripping it tightly. It did little to chase away the chill.

She stalked to the window, feeling bereft and alone, the emotions amplified by the cold. Outside was nearly as dark as inside. The moon was out, but her room did not afford a view of it at this time of night. It was too far along in its arc across the sky.

Tomorrow night was Lady Partridge's ball. Evelyn had spent the last few days thinking of ways to get out of it. She'd never enjoyed the parties under the best of circumstances. She was not prepared to enjoy herself now, when loneliness filled her heart. When each twirling couple would remind her of Gabriel.

She sighed, feeling the tears fill her eyes. If she could wish them away, she would. As it was, she willed them not to fall for as long as she could, eyes wide and unblinking as the moisture built.

I would have thought I'd used up all of my tears.

She had cried in her bed each night, silently letting the misery pour out over her lashes until she felt empty.

She blinked and the tears fell, soundlessly twisting their tracks down her cheeks.

The yellow-orange glow of sunset filtered through the windows. Or maybe it was sunrise. Gabriel peered at the light through squinted eyes. He really couldn't tell anymore.

He lifted the bottle of scotch to his lips and took another drag of amber liquid. The glass was no longer cold in his hand or at his mouth. He'd given it plenty of time to warm up from his heavy-handed touch.

A fist pounded at the door, though it sounded like it collided straight with his skull. Repeatedly.

"What?" he called as his head spun.

He hadn't been this inebriated in a long time, possibly ever. The port he'd tossed back at his dinner party had nothing on the potency of hard liquor. It was a potency he was grateful for now.

I want to forget, he thought, and took another swig. *I want to forget everything.*

Someone knocked again and he slammed a fist on the desk in front of him.

"God dammit man! Come in!" he shouted.

He was more beast than man today—had been since he'd returned from Bath.

She lied to me. He gritted his teeth. *She tricked me, tried to trap me.*

He dropped his head into his hand.

Trap me? That somehow didn't make sense—didn't align with his angry suspicions.

Fuck it is too painful to think. He rubbed his head, trying to massage away the ache there.

"Mr. Stone," Jeffries said from the doorway.

Gabriel chuckled. There was no footman to call on him today. No, he was far too unpleasant today, too unbearable to be around. Jeffries was here to deal with him himself, and he wasn't hiding a single ounce of censure at Gabriel's behavior.

"Mr. Little has brought yet another ledger for you to review," the butler said with a sniff.

"Fine."

Jeffries looked around the room, the mess and disarray it had been in since Gabriel's return. "Should I put it atop this precarious pile of *other* ledgers he's brought you?"

Gabriel was too far gone to care at the judgement in the man's tone. Hells, he was too far gone to care that he was being enough of an *ass* to elicit such condemnation from his usually reserved butler.

"Leave it wherever." He gave a wave of his hand to encompass the entirety of the room.

Jeffries uttered a beleaguered sigh. "As you say, sir."

The man brought the door closed to bang loudly behind him as he left, making Gabriel jolt and wince as the sound ricocheted like stones around his head.

More like bloody boulders.

He let his eyes fall on the stack of ledgers and paperwork that had amassed into a veritable tower atop his desk.

Precarious, indeed.

The whole thing looked like it would topple at the slightest provocation. Much the same as he felt at the moment.

Please, Gabriel, she had begged.

Begged, and he had given her no quarter. He'd decided she was guilty without listening to a word from her mouth.

Truthfully, he had decided her guilt before she had chased

after him—before Miss Harding had told him the truth.

The moment the damned butler had answered the door and the first inkling that she had not been fully truthful entered his awareness, he had cast her as a liar.

She did lie, he reminded himself. *I did not invent that.*

He had every right to be angry with her. He did not need to feel guilt for showing her how much her deceit had hurt him, how she had eviscerated him by breaking his trust.

Then why am I more angry at myself?

Chapter Twenty-Four

The ballroom was too stuffy. Evelyn could hardly stand it and she had only been inside for thirty minutes at most. How had she ever survived hours upon hours at these things in London?

The strings started up again, couples clamoring for space amongst the lines of dancers. Their excitement, and the excitement of her cousin Augusta amongst them, was palpable, but Evelyn shared in none of it.

I do not wish to be here.

She never should have agreed to attend. She had known even days ago that attending a ball would be the purest form of torture, just as it had been during her disaster of a season. In reality, it managed to be even worse than London. In London she hadn't nursed the memories of waltzing with Gabriel, or of the night that had followed.

"I don't think I've ever had this much fun!" Augusta twirled off the dancefloor to Evelyn's side in a flurry of lavender skirts.

She had been more lively and cheerful since they'd arrived in Bath. Each party, even the small ones, seemed to bring her farther from the catty, vindictive girl who had left in the carriage from Porthaven.

Effervescent, Evelyn thought. Augusta seemed effervescent since coming to Bath.

Finally seeing something of the world outside her city is treating her well.

"I do not understand how you can stand there on the sidelines, all dull and boring."

And like that, the Augusta of Porthaven was back.

"I am not in the mood for dancing," Evelyn muttered. "Besides, it is not something I am partial to."

"You seemed partial enough, dancing with Mr. Stone."

Evelyn whirled on her. She had yet to unleash her ire from the other day on Augusta. She hadn't been ready to reopen those wounds when they hadn't even begun to scab over.

"Do not speak his name," she hissed acerbically.

Augusta stepped back at the vehemence in her voice and the anger no doubt simmering in her eyes. For the first time, Evelyn saw a flicker of doubt slip across her young cousin's face.

"I do not see what your problem is," Augusta said haltingly.

Evelyn could not control herself. She stalked towards the girl like a woman possessed.

She didn't know if Augusta had truthfully ruined anything at all with her pettiness. It was possible Gabriel wouldn't have forgiven her lies even if she had come clean to him herself.

But she had to believe the man she had fallen in love with would have listened if she'd just been honest with him without her cousin's heavy hand.

So yes, she blamed Augusta. And she was angry. So very angry—angry at Augusta, angry at Gabriel, angry at herself.

And she *hurt*.

She had been embarrassed, humiliated, truly mortified when Nigel had rejected her so publicly, but she had never hurt like this. She wanted to press her hands to her chest, as if her heart might fall out from behind her ribcage if she did nothing to stop it.

"You have been thoughtless and ill-mannered since I arrived in Porthaven. But what you did—" her words caught in her throat, and she commanded herself not to cry.

Do not become overwrought.

She peered around at the shimmering young ladies and elegantly dressed men. It was a pretty veneer, but it was thin and brittle, and it hid a cask of poison underneath.

It will do you no good. Not in this nest of vipers.

"All I did was tell him the truth," Augusta insisted. "You were the one lying to him, playing games." She stamped her foot.

Evelyn had the uncharitable and uncharacteristic urge to pull her hair. Instead, she fisted her hands in her skirts. Augusta leaned closer, putting herself dangerously within Evelyn's reach.

"*You* said he mentioned marriage. What were you going to do when he made a true offer? What then?"

Evelyn's shoulders slumped and the fight went out of her. She was tired.

The ballroom was suffocating, the walls feeling like they weighed upon her, but it didn't pull her back to London, and she wasn't thinking about Nigel or the discomfort he had caused her.

"I was going to tell him," she whispered. "And I was going to accept. I had already accepted."

Augusta looked at her wide-eyed, mouth parted in shock. She clearly hadn't expected that reply to come from Evelyn's lips.

"What—But how—" she spluttered, then shook her head, composing herself. She scoffed. "The Earl of Sampford was never going to agree to your marrying a tradesman."

"My parents know. I had spoken with Mamma already, and she spoke with my father."

Evelyn touched her hands to her temples. The heightened emotion she had been carrying around for days was giving her a headache.

She looked back at Augusta, the girl's face shifting somewhere from obstinate to stricken.

Good, Evelyn thought. *Let her feel the weight of what she's done.*

"They had already accepted this," she clarified.

Gabriel prowled his study like a caged beast, too wild for captivity and ready to pounce on any unsuspecting fool who disturbed him.

That fool ended up being Lord Hilgrave, who forced his way into Gabriel's office to sprawl across a sofa with a book and a knowing smirk.

"What are you here for?" Gabriel finally snapped, when Theodore had continued doing nothing but stare at the pages of his book for longer than must be necessary, or reasonable.

"Lady troubles?" his friend asked with a wink as he snapped the book shut.

Gabriel scoffed and rolled his eyes. For once, the motion did not send daggers piercing between his eyes. He had foregone drink for the past day and could at least claim a clear head if not a clear conscience.

"Despite what the gossips might claim, I have no designs on Lady Gilbert," Gabriel growled, knowing full well he was being obtuse on purpose and that Teddy could see straight through him. "And," he continued, "any hope and longing in that regards are troubles of my aunt's, not my own."

Teddy laughed but shook his head at Gabriel.

"I wasn't talking about Jane Gilbert."

"Then what are you on about?" he grumbled.

"Oh, I don't know. Perhaps a certain young lady you were waltzing with at the assembly."

"There is nothing between us at all to speak about," he insisted firmly, but Teddy continued to look at him with that condescending smirk plastered across his face.

"Yes. Lady troubles, indeed."

"She lied to me, Teddy." Gabriel finally broke. "The whole time."

Lord Hilgrave frowned. "The whole time you danced?"

He was intentionally goading him, and Gabriel fought the urge to hit the man. It was an urge that became more difficult to ignore the more Theodore seemed intent on riling him up.

"For weeks, Teddy. *Months.* She let me think she was someone else entirely, for months." Gabriel shook his head in renewed disgust and resumed his pacing. "She is a *lady* and her father is an *earl.*"

He spit it like an accusation—like *lady* and *earl* were naughty words that could get him in trouble.

"Yes, the Earl of Sampford, if I remember correctly."

Gabriel spun to face him, eyes bright with his volatile emotions. Teddy tapped his chin, staring off far away, as if deep in thought.

"You knew?"

"Yes, well, you do recall that I spent the early parts of the season in London this year. I recognized her almost immediately at that assembly ball, though it took a moment to place her." Teddy laughed. "I never thought I'd see her dancing a waltz, least of all with you. It quite threw me."

"Well, it's over and done with."

"Why?" he asked, incredulous.

"She lied to me!"

"It wasn't such a very big lie."

Gabriel looked at him in exasperation.

Lord Hilgrave had an answer for everything it seemed. Though all of his answers were of the infuriating *so what* variety.

"You know how I feel about dishonesty, especially after that debacle with Jane. I will not be another second-place suitor, passed over when a better option comes along."

"You know, the two of you might have more in common than you think," Teddy muttered.

"We have nothing in common," he grunted, feeling more defensive than he had at the beginning of this conversation. "She lied about who she is. I asked her to marry me, and she *still* lied. How can I possibly trust her now?"

Theodore let out a low whistle as he took in the magnitude of what Gabriel was saying.

"Alright fine. It was a fairly sizable lie. But is it such a terrible surprise to find out? Here you thought she would come from nothing, and instead you find out she's the daughter of an earl. Some men would consider that good luck!"

"Some men are fools," Gabriel countered,

"And you are certainly not a fool," Teddy quipped.

Gabriel sighed and raked a restless hand through his hair.

"It feels like the last time, all over again."

Theodore shook his head.

"She isn't Jane, Gabriel. For starters, she's a grown woman and Jane was just a girl."

"She's practically the same age as Jane was then!"

Theodore chuckled, though there wasn't much humor in his voice.

"Do you know how young these nobs marry their daughter's off? She's practically an old maid to that lot."

Gabriel scoffed. "That's utterly ridiculous."

"Like it or not, it's the truth. Even if her parents didn't force her out in society at an exceedingly young age, she's still been through several seasons of rejection, at least." Theodore looked at him like he stared into his soul, gauging the weight with which his words struck him. "I imagine that sort of thing, and the looming threat of spinsterhood, matures a person rather quickly. And besides, she'd never run off with any Sir Gilbert." Theodore laughed. "He'd hardly be suitable company for her, even if she were an old maid."

Gabriel let out a snort in surprised disbelief at what his friend had just said. It was a pointless argument.

"And what does that make me?"

"Precisely," Teddy countered. "And she was willing to marry you anyway!"

Gabriel sighed and moved to the large, wide-backed chair across from Theodore. He sank into it with such force the wooden legs groaned.

"Was she though?"

His friend gave him a quelling look. He knew he was being petulant now, but he didn't want to be told it.

"Fine. Perhaps she was willing to marry me. That still doesn't make me her preference. It's the same as Jane."

"You've absolutely no proof of that," Teddy insisted. "Besides, she doesn't need anyone else to make her a lady. She was born into it."

"Yes, I know. What exactly are you getting at?"

Theodore turned thoughtful a moment, as if considering something he hadn't thought of earlier. It made Gabriel nervous.

"Well, I suppose she could trade up for a Marquess or something. Even a Viscount would be better than a Mister, wouldn't he?"

Gabriel choked on a self-deprecating laugh.

"Thanks, Teddy. That makes me feel so much better."

"No but think about it."

"I'm trying not to."

"Never mind all that," he said with a dismissive wave of his hand. "My point is, she has far more prospects than Jane Thomas ever did, and still she picked your sorry self."

"Or so she claimed," Gabriel reminded him, unable to let go of his fear that one lie might well hide another.

"Well, how did she seem when you showed up in Bath? Unannounced, I might add."

Gabriel opened his mouth to snap out something caustic, and fueled by the angry memory of Bath, but paused. It would be a lie to say there hadn't been fear in her eyes when he'd leveled his worst glare at her, but he couldn't say what that fear was of. Did she fear him finding out and being angry with her, or her family finding out about her terrible, low-class secret.

How had she looked before he'd tried to intimidate her?

When she had rushed to him down the pavement that lined the Royal Crescent. When she had tried to *stop him* from leaving.

She smiled at me.

"Happy, I think?"

"Is that a question?" Teddy laughed.

"I don't know."

Teddy nodded sagely, as though this was still the answer he'd expected, and Gabriel was helpfully proving his point for him.

Perhaps he was.

"Not ashamed then?" he asked. "Or terrified? Not desperately trying to hide you away or run you off?"

No.

He had shown up completely unexpectedly, had knocked on her door without invitation, and threatened to expose everything between them to her people.

"Well?" Teddy prodded.

"No."

"Hmm. Imagine that."

Being happy to see me doesn't mean she would have actually married me. And the fear was still there, even in the way she had called my name.

"That still doesn't mean she had any intention of honoring the agreement between us. An agreement that no one knew about. It's hardly enforceable."

Lord Hilgrave winced, and his face turned serious. It was a look Gabriel was unused to seeing on his friend's typically blithe features. Teddy frowned, looking as though he was reluctant to share whatever he was going to say next, and Gabriel couldn't for the life of him imagine why that would be.

"As to that, I'm fairly confident when I say she would not have broken any engagement between the two of you, no matter if it was officially recognized or not."

Chapter Twenty-Five

"**I** don't know how you can possibly make a statement like that. You do not even know her."

"No, but you do. Does she seem the fickle sort to you? And I mean really. Not through some distorted lens of hurt."

Gabriel didn't answer. He didn't have to. He knew Teddy could see the answer on his face and in the way his shoulders settled down, as if all of the puffed-up anger had been drained from his body,

"I know it wasn't right of her to lie to you for so long, but did you consider she may have had a fair reason for giving a false name in the first place?"

"And how do you suppose that?"

"Don't forget, I spent a fair bit of time in London. I'm quite aware of all the most sensational gossip."

"Sensational gossip?" he choked. The two words could never be paired with Evelyn's name. "Evelyn is not the type to be associated with *gossip*. She is too—" he floundered for the word, "good."

"Yes well, London society doesn't hold the same standards as you."

Gabriel frowned, not liking the turn this conversation had taken. No matter if she had lied to him, Evelyn was too honest and decent for there to be gossip about her. But the absurdity of it didn't make the suggestion anger him any less.

"I would watch what you say, Teddy. You are dangerously close to insulting her character and I won't have it."

"Oh, it isn't her character that's at fault. Not in *that* sense, at least."

Gabriel jumped to his feet, his earlier anger at Evelyn quickly replaced by anger at the implication in Teddy's words.

"There is *nothing* at fault with her."

"Except for her lying to you?"

Gabriel didn't acknowledge him. He was breathing heavily now, incensed at the mere thought of anyone maligning Evelyn's name.

He didn't question the way his ire jumped so easily to Lord Hilgrave. It was like he was desperate to shield her from his emotions, however he could. Even if it was only by shifting his focus, and now the bubbling anger at her lies that he had been feeding for days was fully directed at his friend—and, apparently, every member of London high society.

Teddy continued as if he hadn't noticed the rising tide of Gabriel's mood.

"Surely you have noticed that she's not quite like other young ladies, Gabriel? She isn't exactly normal."

How dare he?

"She is perfectly normal. Better than normal."

"She's bookish, Gabriel."

He looked at Theodore, affronted. So what if Evelyn was *bookish*. Who cared? He certainly didn't. Hell, if she hadn't been so damned bookish, he might not have had his chance to meet her.

"You say that as if it's a bad thing."

"In London it is a bad thing," Theodore snapped, exasperated.

He seemed tired with Gabriel for not already understanding the capricious whims of the *ton*. They were whims Gabriel would gladly *never* understand.

"She is a socially awkward bluestocking who spends more time glued to the wall than talking or dancing, and couldn't land a husband if she paid him!"

"How dare you?" Gabriel growled, his voice dangerously low.

Theodore put his hands up in surrender.

"I am just telling you what everyone else says!"

"Then they are idiots, the lot of them."

"I do not disagree with you there," Teddy muttered beneath his breath.

"It is preposterous. Absolute rubbish!"

"Yes, well regardless. It's what they all said. And that was before the *incident*."

Gabriel felt his insides go cold at the way Theodore said that. What on earth could have happened to make matters worse than her peers saying such nasty things about her?

"What incident?"

Theodore winced, not for the first time since he'd begun, and now looked truly reluctant to go on.

"There was a young gentleman. A vile little toad," Teddy grumbled. "It seems the fiend quite shamelessly strung her along while courting another girl."

"What?" Gabriel could hardly understand what Theodore was saying.

"I was there when it all came out in the open. She confronted him after word came out about his *engagement* of all things, and he proved a right rotten scoundrel."

Gabriel could feel his blood boiling.

"Set her down most viciously," Teddy added. "He made it out as if she had conjured the whole thing up between them, though the rumor mill certainly didn't stop there."

"They've questioned her innocence?" Gabriel bit out.

"Not exactly," Teddy said, shaking his head. "It has been suggested that she—*perhaps*—would have been better off trapping the man in marriage." Theodore's voice had gotten so small it was barely audible in the face of Gabriel's rage. "Since she is so unlikely to find a match otherwise."

Gabriel would find the man and plant his fist in his face.

But Theodore was still speaking, as if it were possible for there to be more—for it to get worse.

"It turns out, the lordling's father had all but cut him off for his staggering gambling problem, and he had needed a wealthy backup in case his first choice of bride fell through, so to speak."

"I do not think I understand," Gabriel said and swallowed hard.

I have been kissed before. But not properly, because the villain had only wanted her money. *And the connection to a title,* he realized.

Christ.

"I'll say it plain, Gabriel. Lord Nigel Sedley let Evelyn think he loved her, secretly courted her, wooed her—just so he could pocket her dowry if the other girl's family balked at his increasing debts," Theodore said. "He humiliated her, Gabriel. In front of all society—every single one of her peers. And he was unspeakably cruel about it. He made her a laughingstock. They said vile things about her behind her back, and worse things when they knew she could hear. They are still talking about it," he grumbled.

"Fuck," he bit out.

Gabriel stalked to the window, slamming his hands against the casing to stare sightlessly outside. All he could see was the hazy impression of Evelyn's stricken face swimming in his vision.

"Fuck."

Teddy nodded his agreement with that sentiment.

"I've made a mess of this, haven't I?" Gabriel asked.

Teddy sighed. "You, my dear friend, cannot help but get in your own way."

Gabriel pushed off from the window and turned. "I should go to her." He frowned. "If she will even see me."

Lord Hilgrave rose from his seat to clap a hand on Gabriel's shoulder. "That same rashness is what got you into trouble in the first place," he reminded him.

"I cannot just sit here doing nothing!" He burned with frustration. Gabriel cast around himself as if the room would present the answer to him.

"Write to her," Theodore suggested.

I will write to her. He could only hope it would be enough. *And if it isn't I will* walk *to Bath if I must and beg her to speak to me.*

Drops of rain tracked down the drawing room window, painting a lattice of rivulets that blurred the parkland outside. Evelyn dropped her forehead to the open book at her face, the pages tickling against her brow.

She hadn't read more than a page, and if she had, she certainly hadn't absorbed any of it. She might as well have spent the morning slouched uselessly across the settee, in a trance.

"You are still like this."

Evelyn hadn't heard anyone come in and she started, snapping the book closed suddenly, letting it fall to her lap. She looked up in surprise.

Augusta.

She was not the person she wanted to see just then, and she was the last person she expected would seek her out. They hadn't spoken since Evelyn had lashed at her at the Partridge ball. It had been nearly a week.

"I would like to be alone."

Augusta shifted in the doorway, her slipper scuffing the ground. She looked uncomfortable in Evelyn's presence.

Good.

It was an uncharitable thought, but Evelyn could do nothing to stop it. She knew she was at fault for lying to Gabriel in the first place, but she still harbored resentment towards her cousin that she could not put aside. Not yet.

"I just wanted to say—" Augusta halted, frowning, then spoke in a pained rush. "I understand if you do not wish to speak to me ever again."

Evelyn loosed an agitated sigh at her cousin's dramatics. Even in her apology, Augusta managed to make herself sound mistreated.

"And I would have every right," Evelyn snapped.

"I know."

Evelyn watched the rain cascade down the window. It had gotten stronger, and wind whistled at the glass.

This is not entirely her fault.

Gabriel might have reacted similarly if he'd heard the truth from Evelyn's lips. She just wished she'd had the chance to try for herself.

You had many chances.

It was a truth she didn't like to think about but one that haunted her nonetheless—that she had brought this upon herself.

"I am feeling snappish, and I am taking it out on you," Evelyn acknowledged. It was still just short of an apology, but it was the most she could manage at the moment.

Augusta clasped her hands in front of her but did not leave the outline of the doorway. Evelyn didn't think she could look more uncomfortable.

"Tell me whatever it is you want to say." She gestured to the seat across from her.

Augusta froze, going more rigid if it was possible. She teetered between entering the room and running to hide behind her veneer of smug disdain.

"I promise to listen," Evelyn said.

Augusta took her chances with Evelyn and accepted the offered seat.

"I didn't mean to hurt you," she said, then looked at her hands with a heavy sigh. "No, I suppose I did mean to hurt you. But I did not realize what I was doing."

It was more honesty than Evelyn had expected. Augusta frowned down at her hands, as if struggling to puzzle out what to think—the words to say.

"I didn't think I was doing any real damage," she confessed. "It seemed more like a game." Augusta winced. "That sounds far worse than I meant it."

She looked up pleadingly at Evelyn. "I just mean— It never occurred to me that you might be *serious* about him.

About a future with him."

"Why is that so difficult to believe?" Evelyn asked, exasperated.

It was the same she had heard from her aunt, and clearly a sentiment shared by *Mrs.* Harding, if Augusta was expressing it now.

"He has no title, no connections. No family."

"He has sisters."

Augusta huffed. "That is not what I mean, and you know it. He does not come from a *good* family—not by your standards anyway."

"What do you know about my standards?" Evelyn asked baldly. "Do you think I care for the expectations of the *ton?*"

I have spent nearly 24 years caring little for what people think and suddenly, I supposedly care more for a blasted social hierarchy than anything else?

"You are the daughter of an *earl.* You are meant to marry your equal. Or at least someone with a title."

"Yes, well, I have not had much luck with those," Evelyn muttered.

Augusta looked at her quizzically. "Is that what you like about him?" She seemed genuinely curious.

That he is not a lord? Evelyn laughed.

"No. Although, perhaps somewhat," she corrected. "I like that he does not have the same biases and preoccupations as the men in London." She smiled softly. "Mostly though, he just makes me happy."

"Mamma," Evelyn called as she descended the stairs to the ground floor.

It was late enough that her mother would have quitted her bedroom, and early still that she might find her in the morning room. She moved down the hall towards the back of the residence, her feet gaining speed as she came closer.

Why must this house be so large.

"Mamma!" she called again. She was beginning to feel breathless.

She heard the clatter of cup against saucer from the morning room and her mother's call of "Evelyn," from within. She stopped with a hand gripping the doorway when she reached the morning room.

"I must go to Porthaven," she panted. "Immediately."

Chapter Twenty-Six

"**I** thought you wished to stay in Bath longer."

Yet Lady Sampford did not look remotely surprised at her daughter's sudden outburst.

"I lied about seeing him when he came to Bath. I did see him." She was still breathing heavily. "I saw him, and we fought terribly."

"Oh, dear," her father said from behind his newspaper. She hadn't even noticed him when she'd first come in. "Why didn't you tell us?"

Evelyn looked up at the ceiling. "I do not know." She was just as lost trying to understand what she had been thinking as they were. "I was upset and embarrassed."

"What was the fight over?" her mother asked.

She fidgeted uncomfortably. She had told her mother a little of what she had hidden from Gabriel, but she didn't know if her father knew. It terrified her to admit when she was already ashamed of how much she had muddled everything.

"I already know about *Miss Price*," her father said.

"Yes, well, he does now too."

"And he did not react well to you telling him?" he asked.

Evelyn winced. "I was not the one to tell him."

Her father gave her a wide-eyed look of understanding. Her mother stifled a groan behind her hand.

"Needless to say, it was received even worse than I could have imagined, having come from someone else."

"And that is why he left," her father concluded.

Evelyn nodded.

"You wish to return to Porthaven so that you may speak with him?" her mother asked.

"Yes."

Lady Sampford gave her a gentle, pitying look. "He still may not wish to listen."

"I do not think he will be completely opposed to hearing me now."

"You are sure?" her mother asked, concern etched across her brow.

Evelyn flushed and held up the packet of folded pages she held in her hand.

"Oh," her mother exclaimed.

Evelyn had very nearly forgotten she held them herself.

"I have not been able to bring myself to open any of them," she admitted. "But he has written to me."

Lord Sampford gave an impressed chuckle. "He has written quite a bit, hasn't he?"

A small smile tipped her lips. "I would like to leave as soon as possible."

They arrived in Porthaven in late afternoon. The rain had let up enough that Evelyn didn't risk a soaking by stepping out of the carriage, though mud still lapped at her hem. It splashed beneath her boot as she turned to look back inside the vehicle.

"I can have the carriage take you to Linden Street first," she said. "You do not have to wait for me."

Augusta shook her head. "Just don't forget that I am down here," she teased.

Evelyn gave her a broad smile before turning to the building she knew housed Gabriel's offices. She drew in a steadying breath when she stared up at the large wooden door, preparing herself to knock and make herself known.

The last time she had been here under very different circumstances. She peered up at the partially obscured window, remembering the view from the other side and felt her face heat at the memory that accompanied it.

I should have insisted Augusta go home.

"Good afternoon," an older man with kind eyes greeted when he opened the door.

"I am here for Mr. Stone. Can you tell him Miss Price is here to see him."

The man's face fell as he apologized. "I am sorry Miss. He is not here."

"Oh."

She hadn't been certain where she would find him, but still she felt dejected. It was late enough in his workday that she had thought this would be the best place to start.

"He had something to see to down at the warehouses. It shouldn't be more than an hour before he returns," the man continued. "I can tell him that you called. Does he have your address?"

She nodded and gave her thanks before trudging back to the carriage.

"What happened?" Augusta asked. "If he will not see you, I swear I will take that book of yours to his head."

"No," Evelyn laughed. "Not the book, please."

The two had gone from shaky truce to something closer to amiability during the carriage ride from Bath. Evelyn was sure the hope that reading Gabriel's letters had filled her with had helped her acceptance of Augusta's remorse. It had positively buoyed her.

"He is at the warehouses. I was told he will return within an hour."

"Should we wait for him? It's not like the carriage is going anywhere without you."

Evelyn shook her head but did not give the driver direction yet—considering. She didn't want to delay seeing Gabriel any longer than she already had. It had been over a week since they'd quarreled.

"No. We will not wait here. We will go find him."

Franklin looked up from his desk when Gabriel walked in and peered at him over his spectacles when he thumped the stack of ledgers and documents he held down on the wooden surface.

"Does this mean you've *finally* managed to look these over?" he asked with a quirked brow.

Gabriel grunted at the man's smirk. He blithely wondered if other men were plagued with such constant impertinence.

First Theodore and now Mr. Little.

He rubbed a hand across the back of his neck. Although Teddy might have been right to goad him as he'd done. Gabriel didn't know if he would have been driven to reason without the man's bothersome provocation.

"I have finally looked at them," he conceded, then grumbled, "I have had little else to read."

He had not received so much as a word from Evelyn.

He knew Miss Harding had not returned from Bath, so it stood to reason Evelyn was there still as well. It was not as if she was on the other side of world that she would not have received his letters or had the chance to write back. And he had written to her nearly every day since the first.

At this point, he would have been happy to receive a mere *Go away!* from her.

Anything would be better than this silence.

Franklin made a clearing sound in his throat and Gabriel realized he had been standing unflinchingly, and likely expressionless, at the edge of his desk.

"I came to see if there have been any updates to these registers," Gabriel said, the last few words drowned out by the slam of Mr. Little's door as it swung open.

"Where is he, Little?" Albon Evans demanded as he stomped into the room. He looked at Gabriel, as shocked as if he had struck him. "You!"

"What can I do for you, Evans?"

"You damned scoundrel!" Gabriel had never seen Albon so riled. "What can you do for me?" His voice rose in volume and pitch as he stalked into the room. *"What can you do for me?"*

Gabriel put his hands up in joking defense. He could not imagine what had gotten Albon in such a sulk, but he was hardly intimidated as the man huffed a furious breath and tossed an errant gold curl from his eyes.

"You, Mr. Stone, can tell me where Henry Watkins has gone to."

That gave Gabriel pause and wiped the smirk from his face. "Henry Watkins is being held in your warehouse," he stated. "You were the one with a locked room to hold him until—" he trailed off.

"Yes," Albon agreed, nodding. *"Until the magistrate came."*

Fuck.

Now Gabriel's raised hands were in supplication.

Fuck fuck fuck. How did I forget this?

"I was irritated when I thought he was late. But he isn't late, is he Gabriel?"

Gabriel drove his fingers into the hair at the top of his

head, raking them through the strands in furious strokes.

Fuck.

"I will send for him immediately." He turned to Mr. Little. "Franklin, pen something to the magistrate now. Have it sent out right away."

"Of course."

"Tell me, Gabriel. What good will the magistrate do if he has no suspect when he gets here?"

The rest of Albon's words sank in.

Tell me where Henry Watkins has gone to.

"What have you done?" Gabriel whispered.

"I have not done anything!" Albon snapped. "*You* did not do the one thing you were supposed to do, and now Henry Watkins is roaming Porthaven."

Shame at his behavior since Bath washed over him, coupled with anger and frustration at the idea that Watkins had escaped Albon's hold. And threaded through was the fear of what would happen if the man crossed paths with Evelyn.

Again.

That thought hit him with sickening clarity—that *Henry Watkins* had been the man who'd threatened horrible things to her in that warehouse.

It sent him into a searing rage.

Thank God she is in Bath.

It was his only consolation.

"You let him escape?" he barked as he advanced on Albon.

Evans had gone from belligerent to defensive in the moment of a heartbeat.

"I did not! If the magistrate had been here when he was meant to be, he never would have managed to get out."

"You were meant to hold him *until* the magistrate arrived. How late he is is immaterial!"

"I was only supposed to deal with this for a few days! Dammit, Gabriel. He was locked in a damned storage room. It isn't exactly bloody Newgate."

Gabriel felt a growl of frustration build in his throat and spun back around to prowl back towards Franklin. He put his back to the desk, leaning his weight against it.

All of that work and he is out there, free.

"What of his accomplices?" Gabriel asked, voice low.

"They are still accounted for."

"Because Talbot can keep track of two men better than you can handle one," Gabriel bit out.

"If you thought Stewart Talbot was so much better than me, why didn't you have *him* watch the bastard?" Albon sneered.

Franklin coughed. Gabriel and Albon turned to look at him.

"Am I still writing to the magistrate?" he asked.

"Are you sure you wish to get out here?" Augusta asked as she peered out the carriage window.

The sun had slipped enough in the sky that the tall warehouse buildings obstructed a good deal of its light already. Evelyn tapped the roof to signal the driver let her out. She could see down a shadowed alleyway when the door swung open, and she shuddered as she recalled the last time she'd been here.

I cannot think about that.

"I will be fine," she insisted, more for her own benefit than Augusta's.

She stepped down from the carriage, her already soiled skirts swaying against the dirt beneath her feet. The coachman looked around with some concern, his face expressing the same reservations Augusta had already voiced.

"Are you certain about this my lady?"

She had become accustomed to being treated like anyone else in Porthaven—no extra protections, no coddling, no deference to her family's title.

"David, I will be alright." She smiled at her father's driver.

There was no *John Coachman* for Lord Sampford. He preferred to speak to a man as a man, regardless of his station, and had instilled the same mores in his children.

And I was worried he wouldn't approve of Gabriel? she wondered.

But there was a difference between respecting one's staff and allowing one's daughter to marry beneath her station. It was the sort of thing that would take a driving force to overcome for most men.

Evelyn smiled to herself. She did not think of herself as above his station. And Gabriel Stone was a driving force unto himself.

It was only after she had walked past a row of big brick buildings that Evelyn realized she had not had David deliver her in front of *Gabriel's* warehouse. She fought to think of the direction she had been given, and peered around in an attempt to make the chaos of lanes and buildings make sense.

Please tell me I am not completely lost.

She turned to peek over her shoulder at where the carriage still waited. The sky continued to darken. She didn't want to go back in defeat. If she didn't find Gabriel's warehouse now, she would be obliged to return to Linden Street to try again in the morning.

I need to see him now.

A laugh echoed from somewhere before her and she whipped her head back to the path in front of her. A rough dressed man was blocking her way, a feral grin twisting his already cruel features.

I know him.

Her pulse quickened and she took a hasty step back.

Oh God. I know him.

"I—I was just leaving," she mumbled, taking another step. Then another.

His laugh darkened as his eyes narrowed, and he advanced towards her. He moved quite quickly for such a big man.

Evelyn screamed as his hand fell on her wrist, fingers clasping around until she struggled against his grip. His other arm came out to lash about her waist as he corralled her towards an alley.

"As much as I enjoy those lovely screams, *quiet,*" he snapped in her ear. He stroked a finger down her cheek. "I would hate to ugly your pretty face."

She clamped her mouth shut as a fearful sob fought its way from her throat.

"Evelyn!"

She heard Augusta's shout from far away and the pounding of distant footfalls as her cousin and David both saw what was happening.

But she was dragged into the basketweave of alleyways before either could reach her.

Chapter Twenty-Seven

"You do not need to do this," she stuttered as the man swung them into an abandoned building behind a heavy, brick warehouse.

He pulled a chair away from one of the walls and thrust her against it.

"Henry, please," she tried again.

He chuckled darkly as he yanked her arms behind her, the force of it making her shoulders scream in complaint.

"I haven't decided what I'm going to do with you just yet," he muttered as he tied a length of rope around her wrists.

She fought against the bonds, trying to pull her arms at least away from the chair back, but they would not budge. He had threaded the rope through the slats in the chair somehow.

"I spied you with that bastard Stone," Henry said. "And I know he's the reason I was caged up in the first place."

He spoke more to himself than to her as he paced before her. Then his eyes slammed into hers, the savage glint there making her press herself against the back of the chair, as if she could retreat and get away.

He pointed a dirty finger at her. "Which means *you* told him things," he accused.

He took a slow step towards her.

"You squealed, didn't you."

There was no question in his unhinged voice. He looked wild, crazed.

He's the reason I was caged up.

"Did—" Evelyn swallowed. "Did Mr. Stone arrest you?"

He snarled. "All but clapped me in irons," he spat. "For that, he needs to pay."

Think, Evelyn. Say something—anything.

"I don't see how keeping me here will help with that. Mr. Stone doesn't even know I'm in Porthaven."

Henry tossed his head back with the force of his laugh.

"Doesn't know you're in Porthaven? How dense do you think I am?"

"I mean it! I was gone for nearly two weeks. I only arrived back today," she insisted.

He looked at her contemplatively, his teeth gnashing as he weighed his options.

"It hardly matters," he finally said with a shake of his head. "He'll know eventually." He smiled at her cruelly. "And then he will suffer."

"Where will you go now?" Albon asked as they exited Gabriel's warehouse.

"To Stewart—see if the other two know anything about where Watkins might be holed up."

"You think they'll tell you?"

Gabriel gritted his teeth. *They had better.*

"No honor amongst thieves," he bit out.

"Mr. Stone!"

He turned surprised eyes down the street to see Miss Harding and a man he did not recognize racing for him.

"Mr. Stone, it's Evelyn," she gasped as she reached him.

"What do you mean?" he asked, fear gripping his chest at the look on her face.

She said no more, just shook her head, hardly able to catch her breath. He turned to the man, dressed in what looked like a coachman's livery.

"What has happened?"

"Lady Evelyn has been taken, sir."

His vision went black and then red, and he thought he might have gone blind as everything seemed to still around him.

"What do you mean taken?" It was Albon who finally spoke while Gabriel rasped another breath.

"You are Mr. Stone?" the driver asked him, and Gabriel managed a nod. "I drove the young ladies here to look for *you*, I believe. I didn't like her walking out here alone, but she insisted."

"Someone snatched her from the street!" Augusta cried, finally finding her voice. "Who would do such a thing?"

Gabriel's insides went cold. He had an idea of the type of man who would do something like this. The type of man who had recently escaped imprisonment and likely held a grudge against him and Evelyn both.

Henry Watkins.

He had tried to hurt her once before, had scared her more than Gabriel could ever reconcile in his mind.

He thought of that night in the park, when he had spotted Henry in the dark. The man had taken one look at Evelyn and sneered at Gabriel like he had found his one weakness.

He did, he admitted.

"Watkins did this," he said to Albon and the other man hissed in a breath.

"I can show you where he took her from," the driver said. "I just couldn't find where they might have gone to."

Gabriel nodded, already following the man back the way he had come. "The alleys behind the warehouses can be mazelike."

He turned back a moment to Evans. "You go to Talbot. See if he has any useful information. And if he does," he pointed a finger at the man, "bring as many men as you can. Henry Watkins is a wild card. I will not have her getting injured because of that cretin."

Evans nodded and rushed in the other direction.

"Miss Harding." Gabriel turned to the girl. "The two of

you will show me where Miss Price—*Lady Evelyn*—went, and then you will both wait with the carriage."

Miss Harding nodded nervously.

"This way," said the coachman.

Henry paced in front of her like a beast.

Or a madman.

She tried her bonds again, but the rope would not budge. She could not even find the slightest bit of give in the knots.

"You can still let me go," she whispered.

Henry wheeled around on her and Evelyn winced, wishing she had kept her mouth shut. It was better when he didn't level his crazed focus on her.

"No, no, no," he repeated.

He crouched in front of her so that his face was in front of hers. He laughed when the chair legs tapped at the floor as she tried to put distance between them. He reached a hand to grasp the chair back, putting his face inches from her own.

"Understand this, girl," he snarled. "There is no letting you go. Right now, I am deciding if I want to play with you now or wait until after I've got that lout Stone where I want him."

The breath froze in her chest, and he grinned at her discomfort. She tried to look away, but he gripped her chin in a painful hold.

"He'll be looking for me already by now, I reckon," he drawled. "I'm sure those idiots Talbot's got locked up will have talked by now."

He grinned as if the prospect of being given up by his accomplices excited him.

"Then you know you won't get away with this."

His grin grew wider. "Stone won't do a damned thing once he knows I've got you."

He traced a finger down her face again, but this time the trail didn't stop at her jaw. His touch ran down the side of her throat, and then farther.

She whimpered in panic when his hand harshly cupped her breast. Then he suctioned his mouth to her throat in a lewd mimicry of passion. She gagged at the revulsion swirling in her gut and he bit down hard, making her cry out.

She kicked out and her booted toe connected with his shin. Henry cursed and reeled back from her, a snarl curling his lip as he hissed at her in rage.

Oh God, no.

She shut her eyes as she waited for his raised hand to descend upon her.

The blow never came.

Evelyn squeezed her eyes tighter, worrying it would fall twice as hard when it did. There was a grunt, then a muffled curse. She could hear Henry's labored breathing and a muttered, *"you bastard."*

She allowed herself to open one eye the barest crack, just enough to make out Henry's hunched form squaring off against an even larger adversary.

Her eyes flew open, and her lips parted as she released her

held breath.

He had at least three inches on Henry and was broader across too, and he stood before him with such radiating menace that Evelyn would have cowered had she been under that vicious glare.

"Gabriel," she barely whispered.

Relief flooded her at the sight of him.

He stalked Henry, sizing him up wordlessly, conveying enough hatred with his eyes alone to make speech unnecessary. His gaze didn't stray from the other man, yet Evelyn knew from every shifting muscle and thoughtfully placed step that Gabriel knew she was there. He kept himself carefully situated between Henry and herself—separating them, keeping her safe.

She saw the broken off shaft of wood in Gabriel's hand and the way Henry absently rubbed at his head. There was no question how she had escaped Henry's violence.

She had been lucky. Had Gabriel arrived a moment later, she would have suffered under Henry's blows. Perhaps worse.

Her stomach pitched at the thought, and at the memory of his hands on her body. A shudder ran through her before a flicker caught her eye and she went stiff against her bonds.

She had seen *something*, glinting in the low candlelight— there and then gone. She squinted and leaned to the side as far as she could, trying to see clearly in the creeping shadows that slinked farther across the floor.

Is that—?

The chair teetered with her twisting but still she craned to catch another glimpse of that flickering. The setting sun did little to brighten the room.

Again, Henry shifted his stance and a spark seemed to flare in his outstretched hand. Evelyn's blood ran cold when that flash crystalized into light reflecting off a blade.

I am going to kill him.

Gabriel could picture himself doing it too. It didn't feel like an idle threat when Evelyn was at risk—lashed to a chair, vulnerable, unable to defend herself.

When he'd come in and seen Watkin's raised hand ready to strike, he hadn't even thought. There'd been a discarded beam on the ground, and he'd lifted it on instinct. It looked half rotted but had proved sturdy enough to stun Henry when it had connected with the back of his head.

God, but if I'd been even a second late.

He couldn't even look at her, worried he would lose all advantage over the other man. Right now, he was sure he had the upper hand on Henry, even with his little knife.

The coward.

"I've sent for backup," he told Henry. "Others are on their way. You'll be outnumbered."

They circled slowly, eyes locked, neither willing to let the other from his sight. Henry's sneer didn't go from his face. Nothing seemed to move the man. He was like a caught animal, backed into a corner.

Gabriel narrowed his eyes. It was the one thing that made Henry dangerous.

"I'll be long gone by then."

Gabriel barked a laugh. "I doubt that."

"There'll be nothing to find but a pool of your blood."

He slashed at the air with his blade. Gabriel studied him, waiting for his opening.

He will not get away with this.

The clattering of wood echoed in the barren room, and for a moment Gabriel turned, eyes wide as the chair wobbled on two legs. Evelyn cried out as the seat crashed to the ground. He wanted to go to her, but Henry had looked too, and Gabriel couldn't pass up his chance.

He sped towards him, lunging as he neared, and took the man down at the knees so they tumbled to the ground. The knife Henry held clinked against the floor as it knocked from his hand. Gabriel reached to swat it away, grappling with Henry, who scrambled to reach it first.

Then pain seared his side, like fire burning its way through his gut. He looked down in mute shock at Henry's fist pressed tight against his torso. The man chuckled and Gabriel watched as crimson seeped past the black of his waistcoat to drip down Henry's hand.

Watkins had been faster.

Gabriel stumbled back on his heels, clutching a hand to his side as the knife slipped from his flesh, still gripped in Henry's hand. Somewhere behind him, Evelyn screamed.

A sob ripped from her throat.

No! Gabriel, no!

Her mouth opened without words.

The sounds tearing from her were not human—they were of animalistic torment. Her bones ached and she felt the scratches that lined her arms, but nothing hurt as much as the thought of losing him.

Please, she begged. *I cannot lose him.*

Henry rolled to this side, leveraging himself on one hand to glare at her, breathing heavily. He grimaced at the slick knife in his hand and tossed it across the floor. It clacked against the stone as he leered at her, a sickening smile contorting his features.

Evelyn was still tangled in the loops of rope keeping her bound to the chair. She struggled, trying to free herself, too fearful of what he would do if he reached her. She let out a strangled whimper as she fought futilely to right herself.

Henry bared his teeth like a beast and pushed up onto his knees.

She dragged in a stuttering breath. It was hopeless. There was nowhere to go and no one else to help her. It would be as Henry had said—the others would arrive too late. No one was coming to save her.

She shivered as she stared at the murder in his eyes.

With a crack, Henry was flat on his back—up one moment, pinned to the floor in the next, with Gabriel hunched over his prone form.

"I told you—you will not get away with this," he hissed.

Lost to his own violence, Henry laughed, a bone chilling sound that Evelyn wished she could block out. He shifted and Gabriel grunted in pain, but she couldn't see beyond the unyielding arms that held the other man to the stone floor.

"Close your eyes, Evelyn."

"What?" she breathed, the word half-formed and thin.

Gabriel looked near mad—hair mussed, suit rumpled, eyes wild. He was near enough the light she could see the sweat that dampened his face and that wet mark on his front that seemed to spread as she watched.

Gabriel panted roughly, but he didn't waver. His eyes never left the man's face. It was as if when Henry had struck him, he had unleashed something merciless.

"I said close your eyes," he growled.

He didn't need to look to know Evelyn hadn't listened. He could feel her eyes on him as he pressed Henry Watkins into the floor. There was no need for her to see this. The violence would haunt her.

He shifted his knees, gripping Henry by the shoulders and dragging him with him so he could keep Evelyn at his back. The deranged glint in the man's eyes wavered as he stared up at Gabriel. Something must have shown on his face to get through to him, until Henry could see the dark intent in Gabriel's heart.

He will not get away with this.

Gabriel bracketed him with his knees, keeping him immobile with his weight above him. The movement sent flames licking at his side.

He could already feel the aftereffects of being on the wrong end of a blade, the leak of blood that oozed through the weave of his clothing. It was weakening him.

He blinked back the pain.

When he had tackled Henry the second time, the man had dug his fingers in the wound while he'd tried to buck Gabriel off. Every breath seemed to go right to that gash, leeching his strength along with his blood.

He needed to take care of Henry Watkins now before he collapsed in a useless mess on the floor.

He would be unable to protect her, and the man was unhinged—he would hurt her beyond reason. Albon and the others would never arrive in time.

He kept his eyes on Henry's as he brought his hands down to their rest. He wouldn't allow himself the comfort of escaping the reality of what he did. His hands pressed, fingers tightening around Henry's throat. He would watch the life leave his eyes, no matter the damage it did to his soul.

He shuddered. He would carry the weight of this with him until the end of his days.

I can't let him hurt her.

It was like the moment Evelyn had first smiled at him, the damn he'd kept so tightly sealed against his emotions had strained to burst. She had battered down his walls, blasted the doors off their hinges, and turned him into a man built of desperation and yearning.

He will never hurt her, he vowed.

Chapter Twenty-Eight

Gabriel slumped forward onto his hands, his head hanging low as shuddering breaths wracked his body. Evelyn couldn't see beyond the black wool of his coat, but she knew what lay beyond the wall of his back. She knew it from the resignation in Gabriel's bearing.

"Gabriel," she whimpered.

He heaved a heavy sigh and fell back to sit beside the limp, unmoving body of Henry Watkins.

"He's gone," he whispered.

"Gabriel!" came a shout from the doorway.

Through watery eyes she watched David and a familiar blond-haired man rush through the door.

"My lady!" David cried as he hurried to her side.

She let out a choked sob as he worked to loose her bonds. The other man rushed to Gabriel, who hadn't so much as attempted to rise to his feet. Others raced into the room, but their faces were a blur.

"Gabriel," she cried, scrambling across the floor as the last loop was cast from her skin.

The blond man had helped him out of his jacket and the waistcoat had followed, leaving him in a blood-stained shirt that made her heart clench in her chest to see. He turned a weak smile towards her.

"It looks worse than it is," he assured her.

She nodded but helplessly cast her eyes around her, too frightened to let her sight focus on the evidence of his injury.

I could have lost him.

Evelyn shivered at the blood that stained the floor—the blood that dripped from his sodden shirt. She swayed. She didn't want to see it, would rather look at anything else.

Her gaze fell on the still body staring sightlessly at the rafters and she wailed.

"Cover that up," Gabriel commanded, and one of the men dragged a length of canvas from somewhere to conceal him.

Still, Henry's face would haunt her nightmares.

"Make sure she is okay," Gabriel said, and the other man wavered.

"You are bleeding, Gabriel."

"I'm fine, Albon. Make sure the lady is okay."

Evelyn shook her head and waved the man away. "I am alright. Why won't the bleeding stop?"

Albon peeked again beneath the shirt.

"It has," he told her. "Or at least slowed nearly enough." He looked at Gabriel with a relieved smirk. "He's right when he says it looks worse than it is."

Gabriel shifted closer and gasped a pained breath. "I don't think it is even all mine," he said. "The fool's hand slipped—he was just too frenzied to notice."

He pressed his wadded jacket against his side and peered at Albon. "I'm surprised you dove into the trenches. You'll be scrubbing this mess from your hands for days."

"Gabriel, please." He sounded exasperated with him. "I could hardly leave you to bleed out on the floor."

"I won't bleed out," he muttered.

Albon huffed, a small smile teasing his lips.

"Then I got my hands dirty for nothing."

Gabriel barked a laugh and Evelyn felt a hysterical giggle bubble up in her chest.

We're going to be okay. Oh, thank God. We're going to be okay.

"Evelyn!" Augusta called from the door. She looked around the room, noticing the state of things, the blood. "Goodness," she whispered. Her voice had become suddenly reedy and weak before she slipped to the floor in a flutter of skirts.

"Christ," Gabriel muttered.

"I'll see to her," Albon offered and pushed to his feet. "You are sure you're okay?"

"Go." He stared after the man as he hurried to Augusta.

Augusta was rousing, her swoon lasting no more than the

time it took her to reach the floor. Mr. Evans was at her side in an instant, concern marring his brow as his eyes seemed to scan every bit of her face.

There was a quizzical look in Gabriel's eyes. "I don't think I've ever seen him so *entranced.*"

"You think—? With my cousin?"

He shrugged one shoulder. "Stranger things have happened."

Evelyn smiled at him. They were certainly a stranger thing.

"I suppose her mother would be happy for it."

She looked at the young gentleman as he hovered over her cousin. They certainly made a fine picture.

Gabriel chuckled. "We will find out soon enough."

She looked at him quizzically.

"Mr. Harding returns soon, does he not? I imagine he will convince his wife and daughter of their good fortune once he realizes Mr. Albon Evans has a soft spot for his daughter."

She watched as Augusta righted herself, then gazed up at Mr. Evans.

Augusta might see that good fortune herself already.

She turned back to Gabriel and frowned.

"You are really going to be alright?" she whispered.

He nodded, then looked at her with a solemn bleakness.

"If you'll forgive me for being such a complete ass."

She closed the distance between them, reaching to cup his face in her hand when she was kneeling in front of him.

"I came to ask you to forgive me."

"There is nothing to forgive," he swore. He touched a

finger to her lips when she would have argued. "It doesn't matter if you lied, why you lied, what lies you told. I should have listened. I am so sorry that I didn't listen, Evie."

That name.

She smiled, that name alone feeling like the final signal that things would be well—that they were *safe*.

She pressed her lips against the finger still resting against her mouth. Gabriel sighed and leaned to kiss her but winced and sat back with a curse.

"Damn but that hurts."

"What is this fellow's name who is coming to see Papa?" Edmund asked from his seat near the window.

"Gabriel Stone."

She rolled her eyes. He was just trying to antagonize her. She had told him his name at least three times that morning alone.

"And you are sure you wish to marry him?"

She gave an exasperated sigh and crossed the room to look out at the view of the Crescent. She smacked her brother's arm as she passed.

"Ow!" he complained, reeling from her dramatically.

"You, Edmund, are a pest," she asserted.

"I am just looking out for my little sister," he insisted defensively.

"You are just trying to get under my skin."

"Payback for all the years you pestered *me* as a child," he muttered.

"Edmund Pricewinters!" she exclaimed. "I have never in my *life* been a pest. That is a distinction you alone have the honor of holding."

She laughed and Edmund smiled back. She liked seeing him happy like this, teasing. He was usually so carefree, but the last time she had seen him, when they'd both been at Haythorne House, he had seemed different—distant.

"Is everything alright with you?" she asked with a frown.

It concerned her that he didn't answer straight away.

He stood and joined her at the window gazing out as he swallowed, brow furrowing under the weight of whatever had been plaguing him.

"You know I am always here if you wish to talk," she told him. "Whatever it is."

He shook his head and sighed. "It is nothing."

"If you are sure?"

He smiled, pushing whatever concerns he carried behind him. She wondered if those worries had always been there, and she had never noticed them past that cheerful mask.

"Ah. That is him, is it not?" he asked, drawing her attention to the carriage parked in front of their home, and the tall, masculine figure that emerged.

"He certainly is a rather big man."

She pushed Edmund's shoulder again with a laugh. He turned with a smile and started towards the door.

"Well?" he asked. "Are you coming?"

"He's here to speak with Papa," she reminded him.

Edmund's smile turned impish. "Yes, but we cannot listen

at the door if we stay up here."

She laughed freely and he winked.

Gabriel clasped his arms behind his back. He didn't think he had ever been as nervous as he'd been sitting in the Earl of Sampford's study, asking for the man's blessing to marry his daughter.

He'd been scrutinized, studied—his worth weighed and measured against what standard, he did not know. He released a held breath with a sigh.

But he hadn't been found lacking. That much had been clear when the stiff, starched Lord who had questioned him for what felt like a lifetime, dissolved into a broad grin as he stood to clasp Gabriel's hand and thump his shoulder. He had smiled like giving over his daughter to a mere tradesman made him the happiest man in the world.

Gabriel released another stuck breath. He didn't have the temerity to question it. He was too selfish for that.

Questioning the Earl of Sampford's apparent approval seemed a good way to force reality back into whatever dream world he had entered.

He tugged at his neck cloth and craned to peer down the hall, waiting for Evelyn to join him. If he was being honest, it was all rather intimidating—the house and the people themselves, of course, but the overwhelming acceptance they had bestowed upon him as well.

He huffed a laugh.

If he'd been told a decade ago that one day he would be

here, in an earl's home, ready to officially engage himself to the man's daughter, he would have thought it a ridiculous joke. To think it would be a damned *love match*, he would have said was insane.

A love match.

He thought the words hollowly, almost as if he didn't quite believe them. They were the words the earl had used, the words the countess had used as well.

A love match, for me. With the daughter of an earl.

He laughed again. It was nearly impossible to believe, but it sent butterflies flittering around his stomach, nonetheless.

"Gabriel," he heard from the end of the hall.

He turned to see Evelyn rushing towards him, her feet barely seeming to touch the parquet floors. "How did it go?"

"Well, I think," he said with a bemused shake of his head. "I think your father might actually like me."

"Why do you sound so surprised by that?" She smiled at him in a way that tugged at his chest.

"He is not what I expected," he admitted.

She scrunched her face in contemplation. He wanted to kiss her right there. The only reason he did not was because of his awareness of where they were, and who could spot them at any moment.

"Am I what you expected?"

He smiled at that.

Lady Evelyn Pricewinters was without doubt the farthest thing he would have expected of a *lady* as she could get. He thought of Lady Gilbert, even the preening and simpering of

Miss Harding and her mother.

No, you are not the least bit what I expected.

He stepped closer, becoming less concerned for who might see when she'd become flustered at his nearness. He tipped her chin farther up with the pad of his finger, so he could stare down into her dazed, hooded eyes.

"Who could ever expect perfection?"

Chapter Twenty-Nine

"**I** think I might collapse!" Evelyn exclaimed.

Gabriel swung her into the room with a chuckle, letting the door slam closed behind him.

"Do not fall asleep on me just yet."

His arm banded around her waist, pulling her to him as his mouth descended for a brief but sound kiss. She felt dizzy when he pulled back and she brought her hands to his chest, her fingers pale against the black silk of his waistcoat. The wine had been plentiful at their wedding breakfast. She may have had a glass or two too many.

"You will have to endeavor to keep me awake." She smiled at him slyly, his reaction immediate and fierce.

"Oh, I do not think I will have any problem with that," he

said with a smug grin, then walked her back towards the bed.

His bed. Though she knew he did not wish to be parted from her at night any more than she did.

Our bed, she corrected.

It made her feel rather delirious.

He danced them across the large bedchamber too quickly for her mind to catch up before the backs of her legs hit the mattress.

"I do not know why I am so nervous," she breathed at his cravat. His perfectly crisp, white cravat, with an enormous emerald tucked into its center.

To match your eyes, he had said.

Her fingers trembled where they pressed against his chest. It was not like she was a blushing innocent. Not anymore. Not with this man.

He brought a hand to her neck, his palm warm against the side of her throat as his fingers carded into her hair. He tilted her face to look at him fully.

"Well," his voice was low and rough, "I have never lain with my *wife* before, so I might be a bit nervous myself."

"You do not look nervous."

He grinned. "Perhaps *eager* is a more appropriate word."

That she could well believe.

Gabriel's hands slid to her waist, and he spun her so that her back was to him, her hands finding the bed for balance. She could feel his fingers at the center of her back, feel the loosening pressure of the bodice as he released the line of hidden hooks.

"It would be a shame to ruin such a beautiful gown," he whispered against her neck as he slid the sleeves down her arms.

She shivered at the way his breath washed against her skin, even as his lips never touched her. She gasped as his quick hands began working on the ties of her stays.

It took but a moment before she was undressed, unlaced, and standing in nothing more than what felt like the thinnest shift ever made. She had purchased it wanting to surprise him, entice him. Now she felt worse than nude.

He dragged her back against him with a hand on her belly and she felt as much as heard his inhaled breath. She could feel his arousal too, pressing through the layers of their clothing— the layers of his clothing.

He was far too in control for her liking, when she stood in little more than a wisp of linen. She leaned back into him, paying special care to the heat of him, pressed against her backside. She smiled at his hissed intake of breath and tipped her head back against his shoulder to catch his eye.

"I think you are wearing too many clothes, husband."

The heat of his gaze turned wild and unrestrained, searing her, as a small smile teased the corner of his mouth. He gave a slow shake of his head and gripped her wrists, leaning close as he walked her much smaller hands forward across the bed, until she was stretched out before him. The height of the mattress forced her up onto her toes.

"Say that again." His breath was hot against the back of her neck.

"You are wearing too many clothes."

"No." He inhaled the scent of her skin. "The other one."

"Husband?" she murmured.

He groaned and pressed his weight against her, rocking his hips so that she felt the hard ridge of his arousal. She wanted no more clothing between them, wanted to feel that hardness sinking into her. But he pulled his hips back, severing that delicious contact.

"My clothing will have to wait," he murmured in her ear. "There's no time to waste if I'm to make you come as many times as I plan to."

She dragged in a shaky breath. "Gabriel, please," she whimpered as his hands trailed up the outsides of her thighs.

She pressed back against him again, earning her a groan that seemed ripped from his throat as he rocked into her again.

"Soon," he whispered.

Then his hands began pushing up the hem of her shift. She felt the cool air on her skin for only a moment before his fingers found her center and he teased through her slickness.

"God, Evelyn. You're already wet," he groaned as he slid a finger inside.

She clutched the sheets in her hands, letting her forehead fall to the coverlet when he withdrew and teased into her again.

And again.

It was slow, agonizing torture.

"I need— I need—"

"I know, sweetheart."

And the gentle strokes became two fingers, thrust inside her. She whimpered into the bedding, moving against his hand as he brought her closer to release. Gabriel leaned into her, the heat of his body surrounding her as he dragged her back up against his chest.

He was everywhere—one hand teasing the base of her throat while his other worked ceaselessly between her thighs. And his mouth traced a heated path up the side of her neck. When she came, it was without warning, a sudden wave that crashed around her as she arched into his arms.

Her shift was over her head and pooled on the floor before she came down from her high.

"Beautiful," Gabriel murmured against her back.

He placed a kiss between her shoulder blades, before turning her to face him. She let her gaze trail the length of him, from the sweep of his dark hair, down to his leather encased feet. She wanted more of him, hated every stitch of clothing that kept him from her eyes and her touch.

"Take this off," she said.

She didn't wait and began the job of peeling the snug jacket from his shoulders herself. She had to stretch up onto her toes just to reach. It fell to the floor in a heap while she moved on to the laces of his shirt.

She heard Gabriel's deep chuckle at her enthusiasm, but a glance down showed that he was already working to free himself of the rest of his clothing.

When he'd shed the last garment, he grinned and lifted her by the waist, tossing her the short distance up onto the bed. She landed with a giggle, but it caught in her throat when she saw the view her new position afforded her—of Gabriel, eyes devouring her, broad chest rising with each deliberate breath. He looked strong. Powerful. Virile. Her eyes trailed downwards of their own accord, and she felt her face heat when they landed between his legs.

He is magnificent.

And he was her husband.

Gabriel all but growled under her gaze and climbed up onto the bed. He might as well have *purred* for all the animalistic carnality in those eyes.

"I promised to taste you again properly when I had the time," he murmured. "But if I do not get inside of you soon, I'm not sure I'll last."

Evelyn whimpered and wrapped her legs around his waist, not caring if she was being wanton. She ran her hands along his back, pulling him closer, needing him closer.

He settled over her and leaned to kiss her jaw, beneath her ear, before claiming her lips. When he pulled back, it was to look down at her with worshipful eyes.

"I love you."

She smiled up at him. His hand slipped down between them.

"I love you," he repeated, and pressed a kiss to her jaw.

She felt the press of him at her center and arched towards his touch.

"I love you," again, as he teased her opening.

"I love you," she gasped. And then her eyes squeezed shut on a strangled moan as he seated himself fully in one thrust.

Gabriel blinked up at the filigreed ceiling. The angle of the moonlight streaming through the window reflected to make the white scrollwork glow. He sighed, blissful. It was dark enough in the rest of the room to be the middle of the night, yet he hadn't felt this rested in years.

A warm body nestled against his side and dark hair fanned across his chest where it tickled at his skin. He smiled down at the top of her head, unable to keep the expression from his face. She looked so delicate there, against the broad expanse of his chest, and he tightened his arms around her, drawing her even closer.

Evelyn sighed, inching nearer, as if to accommodate him—or perhaps to fight off the chill in the room. He drew the blankets up around her shoulders and marveled at the overwhelming contentment that had suffused him. It was a strange feeling—one he had no experience with. But it certainly wasn't an unpleasant one. He breathed a quiet laugh.

"Are you awake?" Evelyn's soft voice brought him out of his thoughts. His arm tightened around her shoulders again.

"You should be sleeping," he whispered.

She shifted against him, a pale hand peeking out from the blankets to brush the hair from her face so that she might see him.

God, but she is beautiful.

It was enough to make his heart clench.

"And what about you?"

She smiled at him and that fist in his chest squeezed. It was the most beautiful feeling he'd ever had.

This woman is mine.

Loving her, marrying her, and now waking up in his home—in his bed—with her in his arms, and he still could scarcely believe it.

"Don't worry about me," he assured her. "I've managed on far less sleep before."

Her hand found his chest and he could have groaned at the feather light touch of her fingers as they trailed down his torso. But they stopped at his side, where the scar still lay, raised and red where Henry Watkins had planted a knife in his gut.

"I do worry about you," she admitted.

He reached to press his own hand against hers, his large palm engulfing her small, dainty fingers. He wished that he could erase the memory of that day from her mind—could take away the fear and uncertainty and horror of everything she'd had to think and hear and witness.

"You heard the surgeon. I was never in any real danger."

He knew it was barely a loose-fitting bandage on the emotional wounds that nightmare had left. He closed his eyes.

It took an effort to banish the image of Henry, staring vacantly at the rafters, so still and harmless in death, from his mind. They were images that haunted him, and he hated that they must follow Evelyn too. He squeezed her hand and opened his eyes, wanting to express all of it, but unsure where even to begin.

"I am sorry you had to witness any of that, Evelyn," he murmured.

What a horrific way to start a marriage.

She frowned, a small crease forming between her brows, and with a small shake of her head, pushed up to her knees to stare down at him. Her little hands pressed flat against his chest, her knee between his legs.

"It was horrible, yes. But I am not nearly as haunted by what I *witnessed* as I am by the thought of losing you."

The fierceness of her words brought moisture to Gabriel's eyes, and he tried to blink it away, but knew her observant gaze could see everything. He squeezed a hand against her hip reassuringly and swallowed the thickness in his throat.

When he thought of everything she had gone through, at Henry's hands and his own, to bring her to that place—on her knees in an abandoned warehouse, both his blood and Henry's covering her hands—

He coughed, looking for a way to change the direction of their conversation. It was more than he could handle just then.

But from her small smile, Evelyn knew how much he appreciated the depth of her concern and her feelings for him. And she knew how much his own heart had become filled with her.

Only you.

He looked up at her, staring down at him with all the love in her heart, and willed her to see the same staring back.

Then he gave her a sly smile as his hand slipped upwards from her hip, over her ribs, to settle over her exposed breast. He brought his leg up to meet the juncture of her thighs as he kneaded her flesh, and groaned when she rocked against him, lost for a moment in sensation.

Then she came to and narrowed her eyes at him in a way that had him grinning like a fool.

"You are a distraction," he accused.

"Oh, Gabriel!" she sputtered and rolled her eyes.

He laughed as she sank back down to the bed with a huff, but he only tucked her into his side once more.

"It isn't even a lie," he chuckled. "I have never met anyone as distracting as you." He let his hand fall to cup her rear and absently rubbed his thumb over her skin.

"You are impossible," she muttered.

"Hmm," he agreed. "And yet you still love me, Mrs. Stone."

She *harumphed* against his chest. "That is still *Lady* to you," she said with all the haughtiness she could muster.

He grinned and he pinched at her behind, earning a yelp and an ineffectual slap on the arm from Evelyn. He pressed a kiss to the top of her head, feeling suddenly emotional again.

"Call yourself a princess if you'd like" He smiled into her hair. "The only title I care about is wife."

Chapter Thirty

The sun was bright as it beat down across the wide stretch of grass. Evelyn smiled. Even the breeze was warm, and when the thin clouds cleared from the sky, it felt like winter—

It feels like winter might hold off forever.

She sighed as she arched her neck, wanting to feel the heat of the sun on her upturned face. It was a feeling that would never get old.

She let herself fall back to the blanket, stretching her arms wide as if she could absorb every last drop of late summer sunlight streaming down. Another shadow moved overhead, blocking the sun from her face and—

Evelyn blinked up at the bright August blue, smiling at the undeniable sense of déjà vu that assailed her.

Another blue sky, another picnic.

Another lifetime was what it really felt like.

Gabriel stared down at her, his mouth quirked in a smirk as she smiled lazily back.

"Mr. Stone," she laughed. "We keep meeting like this. I thought you were a cloud. *Again.*"

He chuckled as he moved around to the side of their blanket. She pushed herself up enough to shift over, leaving more space for her husband to join her.

"What took you so long?" she asked. "I thought I would be stuck waiting all morning for you."

He proffered the bottle of champagne and pair of stemmed glasses in his hand in apology. "I'm sorry. I tried to get away sooner, but Mr. Little's reports were endless."

She frowned at his feigned lightness.

She knew he referred to the meeting he'd had that morning with his foreman—a man whose job seemed to encompass much more than the title implied. News had arrived in the early hours of a wreck washed up along the southern coastline. There was evidence to suggest the debris originated from one of Gabriel's ships, lost at sea months before.

Evelyn knew the news had been a bitter one for him—the likely confirmation of a great loss of life, and he would feel every one of those souls like a weight on his heart.

From the shadows in his eyes, the proof of The Starling's demise had finally come, and he wasn't eager to discuss it further now. She smiled and took the glasses from his hand. She would ask him about it later, when the news wasn't quite so fresh.

"Champagne." She nodded with raised brows at the bottle he still held. "That's certainly an expense for a picnic in our own garden. What in the world are we celebrating?"

She laughed as he grinned roguishly at her, the light twinkling back into his eyes. "Do I need an occasion to buy my wife fine things?" he teased, and uncorked the bottle with a *pop*.

He took the glasses back and poured for each of them. She took her filled glass and shook her head with a smile.

"You do not even like the drink," she reminded him. "You told me it is too sweet."

Gabriel leaned in to steal a kiss, pressing his lips demandingly against her own, and stealing her breath away in the process.

"I think I've developed a taste for sweet things," he whispered against her mouth.

She laughed at his words, still flirtatious even now that they'd been married. Their glasses clinked and she watched him sip from his, before tipping his head back to down the entirety in one go. He grimaced and wiped a hand across his mouth.

"Perhaps it is only certain sweet things I have a taste for," he muttered. He eyed her appraisingly. "I might need a second taste."

The way his eyes narrowed on her lips made it clear he did not mean the wine. The look in his gaze heated her very blood.

"You are incorrigible," she whispered, but he only nodded and plucked the glass from her fingers.

He was above her in an instant, the champagne forgotten,

likely tipped over into the grass somewhere behind him. Her back hit the soft woolen blanket as his body caged her in.

He kissed her again, the slide of his tongue against her own making her toes curl. He traced a finger down the line of her profile when he pulled back, from her hairline to the slope of her neck.

"Don't worry," he assured her. "No one can see us."

She scoffed and turned to look pointedly at the drawing room windows overlooking their expanse of green.

"Except for every servant currently watching from the windows."

He chuckled and placed an open-mouthed kiss to her neck. "My servants do not *watch from the windows*."

She sighed when he ran his tongue along her pulse and arched against him, but her eyes darted back to the windows.

Marie would certainly have no such compunction.

She huffed a laugh. "That seems highly unlikely."

He nipped playfully at her throat. "Fine," he acceded. "Then let them see how I love my wife." He pressed a kiss to the center of her throat. "Let them see how I strive to please her."

A moan slipped from her lips as his mouth dipped lower, hovering above her collarbone.

"There is no striving necessary," she breathed. "You please me, husband."

She could feel his answering smile against her skin.

"I will do more than *please* you. Wife."

Thank you so much for reading

LADY WALLFLOWER IN LOVE

the first book in the Wallflowers in Love series. If you enjoyed Evelyn's and Gabriel's story, please leave a review! It helps more than you know!

I can also be found on Instagram, so give me a follow

@ghsuttonbooks

Again, thank you so much for reading this book. Keep in touch! And keep an eye out for more in the series... Coming soon!

Love always!

Emma Sutton

Some brief words of acknowledgement:

Thank you to everyone who helped along the way, but a very special shout out to my wonderful, most amazing alpha reader (you know who you are). You've been with me from the very beginning of this project, and gave me the blunt, unvarnished, line by line criticism that only a sister can give. It was exactly what this book needed, so thank you, thank you, thank you!